A REGULAR THING

A NOVEL

ALEXANDRA SERRE

Author's note: I tried to follow some NCAA guidelines for college hockey…but there may be some discrepancies

To all of us who have lost ourselves in the world we created in our heads.

PLAYLIST

ESPRESSO | SABRINA CARPENTER

DO I WANNA KNOW | ARCTIC MONKEYS

HOT TO GO | CHAPPELL ROAN

ROLL YOUR EYES | CHANCE PEÑA

THESE DAYS | WALLOWS

HOOKUP SCENE | KACEY MUSGRAVES

YELLOW | COLDPLAY

HATE TO BE LAME | LIZZY MCALPINE FT. FINNEAS

BETTER ALONE | BENSON BOONE

THINGS YOU'LL NEVER SAY | AVRIL LAVIGNE

YOU ARE IN LOVE (TAYLOR'S VERSION) | TAYLOR SWIFT

KALEIDOSCOPE | CHAPPELL ROAN

MATILDA | HARRY STYLES

TRUE BLUE | BOY GENIUS

STILL | NIALL HORAN

SNOW ON THE BEACH | TAYLOR SWIFT FT. MORE LANA DEL REY

CHAPTER ONE

Am I drooling?

VANESSA

This is probably the most embarrassing moment of my life.

I've been stood up.

For the past hour, I've been sitting in this fancy Italian restaurant and people are starting to give me awkward glances as I pick at my fourth piece of bread. My waiter has been by every five minutes to ask if I'm ready to order, and I have no idea how to tell this middle-aged man that I've been stood up by a stupid Tinder date. I want nothing more than to go home and put on my comfy sweats, dive under my covers, and eat an entire pint of ice cream.

Preferably chocolate fudge brownie.

I should've anticipated this. The first red flag is that the guy I'm supposed to meet up with is named *Chad*. I should've known that nothing good ever comes from a guy with a name like that.

Chad is the point guard for BCU—Boston Central University—the school we both go to. We matched on Tinder the other night and he offered to take me out for dinner. And me being me, I accepted—because who would turn down a free dinner with a hot basketball player? He's tall with broad shoulders, biceps that look like he could throw me across the room, and handsome in the way that makes your panties wet. I can't believe I allowed his hotness to blind all my rational thinking.

I'm not even *that* upset that he stood me up. I'm more upset that I wasted a perfectly good outfit on a useless date. I wish he'd at least have the decency to text me that he wasn't coming, then I could've planned for a backup date. I know that sounds kind of slutty of me, but I believe that girls should be able to enjoy dating just like guys do.

I'm not looking for any sort of commitment right now.

I enjoy spending my free time in nonmonogamous relationships. Relationships require you to be too intimate with someone—and not just sexually. You have to be fully open with a person, share all your deepest, darkest secrets and fears. They come to know your favorite food, favorite color, favorite everything. It's all a little too much for me.

At the end of the day, being stood up on a date still stings, even if I wasn't expecting anything more than a good dicking.

The funniest thing about this situation is that I didn't even set this date up. *He did.* He picked a beautiful five-star Italian restaurant and left me sitting here like a complete idiot.

Athletes are assholes.

Honestly, most guys I hook up with are assholes, so again, I'm not surprised. I at least thought that going out with an athlete would be a guaranteed hookup, but my expectations just keep getting lower and lower.

I haven't had sex in three months, and I need a good stress reliever.

I've been on a few dates here and there, but none of the guys do it for me. They're either super egotistical or they have the personality of a door.

I don't think I'm a hard person to please, but God can any man find the clit?

I can't really blame anyone other than myself for the situation that I'm in. I've had a bad track record of only dating guys that my parents would *definitely* not approve of. Am I doing it out of spite?

Most likely.

My parents would rather see me with an *educated man* as they say, which really means that they want me to end up with someone who would fit in perfectly with our family. So that narrows down my dating pool to doctors, business majors, or trust fund boys—all of whom I have *no* interest in dating.

They want me to not only follow in my family's footsteps and live up to the high expectations they put on me and all my cousins, but they also want me to find a partner who precedes the family standards. Or as my mother says, she wants me to date someone with *class*. Whatever the hell that means.

But I couldn't care less about finding a boyfriend right now. And I sure as hell don't care what my family expects of me. Well, *sometimes*. I think I make them nervous because I'm so different from the daughter they were trying to raise.

When I was in high school, they expected me to be on the debate team, be at the top of all my classes, and really strive to fulfill the family name. Instead, I spent my teenage years behind a camera, filming and taking photos.

Don't get me wrong, I wasn't a horrible kid. I filled my time with extracurriculars and was on the honor roll in school, but it didn't matter to my parents, because I wasn't taking classes like AP chemistry or physics. Maybe if I turned out the way my parents wanted me to, I would be in a stable relationship studying law and ready to take the BAR.

But I am *so* far from that.

All I wanted from this night was to get wined and dined by one of the hottest athletes at BCU. Instead, I'm still sitting at this stupid table like an idiot waiting for a guy I know won't be showing up.

To hell with this.

I muster up the courage to wave over the waiter. He strides by with that same pitiful smile he gave me only moments ago.

"Hi, I'm sorry for wasting your time tonight, it seems my date had better things to do. Do I need to pay for the bread?"

"Oh, sorry he's not coming. Don't worry, we comped the breadbasket. Hope your night gets better." His eyes wash over my face and continue to give me the same pitiful look.

All right, that's enough embarrassment for tonight.

I mean, the audacity of this man—no, this *boy*—to set up an entire evening and then bail on me without a single text? I deserve better.

My heels click against the marble floor as I walk out of the restaurant and stand outside while I wait for my Uber to arrive. My fingers fly across my phone, quickly typing out a message to my friends to let them know that I'll be joining them at the bar tonight rather than enjoying myself on a date. Within seconds they respond, anxiously waiting for me to spill about my date. Jokes on them because they're going to get an earful.

My Uber pulls up and I climb into the black sedan, soft curls bouncing as I slide into my seat. I stare at my reflection in the window, and I know that if I were a guy, I wouldn't stand myself up.

When I found out that we were going to this fancy restaurant, I made up an excuse to my parents that I needed a dress for a school event. I told them some lie about going a the political science gala and they practically threw money at me. And since they don't really care too much about what's going on in my life, they sent me money and wished me a good time.

Is it bratty of me to take money from my parents? From an outsider's perspective, probably. But after being emotionally neglected by them for most of my life, I don't mind accepting the money they're willing to offer me.

I will thank them, though, because this dress is to die for. *Literally*. I want to be buried in this outfit. It's a gorgeous black satin material that hugs my body. The bodice is tight with a square neckline and long sleeves that are snug at my wrists. I would live in this dress for the rest of my life solely due to the confidence it gives me. I complemented the dress with simple gold jewelry and pointed black heels—an outfit that screams *I want to go home with you*.

Sorry Chad, your loss.

I watch the busy streets as we drive through the town. Boston is bustling this time of year. With school now in full swing, students line the streets patiently waiting to get into bars and clubs, restaurants overflowing, utilizing their patios while it's still warm enough.

The Uber jolts to a stop and I thank him for the ride. I climb out of the car and turn toward Shaker's. It's the hottest bar around BCU right now.

I shut the door to the car and the driver pulls away as Sydney and Maddie greet me.

Sydney whistles in my direction. *"Wow...*I can't believe you got stood up when you look like *THAT!"* I love when my friends compliment me. I feel like I'm the hottest girl on the planet.

Sydney and I have been friends since freshman year. I wish we had a cool story about how we met, but unfortunately, it's the same old boring tale. We were paired up as roommates in our freshman year and ever since then we've been attached at the hip.

Looking at us, we're almost complete opposites. Sydney is like a golden Barbie goddess with honey-blonde hair, long legs, and tan skin. She shares her tall height and hazel eyes with her older brother—Nate. They also have a younger brother, Ethan, but he looks a lot more like their mother, whereas they take after their dad.

Sydney has that gorgeous defined face that is fitting for a model, while my face is a little more rounded.

Sometimes I feel very inferior to my best friend. I mean she's drop-dead gorgeous and looks like she just walked out of a Victoria's Secret catalog.

"Boys are dumb. All I wanted was a nice dinner and maybe end the night with sex, is that too much to ask for?" It's a rhetorical question, but I wait for an answer.

Maddie, the third part of our trio, rolls her eyes at my statement.

Now, the story of how Maddie and I met is an interesting one. During freshman year I decided that I wanted to have some financial freedom from my parents and save up a bit of money on my own. So, I applied to work at a paint store, and that's where our friendship started.

My first day on the job, the manager introduced me to Maddie, and I was scared shitless. Maddie is the dark and broody type, with her long, jet-black hair, pale skin, piercing blue eyes, and a small horseshoe nose ring. Her resting bitch face made me want to run, but then she introduced herself and we bonded right away over our love of crime documentaries and sharing our trauma with each other. I ended up quitting almost a year later, realizing that the retail life wasn't for me. But at that point I had already introduced Maddie and Sydney, and the three of us became inseparable.

"Your past three dates have been a bust. Maybe you should find someone the old-fashioned way and not on an app." Maddie always likes to point out the obvious. Even when I don't want her to.

Can you blame me, though? Dating apps are so much easier. Most people don't download Tinder because they want a boyfriend or girlfriend, they're on the app to find a casual hookup.

And that's exactly what I want.

Most girls my age want a serious relationship and start to settle down, but why the hell would anyone want that when there's such a large dating pool?

My last real relationship was in high school, and my ex ended up being a dick, so my motto since college started is *casual hookups only*. Ninety percent of my hookups are due to late-night swiping on multiple dating apps. Then there's the stages that follow: texting, asking the same basic questions, meeting, hooking up, and forgetting that each other exists.

I will admit that it does get exhausting after a while. The same routine over and over again. But sometimes it's nice to have that simplicity and forget about it the next morning. And that's my goal for tonight. Especially because it's been a while since I've been with anyone.

I shake my head at Maddie. "You know what, maybe I'll find a good-looking guy tonight and have great, mind-blowing sex. If not, then it looks like I'll be back to my trusty vibrator." I walk past my friends and lead us into the bar.

Shaker's is always busy on a Saturday. It's one of the newest and closest bars to campus in downtown Boston. We're still at the beginning of the semester, so most students choose to party on the weekends rather than study.

We've come here a couple of times during the summer when it first opened, and the crowd is always college students. Some dressed up, celebrating birthdays or other occasions, and others dressed more casually for a fun night out. They always accept our fake IDs, so we couldn't care less about the odd decor. And by odd, I mean the giant electric guitar that hangs behind the bar that's positioned right next to a moose skull and antlers.

We push our way through the crowd and make our way over to the busy U-shaped bar where Sydney orders for us.

Tequila. My arch nemesis.

I don't know what it is about the liquor, but anytime tequila weasels its way into my system, I become an entirely different person. I become someone who is overly charismatic, capable of moving her hips to any beat, and for a lack of a better word, horny. If this is how we're starting tonight, I can already tell that I'm going to be in for a wild ride.

I toss back the first shot with ease. As the alcohol works its way into my bloodstream, I feel the all-too-familiar flush go right to my cheeks. This always happens to me whenever I take a shot.

The second shot burns my throat on the way down. The cheap tequila feels like gasoline in my esophagus, and it takes me a second to compose myself and *not* throw up. Here's the thing about me and tequila, if I'm already drunk, the taste doesn't matter to me. But when we start with it, sometimes the fruity notes don't settle well.

The third shot has my stomach feeling warm and content, as if I'm lying on a beach with a margarita in my hand. My lips pucker as I suck on a lime wedge to take the taste of tequila out of my mouth.

I find that three is a lucky number for me. Whether it's three shots, three drags, or three beers, I'm always at the perfect level. Right now, my head feels light and free, the prior events of tonight have been washed away. My legs move without my brain telling them to, pulling Sydney and Maddie with me toward the dance floor.

I firmly believe that alcohol is liquid courage because there is no way in hell that I'd be able to dance the way that I do if I was sober. As we move with the bass of the song, my thoughts start to slip from my brain. I'm no longer sad about being stood up tonight, but instead the alcohol makes me *mad* that I was stood up. I am so much better than Brad or whatever the hell his name was. See, I don't even remember his name; this night has already improved greatly.

I mean, it did hurt my ego a little bit. Normally I'm the one who calls it quits with someone, and now I'm on the other end of it.

We weave through the crowded dance floor and make our way back to the bar where Maddie and Sydney both order something fruity with an orange wedge on the glass. I settle for something basic yet hard enough to get me where I want to be tonight. A double shot of rum with a splash of coke. I know that without a doubt this rum will pick up my spirits for the remainder of my night.

I quickly down my drink and order another to bring back to the dance floor with us. Maddie and Sydney nurse their first mixed drink and take their time, but I'm ready to party.

We make our way back to the dance floor at the perfect time. The DJ changes the music to something more sensual. I didn't know how badly my body wanted a change in the music. House music is okay to dance to every now and again, but the pounding of the bass sometimes gives me a headache. There's something about R&B music that flows through your body, it's like sex to your ears. The beat of the song has my body moving like my bones are made of liquid. I allow the music to take complete control over me.

The girls and I hip and grind on each other. Maddie is the better dancer out of all of us, but once I have a little alcohol in my system, my hips can move in ways I never thought possible for someone with such bad coordination.

As I'm grinding my ass into Sydney's pelvis I can feel a heated stare in my direction. It's almost like a tingling sensation going up the back of my neck, sending goose bumps across my skin. I turn my head a little to the right and notice the hottest guy I've ever laid my eyes on—tall and tan, messy brown waves tousled on his head, and a lopsided grin that could melt anyone's panties off.

Holy shit, he's hot…and somewhat familiar, but I can't put my finger on it. The alcohol has my brain a little fuzzy.

The hot stranger is leaning against the bar with whom I'm assuming are his friends. He's one of the tallest in the group, easily a head taller than me. His hair is the perfect combo of curly yet fluffy. The plain T-shirt he has on highlights his muscular pecs, and his jeans hug his thighs perfectly. Is this guy made of marble or something? Even in clothes I can tell he's built like a wall.

Am I drooling or did I accidentally spill while taking a sip of my drink?

Our eyes meet for a moment, and I can feel the tension between us from across the room. I feel like I'm in one of those cheesy rom-coms where they spot each other and immediately act like magnets, being pulled toward each other. Because that's exactly what it feels like.

He watches me as I check him out, and if I didn't have any alcohol in my system, I would probably be blushing and turning away. But I feel confident and look sexy as hell, so those little insecurities completely vanish.

As we maintain eye contact, a devilish smirk breaks across his face. I don't know what it is about eye contact, but I find it so sexy when a man can hold my gaze without wavering. Maybe it's a dominance thing or something, but whatever it is, I'm stuck staring at his gorgeous face.

My heart starts beating faster as I watch him saunter through the crowd, making his way toward *me*.

*Oh shit. Okay, Vanessa, be calm, cool, collected. Just because one date ended up poorly tonight doesn't mean the rest of the night will follow suit. Just be cool, don't act like a weirdo, and let the alcohol do the talking tonight…*because I know exactly how I want this night to go.

With me going home with him.

CHAPTER TWO

I might be going to heaven

JAKE

This is one of the best nights I've had in a while.

Why? I just took a body shot between a beautiful pair of tits and I think it was a life-altering experience.

Now, I know what this might look like. A typical college hockey student, obsessed with partying, sex, and having fun. That's not totally wrong. I will admit that I do fall into part of that stereotype, and I'm not ashamed of it.

Boston Central University has been my home for the past three years, and this is my last year playing college hockey before I graduate and head to the pros. I've worked my ass off these past few years to get to where I am today, so if it's considered a sin to go out every now and then, I'll gladly spend eternity in hell.

I personally don't feel like there's anything wrong with indulging in your desires as long as you do so ethically and responsibly.

I try to control how much I go out and drink once the season starts, but my time has been filled with the weight room and practice for the last month and a half. I'm ready to let loose and live a little.

Am I indulging a little more than usual tonight? Fuck yes, but I have a valid excuse. This week marks the first official game of the season, so after tonight I'll be taking things a little easier.

In the meantime, I plan on having the time of my life. One last big hoorah before it's time to get serious.

The boys decided to hit up a local bar called Shaker's. Kieran has been here a couple times since it opened this past summer and I have to say, it was a good thing we let him choose where to go tonight. He said that this place has been a hotspot and the best potential for hookups—looking around, I can confirm he was telling the truth.

Kieran is my best bud, we've known each other since tryouts in our freshman year. At first, we butted heads, but once he actually got to know me, and I used a little bit of my charm, we've been best friends ever since.

Kieran is our star goalie. I've seen this guy become an absolute wall in a game, where no one could get the puck past him. Girls not only fall for him because of his skills in hockey but he's not bad on the eyes either. He's about the same height as me, roughly six foot three, with black curly hair, broad shoulders, tattoos, and green eyes that he uses to get into every woman's pants.

Not to say I don't get my fair share, but Kieran is a tough competitor.

I know it's vain to say, but a majority of our team is a good-looking bunch. Hockey is only part of the attraction.

"Jake, get your ass over here—we're doing shots!" Kieran yells from the bar.

I grab my glass from the bar top and toss it back with everyone else. The amber liquid slides down easily. I'm drunk enough that beer tastes like water and liquor doesn't burn on the way down.

"How the hell did you even find this place, man?" I ask, realizing how different this is from our usual sports bar vibe.

"A girl I hooked up with in the summer asked me to meet her here." He takes a swig of his beer he just ordered. "And it's a great place to pick up chicks. Look around."

I take a second to do as he asks.

This bar is different from most of the places we hang out. It's more rustic than the usual neon lights and sticky floors. This place has dark wooden chairs and tables and a huge dance floor beside the bar.

Shaker's is a unique place. It's almost as if the owners wanted to combine a country sports bar and a club, melding together to make the perfect hangout spot for college students.

The bar itself looks like it's made from stained barn wood with white and gray marble tops. My dad owns a construction company back home, so I'm pretty good with attention to detail.

All of us are standing over by the side of the bar, with Nate and Eli sitting on bar stools and the rest of us huddled around each other.

Even though Kieran normally picks where we go, Nate and Eli always have the final say. They're our captains of the team, so they feel responsible for all of us. It's like they're our parents and we're the out-of-control teenagers.

"All right, listen. I know this is the last weekend before the season officially starts, but I'm warning you all—if *any* of you miss one practice or game because you got too fucked the night prior, Eli and I will beat the living shit out of you and leave you on the ice to freeze."

See what I mean? Daddy Nate—a nickname we dubbed in our sophomore year that he hates—is always putting his foot down when we want to have fun.

Nate is one of my closest friends and roommates. He's easily the biggest guy on our team, taller than both Kieran and me. But he couldn't be more different from the two of us. Nate has more of a preppy boy vibe with his clean-cut look, which is always a hit with girls, even if he doesn't score. His family comes from money but he's not the type to throw it in your face. He always makes sure to take care of everyone around him.

I think sometimes he might take the captain role too seriously and he feels like he needs to take care of us, both on and off the ice. But in all honesty, I think that's what makes him such a good friend.

Eli is the complete opposite of Nate. He's our assistant captain and the other top defenseman, aside from myself. He transferred from Nashville State last year and he's an absolute beast on the ice. He's a year younger than the three of us, but still holds his own on the ice.

Eli is a bit of a fuck boy. He uses his Southern charm mixed with his dark caramel skin, tight short curls, and pierced ears to his advantage. Just about every girl he talks to falls at his feet the second he calls them *darlin'* or *sweetheart*. I say it's his Southern drawl and not his actual game that wins them over.

Eli's mom and younger sister still live in Tennessee. He's not from a middle-class family like mine or a super-rich family like Nate's, but his family is comfortable in their ranch back home.

Similar to Nate, he never judges his friends based on what they do or don't have. And even though he's a fuck boy, he still treats women with respect. Because if he didn't, he knows that his mom and sister would beat his ass. An ethical slut, if you will.

Although Eli and Nate are polar opposites, they make a fire duo—as friends and as hockey players. With Nate's speed and Eli's defense, we're almost unstoppable.

A few puck bunnies litter around our group, letting us take shots from between their tits and hoping to be one of the lucky girls who gets to come home with one of us tonight. Nate rarely goes home with anyone, especially during hockey season. He says he wants to focus on the game, but I feel like he's like me and just doesn't want to commit to anything. Me and commitment go together like water and oil—it just doesn't work.

Eli is sitting next to him at the bar and has a preppy blonde with her lips attached to his neck. Kieran orders another round of shots for us, and suddenly my head is feeling a little fuzzier.

I feel a small tap on my shoulder, and a small blonde stands behind me. She looks vaguely familiar.

"Hey, Jake, how's it going?" *Have I slept with her before?* Sometimes they all meld together. *What the hell is her name?*

I nod at her. "Hey…Brandi. Want a drink?" Normally I try to not sleep with the same girl twice, but this girl has hips I want to grab onto.

She purses her lips in annoyance. "It's Bailey, you asshole."

Shit. Well, at least I was close.

Bailey scoffs and turns around before I can even utter a half-assed apology.

Honestly, I don't know why girls get mad at me for not knowing their names. It's not like I'm out here looking for a girlfriend. Every girl on campus knows me for one thing, hockey...and sex.

Okay, so they know me for *two* things.

I make it known that I'm not looking for a serious relationship. College is all about exploring and having the time of your life before you settle down, and that's exactly what I've been doing.

Don't get me wrong, I'm not out here breaking girls' hearts on purpose. I always tell the girl beforehand that this is just a one-time thing, but how is it my fault if the next morning they're crying because I don't want to take them out for breakfast?

Dating is complicated and messy, and something I'll spend my late twenties doing. But right now, I enjoy going to the bar with my friends, finding a good-looking girl, and making both of our nights full of pleasure. And tonight is the perfect night for that because the bar is absolutely packed.

The DJ changes the upbeat house music to a more sensual song, which draws my attention from the bar to the dance floor. The whiskey has my limbs loose and the music is making me want to dance.

In the middle of the crowd there's a group of three gorgeous women, but the little brunette is the one who captures my eye.

I immediately notice the blonde girl next to her, Sydney, Nate's younger sister. They have uncanny similarities but where Nate is mainly all work and no play, Sydney is more of a free spirit, which is usually why he doesn't allow her to hang out with us. He's too scared she might cause some drama because of something that happened in high school, but I really couldn't care less about the past because she's hilarious, from the few times I met her.

And she also has smoking hot friends.

The two girls dancing with her, I've never met. Nate's sister might be off limits, but there's no rule about going for her friends.

I watch as the brunette grinds her ass into Sydney's hips, moving with the rhythm of the music.

Fuck, I hope that will be me in a few minutes. I want to run my hands up and down her body, touching that shiny fabric that covers her skin. I want to feel her ass grind into me and dig my fingers into those luscious hips.

She takes notice of my long stare, and our eyes lock. She gives me a sly smirk and my dick immediately responds, the front of my jeans feeling a little tighter than when I got here.

She has long brown hair that's curled and falls just above her waist. I wouldn't mind wrapping it in my hands as I fuck her from behind. Her dress clings to her curves showing not only a beautiful set of tits but also a handful of ass. She has these gold, wide-framed glasses that are making me go wild.

I love the whole hot nerdy girl thing she has going on. Much different from my usual type, which is normally puck bunnies and sorority girls.

She's sexy and she's definitely coming home with me tonight.

I lean toward Nate, yelling over the bass of the song. "Hey, man, who's the girl dancing with your sister?" I tilt my head in the direction of the dance floor.

Nate swivels on the bar stool to take a look at the brunette I'm motioning toward. "Yeah, that's Vanessa Nichols. She's Syd's best friend."

Well shit, she is an absolute smoke show. I don't know how I've never noticed her around before. Sydney's definitely never taken her to watch one of our games. What a shame.

She's tiny, maybe five foot four or five-five on a good day. I can tell that even with the heels, I have almost a full head on her. I could easily pick her up and toss her over my shoulder. *Or around in bed.* Hopefully I'll get to try that out later tonight.

Looking back at her I notice how pouty her lips are. God, they would look so good wrapped around me.

Fuck, I'm getting hard in a fucking bar thinking about this chick.

"Know anything else about her?"

Eli chimes in this time, leaning over Nate's shoulder. "She's smoking hot."

"Thanks for pointing out the obvious."

I feel her eyes on me, eating me up from the dance floor. I think it's about time I introduce myself to Sydney's friend.

The dance floor is crowded, but I make my way over to the trio, keeping my eyes on her the whole time. She holds my gaze, and I fucking *love* it.

"Jake Shepherd," I have to yell over the music, but I flash my signature smile and extend my hand out to her, hoping it'll help my game. A gentleman always introduces himself first.

She looks at my hand, confused for a moment, before shaking it. "Vanessa Nichols, nice to meet you."

I pretend like I didn't already know her name and smile at her. "Want to get a drink with me?"

She looks back at her friends, almost as if she's seeking approval to leave them. I get it, girls tend to stick together to make sure a creep doesn't ruin their night, and I don't blame them. I stand there waiting as Sydney assesses me, giving me a devilish grin. Sydney nods at her friend, signaling for her to go with me.

Vanessa grabs my hand and starts leading me to the bar. Her hand is so small in comparison to mine. I follow her like a lost puppy as she leads us through the crowd.

I need to make a mental note to thank Sydney for being a good wingwoman without even knowing it.

Thank you again, Sydney.

We get to the bar, and I put my hand up, signaling the bartender.

"So, what's your drink of choice?" I ask her.

She looks up at me with her big green eyes that are magnified by her glasses. I think glasses on girls are hot as fuck. It fills every guy's sexy librarian fantasy. And trust me, we all have that fantasy. Her eyes are already big, but the glasses help me see how detailed they are, with swirls of gold weaving through her irises.

"Normally rum." She signals toward her almost-empty cup. "But we've been drinking *lots* of tequila tonight, so either will do."

I smile back at her then order two rum and cokes from the bartender. I'd normally opt for a whiskey or a beer, keeping it simple, but for this girl, I'd drink a shot of lemon juice if she asked.

In a moment we both have a new drink in our hands, and I lead her back to the dance floor. The black material clings to every dip and curve in her body, and the low back exposes the sexiest line trailing down her toned back. The sleeves are tight on her arms, showing a little muscle definition. My free hand roams over her as she grinds into me, the fabric feels silky between my fingers. This dress is driving me absolutely crazy.

I lean into her more, my lips finding a spot on her neck. The smell of her shampoo is making me feral. *Coconut? Maybe vanilla.* Whatever it is, it's fucking intoxicating.

I suck on her neck as we dance together, and a soft moan escapes her lips. One I would barely hear if I wasn't this close to her. The music is drowning out everyone, so it feels like it's just me and her alone in a crowded room.

Is that a lyric to a song?

"I don't know if I said this yet, but you are fucking sexy in that dress."

She looks over her shoulder with a small grin on her face. "I know, that's why I got it."

She turns around to face me, looping her arms around my neck. The ice in her drink makes the glass against the back of my neck cool my hormones down.

I'm about to lean in, sealing the space between us.

A few of my teammates join us on the dance floor, which shakes me out of the sex trance I was falling into. Sydney and their other friend, whose name I didn't get, make their way over to us, mixing our groups together.

Suddenly we're going back and forth from the dance floor to the bar to take shots. As we take another shot with my teammates, Vanessa bats her eyelashes at me in the sexiest way possible. She leans up on her toes, trying to whisper in my ear but failing because of our height difference. I lean down to hear what she's saying over the music.

"So, are we going back to your place or mine?"

17

Well fuck, I think I might be going to heaven tonight. Heaven being Vanessa's thighs wrapped around my face.

CHAPTER THREE

The puck bunnies can have him

VANESSA

There is a steady thump at the front of my head that makes me want to vomit. I peek one eye open and notice that there's an arm draped over my body. *A very heavy and muscular arm.*

This is *not* my bedroom.

My eyes slowly adjust to the sunlight that's streaming through the window. The curtains are white and allow way too much light through them.

Oh God, what the hell did I do last night?

Who the hell did I do last night?

I glance beneath the blankets, happy to see my underwear is still on, but somehow the only other item of clothing on my body is a baggy black T-shirt that doesn't belong to me. The bright morning sun makes me wince—the pounding in my head only worsens.

Don't throw up. Don't throw up. Don't throw up.

The last thing I remember from last night was dancing with Sydney and Maddie, then meeting the cute guy who was watching us dance.

Shit, What was his name? It was something small and four letters. Alex? Tate?

No, those both sound wrong.

I turn my head and look over at the nameless guy sleeping next to me. He's much bigger than I remember. The hand that's lying flat across my stomach is probably double the size of mine. If I wasn't so hungover I'd want him to wrap it around me.

I look to the bedside table and find my glasses neatly tucked to the side. At least I was smart enough to not fall asleep with them on. *Again.*

I put my glasses on and glance back at the sleeping giant whose arm still rests on my stomach.

Jake.

Okay, it's somewhat coming back to me now. I remember him introducing himself and buying us drinks. I can't believe he actually stuck his hand out and shook my hand while telling me his name. That is not something that happens often.

This hangover is brutal. I'm never mixing different alcohols ever again. I need a huge glass of water and an ibuprofen, or I might vomit all over his room.

That would be a nightmare.

Slowly I remove his arm from my waist and climb out of the bed. I take a quick glance around the room and find an open door leading to an attached bathroom. *Thank God.* I did not want to explore this potential frat house alone. Who knows who could be lurking in the halls?

Please let this guy have a stash of ibuprofen in here.

I quietly make my way to the bathroom and turn the light on to find some type of medicine. My eyes wince at the LED lights above the mirror. Even I don't have this nice of lighting in my bathroom.

I move to turn off the light switch when I catch a glimpse of myself in the bathroom mirror. My curls from last night are a little tangled and my mascara is smeared. I look completely different from the put-together, hot-as-hell girl I was last night.

I leave the bathroom and quickly scan the room, looking for my discarded clothing. There's a desk tucked in the corner of the room next to the bathroom door that has books neatly situated on its shelf. He has two tall, sand-colored wardrobes along the wall across from his bed, with a TV positioned in between them. In the center of the room is his bed, which has gorgeous white linens. It's easily king-sized and for the brief moment I was in it, it was the comfiest thing I've ever slept in.

I didn't think a guy could be *so* clean. This is completely different from the other rooms I've been in. This guy is organized, and his room is well-decorated, not like the typical blue plaid sheets and a banner saying *Saturdays are for the boys.*

At the foot of the bed, I find my black dress tossed into a ball.

Okay, clearly I didn't care where I discarded *that* last night.

I move to grab my dress and start pulling it on when a groan escapes from the bed. I whip my head to the side to see Jake yawning and sitting up.

Shit. Shit. Shit. Shit.

"Were you going to leave without saying goodbye?" he mumbles, barely audible. His voice is so deep it sends shivers through my body.

I think my feet might be frozen to this spot. I have half of his shirt off my body and my dress halfway up my thighs. I'm also 100 percent sure that my ass is hanging out. Quickly, I pull the T-shirt back on to cover myself.

"Oh, I…uh, don't normally stick around after drunken hookups."

I walk back toward his bathroom to change, and he chuckles low. His laugh is even deeper, it's the sexiest sound I've ever heard. So velvety, yet hoarse at the same time. I could listen to him talk all day.

No. No, I can't. I have to go home.

I close the door slightly, allowing myself enough privacy to change from his borrowed shirt into my dress. It shouldn't matter because I'm sure he saw more of me last night.

Oh my god, Sydney and Maddie are going to freak out when I get home. Do they even know where I am? Did I bring my phone home from the bar?

I walk out of the bathroom as Jake is pulling on a pair of gray sweatpants but still shirtless with his rock-hard abs on display for the world. I have to stop myself from drooling, admiring his toned body. *Of course he's wearing gray sweats.* Why is it that when guys wear them, they immediately become sexier? The cotton material hugs his thighs and the hemline dips far enough for me to see the deep *V* leading to his groin.

I'm definitely staring. I need to stop.

I avert my eyes from his groin, and I'm greeted by his smirk. Yup, he definitely noticed me checking him out.

Fuck. My. Life.

"Just to ease your conscience, we didn't hook up last night." He grabs a shirt out of one of his drawers and pulls it over his head. "We both got shit-faced and came back here. I put you in one of my shirts after you stripped off your dress and passed out."

Of course I did, how classy of me. I did say that I wanted to go home with a guy who would take my dress off me. Guess it didn't really turn out as planned. I should've been more specific.

"But if you're still interested, I mean maybe we can give it a go another time." He winks at me, and my insides turn to mush.

I can already imagine what the sex with him would be like. He seems like the type of guy who would drill into me so hard I wouldn't be able to walk properly for the next week. It would be filled with lust, sweat, and a million different positions, but right now all I want is a coffee and for my headache to stop pounding.

"Well…thanks for the somewhat fun night but I really have to get going. My roommates and I have breakfast every Sunday." *Why did I feel the need to share that with him?*

Jake smiles at me, his teeth so white they could blind me. His fluffy curls fall into his face and he uses his hand to push it back, revealing his gorgeous blue eyes. They're a deeper shade of blue, like a hydrangea. His tanned skin mixed with his chiseled body make him look like a damn Greek god.

I find my phone on the floor next to the bed—*nice one, Vanessa.* It's probably dead by now.

"Do you want to grab coffee or something later?" His voice falters for a moment as I reach for the door to leave.

I realize I never responded about hooking up at a different time. It could be fun, but I don't have time for anything serious, and who knows what he's looking for. Although I have an inkling that he knows exactly how to please a woman.

God, Vanessa, get your head out of the gutter. Stop thinking of him like a piece of meat.

I open the door but pause. Striking out not only once, but twice yesterday has put me in a depressed mood. I'd rather quit while I'm ahead. I'm also late for breakfast.

Hoes before bros.

I smile at Jake but decline his offer. "Thanks, but I gotta get going."

For a second I swear I saw a hurt expression flash across his face, but the second I noticed it, it was gone and replaced by a smirk.

"No worries. It was nice meeting you, Vanessa."

I make my way down the stairs and past a living room on one side and a kitchen on the other. Normally the nosy part of me would take a second to snoop around, but I need to get out of this house and go home to shower.

I grab my heels from the floor and strap them back on before leaving. I don't know how women can wear heels all day. Wearing them for a night out is one thing but wearing them for hours while at work sounds absolutely dreadful. I already know that walking home in these is going to be a pain in the ass, but I'd rather be in pain than have dirty feet.

 I wish I was still drunk, that would make this walk more tolerable.

It also just occurred to me that I never found any ibuprofen.

I shut the door behind me quietly in hopes I didn't wake any of his roommates. The house is gorgeous, definitely not the frat house I was imagining earlier. It's a beautiful brownstone with modern touches in the kitchen and living room that I saw briefly on my way out.

This part of town is mainly college housing. Brownstones line the streets and I check my phone to see where exactly I am. Thank God it didn't die in the middle of the night, or I'd be forced to go back inside and ask for directions.

Luckily his house isn't a far walk from mine, so I start my journey, joining the others who are also going home at nine in the morning on a Sunday.

I arrive back at our condo and wave at our security guard as I head to the elevators. It might seem a little extreme to have a security guard for your building, but it was one of my parents' requirements when buying this place. They wanted to make sure I lived in a *safe* environment, which is funny because home was far from that, with their stuck-up attitudes and high expectations.

I unlock the door and find Sydney and Maddie waiting patiently for me in our living room. I unclasp my heels and throw them onto the shoe rack by the door.

My parents might have paid for our condo, but we've made it our own with funky décor. We have a comfy red sectional in the middle of our living room that we thrifted and paired it with an oval-shaped, glass coffee table. We have a three-bedroom unit on the twelfth floor with floor-to-ceiling windows in every room. From our living room windows, we can see right into the heart of downtown.

My parents never wanted me to stay in a dorm, but at BCU they make you live on campus for your first year, and they couldn't argue with the school. It was one of the main reasons I applied here. To get a sense of freedom and to get the hell away from my family. I could've gone as far as California, but there's something about the East Coast that makes it hard to leave.

As soon as I became a sophomore my parents decided that I needed a place of my own. I was able to convince them to let my two friends stay with me as long as I took a minor in political science—just in case a life in journalism doesn't work out for me. The jab about my major hurt a little, but not enough for me to decline my parents' offer. It's not a bad bargain if I get to live with my best friends basically for free.

I know that Sydney's parents have a lot of money, and she could easily afford a place like this on her own, but it feels useless to ask for either of them to chip in when my parents have more than enough wealth to share. I wouldn't take a penny from my friends, anyway, especially Maddie, who's paying her own way through school.

"*Well, well, well,* did somebody have a fun night? Or should I say, *somebodies*," Sydney chimes in immediately.

I roll my eyes at her. Sydney is always the first one to call people out on their bullshit. I swear she has a superpower that allows her to pick up on everything. Honestly, sometimes she scares me. There is not one secret I've been able to keep from her.

"Actually, I didn't. We got back to his place, and I passed out before I could even take my dress off," I start to explain. "Looks like I'm stuck in a dry spell. Might as well pick up a new vibrator and just swear off men altogether."

I'm a firm believer in self-gratification. But a toy can only do so much. Sometimes it's nice to have an actual dick inside of you rather than silicone.

"You're going to be back on Tinder later tonight, endlessly scrolling and asking our opinion on who's hotter."

I flip them off, leaving them in the living room while I head to my room to shower and change before we go to our favorite coffee shop for breakfast.

Since we became friends during freshman year, we made it a tradition to meet for breakfast every Sunday at a local coffee shop called Caio. They serve the best lattes and the cutest pastries. One time a barista made a cat out of the foam on my latte and to this day it's still the prettiest drink I've ever had.

I open the door to my bedroom and realize I left it a mess. My closet door looks like it's leaking clothes, with shirts and dresses hanging haphazardly off the hangers and different shoes scattered across my floor. I was running around getting ready for my failure of a date last night, and I guess I decided to leave the cleaning for today.

I peel my dress from last night off and toss it into my laundry basket. My attached bath is remodeled to the nines, something my parents said *needed* to be done before moving in. At first everything was pure white, from the marble floors to the tiling in the glass shower. But once I moved in, I painted the walls a deep shade of emerald green and swapped out the matte black features with gold ones. It's much nicer now.

The best purchase I made was one of those rainfall showerheads. I read somewhere that the steam from eucalyptus releases an oil that promotes stress relief, so I made sure every bathroom in the house has some.

Most girls love to soak in a bubble bath for an hour, reading a book and lighting a candle, but that's not me. When I need to relax, I turn down the bathroom light, turn on my *"I need to cry"* playlist, and sit on my shower floor for twenty minutes. Works like a charm every time.

The bathroom steams up quickly and I hop in to rinse off the smell of last night that clings to me. It would take me too long to wash my hair, and I'm craving a hazelnut latte. Hopefully that will help nurse me back to health and take away my nausea.

Fifteen minutes later and I am all showered, moisturized, and ready to go for breakfast.

I slip on my favorite pair of mom jeans and match it with a cream-colored sweater and my Converse. I'm too tired to fuss with hair and makeup, so instead I toss my hair up with a claw clip and quickly brush out my eyebrows. Thankfully glasses have their perks and hide most of my face, so if I'm not wearing makeup, it's not as noticeable. And to be honest, I couldn't care less about my appearance today. All I want is an espresso and to gossip with my friends.

On our walk over to the cafe, Maddie fills us in on some of her work drama. "So, I told the lady that we can't return her paint if it's over a year old and she yelled at me and said she was never shopping here again. Like, okay, lady, as if I give a fuck."

Maddie is a force to be reckoned with. Not only is she a genius but she's also hilarious. Once you get past her tough exterior, you see the small beads of sunshine that is Maddie. She is one of the kindest souls I've ever met.

By the time she finishes ranting about bad customers, which seems to be most of them, we've arrived at the cafe.

I walk up to the counter and order for the three of us while they go and grab us a seat near the windows—our preferred spot. While I wait in line, I take a moment to look around my favorite coffee shop.

Caio is situated on the corner of a less-busy street. It has two walls full of windows, which allow in the perfect amount of natural light. The wall across from the barista station has exposed brick and the others are painted a dusty terra-cotta color. The floors are dark hardwood with a few earth-toned area rugs around the tables and chairs. There's a huge bookcase along the far wall that people can donate books to. I've always felt like it took some inspiration from the coffee shop in *Friends*.

"Order for Vanessa!"

I bring our drinks and pastries over to Sydney and Maddie, who are already chatting about each other's plans for this upcoming week. I take a seat in the cushioned armchair next to the window and start eating my croissant when I look over at Sydney, who has a knowing smirk pulled across her face.

She pulls up a video on her phone from last night. "Do you know *who* you were dancing with last night?"

"Um, well, I know his name is Jake. And, uh…that's about it." I struggle to think of anything else I could remember about him after only meeting him last night. "Oh, and he has a comfy bed I wish I could've taken home with me."

I take another bite of my croissant and I have decided that whoever thought of stuffing a croissant with spinach and cheese is a genius. I hope they're a millionaire.

Sydney rolls her eyes at me and shoves her phone in my face. I watch myself on the screen grinding and dancing in ways my sober self never could. "Ness…Jake plays on the hockey team with my brother. He's well known across campus, if you know what I mean. Big red flag."

She tucks her phone back into her bag. That doesn't shock me at all. I mean, it makes sense that he's an athlete. That would explain why he's in such good shape.

It's been months since I've hooked up with someone, and of course I fumbled *that*. Just remembering his abs from this morning has me all hot and bothered. And if I'm getting all hot and bothered over Jake, then I'm sure there are a ton of girls out there willing to fuck him. Especially at BCU.

Hockey is probably the most popular sport at our university and we're one of the top schools in our division. Last year we almost won the championship but lost to Boston College in overtime. No matter what social circle you run in, you always know the score of last night's game. I'm surprised I didn't notice who he was before Sydney mentioned it. I thought he looked familiar last night.

"Who cares if he's a player? In case you forgot, I sleep around too." I know she's not trying to directly insult me, but if she's insinuating that Jake is a slut, well then, I guess so am I.

"That's not what I meant, and you know it." She sighs and puts her hand on my knee. "Listen, if you want to roll around in the sac with him, I won't stop you. I just think that it's time to stop casually sleeping around and maybe *think* about a long-term relationship for once? There's this cute guy in my accounting class I could set you up with."

I know Sydney has my best interests at heart. All she wants for me is to be in a loving committed relationship, but it's hard for me to get attached to someone like that again. She loves love, who can blame her?

The last time I had a boyfriend was in my senior year of high school. His name was Matt, and we had been dating for about three years until I walked in on him fucking my so-called best friend at the time.

Oh, and how did I find out? I threw him a birthday party at my house and found him drilling into Rachel in *my* bed. At least he got birthday sex from someone, because after that he was getting absolutely nothing from me.

So yeah, I guess the trauma stuck with me and now I have a fear of commitment.

Oh well.

This is why I only do hookups. They're easy and stress-free.

"Well, on another note, I heard he's packing. Care to confirm the rumor?" Maddie rests her chin on her wrist, leaning in closer to me. She always knows how to lighten the mood.

"We didn't hook up and I don't plan on relieving last night any time soon. The puck bunnies can have him." I sip on what's left of my latte and put Jake out of my mind.

Maybe it was a good thing I didn't hook up with him last night

CHAPTER FOUR

Simple, yet effective

JAKE

My ego is bruised.

I'm not the kind of guy who gets his feelings hurt when a girl turns him down. *At least I thought I wasn't.*

It's been days since that fiery brunette left my bed and I can't get her out of my head. Not to sound too cocky or anything, but I've never had an issue with scoring. On the ice or in the bedroom.

If I walked outside right now and asked the first girl I saw to go on a date with me, she'd say yes without question, I have no doubt in my mind about that. If you're on a sports team at BCU, you're guaranteed girls.

But for some reason, this girl—*this one girl*—has ruined me.

Vanessa has been stuck in my head all fucking day and Coach Wilson has been ripping me a new one all throughout practice. It's like I can't get her rejection out of my head. I mean, why would she say no to getting coffee with me? Is my reputation really so bad that it's now deterring girls?

Definitely not.

Normally, if a girl rejects me—which rarely happens—I brush it off and move on to the next. Except this time. It's like I'm on a boat out at sea being lured by a siren call. The siren being Vanessa.

I'm just surprised Vanessa had no idea who I was. I guess I'm not as popular on campus as I thought. *Or she was just pretending she didn't know me.*

Unless this girl lives under a rock or doesn't give a fuck about school sports, she must've heard my name on campus before.

Maybe that is what's drawing me to her, the obliviousness. It's a little refreshing. I'm used to people coming up to me and automatically knowing my name and my stats from the season.

The look on Vanessa's face the other morning showed me that maybe she didn't have any clue who I was. She did, however, look like she was debating whether she wanted to jump my bones or not.

I would love to show her what she's missing out on. I can imagine her sassy attitude comes out during sex, probably a little demanding here and there—most likely a pillow princess, but I don't give a fuck because I *love* giving. I wonder what kind of sounds she makes during sex. Is she a moaner or a screamer?

With the way I go down on women, she'll probably be a screamer.

"Hey, Shep, get your head out of your ass or else you're going to make Wilson have an aneurysm." Nate skates toward me, knocking his glove against my shoulder.

He's right. I need to shake this off. I've been off my game all morning.

Coach made us start practice with a bag skate, having us weave in and out of pylons set up in different patterns. Normally I'm one of the quickest. But today I'm sidetracked by the thought of having sex with a sassy brunette who wants nothing to do with me.

I make it through the rest of practice without seeming like a complete idiot.

Most days I enjoy our morning practices because they make me feel more energized for the rest of the day. The rest of the team despises them. They'd rather sleep in and spend more time in the weight room. The only other guy who doesn't mind waking up before six is Nate. But that's only because he wants to set a good example for the rest of the team.

Every Tuesday and Thursday we have early morning practices that run from six to eight. Coach Wilson has us use the weight room a minimum of three times a week, although the guys and I hit it up more than that. He doesn't care if we work out as a team or on our own, but Kieran, Nate, Eli, and I normally go together on Mondays and Wednesdays since it lines up with all of our schedules. We try to go after classes are done so we can avoid Coach Wilson. His office is located in the athletic building and has a window directly facing the weight room. He always jokes about having eyes on us at all times, but I can see him having the rest of the coaching staff keeping tabs on us.

Lucky for me I'm only on campus for half the day on Tuesdays and Thursdays. After our morning practice I have classes immediately after, then I'm done for the day.

I'm majoring in environmental science, which isn't common for many athletes. A lot of college athletes major in business-based academics, but I decided to pursue a science degree, mainly for my mom. She's a florist back home and is obsessed with environmental activism. During my first year, I took a course about geology and the environment, and I was hooked. It's nice to have a topic I can discuss with Mom when I go home.

And with this major, I get the opportunity to take some pretty dope courses. Last year I took a class that was all about natural disasters. It was pretty wicked learning about different weather patterns and what causes increasingly worse storms every year.

My degree might be useless after I graduate, but I might as well take advantage and learn something fun before I go pro.

When I was eighteen, I got drafted by the New Jersey Demons—which is my dad's favorite NHL team. To say we were stoked is an understatement. The terms of my contract were, once I finish my undergrad, they can call me up to the big leagues or move me to their farm team.

My biggest fear is that after I graduate, they'll decide that they no longer want my rights and then I'll have to wait for another team to pick me up.

It's been stressing me out lately, especially after what happened last year. One of the guys over at Boston College was also drafted right out of high school, but when the time came to call him up, they decided to revoke their rights and not sign him. He didn't play too well in his college career, thinking that because he was already signed, he's fate was sealed. He played sloppy and distracted and it cost him. He's still a free agent with no team wanting to pick him up. *Poor guy.*

The main reason why I'm nervous is that I've had very little contact with the GM of New Jersey—Peter Savinsky. My agent has assured me multiple times that he's been impressed by my stats throughout the years and that I have nothing to worry about, but this is my whole damn career in their hands. I've worked my ass off, proving to them that they made the right decision in drafting me.

All right, I need to stop thinking about it and focus on class. I don't need to stress sweat and have everyone in the room smell my BO.

Astronomy is an entry-level course that I took to fill up one of my remaining electives. Most people don't know this about me, but I really dig learning about space. There's so much to explore and it's all a mystery. It's mind blowing to me. I even convinced Kieran to take this class with me, which was like pulling teeth, but he finally caved when he realized all of the quiz answers can be found online.

Kieran's majoring in business, like most of our teammates. When he was in high school, his parents passed away and left him a shit ton of money that he has no idea what to do with. He says that if hockey doesn't work out for him, he can invest in a company or something.

Our professor spends the next hour and a half teaching us about the basics of our solar system. It's still early in the semester, so some classes are still going through the intro material, which most students find boring, but I find it entertaining. There's a whole lot of shit I didn't know about until I started this course.

Kieran sits next to me, scrolling endlessly on his phone for the majority of class, but I pay attention the whole time, listening to our prof ramble on about black holes and exploding stars.

For the duration of class I didn't think once about the small brunette that was in my bed only a few nights ago. But now I'm convinced that there's something wrong with me because I *never* obsess over a girl.

The last time I had a girl stuck in my mind, I was fourteen, watching Megan Fox in *Transformers* for the first time. That girl lived rent-free in my mind for years, and if you asked any teenage boy at the time, they would also agree.

Maybe the reason why Vanessa is in my head is because we didn't sleep together, and my body just wants to get her out of my system. Maybe if we just hook up once, she'll be out of my system for good.

I keep remembering the way her body moved with mine on the dance floor and the way she would quietly moan when I sucked on her neck. Fuck, I'm getting a hard-on and class is just about to wrap up.

Okay, Jake, focus. Think of vomit. Dead puppies. Eli clipping his toenails in the kitchen. Anything disgusting.

"Are you going to your other class or skipping?" Kieran pulls me out of my thoughts, and *thank fuck* they worked 'cause I'm no longer sporting a tent in my pants.

"Yeah, I'm going. Are you staying on campus or heading home?"

I shove my laptop into my bag as we gather the rest of our things and head outside to the late September air. It's still early in the fall semester, so the sun is still out and it's not cold enough for a jacket yet. Boston winters can be so brutal, I'll soak up the warmth as long as I can.

"I don't have a class until tonight, so I'm gonna head back to the house and make lunch and probably take a nap. My thighs are fucking burning from today's practice." Kieran waves at me and starts heading toward the parking lot. "I'll see you later, dude."

I nod at him and head in the opposite direction toward the Memorial building where my oceanography class is. Oceanography was one of the classes on my course list that really interested me. I mean, who wouldn't want to learn all about the deep seas? We've explored more of space than our own oceans. That's fucking insane, not knowing what lurks in the deepest depths of our planet. There's got to be some wild creatures roaming the ocean floor. Probably giant sharks or prehistoric creatures.

I'm sure if scientists were to find something, they would turn it into a blockbuster movie.

Either way it intrigues me, and my professor for this class is also my academic advisor. He's pretty dope, just a regular, middle-aged, bald guy who drives a truck and loves his cat.

Another perk is that he loves his environmental students—even those of us who have crazy hockey schedules and sometimes miss a class to take a quick nap.

The prof goes off about the basics of the class, and since I already have some basic knowledge of the five oceans and seven seas, I decide that now's a good time to aimlessly scroll through my dating apps.

A lot of the girls here are the same. Or at least their profiles are similar. They love dogs, they drink socially, are looking for a relationship, oh, and they normally have a random quote from a TV show in their bio that's *totally changed their life.*

It's not until a familiar brunette's profile floats across my screen that I stop swiping. For a moment I see those gorgeous green eyes swallowing me through my phone screen. Vanessa's profile is styled similar to other girls, but there's something that stands out to me.

Instead of having a million and one selfies, she only has three photos of herself—two of which include her friends. The rest of her profile is filled with photography. *Clearly that's an interest of hers.* Even her bio is a little different from the typical run of the mill:

Age: 20

Seeking: Noncommitment

Bio: Seriously not looking for anything serious, just here for a good time and maybe a laugh if you're lucky.

Her profile is cute. Simple, yet effective. She gets her point across easily, and I think we could have a good time together. Hell, we had a great time together on the weekend.

Didn't we?

I get so caught up in my own thoughts about her that I tune out the voice of my professor. Or at least I thought I tuned out his voice.

"Mr. Shepherd, is your phone more important than our lecture today?" Mr. Porter calls me out in front of the two hundred–person lecture hall.

Well fuck, my cover is blown.

"No, sir, my apologies." I quickly jam my phone back into my pocket as Mr. Porter continues with his lecture. I silently hope I can get through the rest of my day without thinking about Vanessa.

"I know you did it."

I've been listening to Nate and Kieran go at it for the past five minutes about who forgot to replace the roll of toilet paper. Nate was stuck in the bathroom for ten minutes before I came home to save him from hopping in the shower to hose himself off.

"There's no proof."

Nate rolls his eyes at Kieran. We all know it was him, he's the worst for it. Forgetting to put a new roll of toilet paper out, putting a new garbage bag in the bin, the list goes on and on.

Nate, Eli, Kieran, and I all share a brownstone off campus. Nate and Kieran fork over most of the costs for rent, but Eli and I always chip in for groceries and bills. We each carry our own weight, splitting up who cleans what and who has to do the groceries for the upcoming week. Sometimes, Kieran is a bit forgetful when it comes to household chores, and that's where Nate comes in handy. Not only is he the dad of the team, he's also the dad of our household.

"You're always the one who uses the last of the toilet paper and *never* replaces it."

"Unless you have video proof, you can't pin shit on me." Kieran shrugs, taking a sip from his energy drink.

"You were the *only* one home." Nate's nostrils flare.

This happens on a weekly basis. Whether it's someone not putting a new roll of toilet paper out or someone using the last of the milk and leaving the empty carton in the fridge, someone is always on Nate's shit list.

"I came home and took a nap. Maybe it was Eli. He could've easily come home before his classes and forgot to change it."

35

"I think I might kill you." He throws the empty toilet paper roll at Kieran's head, hitting him directly on his forehead.

"Sorry, Dad!" Kieran yells back as Nate storms up the stairs with a new pack of toilet paper in his arms.

By tomorrow morning, Nate will forgive Kieran just like he always does, and things will be back to normal. Well, at least until Kieran forgets to do something else.

I hit resume on our game. Nothing beats coming home from a long day on campus to play dumb games with your friends. Our current fixation is *Galaxy Warzone*. It's some indie game Kieran found where you play as space marines fighting aliens who are trying to take over your home planet. It's colorful and has lots of shooting, so it's right up our alley. Normally Eli and Nate would be playing some NHL game, but Kieran is all about RPGs or shooters.

"So, was it you?"

"Oh yeah. I came home and took a shit, smoked a joint, and passed out. Must've forgot. Oops."

"You're such an ass." I elbow him jokingly, but my movement made him miss his shot.

"So, how'd it go with the brunette from the bar the other night? I saw her practically running out of the house."

Of course.

I finally have a moment of peace, not thinking about Vanessa, and Kieran has to go and remind me all over again of the girl who turned me down.

"Meh, it was fine."

Kieran is the one who pauses the game this time. He looks over at me, studying my reaction. *Fuck,* he knows.

"Did you strike out?"

I give him a look that gives away my answer.

"No fucking way."

"Shut up."

His eyes go wide. "Oh fuck, you *did* strike out." Immediately he bursts into laughter as Eli swings the front door open.

"Whichever one of you asshats didn't replace the toilet paper, you owe me twenty bucks." Eli drops three packs of toilet paper onto the living room floor. "Nate made me pick up— What the hell are you laughing at, Danford?"

"The notorious playboy finally got turned down."

Eli's mouth falls open. "Shut the fuck up."

I shake my head. "Screw you guys. It was *one time*."

Yeah, and one that I can't seem to get out of my damn head.

"Nate!" Eli yells from the bottom of the stairs. "Who bet that Jake would get rejected before Halloween?"

We hear shuffling from the stairs before Nate appears at the bottom, his phone in hand. "Brody. Said some girl would have her wits about her and turn him down."

That fucker.

As a team bonding experiment, Nate decided to have all the boys make bets during summer training. All random shit, like who would be the first to knock up their girlfriend, who would get the first bloody nose of the season, and of course, betting on when someone would turn me down.

"As if you guys haven't struck out in the past. Eli, a girl splashed a drink in your face two weeks ago. At least I got the girl back to the house."

Eli crosses his arms over his chest. "So I forgot the girl's name, she didn't *need* to throw a drink on me."

"Whatever. Can we change topics now?"

Kieran laughs, "Don't worry, Shep. I'm sure the next girl you go for will put out. Or maybe this girl will be stuck in your head and curse you for the entire year."

"That's so fucked up, I can't believe you wanna jinx the man's game." Eli finally uncrosses his arms and settles on the couch next to us. Nate also joins, picking up two more controllers off the coffee table.

"All right, knock it off, you idiots. Let's kill some aliens and stop thinking about chasing tail, huh?"

Nate's always the one to break up our bickering whether it's at home or it's on the ice. If I had a dime for the amount of times Nate had to break up an argument, I'd be rich by now.

We settle in the living room for the night, playing video games and munching on leftover pizza from the night prior. Conversations range from hockey to girls to what we believe is in outer space—a topic I may have spent an hour on.

If I keep my head preoccupied, maybe I'll start to forget Vanessa. The best thing would be to never see her again, so my dumb brain completely removes her from all thoughts.

It's a big campus, the chances of me running into her again are highly unlikely. *Right?*

CHAPTER FIVE

Is this a joke?

VANESSA

I love my Tuesday morning classes.

My first class of the day is intermediate film studies. We spend the morning analyzing classic films and highlighting common themes throughout cinematic history. This week's assignment is for us to watch *The Godfather* and relate it to the themes we've discussed so far in class.

This class will be an easy A for me because I grew up loving movies. When I wasn't behind a lens, I'd go see a show by myself. There's something comforting about seeing a movie alone, no one around to influence how you feel about the film and being able to absorb what you're watching.

And the popcorn. Nothing on this earth beats the taste of freshly popped cinema popcorn. It's the perfect amount of salt and butter that is impossible to remake at home.

My second class of the day is my digital print lab. Every other week we get an assignment to photograph in a specific style and then the following week we develop the photos in our lab. For our first assignment our professor let us choose our own photography style. Some students love doing portraits, landscapes, or still life, but I personally love nature photography.

I've always dreamed of seeing my name appear under a photo in a magazine like *National Geographic.* If I could work with their environmental team and capture all aspects of wildlife, explore the world, and work at the same time...nothing could be better than that.

Growing up I always loved the outdoors. Anything to do with nature had my name on it. Hiking, skiing, swimming, there was literally no outdoor activity I wouldn't try—even though my coordination isn't the best, it was all about the experience.

I also thoroughly enjoy watching nature documentaries. *The National Geographic* channel was always on when I was home. Sometimes I would fall asleep to David Attenborough narrating about the changing seasons. Now that online streaming exists, I have access to just about every type of documentary possible.

My final class of the day is the one I dread the most and I'm currently sitting in, waiting for the clock to strike five so I can go home. My day goes from having an easy morning to counting down the minutes until I can leave campus. If only I had my morning classes, then Tuesdays and Thursdays would immediately be my favorite days of the week.

Unfortunately, I'm not that lucky.

I wish I didn't have to take this social media class. I don't really care for social media management, but since social media platforms have become so popular, our department head wants communication majors to take a class on how to properly manage an account.

Don't get me wrong, I use social media apps just like every other young adult in North America, but I would rather spend my time in college writing articles to use for my portfolio so when I apply for internships I'll have enough variety.

Yet here I am, sitting in a small classroom with twenty other students, learning the basics of Instagram and how to boost activity.

Journalism and social media is a fourth-year course, mainly for students who are majoring in communication or journalism. It's a project-based class that runs for two semesters and Professor Miles is giving out our assignments today that we'll be working on throughout the term.

"As you know, this is a two-part course spanning over both the winter and fall semester. There will be no exams, as this is solely a project-based class, and you will all be assigned a social media platform to run for the remainder of the semester. The assignments have been randomly assigned so there won't be any favoritism."

I zone out as she goes through the class list, my eyes feeling heavier than they should at this time of day. I idly pay attention as someone gets assigned to run the social media account for the student union, another has to follow the dance team all semester.

I'm lost in my thoughts when I hear her call out my name. "Vanessa Nichols." I raise my hand and her eyes fall onto me. "You will be in charge of taking over the social media accounts for the men's hockey team. They have a decent following, but their website is in desperate need of restructuring."

Hockey?

Out of all things to cover, she assigns me the hockey team?

This has to be a joke. Does she have some secret vendetta against me? It could be that I had this professor last year for another media course, and I may have skipped class a couple times—*okay, maybe more than a couple.* Personally, I blame the university for setting classes that start before eight in the morning.

I'm sure anyone would be thrilled to be stuck with twenty overly handsome athletes for the entire term, but I would rather cover the community garden or the horticulture club. At least that way the content I'd be posting would look nicer in my portfolio.

But no, instead I'll be taking photos and videos of sweaty guys in smelly jerseys. If I wanted an internship at ESPN then this would be perfect, but I don't think National Geographic will care what the score of a college hockey game is.

This might be the end of me.

Am I being too dramatic?

Probably.

Professor Miles finishes giving out the assignments and proceeds with our instructions for the remainder of the semester. Our goal is to either create or improve the social media platforms we're managing during the term. We have four checkpoints throughout each semester where we share our progression of content and followers.

It honestly isn't *that* bad. It could be worse; I could be like Tess Michaels and have to be the social media coordinator for the robotics team. I've seen *Terminator* too many times to know why we shouldn't play around with AI.

Maybe working with the hockey team won't be so bad. Hopefully I can avoid Jake and save myself from an awkward encounter.

41

Oh man, I'm gonna need some luck.

After class I head over to the athletics building to meet with Coach Wilson. Professor Miles said it would be good to introduce myself to him before I randomly start showing up at his practices and games.

I don't think I've stepped into the athletic building since freshman orientation. It's one of the newer buildings on campus and looks the most modern, an eyesore compared to the other historic, brick buildings.

The building is on the other side of campus, near our arena and the indoor track. It's all light gray walls and floor-to-ceiling windows, equipped with state-of-the-art machines and equipment for all of our sports teams. The first floor is filled with conference and study rooms, along with a small coffee shop. If I were an athlete, this would probably be my safe haven. But I'll stick to my own study spots.

I take the elevator to the third floor and follow the directory until I'm standing in front of Coach Wilson's office.

Okay, Vanessa, there's no reason to be nervous. He's just one of the most terrifying coaches in the league, nothing to worry about. If he's mean and scary, I'll reward myself with ice cream and a good cry.

I heard that after they lost the championship last year, he made half the team cry. And personally, I feel like I'm a little more emotional than his hockey players.

I knock lightly on the door and hear a grunt that somewhat sounds like a "Come in."

Hesitantly, I open the door, making sure not to intrude in case I heard wrong.

Coach Wilson stands next to a whiteboard with what seems like hockey plays drawn all over it, but it's all gibberish to me.

I look around, taking in the office. It's lovely—well, as lovely as a coach's office can be.

The athletic building is attached to our sports center where they hold all indoor sporting events, like track and swimming. His office has a huge window along the back wall where you can see right down into the two-storey weight room. I take a quick peek and can see some of the players on the team below working out, luckily Jake isn't one of them.

Coach Wilson puts down the dry-erase marker he was using and turns toward me. "So how can I help you, Miss…"

"Miss Nichols." I extend my hand out to shake his. He has a very firm grip. "My name's Vanessa. I'm assigned to be your team's social media coordinator and photographer for the term."

Coach Wilson nods at my introduction. I take a moment to really look at him, since I've only ever seen him in photos in our school newspaper. He's tall and muscular with ivory skin, built almost as if he's a player on the team, except his hair is short and gray, and he's sporting a thick, but well-groomed, peppered mustache.

"Normally the assistant coach runs our social media, but he's a bit of an idiot. Last year I asked him to upload new video clips to our website and he damn near crashed the whole thing—which is why when Professor Miles asked if we could use a social media coordinator, I couldn't say no. Maybe you can help with the turnouts of fans at our away games. The boys always have low spirits when we don't see red and white filling the stands."

"I will definitely try my best. I'll start looking at the website tonight to get a better idea of what you want posted. If it's okay, I would like to start attending some of your practices so I can get to know the players and build their online profiles so fans can get to know them and feel more connected to them."

"Of course, I'll give you a copy of our schedule for the semester. I'm not sure if Professor Miles told you, but you are required to attend every game, even away games." Coach Wilson walks over to his desk, grabs a paper from a folder, and hands it to me.

"She didn't, but that's not an issue at all." I smile at him as I tuck the paper into my bag. I didn't realize this term assignment would take up so much of my free time. "I'll do everything I can to improve the crowd attendance and work with you guys to expand your social media following as well. It was nice to meet you Coach Wilson, and I look forward to working with you this semester."

"It was lovely to meet you, Vanessa."

After my brief meeting with Coach Wilson, I head back home to process everything from today and start comparing my schedule to the hockey teams.

"So, you get to hang out with the Wolves every day until the end of the season? Remind me again of why that's a bad thing?" Maddie asks as I stab my fork into the pasta she made us for dinner—pesto penne with sun-dried tomatoes.

I love living with roommates who can cook. If I offered to make dinner, I'm sure I would give them food poisoning, which is why I love that food delivery apps exist and anything I want I can get delivered to my door within minutes.

"You get to be surrounded by the hottest guys on campus all semester. I don't see a single issue with this," Sydney adds.

That's the problem. I probably got one of the easiest assignments out of the whole class. The hockey team already has an Instagram and Twitter account. Apparently, hockey boys are all the rage right now. Everyone is obsessed with hockey guys whether they're watching them on TV or reading about them in a book. Maddie has already recommended five different sports romance novels.

"Hmm, maybe she's nervous because she knows that Jake is on the hockey team, and they have some unfinished business." Sydney wiggles her eyebrows at me.

It was only a few days ago when I turned Jake down in his bedroom and tried to delete that whole encounter from my brain.

Boys are trouble with a capital *T*. *Especially* hockey boys.

They're all the same. They're arrogant, cocky, and think that everyone worships the ground they walk on. *Especially* Jake Shepherd. He thinks he is the prince of BCU, with every girl falling to their feet for him. I wouldn't be surprised if he's hooked up with half of the campus by now.

The thought of seeing Jake again after I turned him down is a little entertaining. I mean, how many girls have turned down the great Jake Shepherd?

CHAPTER SIX

Strike out again

JAKE

"Murphy, get your head out of your ass and defend the net!" Coach yells from the bench area, "And Kieran, if you let one more goal in, you can kiss the rest of your week goodbye and spend every free waking minute in the weight room!"

Both Eli and Kieran wave over at Coach, motioning that they heard him loud and clear.

The boys went a little too hard on the booze last night when we went out for wings and beer. Nate told them they'd regret it this morning, but as usual, they didn't listen to his advice.

It's nice to not be on the receiving end of Coach Wilson's yelling for once. We're currently scrimmaging against each other, working on a new play that Nate helped Coach plan out.

Nate is our most powerful player. The other teams anticipate that he'll lead the play, knowing that we try to give him the puck almost every time. Our plan this season is to catch them completely off guard. Coach wants us to explore more plays rather than become reliant on one or two players.

Instead of pushing Nate the puck like we always do, we have Nate start with the puck and drive it down the ice. He'll act like he's going for it, but instead he'll fake a pass to the left and pass right to Sebastian, who's already waiting behind him. Sebastian is our right wing on our starting line. He's a freshman and new to the team this year, but he was scouted all the way from Montreal and has already been drafted to Ottawa once he's done school. This kid has the best slap shot I've ever seen, there's no question he's going to do amazing things when he gets pulled up to the pros.

We reset the drill and start at center ice. Nate starts with the puck and flies toward the defending zone, straight toward Kieran and the net. Eli and I take our defensive positions against Nate, waiting for the play.

Coach likes to split up the first line when we do scrimmage drills like this. That way Eli and I can learn to defend against guys like Nate, Seb, and Levi. In return, they have to try to get past the wall of our defensive line. I don't want to boost my ego more, but Eli and I are such a good defense duo, it's hard for a lot of teams to get by and score.

Even if they do, Kieran rarely lets anything by him. That's why we *almost* won the Frozen Four last year. If it wasn't for Andrew Meyers, the center for Boston College, we would've won. He's one of the dirtiest players in our division, always going for the cheap shots and knows exactly what to say to get under your skin. During the championship game, he said something to Nicholas Phillips, our captain last year who graduated, about his dad who recently passed away. Nick went fucking wild and checked him so hard the ref threw him out of the game. They got a power play and won by one goal.

Since last year, Coach Wilson has been working us hard, coming up with new plays to try out. Coach has some pretty good strategies when it comes to hockey, so I think we have a much better chance of winning this season.

Eli and I are on opposite sides of Nate, trying to distract him and the rest of the second line team from grabbing the puck. Nate closes in on the net and makes it seem like he's about to shoot, when instead, he makes the pass to Sebastian, who is wide open. He slaps the puck, and lucky for Kieran, he blocks it.

We continue practicing this play and a few others until Coach calls it quits for the morning and we all head to the locker room to shower.

"What's the plan after tomorrow's game?" I ask Kieran as I walk back from the showers. He's always the one who plans out where we go after a game. Win or lose.

Kieran pulls his sweater over his head, hair still damp from his shower. "We've got two options, the football team is throwing a party after their game at Alpha Phi, or we can chance our luck at Shaker's."

Two decently good options.

"Let's go with Shaker's."

"I agree," Nate adds as he passes by us in just a towel. "I don't feel like dealing with dickhead frat guys this weekend."

I slip on my jeans and pull my BCU hoodie over my head, my hair almost completely dry. Kieran and I both head toward the door to leave the locker room when Coach peeks his head through.

"Is everyone decent?"

Most of us have already showered and changed, although there are a few guys who take their time, still standing in towels.

"Before you guys head out, there's someone I want to introduce you to."

Coach walks into the locker room with a small brunette trailing behind him.

Oh, you've got to be shitting me. Vanessa?

She's wearing a black cropped sweater that shows a little bit of her tanned stomach, along with faded jeans and white Fila sneakers. I don't know how she manages to look nerdy and casual yet hot as fuck at the same time. This style suits her so well. The jeans are a little baggy and they make her frame look so tiny. It would take zero effort for me to toss her over my shoulder and bring her home with me.

No, I don't want to do that. I want to get her out of my head.

What the hell is she doing here anyway?

"This is Vanessa Nichols. She's going to be the team's new social media coordinator and photographer for the entire season. She has lots of ideas to boost game attendance, so be open to them." Coach Wilson motions to Vanessa. "Would you like to say a couple of words, Vanessa?"

Vanessa smiles at him then takes a moment to look around the locker room, tucking her hair behind her ear. This is every college girl's dream, to be in a room full of good-looking hockey players. I wonder if she's freaking out on the inside or if she really is unfazed by us.

Her eyes settle on me for a moment, and I make sure to give her a knowing smile. The second I do, she averts her eyes back to the rest of the room.

"Thank you, Coach. It's nice to meet all of you. I can't wait to get to know you and build up your team on social media. I would like to have a conversation with each of you to learn about you and your stats, so I'm going to leave this sign-up sheet with Coach. If each of you can fill in a date and time that works for you, I'll be in touch with a time we can get together."

She gives her clipboard to Coach and waves goodbye to everyone. The guys all mumble a nice greeting as she leaves the locker room. I notice a few of them staring at her ass on the way out and that has my blood boiling. If she turned me down, then I highly doubt any of them would stand a chance.

"I'll leave the sign-up sheet in my office. Make sure you stop by between classes and sign up. And boys…" He's now glaring at all of us with his ice-cold stare. "Treat her nicely. She's doing this for a course assignment, and we will not interfere with her work."

After that Coach leaves us to finish getting changed.

Kieran whips his head toward me. "Dude, wasn't that the girl who was sneaking out of your bedroom Sunday morning? The one from the bar who turned you down?"

Kieran was in the kitchen when Vanessa ran off after our weekend encounter and he hasn't let me forget it. He's been constantly chirping me for getting turned down.

"I've seen her around before, she's in one of my photography classes." Levi walks over to me, looking me up and down even though he's a few inches shorter than me. "She turned *you* down?" He hunches over laughing, clutching his stomach as if he just heard the funniest thing ever said. "Wow." He pretends to wipe a fake tear off his cheek. "I never expected Jake Shepherd to be rejected. Oh man, this is going to be so entertaining."

"Fuck you, Brody."

"Hey, Nate, I think you owe me twenty bucks."

Nate shakes his head before reaching into his wallet, grabbing a folded bill, and sliding it into Levi's awaiting palm.

"I really didn't think I'd win that bet."

"Again, *fuck you*, Brody."

He chuckles and leaves the locker room. Levi is a little shit, but he's also like a younger brother to me. I don't want to say that I took him under my wing when he first joined the team, but we've gotten closer over the years. When we first became friends, he told me a bit of his backstory, where he came from and his family life. The kid has a difficult relationship with his dad, so we try to help him where we can—Nate more than all of us.

"This is going to be an interesting season. C'mon Kieran, I need an omelet and a pound of bacon ASAP."

I gather my hockey bag and sling it over my shoulder. I walk fast through the lobby to try to catch Vanessa before she leaves the arena. To my surprise, she stopped before the sliding glass doors leading outside, her phone pressed to her ear.

I slow my pace and make it seem as though I wasn't breaking a sweat trying to keep up with her.

Her face is neutral, almost blank as she listens to whatever the person on the phone is saying to her.

"Mm-hm, okay, yeah. I guess I'll see you at Thanksgiving then. Yeah, bye." She ends the call as I walk up to her, her attention now fixated on me and not her phone.

Her green eyes lock onto mine and it feels like she's swallowing me whole. Her eyebrow quirks up, as if she's studying me, trying to figure out what I'm about to do next. For a second, she looks a little disappointed, but her expression changes the moment her eyes find mine. The disappointment is now replaced with...annoyance. She puts a hand on her hip, waiting for me to speak.

I'm going to have so much fun with her this season. Looks like it's time to turn the charm on.

"*Well, well, well*, it seems that fate clearly wants us together." I smile, trying my hardest to get a reaction out of her.

She rolls her eyes at my comment.

Fuck, I could look at her eyes all damn day, they're a deep green with flecks of gold surrounding her pupils. I don't know how she doesn't have guys wrapped around her little finger.

"It's not fate, it's just a term project." She starts to walk out the doors, and I follow alongside her, not caring if I leave Kieran behind.

"Mm-hm, whatever you say, sunshine. I bet you were happy to get assigned to us."

She stops abruptly, facing me again, sticking her finger at my chest. "Trust me, I wasn't. And don't call me that."

Her tone is hard and cold as ice. I've never had a girl get mad when I gave her a nickname. This might be interesting, getting under her skin while she's forced to be with us.

"Don't call you what, *sunshine?*"

"Yes. That's not my name."

I hold my hands up as if I'm surrendering. "Anything for you, *sunshine.*"

She huffs and I smile at her before running over to Kieran's truck, where he's already waiting for me. I glance back to Vanessa as I climb in. She looks around for a moment, almost in a shocked stance. She averts her eyes back to her phone, puts her earbuds in, and walks in the opposite direction of us. I don't realize I'm staring so intently until I hear Kieran chuckling to himself.

"What?"

"Your face lit up like a kid on Christmas when she walked into the locker room. And you've had that stupid grin plastered on your face ever since." He cocks his eyebrow at me.

"I like a challenge, what can I say?"

"I can't wait for you to strike out again." He laughs.

Strike out again? Not going to happen. It was a one-time fluke. Too much alcohol involved. I know I can win this girl over with my charm.

"Don't worry, I'll make sure it's entertaining for us all."

"Oh man, you're going to make her time with us a living hell, aren't you?"

Am I going to make her life a living hell? No, that's not my style. But am I going to have some fun? *Hell yes.*

CHAPTER SEVEN

I'm going to break his stick in half

VANESSA

Do you ever have something that instantly triggers a bad memory?

Well, for me it's the word *sunshine*. I've hated the nickname for as long as I can remember.

When I was in high school, I had a boyfriend named Matt who didn't like to use basic pet names like baby, babe, or honey. He preferred using the word *sunshine*. He said it was because I was warm and reminded him of summertime. At the time, I thought that it was sweet that he wanted to use a special term of endearment for me. That is until I heard him calling out that name while hooking up with my best friend.

I remember the words as if he spoke them yesterday. *"Sunshine, I'm so sorry. Please forgive me. It was a mistake, I'm drunk, and she looks just like you. Sunshine, please, please forgive me."*

Sunshine.

Sunshine.

Sunshine.

From then on, I hated the word. And now Jake Shepherd has used it twice in the past two minutes and I'm ready to rip my hair out.

I knew working with a group of guys would be different from anything I've done before; I just didn't think that it would be so aggravating from the get-go. Jake's cocky smirk is embedded into my brain and it's all I can think about. He thought he was so clever and funny, thinking of a nickname for me. But little does he know the name just fuels a fire inside of me.

I know I was a bit grumpy, and the irony isn't lost on me. I may have been a little cold toward him, but to be fair, I had just gotten off the phone with my mother, who let me know that she and my father wouldn't be flying down to see me for my birthday. Instead, they planned a trip with their friends to go to Paris.

I mean, am I shocked?

No.

We don't see a lot of each other, especially since I'm in another state. I'll fly home for the holidays or during spring break, but they're both usually too preoccupied with work. When I do go home, it feels like I'm there to visit the city and not my family.

The past few years have been harder on our relationship. I think it has something to do with me becoming more independent and not following their life plans for me anymore. At least on my birthday they try to make an effort to see me—or I guess they used to.

Since I've been in college, they would travel to Boston and bring me to a fancy restaurant and give me an expensive gift I didn't want *nor* ask for. It seems like now that I'm getting older, they don't seem to care as much.

When I was in high school, I thought having careless parents was a blessing. They never gave me a curfew and didn't care who I hung out with as long as my grades never dipped below an A. Looking back on it now, I wish they would've spent a little more time with me. If only they would give up on this idealistic daughter that they've created in their heads and accept me for who I am.

I highly doubt that will ever happen. As soon as I started growing out of the mold they wanted me to fit into, they lost all interest. It seems that the older I get, the less interested they become with my life. When I got accepted into BCU for journalism, my parents weren't exactly thrilled. My mom thought that my photography hobby was just a phase and that as soon as I graduated high school, I would be set on the straight and narrow path they so carefully carved for me.

Their idea of a perfect life for me is to be majoring in political science or business, dating a successful man, and eventually fulfilling my family's incredibly high standards. Unfortunately, I crushed their idea of that life. I can still remember their disappointing faces when I told them that I was studying journalism. Mom threw a fit like a child and didn't speak to me for days.

I wonder how they'll take the news that I'm working with a hockey team for a social media class. That alone might be enough to give my mom a heart attack.

Sydney, Maddie, and I made the executive decision to skip our morning classes today and reward ourselves with a delicious sugary breakfast.

We arrive at the pancake house off campus, and it's packed with other college students trying to get a bite before class.

"Follow me, ladies." Our hostess grabs three menus and leads us toward our table. She seats us at a small booth near the front of the restaurant and places our menus in front of us. I don't even need to look to know that I'll be getting the s'mores pancakes. It's one of their most popular items on the menu and I get it anytime we come here. Something about marshmallow fluff and chocolate chip pancakes in the morning just feels right. I always pair it with an iced latte, and oh boy, I'm in heaven.

Our waitress comes by our table with some water and lets us know she'll be back in a moment to take our order.

"I'm stuck between the French toast and the western omelet," Maddie says.

"You're *always* stuck between those two. Get the French toast. Every time you get the western omelet you always steal bites of my pancakes!" I tell her.

Maddie is like me; we bond over our love for chocolate and sweets. Anytime we go out for breakfast, she chooses a savory option knowing I'll cave and give her pieces of whatever I ordered.

"True." She laughs and places her menu on top of mine, almost as a signal to the waitress that we're ready to order. Sydney is staring at the menu like it's a pop-up quiz.

"What are you gonna get, Syd?" I ask.

She looks up at me about to answer, when her gaze quickly falls behind me.

"Oh, I want to order one of *him,* please." She smirks and points behind us.

Maddie and I turn around to see who she's referring to. Before I can even register his face, Jake breaks out in the widest smile I've seen and makes his way over to our table.

You've got to be kidding me.

Can I not go one day without seeing him?

He takes off his hat to readjust his hair. I feel mesmerized by the action. The soft brown waves are pushed back before he puts the baseball cap back on—backward. *Ugh, that's so hot.*

No. No, it's not hot. He's just some cocky athlete who likes to get on my nerves, even though he makes my insides melt when he smiles at me like that.

Jake squats down beside our table, the movement causing his jeans to grow tight at his thighs, it looks as if he's made out of marble.

Oh God, Vanessa avert your eyes before he notices you staring.

I move my eyes back up only to be met with a knowing smile. Shit, I'm caught.

"All right, Nichols, this is just uncanny now. Are you following me?"

"Jakey, you would love that, wouldn't you?" I watch as he winces at the nickname I give him. Not the greatest, but it's the best I could come up with on the spot. "Trust me, if I would've known that you'd be here, I would've skipped breakfast."

He holds his hand to his chest like I've stabbed him. "Ouch. That hurt, sunshine."

I had a feeling he was going to call me that again.

I roll my eyes in his direction. "What would it take for you to stop calling me that?"

"That's a dangerous question, Nichols." He winks at me, and Sydney kicks my leg under the table. She's living for this.

One of his teammates, Kieran I believe, comes up and grabs Jake by the arm. He glances at Maddie quickly and I swear she gives him the smallest smile. It barely lasts a second before they both move their attention back to Jake.

"C'mon, Jake, leave the girl be."

Jake sighs and picks himself up. "Well, I guess I'll see you around, sunshine." With that last remark, he smiles at me again and leaves with his teammate.

And just like that, I no longer have an appetite for pancakes.

The rest of the week flies by and suddenly it's Friday night and it's the Wolves' first game of the season. As their new social media coordinator, I have to attend every home and away game.

Luckily for me, I have two amazing best friends who are willing to attend every game on campus. I get access to the locker room before and after the game, with the coach's permission of course, so Sydney and Maddie left me to get us seats in the stands.

I find Coach Wilson and follow him to the locker room to try to talk with some of the guys before tonight's game.

I posted a story on their Instagram highlighting tonight's starters, along with some of their stats from last season. I had nothing to do last night besides watch *The Godfather* for my film class, but I got bored within the first hour and decided to do my homework on the team instead.

I mean, how hard is it to run a few social media accounts?

Apparently a little harder than I thought. With over twenty guys on the team, it takes up a lot of time researching each player's stats and history.

I follow Coach Wilson into the locker room, and it's almost like the boys are having a party before the game. All of them are fully dressed in their uniforms, some beginning to lace up their skates while others are doing—honestly, I don't know how to describe what I'm seeing.

There's an old-school rap song blaring from the speaker next to Nate, and in the center of the room are Jake and Kieran, dancing like no one's watching them. Limbs flailing as if they're trying to shake out any lingering nerves before the game.

I wonder if this is some pregame ritual.

I grab my phone out of my back pocket and take a video of the two of them goofing around. My camera would have better quality, but this is way more discreet. The energy in the locker room is electric. It's their first game of the season and you can tell that they're all a little antsy waiting to play.

For some, it's a bittersweet moment, it being their last year playing before they graduate. For others, fresh younger faces are anxiously watching their peers, trying to calm themselves before playing for the first time. I never used to understand how people got emotional over sports. My dad is a huge football guy, and the only time I've ever witnessed him cry was when his team won the Super Bowl. But looking at this group of guys, I think I'm starting to understand why.

"Settle in for a moment!" Nate turns down the music as Coach Wilson starts his pregame speech.

"This is our first game of the season. Keep it clean, skate fast, and don't let a single goal past you." His eyes fall on Kieran with his last word. "You should all have the plays drilled into your head by now and I want to see teamwork on that ice, got it?"

His voice booms off the cement walls and everyone nods silently in response.

"Captain." He nods his head toward Nate. "Anything you want to add?"

The group follows Coach's gaze, watching Nate stand, he taps his stick on the ground to get their attention.

"This is going to be our year, boys. We've trained all summer and spent hours working our asses off, day and night on this ice, and we're going to fucking win. Boston College will play dirty, like they always do—they'll try to make us fall for their tricks, but we're smarter than them. They're going to look up at the scoreboard and wish they would've trained harder. And when it comes time, that championship is coming home with us this season!"

All the guys start shouting, some knocking their sticks against the floor to create more commotion. If you lit a match, it would ignite with their energy.

"All right, let's get out there and warm up!" With Coach's dismissal, the boys start filtering out of the locker room.

I take this moment to go over the video, quickly cropping the beginning of Jake and Kieran dancing. I go to post it on the team's Instagram, captioning it: *Pregame hype.*

As I'm about to hit upload, my phone gets taken out of my hands.

"Who said you could film me without my consent?"

I look up at Jake, who towers over me in his skates. He's always been taller than me, it was one of the first things I noticed. But seeing him in all of his gear, *he's massive.*

Before he can register my quick movement, I snatch my phone back.

"What, are you scared that one of your little puck bunnies is going to see this?"

Jake looks down at me, a smirk splayed across his face. "If anything, the video will only make girls want me more. You were recording, you saw how good my moves are."

Of course he would say something like that.

"I'm allowed to take photos and videos, it's my job, in case you forgot."

"Oh, I didn't forget, sunshine. I just like to annoy you. Enjoy the game. Get some good footage of me out there. Maybe I'll even score a goal for you." He slowly retreats toward the locker room doors that lead to the arena. "And keep a photo or two for yourself. Y'know, for personal reasons." He winks at me before following the remaining teammates out into the arena.

God, he's something else.

I make my way out of the locker room and find Sydney and Maddie dead center in the front row of the stands.

"Did you see any of them naked?" Sydney wiggles her eyebrows at me as I grab my camera out of my bag.

I roll my eyes at her comment. "No dicks in sight yet."

A middle-aged woman sitting behind us coughs loudly. *Oops.*

I turn around and give her an apologetic smile. I forgot that the games are normally family friendly and sometimes we don't say the most PG things.

"Syd, don't forget that your brother is also on the team. So, if I do see anything, I'll report back to you in excruciating detail."

"Ew, okay, never mind, sorry I even asked." Sydney puts her finger to her mouth, pretending like she's gagging from the visual I just put in her head.

We turn our attention to the ice, where the boys are finishing their warm-ups. The teams go to their reciprocal benches, and the starting line takes their place on the ice. The referee holds the puck in between Nate and Boston's center—Andrew Meyers.

As the puck leaves his hand, I feel my heart start to race. Nate wins the face-off, immediately passing the puck to Levi, and they skate into the offensive zone.

When I was researching the team last night I learned a lot about the starters. Nate Archer plays center and is majoring in business—similar to Eli Murphy and Kieran Danford. I swear almost half the team are enrolled in the same classes.

Nate's been on the team since his freshman year. He was the co-captain for the past two seasons, but this is his first year of being captain solo, and his last year on the team, as he's scheduled to graduate in the spring. I'll be sad to see him leave because who will help us lift all our heavy boxes now? The first time I met Nate was move-in day at the dorms. I had just finished unpacking when Sydney walked in, empty-handed, with Nate in tow carrying three boxes. And when we moved into the condo, he was the only person who helped us.

But I can't be mad he's graduating and leaving us, he's moving on to bigger and better things. Nate was drafted to the Boston Broncos when he turned eighteen, but his contract starts once his NCAA eligibility is done.

Levi Brody is the team's starting right wing. Unlike some of his teammates, Levi is majoring in digital journalism. A few of our classes have overlapped in the past, but we've never spoken before now. He's the same age as me, still having another year left to play.

Their left wing is a freshman named Sebastian Xavier. He comes all the way from Montreal on a scholarship and is also studying—like most of his teammates—business.

Kieran Danford is the team's goalie. He plays in basically every game and rarely lets shots get past him. I tried doing some digging on his social media accounts, but this guy is so secretive. All of his accounts are private and it's like trying to penetrate a solid cement wall with a plastic spoon. I guess that's sort of what he's like on the ice too. He definitely has that sexy mysterious vibe going on.

Eli Murphy is the team's assistant captain. He transferred to BCU last year and in his debut game he scored three goals, something uncommon for a defenseman. He quickly proved he was a force to be reckoned with, and earned a starting spot his first year with the Wolves. From what I've seen in game clips online, he's good at checking and making hard hits while hiding it from the refs. He was drafted to the Chicago Eagles in his last year of high school, but he's adamant about wanting to swap to his home state—Tennessee.

The last player in their starting lineup is Jacob Shepherd. Probably the most infuriating of the five in my opinion.

Jake is the other defenseman for the team and has the stats to show that he's one of the best BCU has seen in years. Over the course of last season, he scored more than fifteen goals, which is unusual for a defenseman, had over forty assists, and spent about twenty minutes in the penalty box. Even I cannot deny how talented he is, even if he's absolutely aggravating. He was drafted to the New Jersey Demons when he was eighteen, and they'll be lucky to have him once he graduates later this year.

While digging through Jake's social media last night, I got a small insight into what he's really like. His Instagram is mainly dedicated to hockey and, well, you guessed it, *partying*. When I scrolled through his tagged photos, there were hundreds of photos tagged by different girls, clearly living up to his playboy title.

In certain ways, Jake reminds me a bit of myself, which is scary to think. I get the whole *no commitment* vibe, but I wonder why he's like that. I know why I'm the way that I am and what's led me to make my own decisions. I can't help but wonder if Jake's fine with the playboy narrative or if he's acting like this for a reason.

I guess it could just be that he's hot and is using that to his own advantage. I highly doubt there's a deep side to him.

I pull myself out of my thoughts and revert my attention back to the game.

Levi skates fast, dodging one of Boston's defensemen, and passes the puck back to Nate, who has a clear shot. I angle my camera on its tripod and start filming, knowing Nate will take the shot the moment he gets the puck. The second Nate takes possession, he slaps his stick and gets the first goal of the game. Sydney, Maddie, and I shoot up from our seats and cheer with the other fans in the stands.

Throughout the rest of the first period, no one else can make a goal. Jake gets a penalty for tripping, although I swear the other player tripped over his own foot but made a big enough deal about it that the ref sided with them. It seems like the guys are relying heavily on offense in today's game. I wonder if this was one of the strategies Coach was talking about.

In the second period, Nate is being cornered behind the net and passes the puck back to Jake, who takes the rare opportunity to skate past Boston's offense and score the second goal of the game.

As Jake and Eli skate back toward their defensive position, Jake spots me in the crowd and points. *"That was for you."*

I feel the heat rise to my cheeks as a few people around us stare at me for a moment.

It's not normal for a guy to dedicate a goal to someone unless it's their girlfriend. And I am *far* from that. I don't even think you could call me and Jake friends.

Ignoring his gesture and the smug look on his face, I focus back on the game.

I strategically swap between taking photos and videos. I'm lucky enough to have a good quality camera on my phone as well to get double the content.

A body is checked here, someone slashes there. For a while all I focus on are the players in front of me, and the sound of a puck hitting the boards. I get some good close-ups of Nate and Eli, and an amazing photo of Kieran grabbing the puck midair.

The final buzzer goes off, indicating the end of the third period, marking the first win for the Wolves.

The final score is 3–1.

Their other teammates on the bench hop over the boards and tackle the guys on the ice, celebrating their victory over our rival team. Nate is in the middle of the commotion holding his stick above his head. Jake, Eli, and Levi are also stuck in the thick of it but enjoying every second of their win. I take this moment to snap a shot of the guys all together, smiles splayed across their faces.

Sometimes I forget what it's like to take portraits of people. Being able to capture moments that are so vulnerable and raw, it gives the photos life. It reminds me why I pursued my passion for photography.

I tuck my camera back into my tote bag, now that the game has finished, and my skills are no longer required. I need to get a proper camera bag so I can keep all my attachments together. I've been using an old tote I got from a farmers' market back in Manhattan. It was from this old vintage store, and the print stood out immediately to me. It's this cute beige linen material with a globe and flowers embroidered on it. It has become heavily faded and torn throughout the years, but I can't seem to part with it.

People start to weave their way through the stands to file out of the arena. I make my way past my friends and lead us into the lobby.

"I'm gonna wait for Nate. He'll be so happy I finally attended one of his games."

As much as Sydney loves her family and her brother, she's one of the last people you'd catch at a game. She loves athletes but hates sports. She's quite the contradiction. She's also my ride, so it looks like we're all going to wait for him. I scroll through some of my footage, deleting any shots that didn't turn out the greatest.

When Nate comes out, he spots us immediately, making his way over to where we're standing. And of course, following behind him like baby ducks—Eli, Kieran, Levi, and *Jake*.

"Evenin', ladies, enjoy the game tonight?" Eli says first, his country twang slipping out. "Or were you too busy enjoying *us*?" He leans down, raising an eyebrow at Sydney.

Yeah, he definitely knows how to use that Southern charm

"Eli, dial it back. That's my sister, for fuck's sake." Nate runs his hand down his face before pulling Eli back by his shoulder.

I remember seeing Eli with a few different girls at Shaker's last weekend when we were there. I can understand why, though, he's so damn alluring. His soft warm skin and big lips make him stand out from the rest of his friends.

Sydney ignores Eli and her brother, instead she moves to stand in front of Jake, pointing her finger at his chest. "I assumed I would be the one who got a goal dedicated to her first since I'm your captain's sister, but it seems like Ness beat me to it." She glances back at me and gives me a wink.

I'm so going to kill her when we get home.

"Did you like that, Nichols? I thought it was a good touch. Great content for your little social media accounts too." You can hear the smugness in Jake's voice.

"Yeah, it was lovely, thanks." Hopefully he's picking up on my sarcasm. He uses his shoulder and shoves me to the side a little, very playfully.

"You ladies coming to Shaker's tonight to celebrate, yeah?" Eli asks us.

Before Nate can decline for his sister, Sydney responds. "Hell yes, count us in!"

Nate's nostrils flare for a split second before letting out a sigh. I can only imagine the hell that Sydney has put him through growing up. From the stories she's shared with us, I'm surprised he doesn't have any gray hairs yet.

I don't feel like going out tonight. After what feels like an exhausting week, I wouldn't mind going home and curling up with a book from Maddie's bookshelf. I swear that girl could open a library with the number of books she has.

"I don't know, I have some school stuff I really should get started on and a ton of footage to comb through." That's probably the lamest excuse I could've come up with.

"Ness, you have *all* weekend to work on assignments. Going out for a few hours won't kill you." Sydney stares at me with the biggest set of puppy-dog eyes I've seen. Her big brown eyes are lethal. When she wants something, she knows exactly how to get it.

"C'mon, even Maddie is going to come, right, Mads?" Her eyes dart to Maddie, whose attention is focused on the phone in her hand.

"Uh, yeah, sure." She looks up from her phone scanning the group that surrounds us before her eyes fall onto me. "C'mon, girl, it'll be fun."

"Yeah, c'mon, Ness." Jake drags out the last syllable. "Don't be lame. You scared you can't keep up with us?"

I know he's challenging me. He thinks he can intimidate me into going out with them. Well jokes on him because I don't cave that easily.

"I can't fall behind on my term pro—"

"Ness—wait, is it cool if I call you that?" Kieran starts, his voice is velvet smooth. "Anyway, think of it like a form of initiation. You're an outsider coming in and in order for us to accept you, then you have to hang out with us *outside* of hockey too."

His emerald green eyes put me in a daze. *Jesus, what is it with these hockey boys?*

"See, now you *have* to come out," Sydney pleads.

She's so dramatic. But I love her.

"Maybe for one drink. And I really only mean one." I give her a stern look, but her puppy-dog eyes definitely are winning me over.

I'm caving.

"Hang out with us for the night. What harm could we do?" Nate says as he starts to walk toward the exit, already accepting the fact that his younger sister and her friends are tagging along.

The boys follow Nate out the lobby doors, but Jake falls behind, falling into step with me.

"Captain's orders." Jake slings his arm around my shoulder as we all turn toward the doors. He whispers in my ear before running to catch up with Nate and the rest of the guys. "Looks like we'll be spending the night together, sunshine."

If Jake calls me sunshine one more time, I'm going to break his stick in half.

CHAPTER EIGHT

I'm fucking Jake Shepherd

JAKE

The first game of the year always sets the mood for how you go into every game for the rest of the season.

After winning our first game and *crushing* Boston College, I am on a high. Not literally, although a joint wouldn't be the worst thing right now. My knees hurt a little from today and a few little hits would help the pain melt away.

Honestly, after every win I feel like I'm flying and there's no better way to celebrate than going out with your friends. We even convinced Vanessa to come out with us. I think my teasing might've been the final nail in the coffin. Watching her eyes narrow to mine, meeting my challenge. She's feisty.

I don't know what it is that keeps drawing me to her. It's like she's a magnet and I'm a giant sheet of metal. Even if it's only for a minute, I find myself wanting to be near her.

Talk to her.

Annoy her.

Fuck, I need to get Vanessa out of my system.

I'm fucking Jake Shepherd. If I really wanted to, I could get any girl in this bar tonight. And yet here I am, watching the door, waiting for her to walk in like I'm a fucking dog waiting for its owner to return home. *God, this is pathetic.*

If I could sleep with her once, that would get her out of my head. *Right?*

Kieran already thinks I'm obsessed with her, but I wouldn't call it that. *I'm intrigued.* Maybe a scientist can scoop out my brain and analyze why I can't get that small brunette off my mind.

It goes against my nature to want someone *this* badly.

"Shep, stop watching the door and drink this." Kieran shoves a beer into my hand, reminding me that I'm out with my friends and need to stop fantasizing about a girl who clearly has no interest in me.

Although she did blush when I pointed at her during our game, and that was so fucking cute.

Cute? What the fuck is wrong with me?

I take a swig of my beer and join the rest of my teammates at the bar.

Shaker's is decently packed for a Friday night, and everyone is here to celebrate our win. People constantly come up to us, congratulating us on our win and we feel like we're at the top of the social food chain. It's like everyone just wants to boost my ego even bigger than it already is.

I'm not gonna complain about that.

But then I see a small brunette walk into the bar, and I automatically think it's Vanessa. That is until the girl turns around and disappointment turns in my gut.

Why am I disappointed? I couldn't care less if she showed up.

Well...I guess I care a little.

I quickly down the remainder of the beer Kieran gave me and rest the empty bottle on the bar. I wave over the bartender, signaling for another, when I see a familiar face walk up to me.

"Jake! That was a sweet goal you made tonight." Caroline sends me a smile as she runs her red-painted nails along my bicep.

"Thanks, Car." I wrap my arm around her shoulders and give her a hug. Caroline and I have been friends since sophomore year. She used to casually date our old captain, but since he's graduated and went on to the pros, she's been hanging with our group. I think she feels more comfortable around this crowd than her own friends. I give her a smile as my eyes rake down her body. She's wearing a tight leather skirt that hugs her ass and shows off her recent thigh tattoo—a crescent moon with stars hanging from the points, it looks fucking wicked.

I grab my beer from the bartender. "What're you up to tonight?"

"I don't know, haven't decided yet." She scans the crowd, scrunching her nose at most of the already wasted guys. "I might end up going home and cuddling my dog." She then eyes me up and down. "Unless someone else has something in mind."

I've hooked up with Caroline a couple of times in the past, before she was dating my former captain, and a couple of times post-breakup. I'm not one who fucks with other people's relationships. I'm not a piece of shit.

Caroline's petite but full of muscle, with dark red hair, peachy skin, and covered in patchwork tattoos. She's a solid fuck and doesn't expect anything afterward. She's the type to sneak in and out in the middle of the night without saying a word.

From what I know, Caroline used to want commitment, but when Nick broke her heart last year, she completely change. Now she's the type of girl who loathes relationships and would rather cut off her arm than date someone.

Hell, I can't blame her. Who would want to be tied down, especially during college?

I turn my head back to Car and as I'm about to respond, the girl who's been on my mind all day finally walks into the bar, her two friends in tow behind her.

Holy fuck, what is she wearing?

"Um, I'll catch you later, Car." I barely give a wave before heading straight for Vanessa.

Sydney is aimlessly looking around for our group, her eyes finding me first, and a wide smile breaks out across her face. She tugs on Vanessa's arm, causing her to turn in my direction.

Vanessa stood out immediately to me. Her hair is curled again and she's sporting a very tight red lace top with leather pants.

Leather pants are so fucking sexy.

I draw my gaze up her body, taking her all in. What stands out the most to me is the red lipstick she's wearing. It highlights her pouty lips and all I can imagine is them wrapped around my cock. Is she the devil? Because she's tempting me to do bad things right now, specifically to her.

"Ladies, glad to see you could all make it." I smile at the trio, hoping my charm will immediately win them over.

"Jacob, lovely to see you again." Sydney hugs me first. "Can you point me in the direction of your teammates? I want free shots."

"They're all at the bar. Tell Kieran I sent you over and he'll take care of you two tonight."

"The two of us?" Maddie questions me, pointing back and forth between her and Sydney.

"I'm going to steal Ness for a little bit, if the two of you don't mind."

Sydney wiggles her eyebrows at Vanessa, and she shoves her friend away in response, mumbling something about catching up with them later. Too bad she's mistaken because I want Vanessa all to myself tonight. After seeing her cheer for us in the stands at the game, I haven't been able to get her out of my head.

"That shirt you're wearing is, uh…" *Hot, sexy, makes me want to take her to the bathroom and make her come on my tongue.* I lose the words before I can even say them.

C'mon, brain, start working.

"What, this?" She references her shirt. "It's a corset top."

She says that as if it's something I should have known.

I have a younger sister, Autumn, who normally fills me in on the current fashion trends and what's going on in the world of celebrities. She's really into fashion and dance, but since moving away from home, I haven't been updated as much besides her weekly text.

"Yeah…well, whatever it is, it's hot."

She rolls her eyes. It seems like that's a reaction I get out of her a lot.

"Is this like a Pavlov thing?" I ask her.

She looks up at me and raises an eyebrow, causing her glasses to shift. "What?"

"Every time I say something, you go and roll your eyes at me. So, I'm asking, did you train yourself to do that every time I speak?"

I lean against the wall next to us, as her mouth falls into the shape of an *O*.

She stays silent for a second, as if she's contemplating a reply to me. I've managed to make her speechless, just for one moment.

"Do you think I'm some dog that can be trained?" Her eyes are sending daggers at me.

Uh-oh, I hit a nerve.

Retreat. Retreat. RETREAT.

"No, uh, t-that's not what I meant." I should take my foot out of my mouth and shove it up my ass, I'm such an idiot.

Her green eyes hold an icy gaze. I can't tell if she's about to yell at me or slice my balls off with her glare. But she surprises me when a smile slowly spreads across her face, and she starts…laughing.

What the fuck?

"That's hilarious. I honestly didn't think you knew who Pavlov was." Her voice is so smooth that it makes me forget that she's assuming I'm dumb. I guess that is what the college hockey player stereotype is—a big oaf with a little brain. Well, jokes on her, she has no idea who I am.

"But to answer your question, no. It's just a natural reaction when someone says something stupid, which you happen to do a lot."

Damn. I don't even care that she just insinuated I was dumb. Her laugh has me in a chokehold. I want to hear that again.

"Sheesh, sorry. I'll work on integrating intellectual conversations between the two of us in the future." This also makes her smile, so I take this as an opportunity. "Can I get you a drink?"

"Sure."

We walk back toward our group, and I order her a vodka cranberry from the bartender.

Most girls like those, *right?*

I grab the drink and give it to her. As she holds the drink in her hand, I see her nose scrunch a little in distaste.

"What? You don't like it?" I ask as she takes her first sip.

"No, it's okay. I just..." She trails off. "Normally my go-to is a rum and coke, but hey, it's a free drink, right?"

"I'll make sure to get it right on your next one. Want to dance?"

She looks to the dance floor, seeing her friends dancing with Levi and Eli. "I'm not really in the mood for dancing tonight. Do you wanna sit down somewhere?"

I'm not the best dancer in the world so I'm a little relieved. The only way I can start to move is if I have some hard liquor in my system. And since the beginning of the season has started, I try to stick solely to beer. Emphasis on the try, sometimes I can be persuaded.

I realize I'm taking too long to answer, and Vanessa starts to fidget with the glass in her hand. "I mean, you don't have to. I was just being polite. I can go hang with my friends."

She goes to turn away, but I reach out and grab her arm before she can get too far.

"Hey, woah, hold on there. You barely gave me a second to respond. I'm fine with sitting and chatting. This can be our little meeting where you get to know me better. You know, for the whole social media thing."

She's clearly pleased with my answer, as she sports a smile again.

Fuck, her smile is so pretty.

I follow her to a table tucked more to the side, away from the dance floor. It's quieter over here, easier for conversations.

As we sit in silence for a minute, I realize we've never really talked before. Only quick conversations in passing.

"All right, sunshine, so what do you want to know?" I lean back in my chair, resting my arm over the back of it.

She sighs loudly at the nickname. "If I ask you nicely to stop calling me sunshine, will you stop or are you going to keep calling me that because you know I hate it?"

"Probably option two."

"Ugh, okay, whatever." She shoos me away with her hand, huffing out a sigh.

I want to know why she gets so worked up every time I call her that. I think it's a cute nickname. She's always so moody and grumpy when she sees me, I think *sunshine* fits her perfectly because she's the complete opposite. What's her deal?

"All right, if you tell me a valid reason as to why you hate that nickname, and not just because it's one I made up for you, I'll stop." I hold my hand up to my heart. "Scout's honor."

"You were not a scout." The disbelief is so evident in her voice.

"Hell yes, I was. Troop number two fifty-six at your service."

This gets another laugh out of her. Before speaking again, she takes another sip of her drink. Either she's really thirsty or she's mustering up some liquid courage.

"Fine. But just to preface, you asked for this trauma dump," she starts. I nod at her, waiting for her to continue. "My ex used to call me that. He said that I reminded him of the sun and that his world revolved around me. Then he cheated on me, so I don't really like to think about it anymore. So I implore you, will you *please* stop calling me that?"

I pick up on her body language as she starts to fiddle with the rings on her fingers, clearly this topic is making her on edge. I feel like there's more to the story than she's letting on.

"Is that it? I thought you said you were going to trauma dump on me?" I ask. "You and your boyfriend broke up and now the word *sunshine* has the same negative connotation as Voldemort?"

"Did you really just compare sunshine to Voldemort?"

"No, I'm saying *you* are comparing it. Who cares if your last boyfriend called you that? Why does it affect you so much if it's just a nickname?"

"*Oh my god*, you just won't let it go." She tosses her hands up in defeat before continuing. "*Fine.* Here's the actual trauma dump *you* asked for. I threw a party at my house for his birthday and caught him fucking my best friend in *my* bed. One moment I was his everything, I was his sun and stars, and the next thing I know, I'm being tossed away like a piece of trash. Now do you understand why I might not like the name?"

Yikes. Maybe I shouldn't have pushed her. But also, who the hell would cheat on her? Sure, Vanessa seems like all sass, but there's some charm about her that's intoxicating.

"Sorry, Nichols." She nods at me, chugging the rest of her drink, licking her lips as she puts the empty drink down. "Maybe let's get you another drink and find a more cheerful topic, yeah?"

Vanessa looks up at me and pushes her glasses up the bridge of her nose. Fuck that was cute. What the hell is she doing to me?

"This round is on me, but when I get back, you better have some interesting or hilarious story lined up to lift my spirits." She hops off the bar stool and heads over to the bar.

I watch her walk the whole way there, hips swaying back and forth with her movement. Those pants hugging every curve of her body. They're so different from the baggy jeans she wore to our practice the other day. These ones are high waisted and tight around her thighs and ass, it's so perfect—small yet round and plump.

As she makes her way back with her drink in one hand and my beer in the other, I make sure to turn my attention toward the TV above the bar, pretending like I wasn't watching her the whole time.

"Okay, Jakey, what's your story? I'm ready to be entertained." She flips her hair over her shoulder, tucking a loose strand behind her ear.

My mind immediately goes blank. The whole time she was at the bar I was looking at her, not thinking of something to talk about when she got back.

"Right, yeah." Oh fuck, I gotta think of something quick. "Uh, I was going to tell you when I fell in love with hockey for the first time."

She makes a face of intrigue at me, stirring the lime into her drink.

"Okay, I'm listening." She leans in, positioning her elbows on the table and resting her chin on her fists. I get lost for a second, staring into her massive green eyes. It's like fields of grass on a warm spring day.

"My dad put me in sports when I was eight because he thought it would help me focus more. And it did. I remember attending my first practice and my coach, Coach Andy, put the

73

stick in my hand and had all of us take turns shooting on our goalie." She scoots closer, listening more intently to me over the music blaring in the background. "I was the first player who got a shot past our goalie, and I remember feeling untouchable. For the entire hour of practice, I left everything off the ice. I didn't think about struggling in school or my parents fighting. Instead, when I went home that night, I thanked my dad for introducing me to hockey, and told him I wanted to be a professional hockey player when I grew up."

I hope she doesn't catch the secret I accidentally let slip.

She stares at me for a moment, a smile still plastered on her face. "That's really sweet, Jake. I honestly thought you were going to tell me a story of when you and your teammates got shit-faced or something."

This time I laugh at her. Most people assume I'm a dumb jock who only cares about sports and getting with chicks—which, don't get me wrong, I definitely care about both of those things, but that's not *everything* I care about. People just don't care to ask the right questions.

"Oh, I'm sure I have a million and one stories about me and the boys. But y'know, I'm a lot deeper than people make me out to be."

"Oh really? Okay, how about I rapid-fire some questions at you, *Mr. I'm So Deep*."

I have a feeling this is going to be interesting.

"What is your biggest irrational fear?"

I don't know what I thought she was going to ask, but this definitely wasn't on my list. I take a moment to think it over besides settling on the obvious.

"I dunno, like…probably an apocalypse, like *Mad Max* or something like that."

She stirs the straw in her drink slowly, her eyes still on me. "You don't think you're capable of surviving an apocalypse? You'd think with all those muscles, you'd have a fighting chance."

I'm glad she's taken notice of my hard work. "I never said I *couldn't* survive an apocalypse, but I'd rather *not* have to scavenge for my life."

"Hmm, okay. I wouldn't say that, but to each their own."

"All right, Nichols, what's your irrational fear then if mine's so lame?" I ask.

"Zombies." She shudders as she says the word. I raise my eyebrow in question, asking her to continue. "I *definitely* wouldn't survive that. If there ever was a zombie apocalypse, I'm out. I will literally take myself out of the equation. There's no way I'm living in a world where I could be eaten alive."

I mean, I would eat her alive, but just in another way.

"Okay, I'll give you an easy one for the next question. What is your favorite movie?"

Oh, this is a no-brainer.

"Technically I have two. The first would be *Jurassic Park* because c'mon, a park full of dinosaurs. You're telling me not *one* person in that movie didn't think it was a bad idea to play around with genetics?"

She looks at me, a bit surprised by my answer.

"And the second?" She takes a sip of her drink.

"Basic answer, but *The Godfather*. My dad showed it to me when I was young, and we watch it every summer."

She looks at me shocked for a moment. Most of the time when I tell people what my favorite movie is, they just agree and say it's a classic. But Vanessa? No. Nothing is easy with her.

"You're joking, right?" She looks up at me in shock.

"No, it's a great film. The acting by Brando is insane. And the movie never drags. Coppola made it not only as a crime movie but to showcase Italian immigration into America."

Vanessa is looking at me as if I have three heads.

"What?"

"Nothing I just…wasn't expecting that answer," she admits. "I have to watch *The Godfather* for my film class, but I almost fell asleep within the first hour."

"You're kidding? It's one of the best films ever created and you're telling me that you almost fell asleep? How do you almost fall asleep to a cinematic masterpiece?"

"I just wasn't that into it. It bored me."

"No, nope. I will not tolerate any slander on that movie. When do you need to watch it by?"

"We're discussing it in class on Tuesday, so I'll probably end up watching it this weekend. Unless I fall asleep again, then I'll just look up the IMDb page and go from there."

I take a sip of my beer before responding to her. "I'm coming over and I'm watching it with you, just to make sure you give it an honest shot."

Vanessa rolls her eyes at me again. No matter what she says, I still believe that's her favorite response to me.

"Whatever you say, Jake." Her sarcasm is evident.

"Ask me something else. C'mon, I thought you said you were gonna rapid-fire at me?"

She looks at me, studying my face. I see the moment a thought pops in her head. "What made you choose environmental science as your major?"

Now she's getting somewhere. I don't remember the last time someone asked me about school except for Kieran trying to coordinate an elective with me.

I take a long sip, emptying my beer before answering. "Most guys who want to go pro tend to study business, economics, or some shit like that. But that shit bores the living hell out of me. I actually enjoy learning about the environment, about the movement of tectonic plates, how to measure past climates, all that shit is just so interesting."

She nods her head as I blabber about my current oceanography class.

"How did you know that was my major?" I ask her.

She freezes for a moment, almost embarrassed by knowing that fact about me before I had a chance to tell her. "I was researching all of the players on the team the other night. I won't lie, I was shocked when I found a few of you guys *weren't* business or human kinetics majors. It was refreshing to know a few of you have other interests besides hockey."

I know that Levi isn't a business major, and a few other guys are in psych or engineering, but the rest of them fall under the business umbrella.

Vanessa finishes her drink. I think the alcohol has loosened her up a bit because she hasn't rolled her eyes at me for the past twenty minutes. I think that might be a record. I should write that down.

"I'm gonna grab one last beer, would you like another drink?"

She contemplates for a moment, staring back from her drink to me. "Sure, why not."

I grab our empty drinks and head over to the bar where a few of my teammates remain seated. The rest of them are either on the dance floor or have left for the night. I put our empties on the end of the counter with the other empty cups and bottles and walk over to Kieran, who has a small redhead attached to him tonight.

"So how's it going over there? Has she rejected you again?" he asks.

"I'm working my charm. Just here to grab some drinks."

Kieran smiles at me, trying hard to stifle a laugh. He turns his attention away from me and back to the girl in his lap.

I try to get the attention of the bartender, but he's preoccupied with a group of girls at the other end of the bar. The only downside to being a guy at a bar is that if the bartender is a dude, he will *always* choose to serve women over men.

It's not sexist, just facts.

I don't really complain much about it because I would do the same thing. Women are beautiful. But right now, I really need to get our drinks and go back to talking with Vanessa. I don't know what it is about her, but I feel like we're very similar. I found out she's really into nature documentaries. It's like this girl wants to be the next David Attenborough.

There's a sense of familiarity when talking to her. It's like when you meet someone and can immediately tell that you'll get along well. Even with her sassy remarks and eye rolls, she has this energy around her that's contagious.

"Jake!" Caroline squeals from behind me and I nearly jump. I turn around to face her, and she has two shots of a dark liquid in her hands. "Do a shot with me, please."

She looks up at me with her pouty lips and puppy-dog eyes. She's always hard to say no to. Caroline is the type of friend to bully you into getting blackout wasted with her. Very chaotic, but *very* entertaining.

"What is it?" I'm a little hesitant to drink the unknown liquor.

"The bartender gave it to me for free, he called it 'three wise men' or something like that. I think it's whiskey. C'mon, don't be a baby."

She waves the shot in front of my face, the way you would taunt a dog with a treat. I know she's doing it just to get a rise out of me.

"Fine, if you don't want it, then I'll just have to take both and get alcohol poisoning, is that what you want?"

Gaslighting at its finest, ladies and gentlemen.

I grab the shot out of her hand. "Give it here. You're a pain in the ass, did you know that, Car?"

"Obviously." She smiles at me wickedly and we clink glasses, shooting it back. Normally I wouldn't touch any hard liquor during the season, but we don't have a game tomorrow, so tonight I'll give myself a break.

The liquor feels like fire as it goes down my esophagus. Whatever the fuck that was, I never want to drink it ever again. I'm not a pussy either. I can take a shot of straight Jack Daniel's or Jägermeister any day, but whatever mixture was in that shot, just isn't right. That was inhumane.

"That was disgusting," I cough out.

"Ditto." She rubs my back with one hand and places her empty shot glass down on the counter. "Well, I'm gonna go dance, come find me later if you're bored."

I wave her off and lean back onto the bar. The bartender finally makes his way back to my side, where I order our drinks. He takes a few minutes to grab a beer and rum and coke, but he finally returns with both drinks. I turn around and start to head back to our table when I notice both chairs are vacant. Where the hell did she go? Did she leave to use the washroom or something?

I take a seat at the table and look around, scanning for Vanessa. My eyes coast through the crowd until my eyes find her on the dance floor, and she's not alone.

She's with Levi.

That little fucker. He was teasing me all day after our game about her turning me down. He's doing this shit to mess with me.

I make my way through the crowd of people, balancing the drinks in my hands until I'm next to them. The look I give Levi causes him to drop his hands from Vanessa's hips.

"Brody, get lost." I stare him down, silently telling him to back the fuck off.

Vanessa turns toward me, realizing I was the reason Levi stopped dancing with her. "Levi, pay no attention to him, I don't know why his panties are in a twist."

They're in a twist because two seconds ago we were hanging out and talking, then I turn around and she's dancing with fucking Levi.

"What do you mean? We were just talking and then you dipped. All I did was leave to go get us drinks, and boom, you're gone?"

"Jake, you were gone for like fifteen minutes. I looked over at the bar and there you were with that little redhead taking shots, clearly preoccupied. Levi asked me to dance, and I said yes."

Was I really gone for that long?

Well fuck, it's not my fault the bartender took a million years to take my order. And when I asked her to dance earlier, she said she wasn't in the mood to dance tonight.

Or did she just not want to dance with me?

Fuck it, when have I ever not said what was on my mind. "So when I asked you to dance earlier and you said no, it's because you just didn't want to dance with me, huh?"

She rolls her eyes at me again. Fuck it.

This time, I lean in closer, whispering in her ear. "The next time you roll your eyes at me, it won't be because I'm annoying you." With that, I walk away from her with both of our drinks and try to find myself a distraction, because holy fuck, do I need to preoccupy my mind with something other than her.

I find Caroline back near the bar, talking with some of the guys.

"Hey, Car, I'm ready to dance now." I hold out my arm, waiting for her to grab it so I can lead us back to the dance floor. If Vanessa wants to fool around with Levi, then she can do whatever the fuck she wants. Just like I will.

CHAPTER NINE

We all share the same guilty pleasure

VANESSA

I think it's time to go home.

Watching Jake stick his tongue down another girl's throat five feet away from me is all the entertainment I need for one night.

It was nice getting to know him a bit better. I guess, for the most part, I did have him pinned down wrong. He's not a super shallow hockey player who only cares about getting in a girl's pants, although looking at him right now makes that hard to believe.

Does Jake know how infuriating he can be?

I mean, who asks a girl to hang out and then leaves her for some random chick at the bar?

Okay, I shouldn't be getting worked up over this. I shouldn't even care what Jake's up to. But I can't lie and say I wasn't a little hurt. I was really enjoying our conversation. I feel like it's so rare for me to find a guy I can actually communicate with. Talking with Jake felt so effortless.

This hasn't completely changed my mindset on him. He went from talking with me most of the night to making out with the small redhead I saw at their game today. She is drop-dead gorgeous, with her defined legs and tattoos, so props to Jake. If he wants to hook up with someone to celebrate, I won't get in the way of that.

I grab Sydney and Maddie from the dance floor, and we push our way through the crowd over to Nate to let him know we're ready to leave. The upside of going out with Nate and his friends is he at least offered to drive us all home.

Ugh, I can't wait to go home to my vibrator and *not* think about Jake.

"All right, girls, hop in," Nate yells while rolling down the passenger window.

Sydney hops in the front of his all-white Lincoln Aviator while Maddie and I slide into the backseat.

"Nate, hold up!"

As if on cue, all of us turn our heads to the front door and see Jake waving at us with the redhead attached to his hip.

Seriously? You've got to be kidding me right now.

If there is a god out there, can you help a girl out?

Jake opens the door next to me and leans in. "Hey, Ness, mind moving over?"

He pushes inside the car, moving me so I'm now sitting in the middle. I don't remember signing up to sit bitch in the backseat.

The girl from the bar is pulled in the car, too, and Jake positions her right on his lap, as if there wasn't any more room back here for her to sit. Could this night get any worse?

"Seat belts," Nate orders before driving off.

I get settled in as Jake pulls his seat belt around him and the girl sitting on his lap. She leans into him as he buckles them in and starts kissing his neck.

I think I might puke. He clearly doesn't have any consideration for everyone else in the car being subjected to this. I turn toward Maddie, sticking my finger to my open mouth, pretending to vomit when Jake and the girl start heavily making out next to me.

I stand corrected, this night can *definitely* get worse.

Jake slides his hands up her tattooed thigh, playing under the hem of her skirt. If I wasn't so annoyed I would compliment the girl on all of her ink, but right now I'd rather vomit on the two of them.

"Please refrain yourselves from fucking while there are other people in the car," I mumble but loud enough to hear Jake chuckle against the girl's lips.

I might open Maddie's door and throw myself out of the vehicle while driving.

After what feels like an hour, but was realistically only twenty minutes, we finally make it to our building. Jake is still preoccupied with the girl from the bar and doesn't notice any of us slip out of the vehicle. We wave off Nate and head inside.

I want to collapse on my bed and suffocate myself with all of my pillows. I am so over tonight.

We wave at our security guard, Greg, as we walk through the well-lit modern lobby.

"Good evening, ladies. Did you girls have a fun night out?"

"We had such a lovely night, Greg. How's yours going?" Sydney boasts. She's the most outgoing of our group, and she and Greg have the friendliest relationship. She always makes sure to bring down leftovers when we have them or give him gifts on holidays, so he feels appreciated.

"It's been quiet so far. You ladies get settled and have a good night." He waves at us before we head to the elevator.

We get to our floor and unlock the door to our apartment. Immediately, we kick off our shoes, and all let out a collective groan of relief, our toes so thankful that they're free of our heels. I can finally feel my pinky toes again after squishing them in tight shoes all night.

Sydney walks over to the couch and plops down, grabbing the remote. "Anyone wanna watch an episode of *Love Island*?"

"Ooh, I'm down for an episode." Maddie takes a seat next to her, wrapping herself up in a pink throw blanket.

They both look at me, waiting for an answer. I'm exhausted from the events of today and don't really feel like watching twenty hot single people mingle for an hour. I'm ready to shower and wash all my makeup off then pass out like a bear in hibernation.

"I think I'm gonna turn in. Rain check?"

"Fine, but you owe us two uninterrupted hours of trashy reality TV." Maddie snuggles further into the couch, tossing one of her horror movie decorative pillows behind her head.

Maddie's secret love is horrible, trashy reality shows. Besides true crime documentaries and horror movies, reality TV is the only other thing she'll watch. She's up to date on the newest shows and keeps us informed on which ones are worth watching, and which ones aren't—even though we end up watching them all. I guess we all share the same guilty pleasure.

"All right, sounds like a plan. Goodnight, love you both!" I shout from the hallway as I make my way to my room. I just need some alone time.

"Goodnight!"

"Love you!"

I shut the door behind me and lean against it for a moment to collect my thoughts.

My skin feels sticky from the sweat and alcohol. *I need to shower.* After being out at the bar and sharing a car with two people basically having sex next to me, I need to cleanse myself. I walk into my bathroom and let the water run. Steam quickly fills the air. I step into the shower, letting the hot water wash over me as all the sweat and makeup drips away. Once I'm scrubbed raw, I toss on a baggy tee and climb into bed, ready for my exhaustion to take over and lull me to sleep.

Except it doesn't.

Instead, all I can do is stare up at my ceiling as my brain continues to be stuck on a loop, replaying the events of tonight. It's like my mind can't move on without making me think of that one thing. That one person.

Jake.

I can't even have my own thoughts to myself, he needs to invade those too.

I have a feeling I won't be getting any sleep tonight.

The weekend flies by. After a nice deep clean of the condo, we all decided to take the rest of our Sunday working on our own school projects and things.

Sydney spent the morning organizing our entire kitchen before heading to the library. She's currently obsessed with watching videos of people cleaning and organizing their homes, so now she's taken it upon herself to declutter our space. Sometimes she can be a bit crazy with cleaning, but I will never complain because the place is always spotless when she gets in one of her moods.

Yesterday I worked on editing a few photos for my digital print lab and I also met up with two of the guys from the team, Sebastian and Levi. We went over basic questions regarding their studying, their hobbies, and of course their stats. I had them meet me at Caio, and talking with them was actually really refreshing. Levi and I joked about how ridiculous Jake was the previous night and Sebastian commented on how Jake couldn't keep his eyes off me until we all left, but I just shoved their comments aside.

I couldn't care less if Jake was watching me all night. At the end of the night, he still went home with one of his puck bunnies, not me.

Whatever, it doesn't bother me.

My late-night overthinking has concluded that my relationship with Jake is purely platonic. I'm going to be civil and nice for the remainder of my term project and then forget that he ever existed.

It's probably time I stop obsessing over this and get my Sunday started, since I've been lying in bed all morning. I need to tackle the heaping pile of laundry I've accumulated in the corner of my room. I don't know why I do it, but I always tend to leave all of my chores to Sunday. *It's probably because I'm a huge procrastinator.*

I pick up the clothes off the floor and bring them to our laundry room. We're lucky enough to have in-house laundry, which isn't too common for apartments. I guess one thing my parents are good for besides money is finding a good place to live. I toss a Tide POD in with the wash then make my bed and organize my shelves.

As I'm organizing the textbooks scattered on my desk, there's a knock at our front door. *Okay, odd.* Maybe Maddie or Sydney forgot their key; highly unlikely, but it's happened a few times before.

I walk over to look through the peephole only to see Jake on the other side.

What the hell is he doing here? I open the door and Jake's standing there in gray sweats and a red BCU hockey sweater.

"Uh…what are you doing here?"

Jake smiles wide at me. "Well that's no way to greet a guest, Nichols. Can I come in?"

He strides past and waits for me to shut the door behind him. As I turn to face him, I don't realize how close he actually is, and I bounce off his chest.

"Geez, you're a freaking giant," I mutter, straightening my glasses.

He chuckles at my lack of coordination. My depth perception isn't the greatest, especially with my eyesight.

I forget how much taller he is than me. How intimidating his frame is. I wonder what it's like to be that tall and what I look like from his point of view. Probably like a mouse.

We're standing in the hallway and silence falls between us.

Okay, not awkward at all.

"So back to my original question, what are you doing here? And *how* did you even get into the building?" I ask, crossing my arms across my chest.

"I called Sydney, and she told the guy at the front desk to let me in." He pulls his laptop out of his bag, holding it with one hand. "Did you forget that we're watching *The Godfather*?"

Oh, so he wasn't kidding about that.

I thought he was joking. I wasn't expecting him to actually show up with his laptop ready to watch a three-hour movie. If I would've known he was being serious, I wouldn't be wearing sweatpants and an old T-shirt.

"You were serious about that?"

"Why would I joke about watching one of my favorite movies? Did you hit your head and lose your memory? Do you even know your own name? What year is it?" he jokes as he removes his shoes.

I roll my eyes at him.

Hmm, okay, maybe it is an involuntary response to him.

"No, I didn't forget, I just didn't think you were serious."

He scoffs at me. "C'mon, Nichols, someone's got to make sure you don't fall asleep." He knocks his shoulder into me, teasingly. "So are we just gonna watch the movie in the hallway or is there somewhere we can sit?"

"Oh, right. We can watch it in my room if you want. Sydney just cleaned, so if we make a mess out here she'll kill me."

"Damn, what kind of mess will we be making?"

I guess I set myself up for that one.

"Speaking of Sydney, where are your roommates?"

"Sydney's on campus and Maddie's at work."

He raises his eyebrows seductively, "Oh, so it looks like we have the place to ourselves."

I ignore his comment and walk down the hallway, he's smart and keeps his mouth quiet as he follows me to my room.

"Straight to the bedroom. Geez, Vanessa, if you wanted to have sex with me, all you had to do was ask."

I turn around and lightly shove him with one arm. "Don't be dumb or you can go home, and I'll watch it by myself."

He holds his hands up in a sign of defeat. "All right, all right calm down. I'm just joking."

Jake plops down on the bed, and it sinks a little under his weight. I sit next to him, adjusting the pillows so I'm in more of an upright position rather than lying down with him. Jake stretches his legs out and I realize that my double-sized bed is almost too small for him. If he were to lie flat I can imagine his feet dangling off the edge of the bed. Now that I'm imagining that in my head, I can't stop the laugh that escapes my lips.

"What's so funny?"

I stifle my laugh. "I'm just imagining you sleeping in this bed and…you just wouldn't fit."

"You'd be surprised how easily I can fit into things." He winks at me, and I roll my eyes in response.

I guess I set myself up for that one. "Turn the movie on you idiot."

"Whatever you say, Ness."

He opens his laptop and queues up the movie. This man really has *The Godfather* purchased on his computer rather than streaming it online like I did.

Hmm, so he wasn't lying when he said it was one of his favorites.

"I'm going to be watching you throughout this entire movie to make sure you don't fall asleep."

My stomach flutters with his words—*he'll be watching me.* I'm imagining his eyes on me throughout the duration of the film, and it makes me feel nervous. His deep blue eyes can be so intimidating I don't want to have them staring at me for hours. I'll sweat through my shirt before we even get five minutes in.

"Now before we start." Jake rubs his hands together. "Do you have any snacks?"

"So let me get this straight, you come here unannounced, ready to watch a movie, but didn't bring any food with you?"

He nods at me.

Of course. He clearly didn't think any of this through. Am I surprised? Not really. It seems like Jake is completely oblivious to his actions.

Without another thought, I reach over to my nightstand and pull open the drawer to grab my secret stash of munchies. You never know when you might need a chocolate bar or a bag of chips. I pass him a KitKat and a small bag of salt and vinegar chips. Immediately he holds the chips by the corner as if it's a diseased animal that he picked up off the street.

"Is there something wrong with the chips?" I ask.

He tosses the bag back to me. "That is the *worst* flavor. What is wrong with you?"

"What's wrong with me? What the hell is wrong with you? Salt and vinegar is the best flavor out there. You clearly have no taste."

"Ness, I think the chips burnt off all of your taste buds 'cause those things burn your tongue as you eat them. Only crazy people like it."

"Well call me crazy then. If you wanted better snacks then you should have brought your own. Now eat your KitKat and hit Play, I don't want to spend all day watching this."

I open the bag and slowly plop a very sour chip into my mouth, keeping eye contact with Jake the whole time. As I chew on the chip, he makes a barfing sound.

Classy.

The chip had more vinegar than I expected and causes me to pucker my lips at the acidity. Jake's not wrong, they do burn as you eat them but that's what makes them so good. The salt and vinegar make your mouth pucker and I can't help myself from finishing an entire bag in one sitting.

"Yep, you're definitely crazy. At least you have good taste in chocolate." He breaks off a piece of the bar and takes a bite.

KitKat is the supreme chocolate in this household. They're Maddie's favorite and her parents send her care packages every now and again filled with all the different flavors. Sometimes I wish my parents knew my favorite candy and would send me boxes of it. Unfortunately that would require them to care to know something about me.

We eat our snacks in silence as the movie begins. I remember the first half hour of the movie, but everything after is a complete blur. At some point I get under the covers, our apartment is always chilly no matter how high we turn up the heat.

"Do you mind if I use the blanket?" Jake motions to the comforter I'm currently lying under. I shake my head and he maneuvers under the covers.

Throughout the movie, Jake makes small comments here and there to help explain the plot better. I hate to admit it, but watching it with someone definitely makes the movie more entertaining—even if it's Jake.

We get about halfway through the movie and the main character ends up in Italy and gets married while the rest of his family remains in New York. I was expecting this to be a sweet ending until the wife unexpectedly dies.

I shoot up from my now-lying position. "She didn't even do anything, and then boom, she dies in an explosion made for Michael. That's so messed up!"

"But that's the point! The movie is showing you how the Italian mob was back then. They were ruthless. If they couldn't go after you, they would go after your family." He explains. "No one was safe, that's the most unsettling part of it all."

"I don't think I could be with anyone who is involved with shit like that. Having a target on your back all the time, never knowing if your family was safe. I would go crazy."

"Oh, so if I told you I was in the mob then we couldn't be friends anymore?" Jake asks.

I side-eye him. "Who said we were friends?"

"Ouch, you wound me." He holds his hand over his heart, as if I had just stabbed him. He smirks at me in a way that makes heat rise to my cheeks.

Can we be considered friends? We've only talked a handful of times. If I wasn't assigned to the team, then I can guarantee Jake would have never spoken to me again.

We finish the rest of the movie with minimal comments from Jake.

"See, it wasn't so bad now was it?"

I stop staring at him so I don't seem like a freak. "As much as it pains me to admit this, you were right. I think it was better to watch it with someone."

Jake nods at my comment and then his face turns to a more serious expression. "So I wanted to talk to you about the other night. I didn't mean to intentionally ditch you."

Well that wasn't what I was expecting him to say. But is that what he should be apologizing for? 'Cause I would rather have him apologize for basically having sex with the girl next to me in the car.

"It's fine, don't worry about it."

He shifts his weight so now he's lying on his side, directly facing me. "No, it's not fine. I acted shitty. I ditched you to take shots with Car and made you wait around. I—Ness, look, I enjoy hanging with you. Even with your sassy remarks and constant eye rolls, you're fun to be around."

Okay, that was oddly sweet.

"That's nice and all, but what about you bringing home that girl from the bar? You were practically humping in the backseat. Did you not care that there were other people in the car?"

His eyebrows furrow. "What, with Caroline? We were just making out. We do it all the time."

Oh God, does he have a girlfriend? Jake doesn't seem like the type from his reputation. But hey, I guess you should never assume.

"Okay, well maybe next time you and your girlfriend could be more considerate of those around you."

"*Girlfriend?* That's cute." He sits up more, resting his arm behind his head. "Car and I are just friends who've hooked up a few times. Nothing more than that. And I'm sorry if we offended you with our kissing."

Hmm, okay, so not his girlfriend. But still, it would've been nice to not sit next to them the entire way home while they exchanged saliva.

"All right, look, Ness, if you don't want to be friends with me then that's cool. I just thought since you're going to be around the team for the whole year, we might as well get along, right?"

He makes a valid point, and I was just saying how I want to get along with everyone on the team. Friday night turned out to be a lot of fun, hanging out with Jake and then dancing with Levi and some of the other guys. They made me feel welcomed, a feeling I didn't expect from a college hockey team.

"Well, I guess we *can* be friends, considering you are lying in my bed."

Jake laughs at my remark. "Yeah, I guess that's true."

I stand up on the bed and stretch. Lying in my bed for three hours has made my back stiff.

"All right, well I'm going to make a late lunch, you hungry?"

Jake looks at the watch on his wrist. "Yeah, I could eat."

Jake follows me into the kitchen, which is spotless thanks to Sydney. I open a few drawers, looking for our frying pan that Sydney must have moved during her cleaning spree yesterday—and yes, a house with three girls and we only have one frying pan, sue us.

After searching for a few minutes, I finally find the pan and grab three different kinds of cheese from the fridge.

I quickly assemble two sandwiches as Jake silently scrolls on his phone in the corner of the kitchen. He's in the doorway, one hand above his head leaning on the trim. I don't know if guys know this, but leaning in a doorway is one of the sexiest positions a guy can stand in.

I try to focus on cooking rather than staring at Jake, but I find my eyes peeking back to him every now and again.

"Voilà, the best grilled cheese you'll ever have." I smile up at him, passing him his sandwich on a plate, pretending like I'm a world-class chef, when really this is the extent of my cooking abilities.

He looks down at the food on the plate and I'm waiting for him to roast me for making such a basic meal.

"Are you a mind reader? I fucking *love* grilled cheese."

"Seriously? I thought you would tease me for my lack of a palette."

"No way, that was one of the first things I ever learned how to make. Grilled cheese was my staple snack between school and hockey practice. I once made one with goat cheese, spinach, and prosciutto, it was fucking fire."

I motion for him to go sit at the table while I slide my sandwich on my own plate. Normally Sydney and Maddie make fun of me for making simple dishes, so it's nice that someone appreciates the basics.

We both dig into our food and start chatting about everything and yet nothing at the same time. I guess this is a step toward being friends.

Jake tells me how Coach Wilson is super hard on them this year because of the small mistakes made in the championship last season.

"It's just ridiculous. He works us so hard some days that I feel like I'm going to pass out or vomit afterward—sometimes both. And now Coach is all about teamwork and not relying on one single player to carry the team, which is good 'cause you do need a strong team to win. I think that's why he made Nate captain, 'cause he's a good leader. I mean, I'm not going to complain about taking more shots, but sometimes Coach can be such a hardass. Especially during early morning practices."

"How early are we talking?" I ask out of pure curiosity. I realize I only gazed over the schedule Coach Wilson gave me. I need to make a mental reminder to myself to review it closely later so I can set up my week accordingly.

"Tuesdays and Thursdays we have practice at six. That way if anyone has morning classes, we have time to take a shower and shit beforehand."

"Six? As in, six a.m.?" I ask and Jake nods. "I think I might die."

Jake pops the last bite of his sandwich into his mouth. "Meh, once you've been doing it for so long, it gets easier."

I guess that makes sense. If you've been training for years and play the sport, your body gets used to early morning practices and late-night games. That's probably why these guys are always in such good shape. But now I'm imagining myself at some of their six a.m. practices, and I don't know how I'll be able to function.

"I'm sure that seeing a bunch of very good-looking hockey players will wake you up in the morning." *Ah, there's that cocky attitude.*

I brush him off and grab both of our plates off the table and leave them in the sink with the rest of my dishes. I have to remember to clean that up before Sydney gets home or she might rip my head off.

"Thanks for lunch. I'm gonna grab my laptop and then probably head out if that's cool?" Jake calls from the dining room.

"Yeah, for sure, I have laundry and stuff to finish, anyway."

I watch Jake go down the hall and turn into my bedroom. I start to clean up the crumbs off the counter and the table when I hear a loud, almost *girlish* shriek come from my room. I drop the crumbs in my hand and race down the hall to see what caused him to scream so loud.

I freeze in place when I enter my room and see Jake standing there holding Geralt. *Kill. Me. Now.*

Geralt is my dildo. My lovely, vibrating dildo that has kept me sane over the past few months.

"This was behind my head the whole time?" He holds it between two fingers, just like the bag of salt and vinegar chips.

I can't stop the laughter that comes out of my mouth. Jake's face is frozen in shock, it's as if he's never seen a dildo before—which I find hard to believe.

"Sorry, I must've forgotten to put Geralt away last night." I walk over to Jake and try to grab the thick blue silicon dick from his hand, but Jake pulls away too fast, putting Geralt out of my reach. His height gives him an advantage and I jump up trying to retrieve the toy from his gigantic hands. "Give it back!"

"Geralt? You named it?" Curiosity laces his voice. "Why the fuck did you name it Geralt?"

I climb up on the bed to gain more height to grab the toy from him. "Geralt, like Geralt of Rivia from *The Witcher? Henry Cavill?*" I make it sound like it's so obvious.

Jake looks at me with the most amused expression and lets out a low chuckle that shakes his chest. "Oh, Ness, you are such a nerd. Do you touch yourself thinking of fictional men frequently?"

I use this moment of reprieve to hook my leg behind Jake's knee to make him fall so I can grab the toy out of his grasp.

My plan ultimately fails when I lose my own footing and we both tumble onto the bed, his body now covering mine. He mostly catches himself, hovering over me, but I can feel his muscular thighs trapping my body under his. His body is hard as rock, I wonder what other parts of his body are this muscular.

He's still holding my dildo in his hand, and I can't help but picture him using it on me. Telling me how good I take it, praising me while filling me up. I can feel the heat rise to my cheeks.

Our faces are just inches apart and both panting slightly from falling and laughing. I never realized how gorgeous his face is so up close. His lips are a little plump and I wonder what it would be like to kiss them, taste them. Even just for a second.

I know we had a drunken moment together, but my brain can't remember what it felt like for our lips to touch. Or how it felt to have his big hands roam my body, to be fully encased by this man's body.

Why is he having this kind of effect on me?

I realize now just how silent the room has become and look up from Jake's body to find him staring at me. His blue eyes scanning, studying my face—it makes me breathless.

His eyes find my lips and they settle there for a moment, and I swear he starts leaning in closer, closing the very small gap that's between our bodies.

"Ness, I am going to kill you! You left a huge mess in the—" Sydney storms into my room and stops dead in her tracks as she sees Jake over top of me, immediately killing whatever was going on between us.

Her eyes are wide, and she smacks her hand over her eyes, retreating her steps out of my door. "Oh my, sorry, didn't mean to interrupt. I'll be in my room with noise-canceling headphones on!"

She pulls the door shut, and Jake and I are left in the same position, him over top of me, our bodies touching in many places.

Okay, this time, I'm actually going to kill her.

"Well, that's probably my cue to head out." Jake climbs off me and stands up, fixing his sweater and pants.

I follow suit and compose myself before he can read the blatant expression written across my face. What the hell was that, and why did my body react so easily to him? His lips were right there and all I wanted to do was crash my own to them. Clearly my hormones are all over the place because my body has been starved of a man's touch for months, but that doesn't mean Jake wants me. We literally *just* agreed to be friends and he's clearly getting it elsewhere.

I think I'm going insane because of him. I need to gain control of myself. I cannot be like this if I have to spend the entire term constantly interacting with Jake.

He clears his throat and I turn around to face him. "I believe this is yours." He extends my dildo out for me to take.

"Yeah, uh, thanks."

Can this be any more awkward?

"So, I'll see you later?" He grabs his laptop off the bed, waiting for me to respond.

"Yeah, I'll see you around." I'm ready to dive into my bed and hide from the entire world. The second he leaves I'm going to scream into my pillow and pretend this didn't happen.

Oh God, please just leave.

My silent prayers are answered as he turns to leave, giving me a small smile as he exits my room. I wait until I hear the front door shut and then fall into my bed, letting out a scream the second my face hits my pillow.

Now would be a great time for a black hole to swallow the world up so I don't have to think about this ever again.

CHAPTER TEN

I shouldn't go there

JAKE

I'm in trouble.

Why?

Because I *still* can't seem to get Vanessa off my damn mind. I'm trying really hard to be friends and keep my dick in my pants, but fuck I have no idea what she's doing to me.

Right now I'm trying to figure out her current mood. We're about an hour into our morning practice, and Vanessa has been sitting in the stands with both of her elbows propped on her knees, her camera sitting idle next to her. Her eyes are a little glossed over, either she's extremely tired or got absolutely shit-faced before coming here. The day she comes to practice hungover will be the last. We've all learned the hard way how Coach treats his players when they come in after going a little too hard the night before. I think it's fair to assume she's probably just exhausted, not used to these early mornings. Give it a few weeks, and I'm sure getting up at the crack of dawn will be a piece of cake.

I remember last year after one of our last tournaments, Nate and Eli celebrated a little too hard and once Coach got a whiff of it, he had them do his *hangover drills,* which mainly consisted of the two of them skating around the rink as fast as they could while we all shot pucks at them. By the end of that practice, Nate and Eli barely made it to the locker room before vomiting all over their floor.

And to make it even more hilarious, Coach had them clean it up too.

Ah, good times.

I wonder what Coach would do if Vanessa came in extremely hungover like that. Probably nothing. That man has a soft spot for her. I bet he would offer her a coffee and Tylenol. I've never seen Coach so nice to a student before. Maybe it's because he feels like she's part of the staff, but it still doesn't change the fact that she's a student just like the rest of his players.

Coach's whistle blows and the noise shakes Vanessa out of her tired state, her eyes flinching at the loud sound. My eyes immediately leave her, and I focus on Coach Wilson.

"Bring it in." He steps out onto the ice. "This weekend we have our first game in Vermont. Bus leaves Saturday morning at five a.m. so be here by four thirty or you can walk there."

We all mumble in agreement knowing he isn't joking. When he gives us a time and place to be, our asses better be there fifteen minutes prior. Coach gives us a curt nod before sending us all to get changed.

Most of us shower and get ready for our morning classes, but all I want to do is put on my sweats and eat a greasy breakfast from the small diner on campus. The cook has a good rep around here. His diner, Tony's, has been here for over twenty years and he makes the meanest bacon and eggs you can find in the area. It's an immediate hangover cure and the perfect remedy after an extensive workout.

I wave off to a few of the guys and stop to chat with Nate, Eli, and Levi before Kieran and I head out. As we're leaving the arena, I see Coach talking to Vanessa in the lobby.

"Hey, man, I'm gonna see if Vanessa wants to come for breakfast if that's cool?"

Kieran looks at me with the biggest shit-eating grin plastered on his face. "*Mm-hm,* it sure is. Meet you at the truck."

Ever since last Sunday, Vanessa and I have been hanging out more. We're strictly friends, as she so plainly laid out to me. Last night Vanessa came over and we watched a nature documentary and worked on school assignments, y'know, stuff that *friends* do. After she left, Kieran gave me shit for striking out again. I tried telling him that we're friends and I'm giving up on trying to sleep with her.

Well…I'm at least trying to get the idea out of my head.

He doesn't believe that girls and guys can just be friends, so he made a bet that Ness and I would probably fuck by the end of the month if we keep hanging out this much.

I told him he could go fuck himself.

We're just friends. Did we have a moment when I found her dildo? *Yes*. And did that turn me on? *Of fucking course*. I couldn't stop imagining what kind of sounds I could get out of her if I used that toy on her.

Fuck. No, Jake, get it together. You're just friends.

I shouldn't go there, but fuck, do I want to.

I walk up to Vanessa just as Coach turns to leave, assuming he's heading back to his office to go over plays for this weekend's game. That man eats, sleeps, and breathes this sport.

"Someone looks a little tired," I say as I walk up to her.

Vanessa's tired eyes slowly lift up to look at me. She's kind of cute when she's tired.

She yawns instantly. "You weren't kidding about early morning practices. The only thing keeping me awake was Coach Wilson's whistle. I think that might be the perfect replacement for my alarm."

I chuckle softly. One thing Vanessa is good at is making me laugh. Sometimes you never know what she's going to say, and it can be so out of left field. It kind of reminds me of how Kieran can be so direct.

"Good thing I have the perfect cure for you, breakfast at Tony's."

She raises her eyebrow. "The grimy little diner on campus?"

"Hey, no judging until you've *actually* eaten the food first. C'mon, Kieran is waiting for us."

Without thinking I instinctively grab her arm, not caring if she wants to come or not. My hockey bag is hanging off my left shoulder and it feels as if it weighs two times the amount it normally does. I'm going to blame that on my intense weight training yesterday and the continuous amounts of slap shots Coach had us do today. I look to my right, seeing Vanessa trailing next to me, my hand still holding on to her small forearm. She looks as if it doesn't bother her even in the slightest.

As I turn my focus back to the parking lot I see Kieran leaning against his truck, the same stupid grin stretched across his face.

"Vanessa." Kieran gives her a nod as I toss my bag into his trunk.

Vanessa is about to jump into the backseat when I shut the door.

"I don't think so, Nichols. Ladies get the front seat." She looks up at me confused, then looks over her shoulder to Kieran, who just slid into the driver's seat. "Don't worry, he doesn't bite."

"Oh my god, I wasn't thinking that! I just didn't know you hockey boys were such gentlemen." She huffs and walks around the truck to the passenger side and hops in. I follow suit and sit behind Kieran.

"Well this is...." She looks around Kieran's custom Ford F-150.

"*Expensive,*" Kieran says quickly as he turns down the hard rock that blasts through the speakers. "All-black leather with red ribbing, heated seats, heated steering, fully loaded with all new tech. *She's my baby.*"

Kieran isn't kidding when he says that his truck is his baby. It was one of the first big purchases he made with the money his parents left him. He's been so stingy about not spending a dime and investing most of it, but after a few bad winters, his old 1990 Jeep Cherokee finally died on him, and he bit the bullet and bought a new truck.

If you ask me, it was totally worth it. Especially 'cause it can fit both of our equipment bags in the back.

"Don't think I didn't see your little eye roll there, Vanessa. Make fun of me all you want, but this is my prized possession. My *only* possession I guess." He trails off.

Kieran isn't someone who will openly tell you about their life. The first time I met him he was so closed off to people. It took him the whole first season to finally agree to go out with the team. He told me he had a childhood best friend who ghosted him out of the blue, and then his parents died shortly after. It must have affected how he now views relationships. I've tried countless times to find out more about his past and that friendship, but Kieran is like an unbreakable safe that's encased in bulletproof glass. He'll only tell you what he wants you to know.

"Sorry, but what's the saying? Guys who drive big trucks must have small—"

"Don't you dare finish that sentence, Vanessa, or I will literally whip my dick out to prove you wrong." Kieran cuts her off midsentence and I can't help the laugh that comes out.

Clearly he's not shy with her anymore.

Kieran has left Vanessa completely speechless with her mouth agape. I have a feeling she's not used to the comradery of guys. Kieran is the type of guy who is so blunt about everything and yet so reclusive as well. The guy is a walking contradiction and I believe that's why he can get so many girls. They're drawn to his mysterious side and then love how honest he is.

"I retract my statement about you two being gentlemen. Remind me to never go out with the two of you ever again." She huffs at the two of us, muttering something along the lines of *You two are such neanderthals.*

The mood on the way to the diner is light. Vanessa talks with Kieran about classes and his interest in drawing. It's a hobby of his that he doesn't share with most people, so it's refreshing to see him open up. Maybe this will prove to him that guys and girls can be friends.

We pull into the parking lot at Tony's, and I grab Vanessa's door before she can climb out, giving me an odd look as I hold the door for her. With the way she's looking at me, it's as if a man has never held a door open for her.

Kieran leads us to our usual spot, the U-shaped booth in the back corner of the diner, and an elderly waitress brings us water and menus to browse. As if we didn't already know what we wanted. The guys and I have been coming here since my first year at BCU.

"I can give you kids a minute to look over the menu if you'd like?" our waitress, Eve, asks us.

"No thank you, ma'am, we'll take three big breakfasts, please, eggs over easy, side of OJ for all." Kieran winks in her direction and causes her to blush. This waitress has served us countless times, and every time we come here, Kieran always sweet-talks to her.

"What if I don't like eggs?" Vanessa challenges him, snatching the menu from Kieran's hands.

"Well, do you?" I ask.

"No, I enjoy them. But next time ask before you order for me." She smacks Kieran on the head with the menu before giving it back to him.

"I'm just making sure you have the best experience possible, Nichols. If you don't like it, then you can punch me in the face later."

"I'll hold you to that."

The diner is one of the few places in the area that reminds me of home. I come from a small town in Cape Cod. There's not much to the town, but we have a small mom-and-pop diner called Gerry & Ginny's, and this place gives me nodes of nostalgia.

Tony's has the same small-town vibe to it. With the checkered tile floors, red and white booths, and an old-school jukebox tucked into the corner. It's almost as if they copied and pasted the diner from home to here.

We start chatting aimlessly and Vanessa fills us in on how her social media assignment is going.

"I spent the past few days meeting with every guy on the team and I've created threads on the team's Instagram about every player and all of your stats." She pauses to take a sip of her orange juice that Eve dropped off. "And I even added a couple of highlight reels from last season. Those videos are making girls go crazy seeing you guys in action."

"We can't help it, Ness, women are just attracted to big athletic men like us. It's in their nature." Kieran flexes his bicep.

"You're right, Kieran, the entire female population is absolutely obsessed with sweaty men wearing the same outfits. How could we possibly turn you down?" As soon as the words leave her mouth, she glances at me with an apologetic gaze.

Well, that hurt only a little.

I don't expect girls to fall at my feet and worship me because I'm a good hockey player. But sometimes—well, most times—girls do fall onto their knees for me, and I can't help but feel my ego get bigger every time.

"Maddie's calling me, I'll just be a minute." Vanessa slides out of the booth and heads toward the front of the restaurant.

"*How could we possibly turn you down?*" Kieran mocks in a high-pitched voice. "Well, she did turn you down. *Twice* may I add." Kieran is chucking to himself, thinking he's so clever.

Asshole.

"The first time she was wasted." I defend myself. "And the second time I asked, she was hungover. I can guarantee that if I were to actually make a play on Vanessa, she wouldn't be able to turn me down."

"*Again.*"

"Huh?"

"She wouldn't be able to turn you down, *again.*" He smirks as he takes a sip of his juice.

"In case I haven't said it today, you're an ass."

Vanessa comes back to the table, her phone tucked away in her back pocket. Perfect timing, too, because I see Eve walking from the kitchen with a tray full of our breakfast. I can't wait to annihilate these eggs. I also can't wait to prove to Vanessa that this place is the best spot for breakfast.

She places the food down in front of us, and I wait to take a bite of my food until Vanessa dips a piece of toast in her eggs. I watch her face as she tastes everything. Picking up her fork and grabbing a few hashbrowns, before popping those into her mouth too. How is it possible for someone to look so damn hot while eating fucking breakfast?

Vanessa notices me staring. "What?"

"How is it?"

"You guys were right. This is the best breakfast I've ever had. Oh, I invited my friend Maddie to join us this morning. She just got a bad mark on her paper and needs a little pick-me-up."

Kieran freezes for a moment, then proceeds to shovel his food into his mouth.

"If that's okay…"

"The more people who witness you eat your words, the better, Ness." I joke with her and finally take a bite out of my own breakfast. My eggs are cooked perfectly, the toast has just the right amount of crunch, and the hashbrowns are seasoned with onions and spices.

Damn, I wish I could eat this every day of my life—but I'd go broke if I ate out for every meal.

"So, Ness, are you excited for the away game this weekend?" I ask.

She takes a sip of her juice, a little bit dripping down the side of her mouth. She flicks her tongue out to catch it.

"I guess so. That last time I went to Vermont I was with my parents, and let's just say I spent more time with my skis than them. It'll be nice to be able to hang out with everyone since we'll all be together, y'know?"

"Oh, just wait 'til you hear Jake's singing on the bus. Then you'll wish you would've driven yourself rather than take the bus with us."

Kieran likes to tease me, but I pick the best music for road trips. Not my fault I'm a god with a playlist.

Vanessa looks at Kieran as if he's joking, but when she realizes he's being dead serious, she turns to me. "Is this about to be an episode of *Carpool Karaoke*? But instead of James Corden, we have you hosting it?"

I smile wide at her, she has no idea how fun our road trips are. "You're damn right, and it's always a fun fucking time, so get your singing voice ready." I hold my hand up, waiting for Kieran to high-five me. Reluctantly, he does, right as Maddie walks up to our table.

"Hey, guys." Maddie greets us, then sits next to Vanessa. Vanessa slides farther into the booth, her knee now touching mine.

"Sorry to hear about your essay."

Maddie sighs but gives me a smile. "My prof is such a dick. I swear he only gave me a bad mark because I challenged his statistics in class. He was using a study from over twelve years ago. If he wants to use accurate data, then he should've used more recent studies."

"What prof do you have?" Kieran breaks his silence.

"Dr. Wesley. He's one of the only professors on campus who teach *Advances in Human Identification*, except he insists on using old research. We're supposed to be learning about the advancements, not about what technology we had in the early eighties."

Maddie continues explaining to us about her class and how her professor is basically a huge douche. He's easily in his sixties and should retire, but because he has tenure at the university, he's going to ride this out until he doesn't feel like teaching anymore.

"Enough about me, what's new with you guys?" She leans back into the booth, crossing her arms over her chest.

I stack my empty plate onto Vanessa's and put them at the corner of the table. "We have a game this weekend in Vermont. That should be an easy win for us."

"Oh, that'll be awesome for you guys!" She looks at Vanessa. "Ness, you're obviously going, so we'll have to do something for your birthday when you get back."

Birthday? I didn't know Vanessa's birthday was coming up.

"Woah, hold up. When's your birthday?"

"It's the fifteenth. Friday." She doesn't make eye contact with me, which raises a small red flag.

Vanessa turns her focus away from us, staring off into nowhere.

I've seen guys dissociate while playing, whether a player on the other team said something to throw them off, or they're just having a bad game. They do it to give themselves space and get a chance to calm down. But I don't know why this topic is causing Vanessa to space out like this. Does she not like to celebrate her birthday? I know some people hate to celebrate them. They would rather hang out by themselves and relax than have a party. Maybe Vanessa's the same way, but she doesn't peg me as the type of person who doesn't celebrate their birthdays.

"Excuse me for a moment, I'm just gonna run to the restroom before we leave."

Maddie scoots out of the booth so Vanessa can squeeze by her.

"Okay, was she acting weird or am I just bad at picking up social cues?" Kieran asks.

Maddie shakes her head. "No, she's definitely acting weird. She's not really looking forward to her birthday this year."

"Did something happen?"

I lean in closer as Maddie looks side to side, scoping out to make sure Vanessa isn't around to hear her.

"Vanessa's parents aren't coming to see her for her birthday, so she's a little upset."

"Are they close?"

Maddie shakes her head, making a face that makes me think that Vanessa and her parents are *far* from being close.

"How come they aren't coming to visit her?"

"They randomly planned a trip to Paris without her." *Oh fuck.* "Their relationship is already rocky enough. This is like the fucking icing on the cake. They don't see eye to eye on everything, especially the decisions she makes with her life, but her birthday was one day out of the year that they actually paid attention to her."

Well fuck, that sucks. I can see why she would be so upset. Having your parents skip out on you is like taking a knife to the gut, but having them plan a whole trip on your birthday without inviting you—well that would just twist the knife even deeper.

"What did you guys have planned for her birthday?"

Maddie shrugs. "Normally we take her to see whatever bad rom-com is in theaters, order food, and then sneak it into the theater with us."

I'm glad Vanessa at least has some good friends to make up for her shitty parents. It's not common for friends to have traditions they uphold every year.

"What if the team helped out this year? We can plan something, like a surprise party. That way it'll take her mind off her parents," I suggest. "She's part of the team now, and we don't want her feeling like shit, especially on her birthday."

"I don't know, Vanessa sort of hates surprises."

"She'll like this surprise. Have her at our place on Friday at six. The boys and I will take care of the rest."

Kieran nods in agreement. I give Maddie my number so we can all coordinate the details of the party. Vanessa walks back from the restroom, and we quickly change the subject to something completely different.

"And that's how I learned to not play with firecrackers." Kieran pretends to finish a story. Vanessa takes a seat, now sitting so Maddie is between us.

She has no idea.

Vanessa's going to be fucking blown away by this party.

CHAPTER ELEVEN

Surprise

VANESSA

My birthday has sucked so far.

Normally when you have a milestone birthday, like turning twenty-one and being able to legally drink with all of your friends, you usually go out and celebrate.

But of course, my life is not normal.

This week started off so strong, and then as soon as the clock hit midnight, my luck went out the window.

My day started with my alarm not going off, which made me late to the arena. Luckily Coach Wilson was too busy yelling at the boys to notice me slipping in ten minutes late. Coach decided to host a last-minute practice before our away game this weekend. I thought the boys already had it tough waking up early two days out of the week, but these random drills and training they have to do would be the death of me.

After practice, I tried editing a video to upload to the Wolves' website, and my entire computer crashed. Thinking the day couldn't get worse, I decided I deserved a treat. Not only because my morning had been shit, but it's also my birthday.

Aren't good things supposed to happen to you on your birthday?

I thought my bad luck had finally stopped. My latte was free since the campus coffee shop gives you a free drink on your birthday, and I got an email from my professor saying that our print lab will be closed for maintenance so now I can spend my Friday at home watching a movie for my film class. I was too excited about my lab being cancelled that I tripped over the sidewalk and spilled the entirety of my drink all over my jeans.

Thus, ending my short-lived good luck streak.

The only positive to my day was that Levi witnessed it all happen and offered to drive me home.

"You really are a clutz, huh?"

I lean my head on the passenger window. "I think my birthday is cursed."

He laughs at me. "I think you're dramatic. Does the birthday girl want a burger before I drop her off?"

I haven't eaten anything all day, and the only treat I got for myself, I spilled. A burger sounds like heaven right now.

"Yeah." I look at him with my best puppy-dog eyes. "And maybe a milkshake too."

Levi shakes his head. "You're lucky it's your birthday."

The two of us have become a lot closer since I've been working with the team. Even though it's only been a couple of weeks, our friendship came easy. It helps that we both enjoy photography and have a class together.

Levi is probably the only friend I'm going to see today.

Sydney and Maddie are both studying at the library. They have midterms coming up, so they've been living there all week. I highly doubt that they'll be home before midnight, considering I fell asleep before they got home last night. I can't blame them for studying, even though this means our regular birthday tradition must be put on hold.

This might be the first birthday I spend solo. No birthday tradition, no awkward family dinner. Just, silence.

I usually loathe going to my birthday dinner with my parents, but this year, I'm a little upset knowing that they willingly booked a vacation instead of coming to see me. I know our relationship isn't the best, but this was the one day a year that was mine. The three of us would sit at a table and talk with no distractions or other family members present. Even if they spend the whole dinner criticizing my life, at least I'm not alone.

It's fine, I don't need them. I've never needed them.

When I get back from Vermont, the girls and I will properly celebrate with Thai food and a movie, and I'll forget what a shitshow today was.

I go through some of the notes I've made with Coach Wilson about the sport. I've asked him to teach me a little so that way when I'm updating the website and their socials, I don't sound like a complete moron. Before, I never would've understood what someone meant when they said a player scored a hat trick or got a penalty for slashing. At least now I won't seem so oblivious and hopefully it'll help gain brownie points with the team.

I wonder what the team is up to tonight.

Besides Levi, no one else has wished me a happy birthday.

I didn't expect any of them to know it was my birthday, but Jake and Kieran both knew. I thought that the former would for sure make a big deal about it and find a way to embarrass me in front of everyone. But nothing. The only thing I've gotten this week are random texts and phone calls from Jake asking me ridiculous questions about myself. The other day he called me and asked if I'd rather drink rum and cokes or Jell-O shots for the rest of my life. *What the hell was that about?*

The questions only got weirder after that.

Maybe Jake is free tonight. Is it lame of me to want to hang out with him even though he aggravates me to no end? There's just something about him that makes him so charming. Everything from his stupid fluffy brown hair that he's always messing with, to his blue eyes that literally trap you every time you're speaking with him, no matter what I do or say to him, he always finds a way to make himself so damn alluring.

> **Vanessa**
>
> *Hey, what are you up to tonight? Do you wanna do something? We could go to the movies or something?*

I mean, it is a Friday night, I highly doubt he's sitting on the couch doing nothing, like me.

Jake

Hey, sorry busy tonight. See u tomorrow bright n early.
Hope you're ready for karaoke.

Figures.

That's fine, I can have a relaxing night all to myself. There's nothing wrong with being in your own company.

But maybe I should get out of the house. I can look over my notes tomorrow on the road.

I could go to the mall and get myself a birthday present. That would at least kill an hour or two of my day. My parents sent me money to get myself whatever I wanted for my birthday, as if that makes up for their absence. Mom normally buys me an expensive gift I'd never want, but this year I guess she decided to finally give up.

Last year I asked my parents for a new lens extension for my camera, and instead my mom bought me this white Chanel bag that probably cost her more than triple the amount of the extension. I ended up giving the purse to Maddie because I had absolutely no use for it, and I saw how much she loved it the second I showed it to her.

Maybe I'll go out and get myself the extender for my camera, take a nice photo of it, and send it to my parents. I hope that ruins their vacation—seeing their daughter spending their money on her *pointless hobby* as they would say.

I think it's time for a change of scenery. The mall, maybe stop at a coffee shop on my way home and treat myself to a chocolate croissant.

That doesn't sound bad at all.

Sydney and Maddie surprised me, coming home early from their intense study sesh. They decided to tag along with me to the mall.

Surprisingly, the mall wasn't too packed for a Friday evening. I got the Sony 2.0X Teleconverter for my camera, and this will be great to use this weekend at the upcoming away game.

The girls decided to give up on studying for the rest of the evening so we can bar hop before I leave. Nothing too crazy since I have to be up early tomorrow, but at least this gives us something to do.

We're about to leave the mall, all of us with a few bags in our hands, when we pass by a salon. A wild thought races through my head.

What if.

Twenty minutes later, we're in the car and I found myself with a fresh new haircut. Nothing drastic, I'm not *that* crazy. I added some layers and curtain bangs for more depth, feeling a little bit better about myself.

"You guys promise we're going to have a chill night, right? Nothing crazy, no strip clubs—especially not after what happened last time."

Sydney laughs at my question. "Oh come on, Ness. Have *some* faith in me."

"To be fair, the last time I let you plan a girl's night out, two strippers ended up driving us home and Maddie got a bloody nose from that girl who was elbowing her way to the front."

"Oh my god, I almost forgot about that!" Maddie snorts from the front seat. "What was that, end of freshman year?"

"Yes! It was after Sydney got us those fake IDs and the strip club was the first place to let us in."

"Yeah, what a wild night." Sydney sighs as she pulls into our parking garage. "But don't worry. Tonight is lowkey. We're going to go out, have a couple drinks, and be home before midnight. That way you won't scare the boys with your cranky attitude tomorrow morning."

Thinking of the road trip tomorrow reminds me of what Kieran told me. I wonder if Jake is actually going to sing the entire way. If I'm going to be subjected to twenty singing male athletes tomorrow, I'm going to need some noise-canceling headphones.

Within an hour of being home, the three of us get ready quickly and head out the door. I picked out a pair of light denim jeans that don't have any rips in them—because most of my wardrobe consists of mom jeans or one's with tears. I also got this gorgeous white corset top with small, ruffled sleeves and it ties together in the back. It's something simple but the ruffled sleeves give it more of an elevated look.

"Is there a plan for tonight or are we just picking a random bar to start?" I ask. I like to make a game plan for outings.

Sydney glances at me in the rearview mirror. "We're only going to one place tonight to make it easy for us. But I have to stop at Nate's to grab something."

We park along the curb in front of a row of brownstones. I see the familiar green garden gnome on their front porch, and I'd be lying if I said I haven't thought about stealing it.

Maddie and Sydney unclip their seat belts. "Are you gonna come in and say hi? I'm sure Jake's here."

"He said he was busy tonight, so I highly doubt it." I unbuckle my seat belt, following my friends inside.

Sydney walks in as if she owns the place, but I guess if her brother lives here, she must've done this a few times. I follow closely behind, the inside of the house seeming so dark when it's barely after sunset. Do they not believe in turning lights on?

"SURPRISE!"

Shouts and cheers come from all over the room as the light flicks on.

The living room is packed with most of the guys from the team, and standing in the center of the room is Jake with a shit-eating grin plastered on his face. Sydney and Maddie stand beside him, but his tall frame makes him stand out. He's wearing black jeans with a white T-shirt and his hair is tucked into his baseball cap that he has turned backward. *Why does he always look so damn charming?*

Above the doorway leading to the kitchen, there's a huge hand-painted banner that reads *Happy Birthday, Vanessa!* and there are balloons and streamers all across the room in my favorite colors—green and yellow.

I can't believe this. I am speechless. I hate surprises, like absolutely loathe them, but this is some grand gesture type shit. How do I say thank you and I hate you at the same time?

"Happy birthday, Nichols." Jake walks up and wraps me in a hug. His tall stature engulfs me in a bear hug. "Are you surprised?"

"Yeah, you could definitely say that."

"Good, this took all week to plan. I'm lucky Maddie and Sydney were able to help me."

"It was so hard to keep this from you!" Sydney squeals while pulling me into her own bone-crushing hug.

"Jake thought of it the other day when we were at breakfast," Maddie confesses from behind me.

He planned all of this in less than a week?

I guess that would explain all his random questions and why my friends were barely home. And here I thought that my friends were busy studying. Who needs stuffy, rich, judgmental parents when I have people this amazing in my life.

Jake grabs my hand and starts guiding me through the crowd of people. Everyone wishes me happy birthday as Jake drags me through the house.

"There are video games in the living room. The boys even made up a *Mario Kart* tournament for us. And in the kitchen, we have what I call the Vanessa special."

The kitchen is filled with an assortment of food and drinks. Their dining room table is littered with boxes of pizza, multiple bags of salt and vinegar chips, along with plain for those who *clearly* have no taste, and a dessert tray full of brownies. Near the fridge they have a selection of sparkling water to choose from and a station for people to make their own version of my favorite drink—rum and coke.

My brain can't seem to form any words. The amount of time and effort he put into tonight, making a menu of all my favorite foods, getting everyone to play my favorite video game. He even decorated the house in my favorite colors.

Why would he do something like this for me?

"Thank you, Jake. I—I don't know what to say."

"Hey, no worries. We obviously had to celebrate your birthday. You're fucking twenty-one, that's a milestone birthday."

114

"This is all so perfect."

How do I tell him that this is the nicest thing anyone has ever done for me? Not even my own parents made an effort to see me on my birthday, but this guy who I've only known for a short time, organized a whole damn surprise party for me.

"I was having such a bad week. And this…" I gesture around the room. "All of this made it so much better."

Is this the moment where we start becoming best friends and I spill my whole life and feelings to him?

Word vomit incoming.

"My parents and I have a crappy relationship, but they really showed their disinterest in me this year. They planned a vacation instead of coming to see me. So I've been feeling kinda shitty about it all." The words barrel out of my mouth before I can stop them.

Where the hell did that come from and why did I feel the need to share that thought with Jake all of a sudden?

Jake's brows furrow in a concerned look. "Ness, that really sucks. I'm sorry that they're neglecting you. 'Cause honestly, that's a fucked-up thing to do, especially on your birthday." His voice is smooth and sincere. "C'mon, let's go into the living room. I'm sure Eli wants to start the tournament, he hasn't shut up about it all day."

I follow behind him, grabbing a rum and coke on our way out of the kitchen.

For a house full of college guys, their house is fairly organized. Even though most of the brownstones in the area have similar layouts, theirs seems a bit more spacious. Their living room has a huge brown leather sectional in the center, and along the main wall there's a giant entertainment system fit with a flat-screen TV in the middle. They have little touches here and there that just shout *man cave*. There are three decent-sized beanbag chairs in front of the TV and they have shelves around the entertainment center filled with various video games for different gaming systems. I guess they all have different tastes in games.

"All right, this is how it's going down. Four players in each race. Everyone is equipped with the same style car so it's even for everyone. Whoever loses is out and has to take a shot.

We'll keep alternating the fourth player until the last race, and at the end, the winner gets to assign ten shots to whoever they want. Any questions?"

He's swapped his sweet Southern twang for a more serious tone. It's cute watching him become so serious for such a simple game.

I'm very competitive and something these guys don't know about me is I fucking *love* my Nintendo Switch. I got it a few years ago as a Christmas present to myself, and I've forced Sydney and Maddie to play games with me whenever I can. These boys have no idea what they're in for.

"Ness, sit over here with me." Jake grabs my hand and pulls me over to one of the beanbag chairs set on the floor. It's almost big enough for the two of us, but half of my butt is definitely in his lap.

I should move.

But I don't.

"All right, we're up first," Sydney announces as she plops into the chair next to us. "Nate, get your tall ass over here. You're playing with me, Maddie, and Ness."

Nate looks over his shoulder from the other end of the living room and huffs. I know Sydney loves to push her brother's buttons.

Jake repositions himself next to me and has his back leaning against the couch so he's in more of an upright position. Eli passes all of us a controller and we start the first race. After forcing Maddie and Sydney to play with me so much, the three of us easily crush Nate. As we all cross the finish line on the last lap, I jump up from the chair on the ground.

"Take that, Nathan! Loser takes a shot. Even the captain doesn't get to back out on this one."

Did I mention that I'm very competitive?

He stands up and towers over me. What is it with all hockey men being so freaking tall? Nate's eyes are so similar to his sisters, except his hazel eyes have more of a deep brown that just blazes right through you. When he stands like this, it gives him such an intimidating glare. Maybe I should keep my competitive side to myself.

116

"You're lucky it's your birthday, Nichols." He grabs a shot off the tray on the coffee table and knocks it back without making a face. It's like the alcohol had zero effect on him.

Nate passes his controller to the next person in the tournament, Eli, who seems way too excited to play this game with us. Unfortunately, we crush his high spirits and, just like the first game, the girls prevail.

Race after race, each guy seems to be taking a shot while Sydney, Maddie, and I remain in the beanbag chairs, waiting for the next loser to join us. We play about ten races until finally we're down to the last two. Kieran and Jake. I feel like they conveniently placed themselves last in the roster so that they have a better advantage. It gives them the opportunity to watch how we play and see whatever weaknesses we have. But the jokes on them, we don't have any.

Kieran sits on the couch behind Maddie. "All right, girls, it's time to taste defeat for the first time tonight."

"You better watch what you say, Kieran, things tend to come back to bite you in the ass." Maddie's comment causes the whole room to fill with laughter.

Within the first lap, Kieran gets the jump on us, swerving in between us and holding onto items until the perfect moment. It isn't until the last lap, the three of us team up and strategically push him back into last place.

"Fuck! That's bullshit, you three shouldn't be able to team up on people. Ref, what the hell was that?" Kieran looks to Eli, who's sitting on the couch, dumbfounded that the three of us have single-handedly crushed almost their entire team.

Eli shakes his head. "Sorry, man, it's a fair game. Also, there's no referee in racing, dumb ass. Now take your shot like the rest of us, give Jake your controller, and sit your ass down."

Jake stands up and grabs the controller from Kieran's hands and replaces it with a shot from the tray. Kieran grumbles something under his breath about how this is stupid and plops down next to Nate and Eli on the couch, tossing the shot back as if it's nothing.

117

Jake comes back to sit next to me again, but this time, instead of leaning against the couch, he's moved so we're shoulder to shoulder. *How have I not noticed his cologne before right now?* The scent is warm and summery, like leather mixed with coconut, reminding me of the smell of the wind on a beach.

Snap out of it.

"Hey, Jake, doesn't Ness look smoking hot with her new hair?" Sydney loves playing devil's advocate, but I know she's only saying that to try to distract Jake. It's one of her go-to tactics—sidetrack your biggest opponent so they don't get an advantage.

Jake looks me up and down, but his eyes linger on my new hair. "Hell yeah, you look great. I'm really digging those li'l angel wings."

He brings his hand up to my face and twirls my bangs around his finger. *Angel wings?*

"You mean my curtain bangs?"

"Sure, but angel wings sounds better."

Hmm, angel wings, that's cute. I feel like that's the only term we should use for curtain bangs now.

"All right, angel girl, ready to get your ass beat?" His new nickname for me throws me off guard and sends a shiver down between my thighs.

I quickly collect myself; I hope he didn't notice the effect he had on me. "You wish, Shepherd."

Before I realize it, the race has started, and Jake completely distracted me with his comment. *Oh, he's good.* He knew exactly how to distract me so he could get the upper hand. I refocus on the game, intent on winning the final race and declaring myself undefeated, but Jake is making it difficult. Out of all of the guys we've played with, Jake seems to be the only one besides Kieran who might be competition for Sydney, Maddie, and I. Jake stays in the lead, constantly getting power-ups at the perfect time to deflect anything that we throw at him. On this track he seems to know every shortcut and exactly where to drift.

It's the last lap and there's not much time left to catch up to Jake, and I do not want to lose. I've spent all night beating everyone in this house at this colorful cartoon game.

I. Refuse. To. Lose.

CHAPTER TWELVE

A hockey romance

JAKE

The boys erupt in cheers and hollers, excited that finally one of us has taken down the elite trio. I join them, shouting and celebrating.

Are we overreacting a little too much?

Probably, but the look on Vanessa's face makes it so worth it. I turn back toward the girls, who are all now standing in front of the TV.

I look down to Vanessa, and I know that I have a wicked grin on my face. "*Well, well, well,* sorry, Ness but looks like I won. And you know what that means."

She looks up at me, hatred beaming in her eyes. Oh yeah, she's a sore loser.

"There are seven shots on the table, and I wonder if there's a birthday girl here who would *love* to take them."

Vanessa narrows her eyes on me, furrowing her brows. I'm well aware I'm pushing her buttons, and I'm loving every second of it.

"But luckily for you, I'm not *that* evil." I look at Maddie and Sydney who are standing next to the coffee table. "Maddie and Sydney each get two, and that leaves the rest for you."

Vanessa rolls her eyes at me. I've come to love that reaction from her. I almost purposely say stupid shit just so I can see her green eyes roll back.

"How did you do it?" she asks, reaching for her first shot.

"Oh, is someone a sore loser?"

"I just want to know how we won against everyone *but* you."

I smile wide at her. "Well, if you would've asked me, you would've known that I bought my sister a switch for her birthday last year and she made me spend all summer playing games with her. I guess you could call me a Mario Kart expert."

She sighs, I know that she's internally cursing at herself for not asking before we started playing. I know she would've come up with a better game plan rather than assuming I was bad like the rest of my teammates.

"C'mon, Ness. Take your shots so we can give you your presents," Eli shouts from the couch.

"Presents?" Her voice is laced with confusion.

"Yeah, presents. Normally you get those on your birthday," Eli explains, as if it's redundant.

"Guys, you didn't have to…"

"Shut it and drink, girl." Maddie holds two shots in her hand and immediately throws both of them back. Vanessa and Sydney follow Maddie's lead, and all of them take their shots one after another.

All of the guys on the team chipped in on a gift for her, but I may have gotten her a little something extra all on my own. I grab the beanbag chair Vanessa and I were just sitting on and pull it next to the table so Vanessa can sit while she opens her gifts. I motion for her to sit down, and she follows my instructions. I think that's a first. As Nate comes down the stairs, Sydney and Maddie both come back in from grabbing their presents from their car. We place the gifts on the table in front of Vanessa, waiting for her to pick one.

"I think the obvious answer is to pick mine first." Sydney beams. From what Nate has told me, Sydney is the best person at picking out presents. It's like she has a sixth sense for picking the perfect gift for someone.

"Okay, fine, give it to me."

Sydney has her gift wrapped in gold paper with a green lace bow on top. Vanessa takes the gift from Sydney and slowly peels apart the paper, trying her hardest not to ruin her friend's handiwork. Eventually she caves, shredding the rest of the paper, a smile spreading across her face as she opens the box and pulls out a cream-coloured sweater.

That fucking smile.

"Oh my god, I can't believe you got this for me!" She tackles her friend to the ground.

"Okay, am I the only one confused as to why you're so excited about a sweater?" Eli asks the question that's on everyone's minds.

Vanessa rolls her eyes at him. "You wouldn't understand, but this is the Taylor Swift cardigan from her Folklore album."

Yeah, that definitely didn't help.

Nate grabs the cardigan from Vanessa. "That's *the* cardigan that she wore? Holy shit, Syd, how much did you spend on that? Mom and Dad are gonna freak."

Sydney snatches it right back from him. "No, you idiot, this is just a replica of it, but it's Vanessa's favorite album and I knew she'd never buy it for herself."

Girls are definitely from another planet. A sweater that looks identical to one that one of her favorite artists has worn…what an odd gift. But with the way Vanessa is looking at it, she clearly loves it.

"Here, open mine next." Maddie passes her gift, which is in a black gift bag and dark green tissue paper.

Vanessa slowly pulls a book out of the bag that has a half-naked man on the front cover. She immediately shoves it back into the bag, clearly trying to hide it from the rest of us.

"Maddie…what is this?"

Maddie laughs, very entertained with how red Vanessa's cheeks are. "It's a romance novel. You were asking for a recommendation, and I found the perfect one for you, a hockey romance."

A hockey romance?

"I'm sorry, did you just say you got her a romance novel about hockey?" Kieran confidently asks, knowing all of us would probably just laugh and make jokes about it.

"That's exactly what I said. Do you need your ears checked, Kieran?" Maddie sneers at him. I don't know what it is with these two, but Maddie seems dead set on disliking Kieran. I wonder what he did to deserve that.

"I thought it would be funny since you're working with hockey players. You might as well fall in love with a fictional one."

Eli perks up when she says this. "Hey, who's to say that she won't fall in love with me? I am quite charming, you know."

"Fictional men are *always* better than men in real life. At least this way she won't be disappointed."

I think Maddie bruised his ego.

"As long as there's good spice in it, I'm sure I can get over the fact that it's about hockey. Thank you, Maddie." Vanessa leans over to hug her friend. Even when getting a questionable gift, this girl is so appreciative.

"All right, now it's our turn." Nate walks over to Vanessa and places the box in her lap.

Most of the guys suck at gift wrapping so Nate took it somewhere to get professionally wrapped. After I told him about her situation, he wanted to make sure that Vanessa got everything and more for her birthday. There's nothing worse than spending your birthday alone.

The fact that her parents could just leave her and not feel guilty makes my blood boil. If my parents ever did that to me or my sister, I know that we wouldn't have a relationship at all. That's not how families are supposed to be.

Vanessa opens the box and pulls out the custom jersey we had made for her. Coach had a couple extra jerseys in his office, and he didn't mind donating one for Vanessa. She holds it up in front of her, putting it on display for all of us to see. It's styled just like our home jersey, dark red with white bold writing and a lone wolf in the center. On the back we have her last name printed.

"Guys…this is…" She goes speechless, taking a moment to look around the room, eyes watery.

"Oh no, please don't cry." Nate huffs from the couch.

Sydney smacks her brother's arm, getting him to shut up.

"This is so sweet, thank you. All of you."

She stands up and hugs each and every one of us, showing how grateful she is for today. Vanessa is so tiny compared to the rest of us, it's almost comical.

"Hey, Ness, I forgot I have a gift for you, but I left it upstairs." I'm not embarrassed to give it to her in front of the guys, but it's something I'd rather give to her in private.

"Please tell me it's not your dick."

Ouch. It's not, but would it be so bad if it was?

"Ha-ha, y'know you really know how to boost a man's ego, Ness." I put my arm around her shoulders and start to lead her toward the stairs. "C'mon, follow me."

I yell behind me to Levi and ask him to grab the ice cream cake from the freezer, so it'll be ready once we come back down. I lead Vanessa up the stairs to my room, passing by Kieran's along the way, I hear Vanessa scoff at the state of his room. I swear Kieran is so anal about having a clean house or car, but when it comes to his room, it's a complete disaster of thrown blankets and drawings scattered everywhere.

We get to my room, and I go to the top drawer of my desk and pull out the small box.

"You're not proposing or anything, right? I mean, Jake, I love that we're becoming friends, but I'm nowhere near ready for any sort of commitment."

She thinks she's so funny, turning me down all the time. Normally girls beg for me, but no, not Vanessa. *Never her.*

"Don't worry, angel girl, I'm not a commitment kind of guy." I walk back over to her, standing in the middle of my bedroom. "Here, open it."

I pass her the black box I've kept hidden from my roommates. It's not anything super sentimental, but I definitely put *some* thought into it. She opens the box and pulls out the custom camera strap I got her. It's dark green and embroidered with flowers and vines. The girl I hired to make it charged me double her rate because it was last minute, but that didn't matter to me as long as Vanessa likes it.

"Jake, this is gorgeous, where did you get this?"

I shrug. "A girl in my astronomy class does embroidery as a side gig. I had her put flowers and stuff along the lead 'cause you said you enjoy nature photography the best." I sound like I'm pussy-whipped and we haven't even had sex. I should just tell her I got it because I think she's really fucking cool, and I wanted to make her smile.

Oh, and I can't stop thinking about her.

All right, now is not the time to confess any sort of emotion. *Keep a blank face, neutral.* This day is all about her and I don't want to freak her out if I say anything else. This is just a nice gesture that I'm doing for a friend. Nothing else.

Well, maybe I want a little more than friendship with Vanessa, but she's made it so evidently clear that that is the last thing on her mind. I don't know how to deal with any of these emotions. I've never felt this way about someone before, wanting to be near them, hear their voice, make them happy. Before, all I cared about was playing hockey and fucking almost any girl who threw herself at me. Vanessa is the first girl who's tested me, pushed me, let me into her life, and I'm weak at the knees for her.

Before I can sink any further into my own thoughts, she kisses my cheek. Her lips are so soft and plump, I want them all over me. Trailing down my stomach, going down even farther where I can wrap my hand around her pretty hair as she takes me into her mouth.

Fucking hell. There's no hope for me.

"You're sweet." She stands back and looks up at me with those big gorgeous green eyes, "But why didn't you want to give it to me in front of everyone downstairs?"

That's a great question.

Why? Well, it might have to do with the fact that Kieran would say that I'm whipped and that could cause me to punch him in the face and start a whole brawl over a small gift. It could also be because I was nervous she wouldn't like it and having her reject me *again* might be detrimental to my ego. My brain is malfunctioning on how to respond.

"I forgot it up here and thought you might like to take a minute away from everyone and the shock from tonight. I know surprise parties aren't really your thing, but we wanted to make sure you had a good birthday." *I wanted you to have the best birthday.*

"Oh, well that's very thoughtful of you. I wasn't expecting this, so yeah, I guess I was a bit overwhelmed downstairs." She smiles up at me, readjusting her glasses. Fuck, she is so adorable.

125

She looks around the room, lingering in the silence that's settled between us. She looks up to me, as if she wants to say something more but stops herself. I stand in front of her, watching her fidget with the camera strap in her hands, waiting for her to say something.

She shifts back and forth on her feet until she decides to break the silence. "I'm gonna use the restroom then head back down, meet you there?"

"Uh, yeah, I'll meet you downstairs."

I head out of the room and down the stairs to rejoin the party.

Why do I feel like there's something else I missed? Something else going on in that pretty little head of hers that she's just not willing to share with me yet.

CHAPTER THIRTEEN

Definitely not normal

VANESSA

My birthday did not suck in the end.

I was absolutely spoiled by my friends, and I couldn't be more thankful for the odd group I've come to hang out with. My parents would probably disprove of my friendship with the hockey team, but I couldn't care less what they think.

Growing up, my parents taught me to believe that all athletes are egotistical maniacs who only care about money and themselves, which is probably why I constantly dated guys who fit that category, so I could piss them off even more. The guys on the team have taught me the complete opposite. Not only did they all split on a gift for me for my birthday, but they also threw me a party to make me feel better. These guys took my feelings into account, which besides Sydney and Maddie, no one ever does.

My parents didn't even bother to call *or* text.

Jake threw me a curveball. I mean, his gift was so sweet and sentimental. Watching his fingers fidget with themselves while I opened it, patiently waiting for my reaction.

I don't know how to interpret his actions. I don't know if he's doing these things because he genuinely enjoys my friendship or if he has some ulterior motive. I know I've joked about not hooking up with him, but I'd be lying if I said the idea hasn't crossed my mind more than once. And sometimes I do wonder what would've happened if we hooked up that first night.

Where would we be right now?

I guess I'm kind of grateful nothing happened that night because maybe we wouldn't have the friendship that we do now. Who knows how well we would get along, especially the whole team dynamic knowing I'd slept with one of their teammates. I value my friendships more than a hookup.

After last night, I felt like I got much closer with the boys. I think I may have even learned more about them than I wanted to. Stories were flying around, someone went streaking across campus in their sophomore year, someone accidentally took mushrooms before going to class, and a certain someone hooked up with his TA last semester and definitely got a better grade because of his *Southern charm*.

If it wasn't for Nate kicking us out before midnight, I'm sure we would've all stayed there until the sun came up.

It's safe to say that I regret staying up late and indulging myself in more liquor than I should have, because now I'm standing in front of the Greyhound full of college boys and hockey staff, and my head is absolutely pounding.

I blame Maddie for getting me to drink one too many rum and cokes.

The only upside is at least this time I came prepared with Advil and a Gatorade to help this minor hangover go away before we arrive in Vermont.

"Ms. Nichols, how are you doing this morning?"

I almost scream as Coach Wilson approaches me. "Oh, hi, Coach, good morning. I'm okay, just a little tired." I can't help the yawn that breaks out.

"Well hopefully the boys won't be too rowdy and let you get some sleep before we arrive in Burlington. See you on the bus. Oh, and happy belated birthday, Vanessa."

"Thank you." I smile back at him, and he heads onto the bus.

Most of the guys have already arrived and loaded their bags into the undercarriage. I cannot wait to find a seat and close my eyes for the entire ride. I could use an extra hour or two of sleep. I drag my feet to the bus and slowly climb up the stairs. My body is exhausted from lack of sleep, so something as simple as climbing the stairs feels like I'm climbing a mountain.

"Vanessa! So good to see you this morning, how are you feeling?" Nate's voice is obnoxiously loud, and he does it on purpose.

I want to stab him with my nails.

He stands up out of his seat and greets me in the aisleway, putting his arm around my shoulder. There's no way he knows I'm hungover. I don't have bags under my eyes or sunglasses to shade me from the bright lights. I'm totally pulling this off.

"I'm fine, Nate. Thanks for asking."

"You sure? No headache or nausea?"

Okay, maybe he does know. I have a feeling he called Sydney this morning to see how we were all doing. If you interrupt Sydney's sleep, she will say just about anything to go back to bed.

"Oh good, I was nervous you were going to be too hungover to sing karaoke with us the whole. Way. There." He pats my head then takes his seat next to Eli.

Nate better be joking because I don't think my head will be able to take it.

"Ness, over here." Jake's voice carries through the bus as he waves me over from the back.

If he's sitting at the back then it's safe to say that there's no way he's going to coordinate a karaoke session. I duck between two of his teammates and make my way to the back of the bus where Jake is sitting with an empty seat next to the window. Across from him are Kieran and Levi—the latter already snoring with his hat covering his face.

I go to put my bag in the overhead compartment, but two very muscular arms reach up from behind me, lifting the bag.

"I think your arms are a little too short to reach up that high, I'll get it for you." Jake's voice is low, as he whispers in my ear.

I most definitely can reach, but I also won't fight him, it's too early for me and my body is ready to collapse into my seat.

"You can have the window if you like, I normally take the aisle when I sit with Kieran."

"Thanks." I attempt a smile, but the tiredness is starting to take over and another yawn slips free instead.

He moves aside to allow me to squeeze in between him and the seats. As I work my way into my seat, I slightly rub against Jake's groin. I move fast, making it seem like I didn't notice us touching and I slump down into my chair. I just need to get into a comfy position and pass out.

"Has Coach noticed you're hungover yet?" he whispers, as if Coach could hear us from all the way back here.

I play along. "I'm very good at hiding my feelings, Jake. If I was deathly ill he would have no idea unless I wanted him to."

"Well, that's a little morbid to say this early in the morning."

He looks down at me with those deep ocean eyes. I wish I was on a beach soaking in the sunshine, lying on the sand, and listening to waves as I fall asleep. Maybe I should listen to ambient sounds the entire trip. That always puts me right to sleep.

"Ness?" He's looking at me, waiting for a response. *Oh God, I completely spaced out.*
"Huh?"

He lets out a small breath that sounds like a low chuckle. "I asked if you had a fun time yesterday."

I really can't focus on anything he's saying because his smile is too pretty. *That's it, I must be exhausted if I'm thinking like this.*

"Sorry, I'm just tired. But I had a great time last night, I really appreciate you and everyone who helped put the party together. I think it was my favorite birthday I've had."

Jake's surprise party last night just showed me that sometimes it's okay to have better relationships with your friends than with your own family.

"Well good. Next year I'll make sure to go even bigger."

Jake smiles down at me. God, he looks so good for it only being five in the morning. With his stupid teeth so white and straight, his fluffy hair tousled perfectly on his head, it's like someone plucked him out of a goddamn magazine.

"Next year? Are you expecting us to remain friends after this season?" I look up at him, waiting for his response.

He flashes that smile of his. "Ness, you can't get rid of me now."

Two seconds ago I was sleeping peacefully, resting my head on the window, until the entire bus started belting out their own rendition of "Sweet Caroline" by Neil Diamond.

Annoyed, I look down at my phone to realize we still have almost two hours left of the drive. Before I fell asleep, Jake was asking me a million questions about photography and why I got into it, and eventually, after talking his ear off for forty minutes about my passion, I finally passed out. But apparently, I didn't sleep for long.

Jake's standing in the aisleway, walking up and down, holding onto his phone, pretending it's a microphone. He's leading the rest of his teammates in his epic version of the song, and none of them seem to mind. Eli and Kieran join him, standing up and waving their arms in the air, making this a whole production. I should film them like this. How often do you see a ton of hockey players belting out on a Greyhound bus?

They're definitely not normal.

I grab my phone out of my pocket and start recording as Levi walks to the back of the bus, singing at me.

"I bet you thought I was joking about the whole karaoke thing," Kieran yells over the sound of his teammates singing.

I stop recording them as Levi takes his seat next to Kieran. I make sure to save the video so I can post it later.

I just scoff and I grab my AirPods out of my bag. "I'm going to turn my music on full blast and hope I can tune you all out."

The boys go at it for another few minutes, that is until Coach Wilson yells at them to quiet down.

At least my headache is almost completely gone now. Some ambient music and finishing off my Gatorade should hopefully do the trick.

I shift in my seat, trying to get into a comfortable position, but I swear they make these seats with barely any cushion in them. I think my butt's gone numb. And of course, to add to my day, my AirPods are completely dead, and I didn't bring another set of headphones with me. *Kill. Me Now.* All I want is an extra hour of sleep before I go into work mode and edit photos and posts before the game.

Jake slumps down in the seat next to me, a wild grin looking down at me. "Good morning, sleepyhead. Did you enjoy our performance?"

"Are you asking if I enjoyed getting rudely woken up by your tone-deaf singing?" My eyes narrow on him, I'm imagining him freezing under my ice-cold stare.

"Geez. Note to self, tired Vanessa is cranky." He ruffles my hair, irritating me even more.

"Will you *please* give me five minutes of peace so I can fall back asleep?"

He leans back in his chair, crossing his arms over his chest. This causes his shirt to go tight around his biceps. "Put your headphones in and pretend I'm not here."

If only I could.

"I can't, they're dead."

He looks at me for a moment, eyebrows furrowing as he contemplates whatever is going on in his mind. He reaches down into his backpack, pulls out his own pair of headphones, and passes me one of the earbuds.

"Here, we can share mine. What do you wanna listen to?"

I quirk an eyebrow up at him. "Are you sure?"

"Yeah, I'll listen to anything. No big deal."

I let out a little laugh. "You might take that back when I tell you what I wanted to listen to."

He looks at me, gesturing to me to continue.

"I like to listen to ambient sounds when I fall asleep. It clears my head so I can fall asleep in seconds."

"Okay." Jake nods his head and pulls his phone out of his pocket, typing away. "Do you want thunderstorms, light rain, white noise, or waves?"

He did not just look up ambient noises on his phone. I sneak a peek over his shoulder and see that he did in fact look it up. *That's so sweet.*

"Um…" I'm about to answer when he continues his own thoughts.

"I feel like you're more of a thunderstorm type of person. You're loud and moody, but fascinating. Just like a thunderstorm."

Okay, is he a mind reader?

"One, you're rude for comparing me to a thunderstorm. And two…you're right." He looks at me with a knowing smirk. "I love falling asleep to storms. Something about them is so calming, it just lulls you to sleep. The rumbling sounds are almost therapeutic. It makes you focus on what's going on outside and not what's going on in your head."

"When I was younger and still at home, my dad and I would sit in our garage and watch the lightning in the sky. It was almost like a tradition of ours. Anytime there was a storm, we would meet in the garage with drinks. When I got old enough he would slip me a beer once in a while without telling my mom. It's one of my favorite memories of home."

Every day Jake surprises me with another small piece of himself. Whether he's sharing a random thought or a cherished memory. I wish I could be as forthcoming as him.

I put the earbud in as Jake presses Play and I try to get comfortable again. I try to cross my legs, but these damn seats could use an upgrade. I'm too squished. I feel like BCU makes enough money from our tuition and their donors that they would be able to afford more comfortable modes of transportation. I toss and turn, trying a million positions but I just can't get comfortable. I should've brought my travel pillow, my rolled-up sweatshirt doesn't do much to cushion my head against the hard window.

Jake must take notice of my discomfort because he grabs my legs and positions them on his lap. "You're moving around too damn much I can't focus on taking *my own* nap."

I thank him for his kindness because now that I can stretch out a bit more and reposition my makeshift pillow, I'm much more comfortable than I was a minute ago.

My brain focuses on the soft sounds of thunder playing in my ear and my body starts to relax. Jake traces small circles on my ankle and this motion becomes so soothing I slip into a much-needed sleep.

I wake up as we arrive in Vermont. We stop at the hotel to check in and drop off our overnight bags before heading over to the arena.

"Everyone, listen up. I'll be giving out your room assignments for the weekend." Coach calls from the front of the bus. "Nate and Eli, room two oh three. Shepherd, you and Kieran are in two oh four. Levi and Xavier, two oh eight." He continues through the lineup until all of the guys unload the bus.

Since I'm technically a part of the staff, I get a room all to myself, which is quite shocking.

I grab my camera bag from above my head and hop off the bus. Most of the guys are grabbing their bags from under the bus but leave their hockey equipment for when we travel to the arena. I grab my overnight bag and join everyone else in the lobby. Coach is passing out the room keys for everyone and I overhear him giving the boys strict rules for the night.

"After the game we'll be going out for a team dinner. Your time is your own after that, but everyone, and that means you, *Danford*"—his eyes narrow on Kieran, I wonder why he's singling him out—"needs to be in their room by midnight. We leave tomorrow at eight a.m. and if you aren't on the bus, then you can walk back to campus."

Well, at least it's not as early as this morning.

I grab my room key from Coach and read over the hotel pamphlet while walking over to the elevators. This hotel has so many amenities, I wish I was here for more than one night. There's an indoor pool, a hot tub, a sauna, a bar, and a gym. So I guess the school cheaps out on transportation but splurges on the accommodations. Well, I won't be complaining anymore.

The doors to the elevator slide open, and as I'm about to hit the button for my floor, Jake lugs his overnight bag over his shoulder and squeezes in between the closing doors.

"What room are you in?"

"Two sixteen, I'm in the block of rooms with Coach and everyone else." I read off the number written on the pamphlet in my hand.

"I'm in two oh four, so I'll only be a couple of doors down, y'know in case you get bored later." He raises his eyebrows at me and winks.

God, he is such a flirt.

"Thanks for the offer, but I'll be taking advantage of that hot tub the moment we get back from the game."

The elevator comes to a stop and the bell rings, indicating that we've reached our floor. Jake motions for me to exit first, saying something along the lines of *ladies come first.* We walk down the hallway, other teammates already checking into their rooms, and Jake stops at his door.

"Well, if you get bored hanging out in that hot tub all by yourself, the guys and I will most likely be in the hotel bar 'til curfew."

I keep walking but turn around to say, "Don't worry, if I miss hockey boys, I'll just read the book Maddie got me."

Jake presses his key to the door, and as the green light flashes, he calls out. "If there are any sexy parts, make sure you send them to me!"

He is definitely something else.

CHAPTER FOURTEEN

Should I be doing this?

JAKE

Normally I sound extremely cocky when I say that I know we're going to win—but tonight we're fucking *crushing it.*

Something has to be up with Vermont University, 'cause their team cannot defend for shit. Their goalie has allowed us to score too many goals within the first two periods, they'll never be able to catch up.

If Kieran let this many slide, Coach would have his head on a stake the second we got back to campus. It would serve as a warning for anyone else who fucks up that badly.

Blowouts are hard to come by, but I have a feeling tonight we'll be celebrating.

It's pathetic for Vermont, considering how much shit their center has been talking the entire game. Austin Trent always talks about how good of a player he is and how his team would be nothing without him.

And yet he hasn't scored a single goal all game.

Trent's had two breakaways tonight, one when Eli was preoccupied with one of their wings, and the other when I may have been looking in the stands to see if Vanessa was watching me. Lucky for me, I'm fast on my skates and Kieran blocked the shot before anyone could even blink.

We're in the third period and only have about two minutes left. There's no way they'll be able to catch up. Even if we pulled Kieran out of the net, we'd still beat them by a landslide. But they'll try anything to get a number on that board to score points for this season.

Trent skates toward our net, but Eli and I are already ahead of him, anticipating his next move. He winds back, setting himself up to try to take a slap shot. I pump my legs faster, trying to get to him before he has the chance to shoot. I'm a second too late and as he shoots, I slide into him, both of us slamming into the boards as Kieran saves the puck.

No whistle, so my hit was clean. I'm pretty good at hitting hard but clean. I don't try to hurt another guy 'cause I know exactly how that feels. But fuck, my shoulder is definitely going to hurt later from that one.

The play is stopped, and Vermont's coach calls for three of their guys to swap.

"That was a dirty hit, Shepherd. You better watch your fucking back." Austin skates over to me, he's the *do you know who my father is* type of guy. He's also notorious for hogging the puck and not being a team player, which is redundant because hockey is *literally* a team sport.

I don't know what it is with a lot of these college captains, but most of them have this superiority complex where they believe that they're better than everyone else. We're lucky to have a guy like Nate as our captain because even though he comes from money, he never makes you feel like a lesser human being. I swear some of these trust fund kids are so obnoxious, it's nice to make them feel like shit during a game.

"Take a good look at that scoreboard, Trent. I'll score another just for you." I wink and blow a kiss at him as he continues to his bench, which only causes him to grunt like a fucking neanderthal.

Some guys are so easy to piss off. *I live for it.*

Shit-talking is all part of the game. It fuels your adrenaline. When someone says something to piss me off I turn into an absolute machine. My mind blanks and my body knows exactly what limits to push itself to. I don't experience that too often, but when I do, the guys know when to back off and let me be.

The clock counts down again as Nate takes control of the puck. He gets over the center line and both of Vermont's defensemen are on him immediately. Their coach has clearly been paying attention during the game because Nate is always our highest scorer. For the rest of the game, Vermont's players will be looking at him closely and playing dirty.

Coach has taught us what to do in this exact situation. If Nate is ever double-teamed, we do what Coach calls *the swing*. Nate keeps the puck tight and close and looks over to Levi who is trying to get an opening.

My turn.

I whistle loudly, skating behind Nate to signal I'm open. Nate flicks his wrist and sends the puck right into my stick. I weave past their forward and have a clean shot right to the net. The only one who can stop me now is the goalie. And given his record tonight, he shouldn't be a problem. I look into the stands for a split second and catch Vanessa with her camera—filming *me.*

Time to give her a little show.

I skate hard and fast toward the net. I've have this trick shot that I like to throw into the mix every now and again. I showed Eli how to do it during our summer training, but he shoots the puck too high every time. But this is something I've worked years to perfect.

During the summer my dad would take me to an indoor rink and work on some drills with me. He's not the best skater, so he mostly would pass me the puck and we'd focus on stickhandling. It was a random summer day, and I was playing around with the puck on the ice while waiting for my dad to lace up his skates. I did this weird figure-eight movement with my stick, and my dad thought it would be a fun trick shot if we were able to incorporate it into a play. For the remainder of that summer we worked on it until finally I came up with my own unique trick shot. My dad calls it *the eighth wonder.*

To successfully maneuver it, you have to be close to the net and give it the force of a slap shot. I scoop up the puck and keep it balanced on my stick. I flick my wrist in a figure-eight motion and send the puck flying into the net. The goalie's glove reaches a second too late.

We win 5–0.

My shoulder is killing me. It's only been a few hours since our game and I can already tell I'm going to need to ice and heat it before bed.

I wish I was in my own bed tonight rather than rooming with Kieran, sleeping on a hard hotel mattress with starchy sheets.

At least this is one of the nicer hotels we've stayed in.

I remember we once stayed at this grimy motel during one of our away games. Instead of staying right in town, Coach accidentally booked us with the wrong hotel, and we were staying in the outskirts. The hotel smelt moldy and had these sheets that looked like they hadn't been changed since the sixties.

But this hotel has good amenities. Most of us have been hanging out at the bar ever since we got back from our team dinner. Some of the guys decided to stay out for a couple of beers, but my stomach is full of wings and beer. I'm ready to do nothing but lie in bed and watch *The Office*.

It's only a little after nine, but the hallways are empty, my bed is going to be so— *That's my best friend's bare ass.*

I cover my eyes with my hand and face toward the door. "God dammit, Kieran, can you put a sock on the door or something next time?"

My voice scares the shit out of them. "Jake, get the fuck out!"

I grab the handle of the door and head out before I catch a glimpse of something I definitely shouldn't.

"I'll be in Eli and Nate's room when you're done," I call out as the door shuts behind me.

I've seen Kieran's ass probably a million times by now. I mean, hell, we all shower in the same locker room. Dicks don't even surprise me anymore. I walk across the hall to Nate and Eli's room. I knock once. Twice. *Three times.* Finally I hear heavy footsteps.

Nate opens the door slowly and the light from the hall illuminates his room. He was sleeping? You've got to be kidding me. We're the same age but sometimes Nate acts like he's years older. He's definitely wiser.

"What?" Nate's voice is laced with sleep and annoyance. As soon as we got back from dinner, he and Eli went straight up to their rooms, no post-game beers with the boys in the lobby bar.

"C'mon, old man, there's no way you were already in bed?"

He looks both ways down the hall, making sure the coast is clear for whatever he's about to say.

"Eli and I ate some gummies at dinner and I'm too tired to even finish the story."

I look up at his face and take notice of how red his eyes are. *Oh, gummies.* Yeah, I take back what I said about him being wiser. You'd think he'd know by now what his tolerance levels are.

"Oh, what happened to Mr. Responsible?" I push his shoulder and he almost loses his balance. *Okay, yup, he's definitely stoned.*

"I thought they were CBD, but I guess I read the packaging wrong. What do you want, Shep?"

"Kieran has a girl in the room, so I need a place to chill for a while." I try to squeeze past him to get into his room, but he puts his arm up, blocking the entrance.

"No, I want to pass the fuck out and I know that your dumbass will put on a movie and you won't stop talking throughout the whole thing."

I don't *always* talk during movies. Most times, maybe, but if there's something I see that I want to talk about or a theory of what the plot twist might be, I have to share it. It would be rude to *not* share my thoughts with other people.

"C'mon, I thought captains were supposed to help their teammates?"

"Yeah, well, not tonight. Go sit in the sauna or the hot tub for an hour. I'm sure that'll give Kieran more than enough time to finish with whoever he's fucking."

The idea of hot water and jets makes my body spasm. It would feel heavenly on my aching muscles. Especially my shoulder.

"Great idea, except what the hell am I supposed to wear?" I refer to my sweatpants and hoodie I'm currently wearing. If I was planning on swimming then I would've brought swim trunks with me, but considering we're here to play hockey, it seemed a bit redundant to pack.

"Sounds like a you problem. See you in the morning, Shep." He shuts the door in my face, and I hear the bolt lock on the other side.

I guess I could always strip down to my boxers. It's not like anyone's going to notice what's going on under all the bubbles anyway.

I head downstairs to the pool; the hallways are still fairly empty, *thank fuck*. Normally hotels are packed with people and families. Kids are always running up and down the halls, playing pranks and knocking on random doors. The occasional businessman sits in the lounge, two vodka tonics deep, flirting with the waitress. It's the same at every hotel.

The only difference about this one is there's no one in the pool this late. Except for one person.

I make my voice as deep as it possibly can go and do my best impersonation of Coach Wilson. "Ms. Nichols, what do you think you are doing?"

"Jesus Christ!" She shrieks, almost tossing her book in the water. "Jake, what the hell, you nearly scared me half to death. What is wrong with you?"

I can't help the laughter that escapes me. I would pay serious money to have that recorded forever. The look of pure horror on her face for a split second, thinking she was caught.

"C'mon, it's a little funny."

Vanessa's eyes look dark as she shoots me a glare that could kill a man. She shakes the book, a few droplets of water falling from her page. It looks fine, minimal damage at most.

I strip down to my boxers and toss my clothes onto a nearby lounge chair. Vanessa's eyes are attached to my body as I walk toward the stairs of the hot tub, and I pretend like I don't notice. She quickly averts her stare as I walk in, making it seem like she wasn't just eye fucking me.

Sneaky girl.

The hot water immediately eases the tension in my body, and I almost collapse onto the bench next to Vanessa. I settle into the corner, the jets pounding against my lower back and my shoulder. The massage feels heavenly. That last hit tonight definitely sent me over the edge in the pain department. I'm ready to sit here for the next hour and let the jets work their magic. *And maybe annoy Vanessa a little.*

I let out a groan in pleasure as one of the knots in my shoulder gets repeatedly hit with the strong water pressure. We need to invest in a hot tub at the house.

"So what are you up to tonight? Drinking wine and reading your hockey porn instead of going out with the guys?"

"No." She looks at me for a moment, then sighs in defeat. "Okay, *maybe* I was doing that. I didn't feel like interrupting and there was nothing good on TV, so here I am." She motions to the wine and book she set down.

"I'm sure the guys would've loved to hang out with you in a bikini." I don't know what it is, but flirting and irritating Vanessa are probably my two favorite things.

"Hence why I came here, *alone*. That is until you interrupted me."

I'm starting to think she loves to bicker with me. The funny thing is, if she thinks this annoys me, she's completely wrong. I will bicker with her until those eyes get stuck in the back of her head from rolling them so much.

"All right, all right I'll keep to myself. I just wanted to come down here to relax until I can go back to my room."

"What's wrong with your room? Not up to your high-class standards?"

"I love how you think I'm just a stuck-up snob. But alas that's not the case." I grin at her as she moves her hand in a circular motion, silently asking me to continue. "Kieran currently has a girl in there and I don't enjoy watching, which is why I'll be here for the next hour."

She makes a noise that is a mix between a *hmm* and an *ugh* sound.

"What?"

Vanessa shifts on the bench, situating herself so now she's sitting directly across from me. "I thought Kieran might've been interested in Maddie, but maybe I was picking up wrong signals."

Huh. Glad to know I wasn't the only one who thought that. The way he acts around her is different from the way he interacts with Vanessa and Sydney. But I would know if anything was going on. Kieran might be reclusive with a lot of stuff going on in his life, but I'm his best friend, he tells me everything.

"Well, she's hot and definitely his type." I lean my head back, closing my eyes and focusing on the hot water. "Enjoy your book and your wine. If I fall asleep and start drowning, save me, will ya?"

She giggles at my comment. "Don't worry, I won't let you sleep with the fishes."

Did she just quote *The Godfather*? Nothing's hotter than a girl quoting one of your favorite movies. Actually, scratch that, nothing is sexier than a girl in a bikini, wearing glasses, and quoting one of your favorite films. *Fuck*, the red fabric over her breasts is so thin I can see her nipples, the smallest movement would have her bare to the world.

Fucking hell, stop being a creep.

I lean back into the water, and it feels like my body is melting away. The temperature is hot, but not burning. The soft spa music playing in the background is just about lulling me to sleep. Until I hear a small, almost inaudible gasp come from Vanessa's mouth. I peek an eye open to see what she's doing. Vanessa is holding her book close to her face, sipping the remainder of her wine.

Clearly there's *something* entertaining happening in her book.

I close my eyes and focus on the distant ache of my muscles being relieved. I wonder what exactly she's reading. All I gathered from her explanation is that it's a romance novel about an NHL player in Vancouver and his best friend's younger sister. I don't know how that could pique anyone's interest, but with the way Vanessa is blowing through the book, it makes me think that there's a huge following for this kind of stuff out there. *Who knew?*

As I sit and relax, the only sounds are the soft music in the background and Vanessa's little reactions to her book. I never knew that watching or listening to someone read could be so entertaining. I want to know what's causing her to laugh, gasp, and moan.

Another sharp breath escapes her lips, and she accidentally runs her foot up my leg, immediately pulling away as she felt the movement.

"Sorry."

I look over at her, my head still relaxing on the side of the hot tub. She never has to apologize for touching me.

"No need, it felt nice."

The heat rises from her chest to her face, and I can't tell if it's because she's embarrassed or the water is too hot for her.

"I think I just got too into the book and forgot where I was." She grabs her bottom lip between her teeth and redirects her focus back to the novel in her hands.

A second later, I hear the clap of the book closing quickly.

"Actually, uh, I—I'm just gonna head back to my room. Y'know…to sleep." She puts down her book on the side of the hot tub and climbs out, walking toward her towel and shoes sitting on the lounge chair. Her cheeks are still flushed, and it's definitely not the water temperature causing the redness.

I swim over to where she was just seated and grab the book before she can come back to get it. She dog-eared the page she was on and I'm curious to see what has her all hot and bothered.

I quickly skim the pages while she dries off, completely unaware of what I'm reading. As I scan the page, it's basically filled with porn, just in written form. Fuck, this shit is hot. Maybe men should start reading this kind of stuff. It definitely would help some guys in the bedroom. *Me?* Definitely not. I've never had any complaints, only praise. But some guys could learn a thing or two.

Before I can react, the book is snatched right out of my hands.

"Excuse me, that's private." Vanessa wedges the book under her arm, out of my reach.

"That's some hot stuff in there, Ness."

Her cheeks turn a deeper shade of red. Is she embarrassed? I would bet any amount of money that she's going to go back to her room to continue to read in private.

"Thanks for the company, I'll see you in the morning." She tosses the small empty bottle of wine in the trash on her way out, waving her hand above her head to signal goodbye. "Don't drown! The team might need you."

A minute goes by, and I try to refocus on relaxing.

Five minutes go by and all I can think of is Vanessa going back to her room to please herself while reading that book. It was clear as day that was what she intended to do tonight. The brief few sentences I got to read even had me turned on. I can imagine her now, splayed across her bed, her fingers gliding in and out—*fuck*, I shouldn't be imagining her doing dirty things to herself. Even if I want to imagine all the dirty things I could do to her.

Another five minutes pass and I sit here, letting the jets pound out all my knots.

Fuck it, I can't sit here any longer.

My feet move without my brain telling them to. I wrap a towel around my waist and spend no time putting my clothes back on. I collect them into a ball, not caring if they get wrinkled or not.

Should I be doing this? She did say that she wanted some alone time and privacy—but how am I supposed to give that to her when I know exactly what she's doing all alone in that room?

I've tried hard to just be friends with her, but I can't stop thinking about Vanessa *that way.* I'll take any opportunity to touch her, even if it's just having her feet in my lap and I'm tracing circles, thinking about her. Thinking about if she likes my touch or thinks about me when she's alone.

My feet stop in front of Vanessa's door.

All right, Jake, you made it this far.

Fuck, I don't know. The proper thing to do would be to leave her alone and go back to my room and just rub one out in the shower thinking about Vanessa touching herself. But when do I ever do the proper thing?

I pound my fist against the door before I can talk myself out of it.

The door swings open after a minute of waiting, Vanessa looks disheveled in a baggy T-shirt and tight pink boxers. "Oh, Jake, hey…" Her hair is tousled and messy, and her breathing uneven.

I think I have caught her in the middle of the act.

"You okay, Ness? You seem to be a little out of breath."

Vanessa's eyes flick back and forth, clearly trying to think of a lie. But I think I know exactly what she was doing.

"Do you mind?" I motion to my half-naked body standing in the hallway. As she takes notice of my lack of clothing, she steps aside, allowing me to come in.

Oh God, what am I doing here?

Okay, that question was redundant. I know exactly what I'm doing here.

I don't think I've ever wanted someone as badly as I want Vanessa. Girls don't normally have this effect on me. I meet a girl, we hook up, end of story. But Vanessa is completely different. I've been telling myself it's because we didn't hook up, and that's why I want her so bad. Except I find myself asking her questions about herself whenever I get the chance. If I see her reading a book or an article, I always ask her what it's about. My brain is hardwired on Vanessa, and it won't stop.

I scan the room as she shuts the door behind me. Her sheets are strewn across the bed. Her book lies open on one of the pillows like it was just tossed aside without a thought.

Yeah, she was definitely up to something.

"Doing a little late-night reading?" I ask, walking toward the bed.

My hand barely brushes the book and Vanessa bolts to the bed as she sees what I'm reaching for. She slaps her hand on top of the book, stopping me from picking it up.

"Don't touch that." She holds the book to her chest, crossing her arms over it as if they're shielding me from the content inside the pages. Too bad I already got a taste, and I know exactly what she was reading.

"Why?" Her face scans mine, but I cut her off before she gives me an answer. "You don't want me to see what's getting you off. What is it? Praise kink? BDSM?"

My assumptions make her blush. "No, it's not that, you snoop."

Vanessa takes a step back but doesn't realize how close she is to the bed and loses her footing. I reach out and catch her at her waist. Lucky for her, I have amazing reflexes. Her chest is rising faster, and I swear I can hear the rapid beating of her heart.

"What's in the book, Vanessa?" I still have my arm wrapped around her waist. I really don't want to let go.

She hesitates, internally debating whether she wants to share this information with me.

"They're not having sex, he's just…eating her out. It's hot." That is hot. I never thought Vanessa would be such an easy girl to please. One tiny little sex scene and here she is all hot and bothered.

"All it takes is a good sex scene and you're all set, huh?"

Now she takes notice of my hand on her lower back and decides to put space between us, pushing against my chest to create more room.

"When you haven't had sex in months, it doesn't take much. Obviously you've never had that issue."

She's right. I never really go through dry spells unless I purposely want to.

"God, it's so embarrassing. Why am I even telling you this?" She walks toward the desk and puts the book on the surface. "Does it make me pathetic that something as dumb as a sports romance can turn me on?"

Definitely not.

"Damn, Ness, if you wanted to fuck a hockey player all you had to do was ask." I wink, my comment causing her to laugh. She could ask me to do anything right now and I'd say yes.

Vanessa rolls those devilish eyes at me. "In your dreams, Jake. I'm perfectly capable of taking care of this"—she motions to her body—"issue without you. I was already in the process of doing so until you interrupted me."

It seems like I've been interrupting her a lot tonight.

I take a seat on her bed and rest against her headboard, tucking my arms behind my head. "Oh please, don't stop on my account."

The frustration is clear on her face. Can girls experience blue balls? 'Cause I think I just cock-blocked Vanessa from finger-fucking herself.

"You're infuriating."

Maybe I can offer my own services. Although the last time I did that, she shut me down. Can my ego handle being turned down again?

Let's find out.

"Well, I guess it's a good thing I stopped by and interrupted you." I stand and walk closer to where she's standing next to the desk.

Vanessa's eyes narrow at me. "What the hell are you talking about?"

I sigh. "Look, I'm great at making women come, and you need an orgasm. Therefore, I'll let you live your hot sports romance fantasy while I eat you out."

And now she's looking at me as if I have three heads. Maybe no one's ever been this blunt with her before.

Her head shakes profusely. "No. *Nope.* No way."

And my ego flies completely out the window. Oh for three. I guess some girls are just unattainable, even for me.

"All right, fine." I put my hands up, backing away from her. "Go back to your hand and your hockey porn fantasy. If you need me, you know what room I'm in."

I make my way toward the door and grab my clothes off the floor. I'm hoping that Kieran is done by now or I'll be sitting in front of my room half-naked.

My hand is on the doorknob, twisting it open when she calls out. "Wait."

I release the handle and turn back to her. She's standing next to the bed, fiddling with the hem of her shirt.

"Do you really want to, uh…"

"Eat you out?" She nods at my question. "Ness, I would do anything you'd ask. All you have to do is *ask.*"

I walk over to her, standing next to the bed. Her glasses magnify the size of her mossy-green eyes and fuck, do they have me trapped. There's a fleck of gold around the rim of her iris that I never noticed before.

Staring down at her I can tell that she's hesitant, fighting with her inner self over what to do. She's probably bickering with her conscience, deciding whether she should go through with this. I'm hoping that the devil on her shoulder convinces her to listen to what she *wants* and not what she *thinks* would be right.

She deserves to have fun. I can't imagine going months without any sort of physical touch.

I tuck a strand of her hair behind her ear and move my lips, so they hover over her exposed neck. I wait to see if she pulls away, if she tells me to stop. I would never do anything that would make her, or any girl, uncomfortable.

Instead, she stretches her neck to the side. I start to pepper featherlight kisses along the side of her jaw. As I make my way down her neck I feel her pulse going erratic under my lips. The sensation causes goose bumps to rise on her skin.

"Tell me what you want, Ness." My throat is scratchy. I feel like I'm parched and she's the closest glass of water. I want to drink her in.

Slowly, I back her up onto the bed, positioning my body over hers. I hover over her, making eye contact as I start tracing small circles on her inner thighs, causing a shiver to go through her body. I hope she doesn't mind my calloused hands, but that's what years of playing hockey will do.

"Ness?"

"Hmm?" My touch clearly distracts her.

"Tell me." I stop my movements, waiting for her to respond.

"Will you…" She looks down between us, squirming under me, getting more impatient with every second that passes, my small touches driving her nuts.

"Sorry, what was that?"

"Will you"—her breath hitches as my thumb finds her clit over the thin fabric—"*please, go down on me.*"

There it is.

"Anything for you, angel girl."

I move down her neck, sucking and kissing the tender skin. I pull her shirt aside when I get to her collarbone, wanting to touch every part of her. She pulls the shirt over her head, exposing the most beautiful pair of tits. I don't think I've ever seen such a perfect pair. Her nipples are pink and hard against her soft skin. I take one into my mouth, sucking and kissing softly, earning soft moans from Vanessa's lips.

As I work my way down, exploring her body with my lips and tongue, I reach the hemline of her boxer shorts. They're light pink with cherries on them.

I wonder if she bought these for herself or stole them from a previous hookup—I guess it's none of my business, though.

She slowly grinds her pelvis into me.

So impatient.

I trace my fingers along the elastic waistband and start pulling them down slowly. So slow, sucking and kissing her legs and I pull them off and toss them onto the floor behind me.

She smells fucking divine. *Coconut and vanilla.* Whatever lotion she has on her body has me salivating at the mouth. Her pussy is the prettiest shade of pink, and the landing strip has me looking exactly where I want to go.

Fuck me, she's gorgeous.

"Are you just going to stare at my pussy or are you going t—" I run my tongue along her center to shut her up. *Definitely impatient.*

I glide my tongue over that sensitive bud of nerves, slowly dragging it up and down her sweet pussy. I suck on her clit and trail kisses down until I reach her opening. Her hands reach me, tangling her fingers around my curls. As I suck and kiss harder she pulls my head in closer.

I'd be perfectly fine if she suffocated me like this.

I tease her with my tongue, slowly pressing inside of her.

"*Fuck*, Jake. Oh my god, keep doing t-that."

I do exactly as she wants, lapping my tongue against her, thrusting my tongue in and out, tasting her. *Fuck, she's so sweet.*

Vanessa moans louder, telling me she absolutely loves the feel of my tongue on her.

"Can I add a finger?"

She responds in between moans. "Yes…please."

I suck on my index finger, making sure it's lubricated for her. I push a finger inside her tight cunt as my mouth moves around her clit. I know exactly the right moves to get a girl to come in under a minute, but I feel like taking my time with Vanessa. I'll make it the best goddamn orgasm she's ever had. I want to make it so any time she comes, she's always comparing it to me. Any time she wants to please herself, she thinks of this moment, because I know that after this I will never think about anything else but her.

Slowly I thrust my finger into her while continuing to play with that bundle of nerves. *Kissing. Sucking.* I give her clit a small nibble, which causes a moan to escape her lips.

Oh fuck, the sound she makes has my dick throbbing in my pants. She tastes so sweet and her pussy is soaking my hand.

I pause for a moment, which causes her to whimper as I pull my finger out. God, she's so sexy.

My eyes meet hers. "I'm gonna add another finger okay?"

Her chest is heaving as she nods.

My tongue finds its way back to her center, running it up and down, earning the softest moans that trickle from her mouth. I push a second finger into her, and I can feel her walls tighten around me. My fingers are soaked from her, I wish it was my dick inside of her rather than my fingers.

No, tonight is all about Vanessa.

I know a vibrator and a dildo can do the trick, but I also know that there is nothing nor anyone that will make her come like I can.

I'm going to ruin everything else for her. Her dildo won't be enough to please her after me. She'll try hard to think about someone else—even that damn Henry Cavill—but every time it'll be me that pops into her beautiful head as she comes.

Am I being a little too cocky? Maybe, but I don't really care. I'm too confident in my abilities.

I slide my tongue in between her, then suck on her clit until her legs start to shake.

"Oh God, Jake."

"Ness, I want you to fucking come all over my face. Do you understand?" She's silent, besides her heavy breathing. She's enjoying this too much, lost in the sensation that's taking over her body. But I know exactly how to make her talk.

I remove my fingers from her and slowly tease her with my tongue.

"Jake, please. I'm so close."

Vanessa seems like she's the type of girl who likes to be praised during sex but also to be told what to do. Sometimes you can just tell by looking at someone exactly what their kinks are. Or I might just have a superpower of knowing what turns women on.

"I said, *do you understand*?"

She looks down at me, those giant green eyes giving me the biggest pouty look as she nods.

"Good." I grab her hips and flip us over, placing her on my face, but she pulls up to balance on her knees.

"Jake, I don't know…" She looks down at me, her eyes falling onto her thighs that rest next to my head. Not realizing it, she lets her insecurities show just for a second, not saying a word but silently saying everything.

Being with someone is intimate no matter the setting. You both are naked and vulnerable. Exposing a piece of yourself even if you don't mean to. I don't want her to feel anything but wanted when she's with me.

"The nicest thing you could ever do to me is suffocate me with these thighs." I take turns kissing both sides of her thighs. The skin is so soft and creamy, I run my tongue along her as I guide her to sit on my face.

The last thing I want her to feel while she's on top of me is insecure. Her body is magnificent. Her skin is velvet soft, and she has the cutest dimples at the bottom of her back that my fingers are loving digging into as I hold her on top of me.

I resume feasting on her like I was moments ago. She rocks her lips against me, loving the friction that she's creating. With the way she's grinding on me, I can tell that she's close.

There's this trick I've learned some girls *really* like.

As she rides my face, I take her clit in my mouth, sucking it as if I could suck her soul out of her body. I slowly graze my teeth along her clit, and it sets her over the edge. She comes with my name spilling from her mouth.

Fuck, her moaning my name gets me so hard, I swear I could come just from that sound. I look down at my boxers and looking at my bulge physically hurts me. *I'll take care of that later.*

Vanessa collapses on the bed, satisfied.

"Well…they were right," she says between heated breaths.

"Who was right?" I ask, facing her.

She smiles and rolls those devilish eyes at me, knowing what she's about to say is going to boost the shit out of my ego. "I've heard whispers around campus since I started working with the team. You live up to your reputation."

Well, that's not shocking.

"I know, but I love hearing that come out of your mouth." My ego has successfully been repaired.

"You're such a dick, did you know that?"

"I may be a dick, but at least I'm great at making you come."

Vanessa grabs the pillow from above her head and swings it at me, hitting me in the face. I grab the pillow and toss it back at her, tackling her back into the bed with me.

How does she have this much energy? Here I was thinking I had just given her a mind-numbing orgasm that should've put her to sleep, but maybe it was just mediocre.

"Clearly I didn't make you come hard enough if you still have energy to start a pillow fight."

She grabs the pillow and places it under her head, as if she's getting comfortable before falling asleep.

"Yeah, as if you'd tongue fuck me all night until I pass out from so many orgasms." Her voice is laced with sarcasm, but I'm going to make her eat those words. If she thinks I won't go down on her until sunrise, she's mistaken. I'll make her come so hard that everyone in the hotel will hear her yelling my name.

"I could do this all night, sweetheart."

Her eyes look over to me, lust written all over her face. "Prove it."

And so I do.

CHAPTER FIFTEEN

Was it the best orgasm of my life?

VANESSA

Last night was a first.

Not for me receiving oral but for coming so hard that I almost blacked out.

Did I make the best decision last night? *Probably not.* In the moment it seemed like the best option. I mean, who would turn down a gorgeous hockey player who tells you he would do *anything*—especially when he offers to go down on you all night and ask nothing in return?

I've never had a guy make me come so hard that I immediately fell asleep afterward, but after four orgasms, I think my body turned into liquid and I passed out once my head finally hit the pillow.

When I woke up this morning, my bed was empty, and my body was more relaxed than it has been in months. There's just something about having an orgasm caused by another person that makes it more satisfying. My vibrator is great, and my dildo has satisfied me more than enough times, but Jake's tongue mixed with his fingers just sent me over the edge and into oblivion. I think he may have ruined my vibrator for me and that annoys me to no end because I feel like that was his intention.

If he ruined Geralt for me, I might have to kill him.

I don't know how to explain the events that transpired last night. I was happily enjoying my evening, reading a spicy romance and sipping on a bottle of wine that I convinced the lobby bartender to give me for free. Then Jake came down to the hot tub and everything changed from there.

At first I was reading a hockey romance, and the next thing I know, I was living it.

When he said he could go all night and I told him to prove it, but I didn't think he was *actually* going to.

Was it the best orgasm of my life? Maybe. Possibly. *Okay, fine, it definitely was.*

Except there's no way I'll be telling Jake that because it will only make him cockier than he already is. I already let it slip last night that he lives up to his reputation, which I think telling him that turned him on even more. He never once asked for anything in return, so I feel a little guilty that last night was all about me.

Normally it takes a hell of a lot of begging for a guy to go down on a girl, but Jake was so willing to do that, it makes me wonder why the hell he *would* do it. I mean, for most guys if they go down on a girl, they expect *something* in return—a hand job or a blowjob. Surprisingly, Jake asked for nothing. He just kept going and didn't mention wanting anything from me. *Weird.*

If it's not sex he wants from me then what is it? Friends don't just perform oral on one another. Is there something more that I'm missing? Is it right in front of me and I'm just an idiot for not seeing it?

No. This is Jake. Golden playboy of BCU. I'm probably just reading way too much into this whole situation.

Unless he wants something more out of this, which I highly doubt. But if that's the case then I really do need to talk to him about this because I'm nowhere near ready to commit myself to anyone. I want to enjoy my single life and work on my photography. I don't have time for relationships.

The second I see him we can straighten all of this out. Although, how do you greet someone who gave you the best orgasm of your life? Do I give him a kiss on the cheek? Give him a hug? Or is a handshake more appropriate?

God, I'm such an idiot.

All I need to do is have an adult conversation and tell him that this can never happen again. It was a one-time thing and I was just needy and hadn't come from a man's touch in months. A moment of weakness, if you will.

His hands did feel like magic. All rough and calloused from hockey. It's almost like I can still feel a ghost touch lingering on my thighs, it causes goose bumps to rise all over my body.

Geez, I'm starting to sound like a teenage boy going through puberty.

The elevator dings, which brings me back to reality.

As the doors open to the lobby, I'm greeted by the entire team lounging around on the couches and chairs, waiting for the bus to pull up. Nate is chatting with Coach Wilson. Eli and Levi are both passed out on a couch while Kieran sits across from them with his sunglasses on. *Yikes, someone must be a little hungover.*

"And here I thought you might oversleep and miss the bus." Jake's leaning against the wall next to the elevators. How did I completely miss him when I got off?

I force a smile. *Act normal.* "Just had trouble getting up this morning, that's all."

Jake's eyes lit up at my statement. *Fuck my life.* That's going to go right to his head.

"I knew I was good, but damn. Good to know my tongue performed well last night." He winks one of those gorgeous blue eyes at me.

Yup, just like I thought. Maybe my subconscious loves to boost his ego because that's all I've been doing these past twenty-four hours.

My brain is in overload, and knowing myself, if I don't talk to Jake before we get on the bus, then I'll put it off forever. Procrastination is one of my toxic traits. I just have to set boundaries. We're friends and what happened last night will never happen again. Even if my body is screaming at me right now to jump his bones. Maybe if I practice it enough in my head, my mouth will actually say the words out loud.

"So about last night—"

Coach Wilson's voice cuts mine off. "Everyone drop your room keys off to the front desk if you haven't already and let's get a move on! I want to be back at campus before nightfall."

It seems a little extreme to think we won't be back until dark; I mean, it's only eight in the morning. Are we expecting heavy traffic or a breakdown?

In an instant, everyone starts moving. Some follow Coach out the front doors while others head over to the reception desk. I fumble around, looking in my pockets for my room key. The only downside to my sweatpants is that they're men's and the pockets go *so* deep. I shouldn't complain, most women's clothes don't have any pockets, or if they do, they barely fit my chapstick—hence why purses exist.

"I'll meet you on the bus," Jake calls out to me as he heads for the front doors.

I finally dig out the card, give it back to the receptionist, and follow the rest of the players out of the hotel. Outside of the lobby, the bus is pulled up to the front door and everyone lines up to stash their bags away before heading onto the bus. The air here is crisper than back in Boston. It feels fresher, maybe because Vermont is known as the Green Mountain state and Boston is always *go go go*.

This is my favorite time of the year. Watching the leaves change from green to various arrays of oranges, yellows, and reds. It's also the best season because I love living in cozy sweaters and cardigans.

Speaking of sweaters, I need to grab mine out of my bag before I stow it under the bus and freeze the entire way home. I'm sure Jake is the type of person who would let me borrow his if I was shivering, but I'd rather just have my own. And who knows how Jake's going to react after I talk to him. I'm hoping he'll be fine with us never bringing up last night ever again. I mean, he's notorious for going out with multiple girls and never settling down, so I can't see why this would be an issue.

I find Jake at the back of the bus waiting to put his bag with everyone else's luggage.

"Jake, can we talk for a sec?"

"Sure." He tosses his bag into the undercarriage, and he leads me to the front of the bus, a little bit away from everyone else to give us privacy. "What's up, Ness?"

The sun peeking through the clouds lightens his facial features. All of a sudden my brain goes blank staring at him. His chiseled jaw. His ocean blue eyes. The way he flicks his tongue out to wet his lips as he waits for me to talk.

Okay, Vanessa, it's time to just rip off the Band-Aid.

"It's about last night."

A wide grin breaks across his face. "I get it, I was so good you came back for seconds. Although from what I recall from last night this would be what…your fifth helping?"

So damn cocky.

"Ha-ha." I shove his arm lightly. "Actually…I was going to ask if we could pretend it didn't happen and never bring it up again. Like, ever. I had a moment of weakness, and you were offering and I just—I took advantage of that whole situation. Can we just pretend it never happened, please?"

Jake's lips stop smiling and he straightens himself as he nods.

My rambling doesn't stop. "I just value our friendship and last night was a mistake and—"

Jake cuts me off before I can continue my word vomit. "No worries. It was just a friend helping out a friend." He nods at me again then heads onto the bus without another word.

Okay, was that weird or am I just imagining things?

Maybe Jake is used to girls following him around like a puppy dog after they hook up, but that's not me. I want to put this behind us and never think about it again. It was just a one-time fluke, and my brain can delete it from existence once I get home. I have an inkling that last night's experience might linger longer than I want it to.

I wish I was back home sitting in the coffee shop with Sydney and Maddie, gossiping to them over lattes about this weekend. I could unload my brain on them while snacking on a warm croissant and listen to them freak out in between bites.

I toss my bag with the others and hop on the bus, hoping to find Jake in the back saving me a seat.

I'm a little bit relieved walking onto the bus as no one really pays any attention to me. I don't know if I was expecting Jake to tell any of his teammates about what happened last night, but why am I feeling a little ashamed?

As my legs carry me down the aisle of the bus, I spot Jake sitting in an aisle seat near the back, head low while he scrolls on his phone. Instead of saving me a seat, he decided to sit next to Kieran, who's currently passed out with his head against the window. I guess early mornings and Kieran don't mix well together.

"I thought we were sitting together on the way home?" It wasn't really discussed, more like I assumed we would be.

"Kieran and I normally sit together on roadies. Levi has a free seat, I'm sure he'd love for you to sit with him." He pulls the hood of his sweater over his head and pops in his headphones—clearly signaling he doesn't want to be bothered.

Okay then.

Levi is sitting a couple rows ahead of Jake, and I turn around to head to the middle of the bus. If Jake doesn't want me to sit with him, maybe I can keep Levi company for the duration of the ride. Unlike the way here, I'm not mildly hungover or tired. I slept so well last night that I feel like I downed a triple shot of espresso.

"Is that seat taken?"

Levi looks up at me with his deep brown eyes that girls definitely swoon over. "Aren't you sitting with Jake?"

The confused look on Levi's face matches my own a few seconds ago when Jake turned me down. He looks over his shoulder and I follow his gaze back to Jake. His eyes meet mine, then quickly avert back to his phone, pretending like he wasn't just looking at me and Levi.

"Guess not." I shrug and Levi stands up so I can squeeze by.

I tuck my bag into the overhead compartment, grabbing the essentials—my headphones and my water bottle. I get situated in my seat, tucking my headphones into my pocket and putting my water bottle in the cup holder attached to the armrest.

Did I do something wrong to piss off Jake? Did I miss something important that made his mood do a complete one-eighty?

I wish Jake would just tell me what I did to put him in such a mood. Was it because I didn't offer to do anything for him? 'Cause if that's what all this is about, I'll be having words with him. Could he be mad at me for what I said outside? No, there's no way. He even said so himself that it was just a friend helping out a friend.

I let out a sigh, maybe too loud because it causes Levi to turn his attention on me.

"Okay, what's wrong, Nichols?"

I don't want to completely unload on Levi, I'll leave that word vomit for Sydney and Maddie. So instead, I just ask, "Are men programmed to always be so aggravating?"

Levi lets out a soft laugh. "No, but that's definitely Jake." He looks over his shoulder to the back of the bus. "And Kieran. They're both in moods this morning. My guess is they both struck out last night and their egos are a little bruised, so they're taking it out on the world."

I know for sure that's not the case for either of them, but I keep that information to myself.

"Is this why you're not sitting with him? Did you guys have a fight or something?"

If we had a fight, it was clearly one-sided, and I had no idea an argument was even taking place.

"No. I just...we..." I can't find the words to explain to Levi what I'm feeling.

Levi looks at me, then behind me where Jake is sitting a few rows back. His eyes are like ping-pong balls going back and forth, until finally it clicks.

"No fucking way. Did you guys hook up last night?"

Ding ding ding, we have a winner!

"Why don't you say it a little louder so the whole bus can hear?" I know that my cheeks are turning bright red, and I lean close to Levi to whisper so no one else can hear. "We didn't hook up. Well...sort of."

"What do you mean?"

"You know, a little past third base, but not technically a home run."

My innuendo hits the mark, and I can tell the second Levi pieces it all together. He chuckles and pulls the hood up on his sweater. "Gotcha."

Am I smart in trusting Levi with this information? He gives me warm and friendly vibes, but I can't put my finger on why.

Levi senses my unease and takes this as an opportunity to change the subject. "Did you pick someone to do your portrait project on?"

I am an idiot. With all of my planning and my hectic schedule, I completely forgot about our assignment due this week for our class. I've been so focused on updating the team's social platforms, that I put my other work on the back burner.

We're supposed to do a few portrait photos showcasing humanity's beauty. I was going to ask Sydney or Maddie if I could photograph them, but Maddie hates having her photo taken, and Sydney's been so busy with her own assignments I haven't had a chance to ask her.

"Not yet. I haven't done much portrait photography, unless you count me taking photos of wildlife as portraits," I confess. "What about you? Who'd you pick as your model?"

"My grandma." He smiles. "She's basically raised me since I was six so I asked her if I could take some photos for a class. She loves that I'm exploring more than just sports, so she's always willing to help me out. I have the photos in the lab, so I can show you when we get back to campus if you want?"

Levi is a little bit of a savior because I was just going to wing it. Somehow I managed to go most of my academic career with very little portrait assignments.

"That would be lovely, thank you, Levi."

"Any time."

Levi and I spent the majority of the ride home talking about different photography styles and what got us into the hobby.

He told me that his dad is a sports photographer and was always traveling when he was younger, hence why his grandma mainly raised him. His mom passed away from cancer when he was five, so it's been him and his grandma for most of his life.

Both of his parents had a passion for photography. His dad currently works for an NBA team on the East Coast, but his mom was all for portrait work. I think that's where he gets his inspiration from. Portraits are great for photos of major life events like birthdays or holidays to preserve sweet little moments.

Once we got back to campus, I followed Levi to our print lab, completely ignoring Jake. If he's mad at me then he can work that out himself.

Levi and I go through all of his prints, and I don't think I've ever met anyone as talented as him. Some people think that photography is just clicking a button on your camera, but it's so much more than that. By looking at the photos that Levi took of his grandma, you can see every piece of life. The wrinkles in her forehead she's collected over the years, a sunspot on her cheek from too much time gardening—it all tells a story. I wouldn't be surprised if I saw Levi's art hanging in a gallery one day.

After the lab I came home to an empty apartment. Maybe I was a little relieved to come home to silence. I feel like I need to de-stress from the weekend. I want to tell Sydney and Maddie about what happened last night, but I don't want them to pester me with a million questions, which I know for certain that Sydney will.

I toss my overnight bag into the corner of my room. Normally I give myself a day to decompress and then the next day I'll go through my clothes and do all of my laundry and boring chores. I turn on some music and take a seat at my desk, ready to go through this weekend's material and put together a few posts for the team's social media. Over the weekend our Instagram page gained over a hundred new followers, and my most recent post, which included a video of Jake smashing someone into the boards, has over fifty comments, most of which are girls drooling through their phone screens. Maybe one of those girls can cheer Jake up.

"Oh thank God, you're finally home!" Maddie's voice carries through my room.

A scream escapes my lips. "Jesus, you scared the crap out of me!"

I don't know how I didn't hear them come home. Normally Sydney flings her shoes off so hard they hit the wall behind our shoe rack, and that's always my cue that she's home. Maddie on the other hand is like a ghost. She's so stealthy that we never hear her when she comes home.

Sydney jumps onto my bed and plops down, holding one of my pillows in her lap. "How was the weekend?"

I swivel around on my desk chair and prop my legs up on my bed. Maddie takes the spot on my bed next to Sydney—snuggling under one of my throw blankets.

"I assumed Nate would be texting your family group chat with game updates."

"Obviously!" She rolls her eyes. "I meant how was *your* weekend. You have guilt written all over your face and we got zero text messages from you last night, so spill."

I swear, Sydney's brain has a built-in lie detector so you can't get anything past her. Even if you *think* you might be able to tell her a little white lie, she'll be all over you within minutes and you end up spilling more than intended. Which is exactly what's going to happen.

Maddie leans up from her sitting position, putting her hands together like she's praying. "Please tell me you finally got laid."

Before I can stop myself from reacting, my eyes go wide, giving away my answer. This causes both Sydney and Maddie to jump up squealing with excitement.

"It's not what you think." As the words leave my mouth, they both stop jumping and plop back down on the mattress, acting as if I just burst their happy bubble.

"What do you mean?" Maddie's eyes glare at me, begging to spill what occurred this weekend.

"Well, I didn't necessarily have sex." They both look at me, waiting for me to continue and save them from waiting any longer. "But a guy did go down on me. Multiple times." I hide my face in my hands, waiting for them to say something.

Maddie speaks first. "Hey, at least your dry spell finally came to an end. And if it was multiple times then at least it must have been really good head."

I lift my head from my hands and look at my two best friends. I look at Sydney for less than a second before she guesses exactly who I did the dirty with.

"Oh you little slut, it was Jake wasn't it?" She says it so plainly.

"How could you have possibly guessed that? All I did was look at you!"

"Yes, but it was a very guilty look and you know I can read you like a book." She smiles big, showing off her gorgeous straight teeth. "So are you guys dating? Or is this just a casual hookup? Are you guys gonna do it again? Please share *all* the details."

I grit my teeth together. I want to scream into a pillow because I don't know what the hell happened or how to explain it. It really did happen so fast.

"It was a one-time thing. I was hanging out in the hot tub, y'know drinking wine and reading. Then he joined me and we were talking. Shortly after I left, he showed up at my room. I was horny and he just…offered to take care of my problem."

"You agreed it was a one-time thing or you *told* him?" Maddie asks.

Oh, I guess I never really considered his input on the situation, I just decided for the both of us that this was the best cause of action.

"Well, I said it first but he agreed."

Sydney smacks her hand over her mouth before saying, "Oh my god, that makes so much sense now."

Did I miss something?

"What makes sense?"

Sydney grabs her phone from her back pocket and shows me a text message on her screen. "Nate texted me earlier asking if he could come here to study. I guess Kieran and Jake are in a shitty mood and invited some girls over to *cheer them up*. You put Jake in a bad mood."

"Well, I don't know why it's my fault he's in a bad mood. If he's being a dick because I didn't offer to blow him last night then he can go fuck whomever he wants—it doesn't bother me," I lie.

"Maybe he's not upset about that. Maybe he's into you and you telling him you just want to be friends absolutely crushed his soul so much that he has to get into another girl's pants to forget about you." Maddie raises an eyebrow at me.

That's definitely not it.

Or at least I hope that's not the case. Because if Jake Shepherd does have feelings for me, I have no idea what I would do.

CHAPTER SIXTEEN

Have fun on your date

VANESSA

This week has thrown me a curveball.

Since school started, I've had minimal contact with my parents. I got one phone call the first day of classes—only so my mom could find out if I was taking any law courses this year. She was *not* happy to find out that I dropped my minor in political science only to swap to film and photography. After that, they only called one other time—a few days before my birthday to let me know that they wouldn't be visiting and probably wouldn't have any service on their vacation.

My parents have money, so not having service in Europe was just a lie they told me so I wouldn't bother them.

I hadn't heard anything since their trip until two days ago. I was leaving campus after my Wednesday classes had finished when my dad's caller ID lit up my screen. Immediately I went into panic mode because my dad rarely calls me, so I automatically assumed someone died.

Someone did.

But not anyone important, as bad as that is to say.

My mom's aunt passed away over the weekend, so my dad called to let me know they were heading back early from their vacation. I didn't know why my dad felt the need to update me, that is until we got to the actual reason for the call. My parents expected me to come home this weekend for the funeral so we would look good in front of my mother's relatives. I hate that side of my family so much.

Okay, maybe hate is a strong word. But I strongly dislike them.

Mom knows why. That side comes from generations of wealth. Somewhere down the line, an ancestor founded a bagel company in New York that's been around for decades. Since then, my family has produced businessmen, lawyers, and housewives. They expect nothing less than perfection.

I grew up spending my summers in the Hamptons with my cousins. We had catered dinners for every holiday, and birthdays always consisted of *very* expensive gifts. It made me want to puke. It still does. Most of my cousins have followed in their parents' footsteps, either holding shares in the family business or becoming a doctor or a lawyer.

I'm the only outlier.

Maybe that's where my resentment comes from. They believe that everyone needs to be financially successful in order to have happiness. But I don't think anyone on that side knows what happiness truly is. My family believes that you should find a partner who is on the same social status. Meaning we should look for companions who attend ivy league schools, wear designer clothes, and know which fork to use during each course.

I think the moment I knew I would never be like my family occurred a few summers ago. We were staying at my aunt Helen's house in the Hamptons and I overheard my mom's siblings talking about my dad. My dad is a successful man, but he wasn't always. When my parents first started dating he was doing his residency, and he was almost broke and drowning in student debts.

Dad's family comes from Brooklyn and is lower class, and that did not sit well with my mother's side. They thought that he was just coasting through college and would eventually drop out once my mom passed the bar. They didn't approve of her dating anyone they deemed less than them.

A.k.a. anyone without money.

My aunt Helen is one of the most judgmental people in our family. She believes that she and my uncle Richard have the poster perfect family and none of us will be able to compare to them. She's a realtor and her husband owns a string of restaurants along the East Coast.

My mom's younger sister, my aunt Amy, is a housewife, but she likes it that way. Her husband, Vince, works in medicine with my dad, and their son, Theo, is only a couple of years older than me. The one thing they all have in common is that they believe they're better than

167

everyone else because they were born *with* money and didn't have to earn it, like my father—which is why they still treat him like an outsider, even though he's made a name for himself.

I never told my parents that I overheard that conversation. I'm sure my dad has lived through enough of my family slandering him. That could be why I resent my parents' money so much. Who needs therapy when self-reflection basically explains all my problems to me.

I ended up telling my dad that the team has an away game that I need to cover so I can't make the funeral. He wasn't pleased, but I overheard my mom telling him it was useless to try to convince me otherwise.

The team doesn't have an away game this weekend, just the one game on campus today that I'm currently filming. My parents have never paid attention to a single school email or asked me about anything photography related, so really, there's no way they would find out.

To add to my weird week, Jake has barely spoken to me since we got back last weekend.

Usually I see him before practice starts, we share a small conversation, he normally makes a joke and I pretend it's funny, and he even surprised me a once or twice with a hazelnut latte. This week he's barely muttered a hello.

I guess I could always do the adult thing and actually talk to him. I said hello to all the guys this morning when they walked into the arena, and Jake seemed to be in higher spirits than this entire week. Maybe that's a good omen for me to talk to him once the game is over.

The arena feels colder than it usually does in October.

Normally the stands have heaters, but they only turn them on in the colder months. Next time I'll plan better attire besides a long sleeve and jeans. I decided to wear the cardigan that Sydney got me for my birthday because normally it's cozy. But I've realized that being cozy in my home with the heat turned on is much different from the temperature in the arena. The small gaps in the woven material allow a chill to dance across my skin.

At least the game is almost done so I can go home and snuggle under some blankets for the rest of the night while I edit my footage from today and update the team's socials. I've restructured the layout of the team's website so it's more user friendly. Whoever was responsible for the maintenance of the website before clearly didn't know what the hell they were doing. There was no drop-down menu for people to navigate, and the link for the live streams was expired. It took me almost a week to get everything organized.

It's near the end of the third period and we're currently winning 3–1 against Northeastern University.

The opposing team is really good. I can tell by the way that they play that their captain is quick on his feet and can change a play within a second. If he notices Nate make a gesture or give Jake or Eli a look, he's already switching his own game plan. It's made for quite an enjoyable game and some great content.

Having a home game has its perks. Maddie and Sydney keep me company whenever the boys play on campus. They get to sit and relax, watching the game and sipping hot chocolate while I walk up and down the aisles, trying to get good shots of the team. My hot chocolate has probably turned to ice by now, which is why I normally opt for an iced drink when I come here.

I turn my attention to the scoreboard and watch the time tick down. There's only two minutes left, and Northeastern has the puck. Their left wing passes it to their center who is skating past the center line. I've seen the guys during practice skate so fast that if you blink, they're suddenly on the other side of the ice—but this guy, he makes them seem like snails. It's like there's a gust of wind pushing him toward our net. He swipes by Eli, shifting his weight onto one skate. Jake skates fast, desperately trying to get to him before he can shoot.

At the same moment Northeastern's player sends the puck flying at the net, their right wing slams into Jake, knocking him into the boards. *Hard.*

Kieran's attention is so focused on his best friend that he misses the puck that flies right past his head. I turn back to where Jake lies crumpled on the ice, gripping his left shoulder.

Crap, he's not getting up—which means the hit was worse than I thought.

My heart beats erratically. I always knew sports could be dangerous—hockey being one of the worst. The number of times I've watched fights break out or someone accidentally getting checked too hard into the boards makes a shiver run down my spine.

Please let him be okay.

Everyone in the stands gets up to see the commotion. The ref waves his arm in the air as he blows his whistle and skates over to Jake, waving over Coach Wilson. Silence falls on the crowd as Coach makes his way over to Jake, and the rest of his teammates, who are surrounding him on the ice, blocking the audience's view. After a few moments, Nate and Eli help Jake stand up and gain his footing back. He's still gripping his shoulder as Coach guides him back to the bench. Jake disappears into the locker rooms, most likely going to see the team doctor. Coach puts in Dawson McNeil, the second-string defenseman, to finish the remainder of the game.

I shove my camera back into my tote bag and rush through the crowd. Hopefully I can get into the locker room.

The lobby is almost empty, everyone still in their seats as the game dwindles down. I make my way through the double doors that lead to the locker rooms. As I'm about to enter, the buzzer goes off, indicating the end of the game. The doors at the end of the hallway swing open and Coach Wilson walks quickly, headed straight toward me.

I stop in my tracks, taking my hand off the door and slowly backing away toward the exit doors. Behind Coach, like a row of ducks, the team follows him into the locker room.

It's probably best to wait in the lobby with everyone else until Jake comes out. What was I going to do anyway? I'm not a doctor. I wouldn't know the first thing about sports injuries.

Maddie and Sydney are patiently waiting for me in the lobby, near the concession stand.

Maddie is the first to see me. "Is Jake okay?"

"I don't know, I was going to check on him, but the whole team just showed up."

Sydney touches my arm, sensing my unease. "Their team doctor is great. Last season Nate twisted his ankle and was out for a few games, but they have a great physiotherapist on campus. I'm sure he'll be fine."

Sydney tries to relieve my anxiety, but I can't help but be concerned. Even though we've barely spoken this week, that doesn't mean I'm not going to worry about him when he gets hurt. Jake is still my friend, even if we're not speaking.

It also doesn't help that I haven't been able to get him off my mind since Vermont.

I take my camera out and scroll through the footage from the game, desperately trying to occupy my mind until we get an update or the boys come out, whichever happens first.

It feels like forever, but finally the players start filing out, one by one.

Kieran pushes the door open with a powerful force, smacking it off the empty wall behind it. *He looks pissed.* His nostrils are flared, and he has his headphones jammed in his ears. His posture gives it all away, he's mad because he let that last shot in. I'm sure Coach Wilson gave him an earful after the game.

Maddie grabs my arm, pulling my attention away from the double doors. "I'm gonna head out, I have a paper for biology due on Monday. Let me know how Jake is. I'll see you guys at home."

Maddie gives me a hug before taking off. I turn my focus back to the doors that lead to the locker room. Jake is one of the last guys out, followed by Nate and Eli.

Nate spots us immediately, directing the other two to follow him.

"Well boys, that was an entertaining game." Sydney laughs, trying to break the awkward silence that immediately falls upon the group. "Jake, you should really *check* Vanessa's footage after."

Nate drags his hand down his face and sighs in response to his sister, not admiring her puns.

Jake laughs, though. He runs his free hand through his hair, which is still wet from his post-game shower. "I think I might pass on that one, Syd. Don't feel like watching myself get plowed into the boards."

My eyes trail across his body, scanning for any visible injuries. *None.*

He doesn't seem to be in any discomfort. But he's also wearing an all-black suit that constricts most of his movement. He has his hockey bag slung over his right shoulder, keeping any weight off his left side.

I try to push the concern out of my mind. I need to talk to him. It's been over a week and I want to know why he's ignoring me.

"Jake, can we talk for a sec?" Without thinking, I take hold of his arm. I don't grab it too tight, remembering that he was just hurled into the boards less than twenty minutes ago. He winces at my touch, so I pull my hand away, not wanting to injure him any further.

I head toward the front of the lobby and Jake follows my lead away from our friends for some privacy.

Our friends?

It feels weird for me to call Nate and Eli my friends, but I mean, technically we *are* friends. They threw me a damn surprise party, so if that's not what friends do, then teammates sure are generous. I've also known Nate basically as long as I've known Sydney, so that makes us friends by proxy.

We stop next to the entrance doors of the arena. Almost everyone has left by now, just a few friends and family straggling behind.

"That was a hard hit, are you okay?"

"I'm fine." His voice is sharp as he plops his equipment bag onto the ground next to us, encasing us into the corner near the front doors. "What's up?"

This feels like déj*à* vu.

"Is everything okay? Like between me and you?"

His eyes widen in shock at my words, as if I just asked a dumb rhetorical question. "Of course it is, Ness. What makes you think we aren't?"

I don't know, maybe the lack of conversation between us this week or responding to my texts with one word.

"I feel like things have gotten awkward between us, and I wanted to double-check that we're good."

The side of his mouth lifts into a half smile. "Don't worry, angel girl, we're good. You asked me to not bring it up again, so I haven't. I've kept it up here with all my other secret hookups." He points his finger to his head. "I've just had a lot going on this week."

"A lot, meaning?"

Call me nosey, I just want to know where the disconnect was between us.

"I had a few assignments due this week and I had to get an extension on my environmental ethics paper, my mind was a little preoccupied." He tightens his jaw. "Don't worry, Nichols, we're good."

I guess I'm going to have to take his word on this one, even though my gut is screaming at me that there's something I'm missing.

Jake lifts his bag off the floor and pulls the strap over his shoulder. The bag has to weigh easily fifty pounds with all of his gear. I think if I tried to lift it, I'd fall over and probably get crushed by it.

"I have to watch *Good Will Hunting* for my film class if you want to come by and watch it later? I'll make sure to get good snacks, even though I still firmly believe salt and vinegar chips are superior."

Jake fiddles with the strap on his shoulder. "I'm hanging with some of the guys on the football team. They're having a party after their game tonight."

He rotates his left shoulder in small, strained circles, like he's trying to gauge how much movement he has. That last hit of the game definitely did some damage and I feel like Jake is the type of person who will just ignore it until it becomes a bigger problem.

"Do you think it's smart to go out and party when you're clearly hurt?"

My question makes him stop his movements, and his eyes flash to mine, full of angst.

"Like I said earlier, I'm fine. And I already told Kieran that I would go with him to the party tonight, he set up a double date."

Right. I almost forgot for two seconds who I was talking to.

I can feel my eyes widen at his words. "Okay. Well, remember, no glove, no love."

What the hell did I just say? There is something seriously wrong with me.

"You are so weird, Ness." Jake laughs and wraps his *somewhat* injured arm around my shoulder as we make our way back to our group of friends, everything feeling like it's somewhat back to normal.

I thought that after the game I would spend the rest of my Friday night in bed watching *Good Will Hunting*, cozying up in my pajamas and a pint of ice cream, but my plans never seem to go the way I originally planned them to.

Maddie's been working on an assignment since the end of the game and Sydney went out for dinner with her brother and her parents, who decided to visit this weekend. But somehow instead of being with my own company, my night ended up with Levi sitting on my couch, watching the movie with me.

I was fully prepared to have an evening all to myself, until I got a text from Levi asking if I wanted to hang out. His text caught me off guard, mainly because I'm not used to being friends with so many people. My list of friends used to consist of two people: Sydney and Maddie. But now it seems that I've added a few more names to that list.

Levi told me that most of the guys were going to a frat party and he didn't feel like drinking, since they have another game tomorrow afternoon. I don't blame him. Playing hockey with a hangover is probably the worst thing you could do. That, or listening to Coach Wilson's whistle. Hearing that high-pitched noise after you've spent a night drinking is like hearing nails scraping a chalkboard. A shiver runs down my spine just thinking of it.

Since I've started working with the team, I've gotten to know a few of the players on a more personal level—Levi being one of them. I think we can get along so easily because we have a lot in common. Both of us were isolated from our families at one point in our lives, we're both only children, we both love photography, and we also share the same love of salt and vinegar chips.

So take that, Jake! Someone else is just as weird as me.

For our movie night, I grabbed a few blankets and threw them onto the sectional in the living room. Levi was nice enough to bring snacks with him. I may have requested the chocolate fudge brownie ice cream, but he also showed up with a handful of other treats, including pretzels, sour peaches, and salt and vinegar chips. The perfect combo for a movie night.

"I'm gonna grab a Diet Coke from the fridge, do you want something to drink?" I ask as Levi gets the movie queued up on the TV.

"Just water, thanks."

I walk into the kitchen and grab our drinks and two spoons before I settle back onto the couch. I grab a blanket and offer one to Levi, who politely takes it from me.

"Hey, I forgot to thank you for helping me with the portrait assignment this week. I was nervous our prof wouldn't deem the shots as portraits, but he loved them."

He smiles sweetly at me. "No problem, it's nice to have someone I can talk to about photography. Sometimes Kieran will talk to me about it, since he likes to draw and stuff, but they don't understand all the technical terms."

I understand that all too well. Anytime I try to explain anything about photography to Sydney or Maddie they just smile and nod. They're my friends and they are more supportive than anyone in my family about my passion, but I don't always want to bore them talking about different lenses or editing software.

I grab the remote off the couch and start the movie. Levi grabs his bag full of snacks and empties the contents in front of us. He readjusts himself so he's sitting in the corner of the couch with the fuzzy pink blanket laid across his lap.

This is hilarious to me because Levi is the type of guy who wears khaki slacks and cream sweaters, but today he's sporting black sweatpants and his BCU hoodie. Seeing him like this is so out of character, but it's also adorable.

I lean forward and grab the package of sour peaches and snuggle back into the couch, resting my legs on the cream-colored ottoman. We sit and watch the movie, mainly in silence—but it's comfortable.

Robin Williams's character gets introduced to Matt Damon, and their first interaction has me reeling. I think if someone ever talked to me the way Matt Damon's character does, I would slap them. That's why I could never be a therapist.

The movie is cut off by three loud knocks at my front door.

Levi grabs the remote to pause the movie, and gives me a look that asks *Are you expecting someone?*

I swing my legs off the couch and walk over to the front door. Through the small peephole, I see Jake standing on the other side, clad in light jeans and a plaid shirt that's unbuttoned showing a white tee underneath.

"How did you get up here?" I swing open the door but keep it half closed, unsure why Jake suddenly showed up here.

"Your security guy loves me." He peers into the living room, his eyes stopping when he sees Levi. "What's Brody doing here?" Jake's jaw flexes as he keeps his stare locked over my shoulder, eyeing Levi, who's currently lounging on the couch in the mess of blankets I left.

"Who, Levi?" I point behind me, where the man in question is aimlessly scrolling on his phone. "He asked if I was free tonight, so I invited him over to watch a movie. I thought you were going to a party."

Jake takes a step into the foyer, his tall frame makes the hallway feel so small.

"I was." He narrows his eyes on Levi before turning his attention back to me. "I mean, I still am. I was going to see if you wanted to come."

His eyes linger on me, swallowing me in his gaze. I really wish I wasn't in sweatpants right about now. Why wouldn't he have asked me earlier when we were literally talking about our plans? That makes no sense.

"I thought you were going on a double date."

"Kieran canceled our plans."

"And you decided to just show up at my house rather than text or call me?"

He's quick and sharp with his response. "I was on my way to the party and was passing by your building."

An awkward silence falls upon us. I hear Levi hit Play on the movie. Most likely so he can pretend he's not eavesdropping on our conversation. But he definitely is.

"So, do you want to come?"

"And what, ditch Levi?"

Jake shrugs. "He wouldn't even care, he would probably come with us anyway."

"No." I need to watch this movie and write my reflection paper before tomorrow's game so I can submit it before our next class. If I wanted to go out, I would've. "I'm in the middle of something. If you wanted to hang out, you could've said yes when I asked you earlier. I'm not going to cancel my plans just because you changed *your* mind."

Jake rolls his eyes. I think that's the first time he's ever rolled them at me. Normally it's me who gives him the sassy attitude.

"I'll see you tomorrow. Have fun on your date."

Before I can respond, he turns around and heads out the door, shutting it behind him.

What the hell?

I want to run down the hall and yell at him for assuming that just because I'm hanging out with a guy, it means it's romantic. Why does it even matter? He was about to go on a double date tonight, it's not my fault his plans fell through.

Levi turns the volume down on the movie as I join him on the couch.

"Well that was a little awkward." He breaks the silence.

I raise an eyebrow at him. "What was?"

"That whole interaction. Jake's face was as red as your fire extinguisher."

"He's just annoyed that I wouldn't ditch you to go to a party with him."

"No, I think he was mad jealous, Nichols. You should've seen the look he gave me when he walked in here. I think he might kill me tomorrow before our game."

Levi's being dramatic. Jake wasn't jealous, he's just used to getting what he wants.

"He's definitely not jealous. He's mad that things aren't going his way." I wave off Levi's comment. "Anyway, I'm sure he'll find a girl at the party who will take his mind off me rejecting his offer."

I snuggle back into the couch, suffocating myself with blankets. Thinking about Jake at that party tonight, flirting and talking to another girl, it makes that little green monster come out. I wish Jake would've accepted my invite earlier, but I'm a fool to think that he would choose me over some party.

I'm sure he values our friendship, but sometimes it stings, always being peoples second choice.

CHAPTER SEVENTEEN

Welcome to my funeral

JAKE

Tonight, we lost our first game of the season.

I don't know what was going on today, but we were fucking horrible.

Nate carried the team, as always, but it wasn't enough to get us out of the hole that Kieran and I dug us into. I just know that once we get out of the showers, Coach will be waiting for us, ready with a lecture and a good scolding.

I don't normally brag about how good of a player I am—okay, I *try* not to brag all the time—but I'm a fucking good defenseman, but today, I shit the bed. I skated slower than usual, allowed multiple guys to slip past me, and overall played like shit. My shoulder was bothering the hell out of me, an indicator that I should've stayed home last night and iced it instead of going out.

My head wasn't in the game. It felt like I had a lingering brain fog from last night.

Kieran seemed to be in the same boat as me, which really did us in. He let in three goals before the third period, so Coach pulled him and had our second-string goalie play the remainder of the game. I don't think I've seen Wilson's face so red during a game since last year's championship.

The culprit: alcohol.

Last night, Kieran and I may have overindulged at the frat party. I showed up solo, but an hour into the night, Kieran showed up moody as hell.

Was I upset that Vanessa chose to hang out with Levi over me? Yes. I just don't understand her. One minute she's moaning my name and tugging my hair, and the next she wants to *just be friends.*

I don't even want any sort of commitment, but the fact that she can so easily toss me aside hurts more than it should. I'm not the kind of guy who gets jealous over a girl because normally there's no competition. But here I am, whining like a baby because, for once, I didn't get the girl.

Geez, I need Kieran to punch me in the face.

Speaking of Kieran—I don't know what got into him last night, but I don't think I ever saw him without a drink in his hand. I know if Coach gets a whiff of this, we might get benched for the next game. He's not a huge fan of us partying during the season, but he especially hates it when we come in hungover and it affects our game.

To be honest, we were both in shit moods and drowned it in bottles of liquor and girls.

Was it the best distraction? No, but it worked.

I drank until I stopped picturing Vanessa with Levi. They could've been hanging out like friends, but the ruffled blankets on the couch had me thinking otherwise. Levi plays the long game. I've seen it firsthand. He becomes their friend first and then swoops in like Prince Charming. I wouldn't be surprised if he was doing that with Vanessa right now.

I don't understand what she sees in Levi. I get that they have *some* things in common— they have the same major, they both like photography, and they both *love* to annoy the shit out of me. Maybe that does intimidate me a little. There's something about Vanessa that throws me off my game. It's like she's the outlier in a code and I have no clue how to fix it.

After that night in Vermont, things have felt tense between us. I don't know how to deal with a situation like this. One moment she was begging for more, and the next she was asking me to never speak of it again, as if her taste wasn't still lingering on my lips.

I may have been avoiding her at practices this week, but I feel like she felt ashamed after we hooked up, and that's not something a guy wants to think about. I'm hoping she doesn't regret it, but she's so goddamn confusing. How can she go from having me between her legs to hanging out with fucking Brody?

I'm calling bullshit.

I don't think she'll be able to resist me if she gives me the chance. I'm told I have quite the charm, and I already know what pleases her. I'll be her friend. But the second she asks for more, I'll cave.

"Shepherd. Danford. My office, now!" Coach's voice booms through the locker room.

Fuck. I knew he was going to say something.

My hair is still wet as I towel the rest of myself off and head to my locker to grab my clothes. Putting on a suit after a shower always makes me feel like I'm some top shit professional, but right now I feel like I'm about to walk into my funeral. Coach is going to eat me and Kieran alive.

Kieran eyes me from the corner, making a face that screams *We're in deep shit.* I nod at him, silently agreeing that we're definitely fucked.

We make our way over to the office that's adjacent to the locker room. Coach only really uses this office before or after a game, other than that, I think he enjoys his new and clean office in the athletic building. The downside to this office is that it's right next to the locker room and has wall-to-ceiling windows, so all the guys are going to witness the scolding we're about to receive on their way out of the arena. Nate and Eli are already leaning against the wall, shaking their heads as we approach the office door, waiting for the show to start.

Assholes.

Coach Wilson's face is beat red, and he rubs his fingers across his chin. This is not going to end well.

He looks up and sees us standing outside the office like we're waiting for an invitation to go inside. "Get your asses in here."

Welcome to my funeral.

Kieran leads the way, and I follow him through the door frame, shutting the door behind me in hopes of drowning out the incoming screaming.

"Sit down." Like robots, we follow Coach's instructions and sit in the worn-down office chairs. "What the hell happened out there today?"

He stands from his desk so he can look down onto us—making us feel small. Even if Kieran and I were to stand, Coach still towers over us. He's like a goddamn skyscraper. I always wondered why he never played basketball when he was younger. I feel like that would've suited him so much better than hockey.

"So are either of you going to start talking or are you just going to sit there with your hands in your pockets?" His eyes scan between the two of us as we sit here silently, shitting our pants.

I pipe up first. "Sorry, Coach, I was having a bad game an—"

"A bad game!? Your defense was *shit* today, Shepherd. You looked like a ballerina with the amount of times you spun around. You couldn't keep up with a single player and normally *you* are one of the fastest on the team. You let us down today."

Fuck, I hate it when he takes the disappointed route.

"And *you*." His eyes dart in Kieran's direction. "Sure, Jake let the puck get past him, but *you* are supposed to be our best. For fuck's sake, you're our star goalie, Danford. You let in three shots before the end of the second period. I expected more from you, what the hell is going on?"

Kieran's face is stone cold, no expression or thought visible on his face. He's a very closed-off guy; someone who rarely shows emotion unless it's around his friends, but he's always honest with Coach Wilson. Seeing him act this way makes me wonder if there's something else going on in his life that he's not telling me or any of the guys.

Kieran grips the armrest of the chair and lets out a sigh, still not looking Coach in the eye. "Nothing, Coach, it won't happen again."

Coach Wilson sighs and slumps back into his chair. "Look, you two are both very talented players. I'm only getting on you because we have scouts coming next weekend and I want the two of you, especially you"—he points at Kieran—"to be on your A game. Some of the guys on the team didn't get drafted, so this will be a great opportunity for all of you. Whatever made you two play like shit today, figure it out before next weekend or we will be having an entirely different conversation."

Shit. I know I already have a contract, but it still lights a fire under my ass. Kieran hasn't been signed to a team, but he doesn't even know if he wants to go professional. This has been my dream since I held a stick for the first time. I always knew that I wanted to play for the

NHL and become a hockey legend, but that won't be attainable if I continue to play like an idiot.

If New Jersey sees that I'm playing like shit, they could choose to not sign me once I'm done college. I need to make sure that I'm playing my best in case they *do* decide that and I'm left without a contract. I need to stand out to scouts so if I become a free agent, someone will hopefully pick me up.

I look over to Kieran, his face still blank, like Coach's words had no effect on him. We haven't talked much about Kieran's plans after school. Anytime one of the guys brings up where we want to play, he just brushes it off. It's almost as if he still doesn't have a clue about what he wants out of life. But hey, who says you need to have your life figured out at twenty-one?

"Get out. Go home. I'll see the two of you at practice on Tuesday." He waves us off with his hand, I stand up and grab Kieran by the collar of his shirt, and we both move our asses, shuffling out the door.

I can't say that I'm not a little relieved Coach didn't reem us in too hard. I thought he would rip into us a little harder, but I won't complain that we got off easy. I kind of want to know what made Kieran so spaced out today. I've seen this guy play hungover multiple times, but there was something off about him.

Eli clasps his hands on mine and Kieran's shoulders. "You guys are lucky, I thought Coach was going to eat you two alive."

"I was betting that he would throw his clipboard, so now I owe Eli five bucks." Nate pulls his wallet out of his back pocket and slides the bill into Eli's hand.

I drag my hand down my face, taking a minute to process. "No, he decided to use the disappointment card on us today." I grab my bag from the hallway and lead the way out of the arena. "C'mon, let's go get food. I'm starving."

The parking lot is mostly empty, only a few cars littering the pavement. Kieran unlocks his truck and I toss both of our bags into the trunk as Eli and Nate pile theirs into Nate's SUV.

I'm glad Kieran normally offers to drive us to games and practices because I can barely fit in my Jeep with just my bag. Imagining the two of us with all of our gear in my 2006 Jeep Wrangler…yeah, it just wouldn't work. Our bags would have to be strapped to the roof.

"So where should we go?" I lean against the passenger door, waiting for someone to suggest somewhere to go.

Eli chimes in first. "We could go to the diner or to Outlaw Roadhouse."

Nate shakes his head. "No, I went there the other day with a few of the guys and my stomach is still recovering." He holds his stomach as if he can still feel the pain.

The four of us bicker back and forth, suggesting restaurants only to be turned down by each other. It feels like I'm trying to convince my sister to go out. Anytime my family wanted to go out for dinner, Autumn would always be the most indecisive.

I should give her a call soon and check in on everyone.

Finally, Nate takes control of the conversation. "If we can all agree to go to Wing Shack, I'll pay for everyone just so you all shut up." There's a reason we call him *Daddy Nate*.

We all respond at the same time. "Deal."

Kieran and I follow Nate and Eli the whole way to the restaurant, and I shoot my parents a text letting them know how the game went. Per usual, Mom tells me not to dwell on the negative and Dad offers words of encouragement.

I wish they could come to more of my games, but they're always tied up at home— whether my sister has a dance recital or they're both stuck at work.

My mom is *always* at her flower shop, putting together these intrinsic bouquets that people come from all over to buy. She has one of the most successful shops in Cape Cod. Dad has his own construction company that he built from the ground up, so he's normally dealing with a million and one things. He used to always say that his business feels like a third child, and sometimes it feels like he puts a lot of attention on it. I can't complain because he gave our family everything we've ever asked for.

We pull into the restaurant faster than expected. We may have casually raced down the road, seeing who could get there first. Somehow Nate always wins. Even though Kieran's truck can pick up speed like it's a feather, Nate is quick and smooth with his driving.

The restaurant isn't super packed for a Saturday, which is refreshing. Our waitress brings over our drinks while we wait for our food. There's something about having a big dinner after a game. I could easily eat five pounds of wings after working out.

I take a sip of my Coke, the sweet taste bringing me back to summers in Cape Cod. My mom would always stock the fridge full of pop but then refuse us from having any until at night. I guess I'm a little thankful for that because now I don't find myself addicted to drinking carbonated drinks all day.

Kieran is sitting in the corner of the booth, paying no attention to Nate, who's been lecturing us for the past five minutes on our game play. It never feels good to have your captain rip into you for playing badly, but we played *really* fucking badly today. So if Nate needs to release all of his pent-up stress by talking to us, you bet your ass I'm going to let him.

"I just don't get it, Kieran. What's with you, man? You were perfectly fine this summer during camp, but since the actual season started, you've been off your game." Nate takes on multiple roles with our team. Captain. Dad. *Therapist*. We should probably pay him for everything he does for us.

Kieran finally peels his eyes off the table to take a sip of his beer and shrugs. "I've been dealing with family stuff, so my head has been a little cloudy. Sorry if my family issues cost us the game." His tone is laced with sarcasm, as if he doesn't care that we just had our first loss of the season.

If there's some family drama going on in his life, that's never good. After his parents died, his uncle became legally responsible for him. I know he doesn't like to visit his uncle often, since he and his dad are twins. *Were twins*. It's hard for him to see his dad's face, even if it really isn't *his* dad.

Nate's face immediately softens. "Do you want to talk about it?"

185

Kieran fixes his posture, now sitting up straighter. "No. It's honestly nothing, I just let it get to me today." He stares at Nate before averting his eyes back to the table. "I'm sorry we lost, I promise I'm fine."

Nate's jaw is as solid as stone as he gives Kieran the biggest stare down I've seen. He knows that Kieran is purposefully keeping information from him. But Kieran isn't one to share his feelings with us. It's very rare that he even lets *me* into his life, but to bring Nate, Eli, and the rest of the guys into his life—he's just too secretive for that.

Nate deems his response good enough and nods at Eli to take over the conversation so the awkward tension can die down. It's a tactic they've always done. He starts the conversation, gets you talking even when it's uncomfortable, and then he lets Eli swoop in and change the mood so you don't feel like a complete bag of shit after dumping all your emotional trauma onto him. It's almost like a weird version of good cop, bad cop.

"So, Jake, are we ever going to talk about what happened last weekend or are we just going to ignore the elephant in the room?" And sometimes Eli likes to pry too.

"Yeah, my sister mentioned something *may* have happened between you and a little brunette who just so happens to work with our team." Nate raises an eyebrow at me.

Fuck.

"Oh look, our food." Our waitress saves my ass as she walks up to the table carrying a tray full of chicken wings.

I'm silently grateful for her presence. She takes a moment to put down the mass amount of food we ordered: four orders of wings, three orders of fries, and an order of jalapeno poppers.

I plop one of the small fried sticks in my mouth as Nate asks, "So back to the conversation, are you going to tell us what happened or leave us to our own imaginations?"

"And you know how dirty *my* imagination is. Is that really what you want? You want me to picture Vanessa all naked an—"

I don't let Eli finish his sentence before I have his shirt fisted in my hands. "First off, it's none of your *fucking* business, and secondly, keep Vanessa out of your perverted thoughts Murphy...or you won't like what happens."

Eli plucks my hands off his shirt and pretends to dust himself off. "Mm-hm, they're definitely screwin' around."

The boys chuckle at my quick defense, easily showing them my cards.

"Anyway, it doesn't matter." I force myself to take a bite of a wing, now feeling like I lost my appetite thinking of that whole situation.

As if they can't tell already by my facial expressions, Nate continues to pick at me. "Do you like her or something? Is the notorious slut, Jacob Shepherd, finally smitten by someone?"

"Smitten? What are you, eighty?" Eli smacks his arm.

I rest my head in my hands; this is *not* a conversation I want to be having. Mainly because I've been wracking my brain trying to figure out what they hell is going on between us. I feel like a broken record going over it again and again.

Do I have feelings for Vanessa? *Maybe.* But she doesn't seem to have much interest in me other than being my friend, so I won't take it any further. If she wants something more, the ball is in her court.

Or the puck is in her stick.

Okay, no, that just sounds wrong. Dad joke gone bad.

All I know is that seeing her the other night all cozy with Levi has a knot in my gut.

"No, I'm not *smitten,* Grandpa. I'm still the same old Jake that you all know and love." That's a lie, but I don't want the guys to think that I'm obsessing over someone. Especially someone who's turned me down more than once.

"Prove it then. Because I haven't seen slutty Jake since that night at Shakers with Caroline." Nate *knows* exactly how I feel—it's like a damn superpower—and he knows that I won't turn down a dare. "Go over to that girl sitting at the bar and get her number. If you get it, then we know that you're still the same old Jake."

Okay, this is easy—I can get a girl's number in my sleep.

"Fine." I pry the remainder of meat off my chicken bone and wipe my hands on my napkin before getting up.

The guys all have their attention fixed on me as I saunter over to the bar. The girl in question has honey-blonde hair down to her waist, and the tiniest pair of denim shorts I've ever seen someone wear in public.

Isn't October too cold for shorts?

"Hey, how's it going?" She looks at me, unamused, with her big lips tight in a straight line.

Okay, not a strong start, but I can fix this. "Do you go to BCU?"

"Yeah." She pauses, looking me over once more before her eyes get big as if she's recognized me. "Do you play on the hockey team?"

"Yeah, Jake Shepherd. Nice to meet you, are you a hockey fan?" I extend my hand and shake hers. It's a move I pull on girls that seems to work every time. For some reason, they never expect a guy to shake their hand—it throws them off guard every time, and then I swoop in with my undeniably good charm.

"Didn't you guys lose your game tonight?"

Ouch.

"Uh—yeah."

"Damn, that sucks."

God, I do *not* want to be having this conversation right now. I'm not even slightly interested in this girl, and I'm just wasting both of our time.

"Anyway, my friend over there"—I point at Eli, who's too focused on his chicken wing to notice—"he wanted me to ask you for your number."

Eli told me that I had to get her number. He never said that it had to be for *me.*

"Really?" She looks over my shoulder and eyes Eli. "Oh, he's cute. Yeah, you can give him my number." She grabs my phone out of my hand, immediately adding her number into my contacts. Hannah, with a purple heart.

Yeah, she seems like the type to give herself an emoji next to her name.

"Great, thanks. He'll be stoked."

I turn back around and head back to the booth. The guys focus their attention back on me as I slide back into my spot, my phone unlocked in my hand with the screen on her contact info.

"See. I'm still the same old Shep. Nothing has changed."

As soon as the words leave my mouth, the blonde from the bar appears at our table.

Oh fuck me.

"I'll be waiting for your call." She winks at Eli, who looks dumbfounded for a second. He finally acknowledges the girl, giving her a nod.

As soon as she gets out of earshot, the boys stop stifling their laughter.

Eli immediately starts laughing. "I can't...believe." His laughter takes over again. "You have *no* game, brother."

"Nothing has changed, my ass. Something is definitely going on with you." Nate shakes his head then takes a sip of his drink as Kieran and Eli continue to howl in hysterics.

"Fuck you guys," I mumble before downing the rest of my Coke.

CHAPTER EIGHTEEN

Are you becoming a puck bunny?

JAKE

Studying the stars is one way I like to keep my mind occupied from all the other shit going on in my life. After the relentless teasing from the guys yesterday, I decided to spend my Sunday in the library catching up on notes and assignments.

Unlike the typical college athlete stereotype, I don't like to fall behind in class, and I find I can study better at the library. The atmosphere here is different—everyone is focusing on their own work whether they're studying or working on a paper. It motivates me to concentrate.

Or maybe the environment just helps my ADHD brain focus.

I've let myself get a little behind in my astronomy class, but I didn't think that an intro level course would have so many articles to scour. I have a paper due on Tuesday that I haven't even started yet.

For the past hour I've been reading every article since the first day of classes and haven't found one that inspires me to write a whole four-page essay. There are countless topics to choose from, like black holes, the different types of light, discussing the development of telescopes and satellite imaging—and yet I'm still stuck.

A coffee break might just be the remedy I need to help me get into the groove of things. A little caffeine will give me the boost to trudge through the next couple of hours and write a B-worthy paper.

I shove my laptop in my bag and head down to the lobby to grab a coffee from the cafe. I spent a lot of time here in my freshman year. Kieran and I used to sit in the cafe pretending to be on a study break when we actually just came here to pick up girls. Some girls loved the smart athletic look, so Kieran and I ate it up. By the time winter semester came around, we had to change our game for something new.

I walk up to the counter, shaking off the nostalgia that it brings, and order a large black coffee. *I need this to last until my paper is done.*

"Shep." Levi's voice sounds from behind me, fist-bumping me as I turn to meet him. "Hey, man, how's it going?"

"Good, good. Just grabbing a coffee on my study break."

He leans against the display case that's full of baked goods. "How did the talk with Coach go? I probably would've shit my pants if I was in your position."

"Not bad actually. Kieran and I were lucky to leave the office intact. He didn't rip into us as hard as he could've." It isn't until now that I notice the small figure emerge from behind him.

Vanessa.

She looks up at me, holding tightly onto her laptop in her arms, and smiles at me through those huge glasses.

I fucking love those on her.

Today she has an oversized plaid shirt unbuttoned with a black tee underneath. Her leggings cling to her body, defining her calf muscles, and her platform Converse do nothing to increase her height next to me and Levi.

She brings an immediate smile to my lips. "Hey, Ness, what's up?"

"Hey." She adjusts the bag on her shoulder. "We just met up to work on some assignments."

I turn back to the cashier and grab my coffee from him, tossing the extra change into the tip jar.

"Oh man, I meant to ask, is there anything I need to bring to the party next Saturday?"

For the past three years, Nate and I have put on one of the best Halloween parties on campus. It's invite only, and it seems like every year it gets crazier and crazier.

"If you could scoop up some extra napkins and ice on your way over, I'm sure Nate would be happy. One less thing for him to obsess over."

Vanessa looks back and forth between me and Levi. "What party?"

"We're gonna have a Halloween party after the game if you wanna come."

I see the hesitation spread across her face for a moment.

"Sydney and Maddie are more than welcome to come too. But you guys *have* to dress up."

It's a rule we have. *No costume, no entry.* There's no point in hosting a party on Halloween if people aren't going to dress up. I feel like that goes against everything that the holiday was meant for. It's a day made for young kids to get free candy and for college students to get absolutely smashed while wearing the most random fucking outfits.

Her teeth graze her bottom lip as she decides. "All right, sounds like fun. We'll be there."

Levi looks down at his watch, cursing under his breath. "Oh shit, I'm late to meet Seb. I'll see you around later?" Levi gives Vanessa a hug before heading toward the front doors and shouting back, "See you at practice, Shep!"

I look down at Vanessa, whose cheeks have the smallest tinge of pink. *Is she into Levi?*

"So is this why you didn't want me to say anything about last weekend? Because you're into Levi?" I raise an eyebrow at her, teasing.

Her eyes automatically roll into the back of her head. "I don't think that's any of your business."

"I thought we were friends, Ness, you wound me." I bring my fist to my chest, acting as if she just stabbed me.

"You're so annoying."

She starts to walk toward the front doors that lead to the parking lot and I follow into step next to her.

I tickle her side. "Yeah, but you love when I annoy you."

The look she gives me makes me wonder what's going on in her head.

VANESSA

I hate to admit it, but I think I do love it when Jake annoys me.

He never fails to bring a smile to my face with his dumb jokes and goofy personality—but I will never tell him that because I truly believe he will never leave me alone until I die.

"So…" He stops on his heel, leaning his back against the floor-to-ceiling window with his arms crossed over his chest.

He looks so put together. His curly hair is tousled perfectly somehow. His jeans are worn in, the way your favorite pair fades over time, and his black long sleeve clings to his toned body. Whether he's wearing everyday clothes, a suit, or his hockey uniform—*he always looks perfect.*

Jake's so different from Levi. Levi is a sweetheart, and I absolutely cherish the friendship we've started to build, but where Levi is dark and gloomy, Jake is sunshine and smiles. Our friendships are so different, and I find myself craving Jake's presence more and more. Being around him brings more light into my life.

When I hang out with Levi, we normally talk about school or photography, with Jake, anything is on the table. It makes me look forward to seeing him because I never know what's going to come out of his mouth.

"You and Levi have been spending more time together, is it anything serious? Anything I should know about?"

Okay, I take back what I said about loving when he annoys me.

"Since when are you so curious about my life?"

"I'm always curious about you, Ness."

My heart skips a beat at how fast he responds. I swear, sometimes this boy just says things that make me feel like I'm being swept off my feet. Who even says things like that?

"Seriously, why are you so concerned about my friendship with Levi?" I press.

"I'm just watching out for my friend, that's all."

"You didn't seem to be watching out for him when you asked me to ditch him last weekend to go to a party with you."

His nostrils flare, as if I struck a nerve. He was like this the other day and I got the weirdest vibe from him. Levi accused him of being jealous. *As if.* I don't think that Jake could ever be jealous of anyone. He could get any girl he wanted with the snap of his fingers.

I squint my eyes and cross my arms, staring up at him. "Are you jealous of Levi?"

His back straightens, pulling him away from the wall and puffing out his chest. "*Me? Jealous?* Fuck no."

Just like I'd thought. Levi is definitely delusional thinking that Jake would be jealous over someone like me.

"Okay, well, Mr. Nosey, I have no intentions of dating Levi because *I. Don't. Date.*" I poke his chest with the last three words.

Jake studies me, watching my body language, as if he's trying to read my mind.

"So what, are you becoming a puck bunny or something?"

His question feels like a slap to my face. I don't have anything against girls who hook up with guys solely based on a sport they play, but I'm not one of them. And I know he didn't mean it as a compliment.

I take a step back from him, moving closer to the doors. "What the hell, Jake?"

"I mean, you get *randomly* assigned to work with the team. You become friends with me and we hook up, and then boom, you move down the roster onto Levi. Sounds like something a puck bunny would do."

As he speaks, his eyes never land on me. It's like he's looking right past me and doesn't care that his words are hurting my feelings. My cheeks immediately heat and I can practically see how red they're getting from his accusation. I don't know where the hell his attitude came from, but I'm not into it and I won't tolerate him degrading me—*especially* in public.

"Fuck you, Jake. I asked you to keep that between us."

I don't let him respond, I turn around and head out the front doors to the library, praying that Maddie is already waiting for me in her car.

The late October air carries a chill that causes goose bumps to litter my skin. I wish I had brought a jacket, but I wasn't planning on standing in the cold while waiting for my ride.

I feel his soft grip on my arm before I hear his words fall from his mouth. "*Shit.* Ness, wait, please."

I face him and feel like there's steam coming out of my ears. "You don't see me commenting on your sex life, so stay the hell out of mine."

I should pump the brakes on my words. But I can't. I've lost complete control of the car and I'm going full speed ahead.

"You've slept with half the girls on campus, Jake. How *dare* you accuse me of trying to sleep with the whole damn team. In case you didn't know, I can be friends with whomever I please, and that doesn't mean that I'm sleeping with them."

His face crumbles as I tear into him. Deep down, I know that he didn't say that to me because he actually believes I'm a puck bunny. But it still stung. Whatever his reasons are, I don't want to hear them. I couldn't care less about what he has to say right now.

"Ness, I'm sorry, I don't mean to be such a dick."

"Sorry if I bruised your ego, but that doesn't give you the right to tear me down!"

I'm tired of explaining myself. I shouldn't have to feed his ego and make him feel like he's the only guy I can be friends with. Levi is right, he does sound jealous, but I have no idea why he's acting this way.

My phone vibrates in my hands, signaling that Maddie pulled into the parking lot, and perfect timing too.

"My ride is here, I'll see you later."

I don't wait to hear his response. Instead, my feet fly down the stairs and pull me to the parking lot where Maddie patiently waits for me.

Should I have slut-shamed Jake after he accused me of sleeping around with the team? Probably not. But in the moment, it felt right. I just don't understand what's going on between us. Maybe it is sexual tension, but I feel like that only comes from one side—*me.*

In all honesty, after Jake and I hooked up, it's been so hard to forget him. Every time I try to get off, whether it's with Geralt or my small vibrator, it's always Jake's name that escapes my lips. I'm always picturing *him.*

I'm messed in the head.

I'm the one who told him to forget it ever happened, and yet I'm the one who can't seem to forget that night.

Maddie immediately notices my mood the second I sink into her passenger seat, tossing my laptop onto her backseat. Her pants are covered in paint from work, and I'm a little glad I quit working at the paint store after only a couple of months.

"Why do you look like someone just punched you in your tit?"

I sigh, immediately venting to her. "Jake called me a puck bunny because I hooked up with him and now I'm hanging out with Levi. Even though Levi and I are just friends, he's acting as if I want to suck each player's dick."

"What the fuck? Who does he think he is?" She scoffs as she pulls out of the parking lot. "Do you want me to go kick him in the dick or something? Because I'll do it."

I cherish my friendship with Maddie. She's the type of friend that you could call at any time of the day and she would answer. I'm sure she would even help me hide a body if I asked, and knowing her knowledge with forensic science, she would also make sure we would never get caught. Having her and Sydney both in my life seems too good to be true sometimes. I wouldn't trade them for all the money in the world.

"No, it's fine." I bite at the inside of my cheeks, something I do when I'm anxious. "I mean, it's not fine, but everything feels so messy."

"Girl, I need you to elaborate. What the hell has been going on with you recently?"

What has been going on with me?

I don't feel like myself. I feel like I'm misguided and confused. Mainly with all of my emotions. My relationship with my parents is rockier than ever, and that's definitely taken a toll on me. Other than that, the only other thing in my life that has been on my mind is Jake. And I hate that he's constantly on my mind.

Sydney once told me that Jake and I were perfect for each other. We both hate commitment, we love the environment, and both of us are nerdy as hell—even if Jake doesn't show it all the time.

I never believed her until the night in Vermont.

Since then, he's spun my world around. I can no longer go a day without thinking of him and it's been driving me crazy. I've been going crazy wondering if he's been with anyone since me, if he's seeing other girls, if he hooked up with me just because I was there. These thoughts are constantly going through my head and sometimes it becomes too overwhelming.

"Oh, also, we're going to a Halloween party on Saturday at Nate's place."

A wicked grin grows on Maddie's face. "I have the *perfect* idea for your costume."

She spills her idea to me, and I absolutely love it.

CHAPTER NINETEEN

Fine, let's make a bet

JAKE

There's a fire lit under my ass.

After Coach's talk with us last week, I made it a point to prove to him just how determined I am. I've put so much sweat and blood into this sport to be the player that I am today. I felt the need to prove that last week was just a fluke and that my shitty performance won't become a regular thing.

We had back-to-back games with UConn this weekend. Before the first game, Coach told us that there were going to be scouts this weekend. He knows that if he gives us the heads-up it will make everyone focus and play their hardest. Definitely a smart strategy.

Last night, I brought my A game and we won 4–0. My defense was impenetrable, the players could barely get past me without me tearing into them and stealing possession of the puck. My agent even sent me a message this morning that he got from the Demon's GM, raving about how well I played.

Today, I played like a fucking god. UConn desperately tried to avenge their loss from last night, but they found themselves in the same spot as the night prior. I played hard as fuck and I think I can thank my overthinking jealous self for that.

I've been mentally beating myself up all week for the way I spoke to Vanessa at the library. I fucked up calling her a puck bunny the other day. I don't know why I said that.

Okay, that's a lie, I do know why. It's because I'm maybe a *little* bit insecure about her relationship with Levi. Her "friendship," as she calls it. I should know better. I've come to know Vanessa's character and she doesn't seem like the type to make friends and then drop them the second she meets someone new, but it doesn't change the fact that I feel like our friendship has been affected.

I royally fucked myself in that situation though, and I have no idea if she's actually going to show up tonight. She's been ignoring me, and rightfully so. At practice, on campus—anywhere she sees me, she acts as if I'm a ghost, pretending I don't exist. Yesterday she didn't say a word to me at the game. She didn't come into the locker room before the game. She spent the whole game in the stands taking her photos and videos, and after the game, she was nowhere to be seen.

Today, she barely looked at me when she came into the locker room to talk with the guys pregame. I even tried to make a joke to lighten the mood between us and all I got in response was one of her famous eye rolls before putting all of her attention and focus on the other guys.

I guess I'll take the silent eye roll over her not acknowledging me.

It stung a little, having her eyes pinned to everyone but me. I want all of her focus on me, all the time. Just like how I can't seem to take my eyes off her when she's in the room.

I sound like a mopey fucking idiot.

"Just so we're clear, if anyone even thinks about going into my room tonight, I'll bring you to my family's ranch and let the pigs eat you." Eli's voice calls out from the showers.

Nate ruffles his towel through his hair. "Eli, no one wants to go into your room."

"That's not what your mom said last night."

Nate whips his towel across the room, smacking Eli directly in the face as he walks into the room. Nate's a little protective of his family. But that's also why we love him so much. Daddy Archer, always there to save us when we need him.

"Do you guys have your costumes? Booze? Food? Did we forget anything?" Nate goes over the list on his phone. I swear this guy makes a note in his phone for everything.

"Yes, Dad, everything is taken care of."

"Just making sure. Sometimes it's hard to trust you idiots with parties."

Kieran chimes in on the conversation. "Nate, it was *one* time, you've got to let it go. I didn't know that the goat would freak out like that."

Last year, Eli, Kieran, and I took it upon ourselves to plan Nate's birthday party.

Personally, I thought I did a good job, because normally I knock it out of the park. Nate loves animals, so Kieran thought it would be a great idea to have a petting zoo in the backyard. Eli's family has a friend in the area that has a small farm and offered to let us borrow a few small farm animals for the afternoon.

I got everything set up, even had a pen with hay in the backyard. It all was going so smoothly until someone took a photo of a goat with the flash on and it started running rampant through the yard, causing all the other animals to go crazy. Tables were knocked over, glasses and food were tossed around. It was quite the show.

It took us two full days to clean the mess, and Nate never really trusted us again with planning.

"Did you invite your sister to the party tonight?" I ask Nate, fishing to see if Vanessa will be tagging along with her friend. I invited her the other day at the library, but I feel like after our altercation, she might not want to be near me.

Before Nate opens his mouth to respond, Levi's voice cuts across the locker room. "Yeah, Syd's coming with Vanessa and Maddie. I'm gonna pick them up on my way over later."

Of fucking course he is.

My voice cracks. "Oh cool."

I hope that came out smoother than it sounded.

Levi and I are cool, but it still doesn't take away the pang of jealousy in my chest every time I see Vanessa with him.

She claims that they're just friends, and I'm trying hard to believe that. I feel like I'm the one who pushed them together. If it hadn't been for me sitting with Kieran on the bus ride home from Vermont, they would've never bonded and maybe I would be the one picking Vanessa up tonight.

I've been listening to Chrissy, a sorority girl, babble on about the volunteer work she did in the summer for the past ten minutes and I've never wanted to gouge my own eyes out more than I do right now.

The amount of crappy conversations I've had to pretend I'm interested in just to hook up with a girl is a little depressing. It could be that I keep going for the same girls over and over again—puck bunnies. *I'm exhausted.* I'm tired of the same old routine. I flash them a smile, shake my curls, and suddenly they're putty in my hands.

I want a challenge.

I want someone who makes me work for it. Someone whose conversation actually intrigues my interest and doesn't ask me for the millionth time what position I play or how much money I could make if I go pro.

The only girl who remotely fits that bill is Vanessa and she currently isn't speaking to me.

"Jake?"

I shake my head, refocusing on Chrissy, who's standing in front of me with her arms crossed over her chest and a sour pout staring at me.

"Yeah, that's crazy." I have no idea what she just said.

"You weren't even listening to me."

She's right, I wasn't. I know that it's rude of me to blatantly ignore her, but I'm ready to chug the beer in my hand and go drown myself in the bin full of bobbing apples.

"Sorry, I—" Kieran slips past me and I take it as an opportunity to get the hell out of here. "Kieran! Hey, man, let me help you grab more ice."

Kieran stops in his tracks, giving me a very confused look. I quickly motion my eyes to the small redhead next to me and he immediately realizes I need an out.

He clasps his hand on my shoulder. "Oh, thanks, buddy. Sorry, Chrissy, I need to steal him for a quick sec."

Kieran ushers me into the living room, away from the sorority girl. *Thank fuck.*

"Thanks, man, I was drowning in there."

"Yeah, I could tell you weren't interested. Y'know, since she wasn't Vanessa." I shove him as we move into the living room that's fully decked out in Halloween decor.

Nate loves to plan a good party. After the game, we all came straight back to the house to decorate. There are spider webs draping through the house in the corners of doorways and windows, a cauldron in the kitchen filled with drinks and dry ice to give a boiling effect, and so many pumpkins that it looked like we robbed a pumpkin patch.

We stayed up late last night carving most of them but stopped once we reached twenty. Kieran took pride in carving classic horror villains into pumpkins while I went the easy route and did basic jack-o'-lantern faces. Eli set up a crime scene in the living room with fake blood and caution tape wrapping from the coffee table to the entertainment center. He said we can use the tape for limbo later—I don't think anyone will really want to do that, though. All the food and beverages are themed for the night with sandwiches that look like eyeballs and punch that looks like blood. We honestly went all out.

Our front door swings open and an influx of people make their way into the crowded living room. I scan the group of people that just walked in, immediately finding Levi dressed up as a biker, a few bags of ice in hand. Sydney is dressed as a fairy and Maddie a vampire. My breath is knocked out of my lungs when my eyes fall on Vanessa as she walks in after her friends.

Oh, fuck me.

Levi spots me and Kieran immediately, leading the trio of girls our way.

"Guys, this party is fucking awesome." Levi looks around the room, noting the decor.

"How did you guys pull this off? There's no way Nate was in charge of this." Sydney's eyes are wide as she takes in the room.

Sydney really has no idea how much her brother loves to plan a party.

"Hey, Ness." My voice comes out higher and scratchier than expected, but holy fuck her in *that* outfit has my dick pressing against my boxers. I'm glad that my cowboy costume isn't skintight or else everyone would see the woody that I'm currently sporting.

I take my time, drinking her in. Vanessa's jaded eyes peer up at me as my gaze roams over her body. She has nothing on but a hockey jersey, fishnet tights, and bunny ears.

She's a goddamn puck bunny.

Her brown hair falls over her shoulders in curls, but two sections at the front are braided back into small buns that rest in front of her bunny ears. Her angel wings fall free, framing her slender face. I want to grip her chin and pull her into me.

Her glasses are missing, which shocks me because I don't think I've ever seen her without them. She must be wearing contacts because I know Vanessa can't see a damn thing without them.

I break the silence. "I like the outfit."

"Thanks, I thought it fit me *perfectly.* You know, since I'm a puck bunny, after all." The smile she gives me is riddled with sass as she grabs Maddie and Sydney's hands, pulling them into the kitchen.

My gaze is locked on her as she walks away, hauling her two friends to the booze table. She bends over the table, giving me the absolute best view in this whole house. Her ass is so perky and round, I watch as the fishnets trail up her legs and disappear under her jersey.

And that's when I notice the name and number plastered in black letters on her back.

Brody. 18.

VANESSA

I knew exactly what I was doing when I threw this costume together.

After our little altercation at the library and venting to Sydney and Maddie about Jake, Maddie came up with the best idea for my outfit. *A puck bunny.* Since Jake accused me of wanting to sleep with the entire team, I thought to myself, what would be better than becoming one?

When I told Levi about the costume idea, he was more than willing to help me. He even offered up his jersey, saying that it would make Jake even more jealous than he already is. I think his exact words were *"Jake is going to go feral when he sees you in this."*

Up until two seconds ago, I didn't believe him. But looking at Jake from the corner of my eye, his eyes are wide and breath fuming. Does the idea of Jake being jealous turn me on? Maybe a little.

Okay, a lot.

I've been in denial, thinking that there was no way that Jake was jealous of Levi, but tonight only confirmed what I've clearly been too blind to see.

Even if he doesn't have romantic feelings for me, there is definitely some sexual tension between the two of us and I think it's time for us to resolve that. Things have been strained ever since Vermont, and the only solution is we need to hook up and get over it. I've never been one to shy away from what I want, and what I want right now at this moment is Jake Shepherd.

"Well don't you three look lovely tonight." Eli walks up to the table, rescuing me from my thoughts. He's dressed as a firefighter, except he's shirtless. His warm skin and abs probably have every girl in here fawning over him. He has on tan overalls and a bright red firefighter hat that matches suspenders. Eli slings his arm around Maddie's shoulders. "If you're looking for a neck to bite into later, darlin', come find me."

Before Maddie can respond, Kieran appears out of nowhere—as if he just poofed into existence. "Get your arm off her, you dickhead."

Maddie makes a scoffing sound, narrowing her icy blue eyes on Kieran. "I can speak for myself, thank you very much." She slowly turns her head so she faces Eli, who now looks like he's contemplating his life with the glare that Maddie is giving him. "Eli, kindly take your arm off me before I snap it in half and make you use it as a hockey stick."

Eli's eyes go wide and he snaps his arm back to his side before Maddie can follow through on her threat.

She's not joking either. Last year, Maddie made Sydney and I take self-defense classes because according to her, you can only rely on yourself.

"You girls are no fun." Eli pouts, pushing out his bottom lip. "Are you down to play beer pong at least? Nate picked up glow-in-the-dark solo cups and Jake painted the balls to look like ghosts."

I think we're all still a little shocked by how well-decorated this party is. Out of the few years I've known Nate, I've never known him to be a good party planner—that could also do with the fact that the three of us normally weren't invited to their parties before this year.

The fake spider webs look creepily real, with tiny plastic spiders dangling from strings. There are LED lights strung around the whole house, giving a red or orange hue to each room. Everything from the food and drinks down to the party games they have set up are all planned so perfectly. If the NHL doesn't work out, maybe Nate can look into becoming a professional party planner.

Sydney looks at me like there are stars in her eyes. "Vanessa and I will play. We're unmatched." She tosses her hair over her shoulder and I'm surprised it doesn't get caught on her fairy wings. She has a crown of braids on her head and the rest falls in gorgeous honey waves.

Her answer brings a smile to Eli's previously pouty face. "Beauty. Let me grab Jake and I'll meet you two on the patio. Nate made us set it up outside so we wouldn't cause a mess. He never lets us have any fun." Without another word, he disappears into the crowd.

I'm a little excited to play against Eli and Jake. It's time for me to redeem myself. After Jake won against me in the Mario Kart tournament on my birthday, he never let me forget it. Now it's my turn.

Sydney and I grab a cup of punch—which is 90 percent rum and 10 percent juice, and head to the patio, leaving Maddie talking with Kieran.

The backyard is littered with pumpkins of all sizes and colors, some carved and some still perfectly intact—I wonder how many will be destroyed by the end of the night. There's a stone path leading from the deck all the way to the back of the yard, where a group of people occupy the wooden benches surrounding a small fire pit. *Are these even legal in the city?*

Tying the whole backyard together are strings of pumpkin-shaped lights draped from the wooden beams of the deck to the trees lining the fence. The beer pong table is lined with glow sticks, and all of the cups glow in the dark, illuminating the black tablecloth. The small white pong balls are decorated like tiny ghosts, and it's one of the cutest things I've ever seen.

Most of the parties that Sydney drags me and Maddie to consist of a single keg, loud music, and plastic folding chairs. It's nice to finally go to a party that seems like it was somewhat planned.

The only positive to those crappy frat parties was that Sydney and I crushed just about everyone in beer pong. I think we may have lost two games in our entire college career, which is pretty impressive if you ask me.

"Eli looked *so* sexy in that costume," Sydney spills to me as she takes a sip of her drink.

I know exactly how this will play out if Nate overhears her saying that. "Eli? As in your brother's *best friend*, Eli?"

As if my words bring her out of the fantasy she was just living in, she blinks at me with a frown. "A girl can still appreciate a fine-looking man." She winks at me as Jake and Eli slide open the patio doors to join us.

Now I take a good look at Jake.

Oh screw me, he's hot as hell.

I don't know what I was expecting him to dress up as, but for some reason I didn't imagine him as a cowboy. With dark denim jeans, a brown velvet vest, and a dark suede cowboy hat—the look fits him well. The vest is left open, which gives the best view of his abs, and I have to stop myself for a second to make sure I'm not drooling.

I bet he looks better than the model on the costume's packaging.

"I hear you two lovely ladies are the people to beat tonight." His words are light and make my stomach flutter.

He walks over to the table and sets down his drink, picking up a ball and twirling it in his hands.

"Vanessa and I have never lost a match before, so you better be careful, Shepherd. We don't want to crush your ego too much tonight."

Sydney winks at him and I feel like I might need to knock on wood if she keeps boasting about how good we are. Anytime you get too cocky, it always comes back to bite you in the ass.

Eli slings his arm around Jake's shoulder, looking between him and me. "Well, let's get the game started then. It'll be fun to see Jake lose something for once."

Sydney and Eli face off, and she wins. We take turns throwing the ball back and forth between teams. Anytime Sydney or I would sink a cup, they would take one in return. We alternate between dumb trick shots, most of them missing their mark.

It feels so refreshing to hang out and laugh with Jake again. I know I've been purposefully ignoring him, but I have my reasons. It's nice to be in his presence again, and it wouldn't hurt if we demolished them in the game.

I eat my words as Eli's toss lands perfectly in the cup in front of me, leaving one cup left on both sides. Jake's smile grows and he tips his hat at me, signaling for me and Sydney to drink.

Our eyes connect and I feel the heat go straight to my core. His features are darker outside with the lack of light and it has my senses on high alert. He watches me as I take a sip. I don't break eye contact as I lower my cup back down to the table and grab one of the balls.

"You may have won against a couple of frat guys, but they're no match for me. Nobody can compare to me, angel girl." Jake's voice is low and sultry, and my palms are suddenly sweaty.

He's trying to throw me off, *I know it.* Just like he did at my birthday party.

The music is almost completely cut off outside, the only thing you can hear is the crackling of the fire and the conversations behind us.

"This puck bunny is craftier than she looks."

Jake's stare is still fixed on me as he raises an eyebrow at my words. "Oh really? Care to make this interesting? How about we make a little bet?"

He knows I'm too stubborn and competitive to say no to a challenge.

"Fine. Let's make a bet."

He motions for me to go first and I think for a moment, finding something that Jake would be terrified to do. "If you miss this last shot, you have to prank call Coach Wilson and tell him you got arrested and need him to bail you out."

Jake only smirks at me, letting out a small laugh. I have a feeling his terms are going to be much, *much* worse.

"Okay, fine. But if I win, you take off Levi's jersey and have my name and number plastered on you for the rest of the night."

And just like that, it all clicks. I *knew* that wearing Levi's jersey would make him jealous. I just had no idea exactly how jealous he would become.

I narrow my eyes on him, and the word rolls right off my tongue. "*Deal.*"

He chuckles to himself, as if this conversation is amusing for him. Jake walks over and holds out his hand for me to shake—to agree to our terms.

I place my hand in his and he pulls me close, whispering so no one else but me can hear, "Just remember, if you miss…you're mine."

His words make my knees shake. Jake walks back to his side of the table, and with all the cockiness in the world, he puts his hand over his eyes and shoots the tiny plastic ball that looks like a ghost into the last solo cup.

Fuck me.

Eli grasps Jake's shoulders, yelling and cheering for his teammate.

"Your turn." Jake motions to the cup in my hand and I take a drink.

Sydney gives me a reassuring look. If Jake does a trick shot, then I have to—I know the rules.

"Does a backboard count as a trick shot?"

Eli straightens his firefighter hat. "Sorry, darlin'. This has to be *all* you."

"Just close your eyes and toss it, Ness. I got it in, so it can't be *that* hard, right?"

Jake's taunting only fuels my need to win even more. I stick my tongue out dramatically at him before putting my hand in front of my eyes.

Okay, Vanessa. Visualize the cup. You can do this.

The moment I feel the ball leave my hand, I open my eyes to watch my ball float toward the cup, only for it to bounce off the edge and roll off the table.

I am screwed.

Without a single word, Jake scoops me up by my waist and hoists me over his shoulder. "Time to change."

CHAPTER TWENTY

I don't have any pants

VANESSA

"Jake, put me down!" My arms flail around him, but ultimately do nothing to help me get out of his grasp.

Let's be honest, do I even want him to put me down?

He smells so good, like vanilla and tobacco. It doesn't sound like the best combination, but whatever cologne he has on, I want to drown myself in it.

Jake carries me into the house, up the stairs, and into his room before playfully tossing me on his bed. I've missed the soft cushion of his king-sized bed. The duvet is so fluffy and soft, I want to bury myself in it.

I watch as Jake walks over to his wardrobe, pulling out his own jersey to replace the one I'm currently wearing. He turns back toward me, extending his arm out with the jersey in his hand. "A deal's a deal, Nichols."

I roll my eyes and stand up from the bed, taking the shirt from his hands. We stand in the middle of his room, neither of us moving.

His voice is quiet as he looks down at me and asks, "Are you still mad at me?"

Jake's question takes me by surprise. I know I've been a little cold toward him the past few days, but I didn't think that my absence would affect him. Like, at all. I mean, he has his choice of friends and girls at his disposal. Why would I make a difference?

"I'm not entirely thrilled that you basically called me a slut in the middle of the library."

"Ness, I'm so sorry. I was having a bad day and took it out on you for no reason." He takes off his hat and runs a hand through his curls. "Seeing you with Levi, it just—I felt like you were replacing me with him."

It's so weird seeing Jake be so vulnerable with me. Sure, we've talked about some deeper topics here and there, but I don't think we've ever actually discussed our feelings. We've definitely have never discussed our feelings about each other.

"I never should have accused you of trying to sleep with the whole team. I think I was just jealous that after Vermont, you decided you didn't need my friendship anymore."

I feel my face soften with Jake's words. It doesn't excuse the way he spoke to me, but it definitely gives me some insight. I didn't know Jake Shepherd could actually share his feelings, especially with a female. This whole time he thought I was choosing Levi over him. But really, I was hanging out with Levi because I didn't know how to control myself around Jake.

Ever since that night in Vermont, I haven't stopped thinking about him. I catch myself reminiscing on the way he looked in between my thighs with my hands tangled in his curls, the feeling of his hands on my body. Every time I'm around him I have to control myself. I have to stop myself from thinking about him. It's so aggravating thinking about him *all the damn time*. Hanging out with Levi gave me a reprieve. He's a great person to bounce my thoughts off, but never once did I think about Levi the way I think about Jake. Talking with Levi allowed me to think about my feelings and what I should do with them.

And I think I've come to a decision.

The words pour out of me like I couldn't hold them in for another second. "Jake, I wasn't trying to replace you, I was using Levi's friendship as a distraction so I didn't have to deal with my feelings for you."

His eyes go wide.

Oh no.

I shouldn't have said anything. I should've kept my sassy demeanor and changed and walked right back down to the party to rejoin our friends. This is dangerous territory.

His posture straightens. "Feelings?"

"Not *feelings*, but…" I try to recover, but ultimately fail. "I can't stop thinking about that night. As much as I want to get you out of my head, I can't. You were right, okay? I can't stop thinking about you."

Jake stares at me, but I can't tell if it's in awe or disbelief.

I can't believe I just said that. *What is wrong with me, and why can't I just keep my thoughts in my head?*

The bass of the music is the only sound that leaks into the room. My face is flushed and I can feel the heat burning in my cheeks.

"You know what, I'm gonna go get changed in the bathroom and head back downstairs." I try to excuse myself from this awkward situation, but Jake grabs my wrist, stopping me in my tracks. I feel his breath on my ear, and it sends shivers down my spine.

"You haven't been able to get me out of your head, huh, angel girl?"

He circles his thumb over my wrist, which makes goose bumps rise on my skin. I shouldn't be reacting this much to a single touch. I swallow my thoughts and put on a mask of confidence.

"You know what they say, save a horse and ride a cowboy." I motion toward his hat and a deep chuckle escapes his throat.

I look up at him as he towers over me. I want to be suffocated by his body.

His cocky white smile is plastered on his face. "I was wondering if anyone was going to use that line on me tonight. Thought the cowboy outfit might just do it for someone." He lightly grabs my chin, forcing me to look up at him. "Guess it worked on you."

Jake pulls me into him, crashing his mouth against mine. His lips are full and he tastes of alcohol and mint. I want him to swallow me. He moves his hands, trailing from my chin down my neck, one resting on my collarbone. His hands are rough and calloused from years of playing hockey. I want to feel them explore my body. I wrap my hands around his neck, pulling him closer. I want more of him. *I want all of him.*

He detaches his lips from mine, panting. "Ness, if we do this, I'm going to wreck you. I'm going to ruin you for everyone else. No one else in this world will be able to compare to me. So, I just want to make sure you're okay with that."

Hmm, let me think for a second. Yup, I am more than okay with that.

I answer him by grabbing his neck and pulling him back down to me. I open my mouth and allow his tongue to intertwine with mine and my hands move to his hair, knocking off his hat. I need to tell him just how much I love his curls.

One of his hands settles on my neck while the other gets lost in my hair. God, not only is he good at eating pussy but he's also an excellent kisser.

I break the kiss and look at him with a devilish grin. "Didn't you say that you were going to *wreck me*? I thought you always made good on your promises." I can see the hunger in his eyes, and I know that I have him hooked. "If you can't do it, I'm sure I can find someone else at this party who can. Maybe Levi. I am wearing *his* jersey after all."

That last sentence is what breaks our heated gaze and makes Jake go feral. I shriek as he picks me up and tosses me onto the bed. I've always imagined being picked up and tossed around, but most guys I've been with have been so vanilla and boring. *God*, he's so hot.

All I can think is that I want *more, more, more.* My heart beats harder, pumping blood through my body that goes straight to my core. I've never wanted to have sex more in my life than I do right now.

He pulls off my boots, before pointing at the shirt covering my body. *"Take. It. Off."*

I look up at him, biting my lower lip, knowing that it's making him crazy that I'm not listening to his commands.

"Ness, take it off, *now."* His eyes burn into me.

I slowly peel off Levi's jersey and toss it on the floor. I grab Jake's jersey that was haphazardly thrown on the floor during our heated make out. I go to pull the shirt over my head when it gets ripped out of my hands.

"One day, I'm going to fuck you while you're only wearing my jersey. But tonight I want to see all of you."

Jake flicks off his cowboy boots and leans onto the bed, grabbing me by my hips, he pulls the both of us up farther onto the bed. He kisses me as we lie in the center of his bed. My head rests in between two of his pillows as his mouth moves from my own down to my neck, slowly sucking and nipping at the tender skin. He works his way down, stopping at the red lace bra covering my breasts. I may have worn a matching set tonight under my costume.

A girl can never be *too* prepared.

I instinctively lift up and arch my back so he can reach to unclasp my bra. We move quickly together as I pull the straps down my arms, and he attaches his mouth back to me. Finding my right nipple, he tugs it in his mouth—his tongue lapping and sucking. The sensation from his tongue shoots right down to my core. I can feel myself soaking in my panties.

Jake's mouth moves farther down my stomach and then stops at the hemline of my fishnets. He looks at it as if it's a barricade that he wants to break through. Jake's icy blue eyes look up at me in a pout, as if he's asking for permission to take them off.

I look down at him, wanting to take a mental picture of him because it's one of the sexiest sights I've ever seen. I nod at him, giving him his answer.

Without waiting another second, he leans down and rips the fishnets apart. "You have no idea how badly I've wanted to do this all night."

His lips attach themselves to the inside of my thighs, trailing kisses up and down. *Sucking. Biting. Teasing.* His touch is making my body pulsate and I want him in me. He hooks a finger around my panties and he lets out a hot breath.

"Jesus, Ness, you're already so wet for me." His lips brush against me, and slowly his tongue traces over me. As he does this, he moves an arm up and grabs my nipple in between two fingers and adds the tiniest amount of pressure. It's so sensitive and light it has me squirming.

Jake takes his hands and presses them down on my hips. "Stop moving, angel girl."

That nickname has me whining. I don't know why he likes it so much, but I love that he keeps using it.

His tongue strokes me, and his lips suck gently. The feeling alone is one that could send me over the edge at any second. I try to remember the last time I've been touched like this, but I can't. I can barely form thoughts in my head as Jake's touch sends waves of pleasure throughout my body. No one has ever made me feel like this. I feel desired and sexy. He is nothing like what I've experienced before with other guys. It's soft and tender, yet heady and full of want.

I tug on his curls, focusing his attention on me. He looks up at me, lips glossy.

"I want *you*, please," I beg, making my eyes bigger and pouty, which makes him melt into me.

"Anything for you." He's up in an instant, his hands finding his belt and unbuckling it. The buckle rattles as it hits the floor with his jeans and vest.

"This might sound weird but…" I look him up and down, taking him all in. Every part of him is all muscle, and he has a small freckle next to his left nipple. "Will you keep the hat on? It's kinda hot."

"Aren't you a little kinky, Ness." He straightens his hat before leaning over to his nightstand, pulling out a condom. He puts the wrapper in between his teeth, ripping at the package.

As he does this, I lean forward, pulling down his boxers. The fabric is tight like spandex and does nothing to hide the massive bulge at the front. His dick springs free and…*oh my god, I am screwed.*

I've felt his dick before, but there were always layers of clothes between us. Seeing it in front of me right now, in its glory—that thing is going to split me in half.

"Are you okay?"

Am I okay? I don't think I'm even thinking straight right now but I don't care. This could mess up everything between us, but I find myself throwing caution to the wind. I want Jake, and I want him all *now*. "Wreck me, Jake."

"You got it, Nichols." He tips his hat at me, and that devilish grin reappears.

He grabs at my panties, and pulls them down my legs, tossing them on the floor with the rest of our clothes. He positions himself in front of my entrance. He runs his dick up and down slowly, pushing into me at a wicked pace. I move my hips, wanting him in me faster.

"Slow down, baby, you might need a second to adjust to me."

As he pushes in deeper, I feel myself stretch to fit him. It's uncomfortable, but only for a second. He plunges in all the way, and I swear he hits something inside me that almost makes me scream. I clasp a hand to my mouth as he fills me, not wanting to be too loud, especially since the house is filled with people. He starts thrusting in even, long movements. He pulls out slowly, then thrusts back harder. Each time he moves, it sends pleasure rippling through me.

My nails attach to his back, digging in, pleading for him to go faster. I moan his name as he starts thrusting harder, causing his hat to fall onto the mattress beside me. I place my hand on his chest as I move to grab it. He stops moving long enough for me to push him off.

I shove him back onto the mattress and climb into his lap, grabbing his discarded hat, and placing it on my head. "My turn to ride."

I adjust the hat on my head as I lower myself onto him, and he feels much bigger in this position. If we do doggy, he would probably kill me.

I go agonizingly slow over the tip and Jake bucks his hips a little at the sensation. His finger finds my clit and rubs small circles. I lower myself all the way, stretching over his thick base. I work my hips, grinding and riding his cock. Our breaths are mixed together, both of us panting and moaning as we move with each other—our lips barely touching. Feeling his breath on mine turns me on more.

Jake grabs a hold of my hips with one hand, making them move in sync with his, his other hand still rubbing me as I ride him. I can feel that familiar tingle settle low in my stomach, telling me that I'm close. He thrusts his hips up as I grind on him, the friction only increasing the high I'm about to ride.

"Jake. I'm going t-to—" He cuts me off with a kiss.

"Come for me, Vanessa." His gruff voice against my lips sends me over the edge. I feel like my body convulses with the pleasure coursing through me. I can't control the words as they escape my lips. "Oh God…Jake, oh God."

"That's right, baby, I'm *your* god."

I completely let loose, melting under his touch. My brain feels like it's full of stars, and I'm floating in the night sky.

As I come down, he flips us over and starts to drive into me as he reaches for his own release. I feel myself clenching around him, gripping onto him as he fucks me. I can feel another orgasm creeping up on me. I don't think I've come more than once during sex.

His thrusts become slower, and harder as he reaches his climax. My name slips from his lips as he comes and it sends me over again, coming with him. He rests his forehead against mine, and we both lie there for a moment, panting.

Jake collapses next to me on the bed. "Fuck, that was even better than I've imagined."

"How long have you been imagining us having sex?"

"Probably since the night I met you at the bar." He winks at me, then turns over, tossing the used condom into the trash can next to the nightstand.

He turns back over, pulling me into his side. "How was it…for you?" A curl falls over his face as he asks me an intimate question.

How was it for me? I don't think a man has ever asked me how the sex was afterward. Normally I'd put my clothes on and get the hell out of there, or if they were at my place, I would kindly ask them to leave. The sex with Jake was *mind blowing*. I've had decent sex in my life so far, but this. *Him*. This was on a completely different level.

"Your reputation definitely precedes you." I look up at him, smiling at his goofy smirk.

We allow ourselves to lie here together for a few minutes, soaking in the afterglow.

It's not until I break the silence that we stir. "We probably should head back downstairs before people start to notice that we're missing."

"Oh, I think people know what was going on with you screaming my name and all."

I roll my eyes at him before hitting him with a pillow. "You suck."

I head to the washroom quickly to clean myself up, grabbing my underwear and bra along the way. When I emerge from the room, Jake has his pants pulled back on and holds his jersey out to me.

"We made a deal, I believe this is yours for the night."

I grab the red jersey from his hands, with the number twenty-four plastered on the back with his last name. I pull the heavy fabric over my head. Jake's jersey is definitely a bit bigger than Levi's. His sits a little farther down my thighs, and I look to the floor and see the torn piece of fabric that used to be my fishnets.

"I don't have any pants now."

Jake turns toward me and looks me up and down with a wicked grin. "Don't worry, mine's longer, so it covers you—but if you want, I'll stand behind you all night so no one can see your perfect ass except for me."

I smack his shoulder, and he lets out a thick laugh.

What did I get myself into?

CHAPTER TWENTY-ONE

Friends who occasionally have sex

VANESSA

I got fucked so hard it rewired my brain.

We've been sitting at our regular table at Caio for half an hour and I don't think I've uttered a single word to Maddie or Sydney. My subtle *aah*s and *ooh*s are sufficient enough responses for them today. My head is so scrambled that I ordered the wrong latte and I've been ordering the same thing since we began coming here. So that's a bit alarming.

Sydney started off the conversation delving into all the details from last night. She made sure to tell us about how Nate refuses her from dating anyone on his team—but that didn't stop her from making out with some random guy attending the party.

"Nate may have given him the death glare, but it was *so* worth it. We're gonna go out next week!"

"Girl, you're a hopeless romantic and yet you're going to give a football guy a chance?" Maddie's question alerts me. "Please be careful, we all know what happened the last time you dated an athlete."

Sydney waves off Maddie's words. "Yeah, yeah, I know, he broke my heart and I went into a Netflix coma for a week. Don't worry, he's different."

"You didn't leave your room for a week and definitely didn't shower. We had to light candles around the house so you wouldn't stink up the place."

Sydney shoots Maddie the finger.

I can't believe I almost forgot about that. It was our sophomore year and a guy on the lacrosse team asked Sydney out. She's very into the tall, muscular type, so he fit her standards perfectly. Well, that is until she found him making out with two sorority girls in the quad.

When I say she was a complete wreck, I mean the same sweats for three days, hair in a rat nest on the top of her head, and an endless supply of cupcakes.

Maddie quickly changes the subject to her co-op assignment. For the semester, she gets to work in the hospital morgue to learn about autopsies. Between that and work, she's rarely home. I listen to her ramble on about a few different cases she's helped with so far, making sure to leave out all details regarding the people she works on. You know, all that doctor-patient confidentiality stuff.

I probably should tell my friends about the events from last night, but I have no idea how to bring it up without them making a huge deal about it.

After we left Jake's room last night, we pretended as if nothing happened. The two of us rejoined our friends and I was teased endlessly about losing beer pong. We enjoyed the remainder of our night, acting as if nothing happened between the two of us.

"I told my professor that it's not fair that we're graded as a group when I single-handedly wrote the entire cost analysis report." I tune back into the conversation and realize that Sydney is now explaining the latest gossip going on with one of her class assignments.

"And what did your prof say?" I ask, pretending as if I was listening to the entire conversation and not involved in my own thoughts.

I know, it's rude of me to tune out my friends, but somehow my brain manages to block out everything when I'm internally debating with myself.

"She said that she's going to do an evaluation at the end of the project and wants me to document every email I send to my classmates to see how they're basically leaving me with all the hard stuff."

Sydney huffs out a breath. I've been in the same position before where you put all of your effort into something and the other members of your group just coast on you. It's not fun, and I do feel sorry that she's going through this. The last two years of your degree are significantly harder, and having a bad team on a project definitely doesn't make it any easier.

"Ness, you've been awfully quiet since we got here, is everything okay?" Maddie rests her hand on my knee, and I know that the second I look at her, I'm going to crumble.

Sydney's eyes narrow on me, as if she also knows something is up. "Yeah, normally you *love* gossip. Are you hungover?"

She holds the back of her hand up to my forehead, checking if I have a temperature.

I can't take it anymore. I'm terrible at hiding things from my two best friends.

"No, no—I'm fine. Just the usual, y'know, didn't get enough sleep, ordered the wrong coffee, I may have slept with Jake last night, and I have a progress check-in this week for my social media class that I'm stressing over."

Sydney shakes her head in disbelief. "Hold on. Rewind. What did you just say?"

Did I really think that I could drop that bomb in the middle of a sentence and hope they wouldn't pick up on it?

"You had sex with Jake?" Maddie's voice echoes in the small cafe.

Suddenly everyone's eyes are on us and our intimate conversation. I shrug and smile as everyone puts their attention back on themselves.

I nervously take a sip of my drink before speaking. "Yeah, it sort of just...happened?"

"Sex doesn't *just* happen, Vanessa. Oh my god, I totally predicted this! I told you!"

I had a feeling Sydney was going to say that.

"Where did this happen? The bed? The bathroom? *The shower?* Ooh, was it against the back of his door? That's always super hot when they can pick you up and drill into you." Sydney's eyes are wide with wonder and imagination.

"His hands are massive so I bet he's packing," Maddie adds.

"Oh my god, *yes*—is it as big as people say it is?"

"Who initiated it?"

I put my hands up in defense, stopping their ongoing questions. "Okay, can you two calm down? Aren't we supposed to be working on assignments and studying?"

Maddie looks at our laptops, unopened on the table in front of us. "Yeah, but this is *way* more interesting than studying the anatomy of the human body."

"We could always discuss the human anatomy of Jake Shepherd." Sydney wiggles her eyebrows at me and I throw a piece of my croissant at her.

"Okay, we'll stop being crazy, but you have to admit, this is insane. Can you blame us for wanting to know all the details?"

My eyes look around us, making sure everyone has gone back to their own business before scooching closer to my two friends. "Okay, fine."

Sydney claps her hands together as she stifles a shriek, knowing it would only cause more attention on us.

"So I may have had a teeny, tiny, micro-sized crush on Jake since the first night we met."

"I knew it!" Maddie clamps her hand on her mouth before composing herself. "Sorry Ness, continue."

"I know I said that he was annoying the first week or so, but he's just...becoming his friend made me see a much different side of him."

"Yeah, and you definitely saw another side of him last night." The two of them burst into a fit of laughter at Sydney's comment.

"Anyway." My eyes send daggers at them until they stop snickering. "We went up to his room so I could change into his jersey, and instead of me changing, I ended up telling him that I wanted to ride him like a horse. And then proceeded to do so."

I take another sip of my drink as Maddie and Sydney both look at me, their mouths wide open.

"Holy shit, I can't believe you had the balls to say that to him."

"And I can't believe that line worked on him. Men are so easy." Sydney leans back into her chair, taking a bite out of her pastry.

"So, what does this mean?" Maddie asks the question that's been on my mind all morning.

If I'm being honest, I don't know where this puts our friendship. I know I'm sexually attracted to him, and I love spending time together, but I don't date. *He* doesn't date either. We're basically the same person in different fonts.

We haven't talked since last night, but maybe this is something we should discuss. I mean, he did say that he was going to ruin all men for me, and I honestly think he might have because I haven't opened a single dating app since the night at the hotel.

"I don't know, but I'm sure we'll discuss it sometime this week. I have assignments I need to work on, so how about we head over to the library and forget about this conversation for a little while." I smile at my friends and they nod in agreement with me.

I'll focus on schoolwork today and figure out what to do with my feelings another day.

Vanessa
Are you free today?

Jake
I have a break between 12-1 if you wanna grab lunch on campus?

Vanessa
Ok, I'll meet you in the student center.

Jake
See u soon, angel girl

Wednesdays seem to be the one day of the week that no one wants to show up for class.

I don't know if it's the midweek slump that deters people from attending classes or the weather getting colder, but either way—I'm not mad at the empty campus. My creative writing professor let us go an hour early because there was only a third of the class that showed up today.

Professor Miles canceled class due to being sick, and she gave us an extension on our weekly check-in, which is heaven sent because I rushed through it on the weekend and now I have time to clean up my work.

Things have been looking up for me this week. Now all I need to do is speak with Jake and figure out whatever the hell is going on between us. I don't regret hooking up with him. I mean, he did give me the best sex of my life so far, but I'm scared that us getting together could affect our relationship. I had it in my head that if I hooked up with him once, that it would be enough. *But it's not.*

I don't know what's wrong with me but I crave him. Geez, I sound like every other girl on campus.

My mind has gone back and forth trying to figure out what he wants. If he wanted to hook up just once or if he's willing to do it again. If I'm just another notch in his bedpost, which, if I am, who am I to judge that?

The constant thinking has my palms sweaty as I open the door to the student center. I immediately spot Jake sitting in the atrium, his messy waves tucked underneath a backward baseball cap, light denim jeans, and a thick dark green flannel jacket.

As if he can feel my presence, he looks up at me with the sweetest smile before standing up to greet me.

"Hey, Ness, how's your day going?" He pulls me into a hug and the heat he's emitting warms me up from the cold November air.

It felt like the second October was over, the chill that comes at the end of fall rolled right in. I bet we'll have snow by Thanksgiving.

"We got out early, so I'm done for the day, you?"

"Two classes later this afternoon, but they're both easy." Jake moves to grab his bag off the ground and slings it over his shoulders, "Follow me, I'm taking us somewhere for lunch."

Before I can respond, he's already moving toward the exit that leads to one of the many student parking lots. My tiny legs move quickly to catch up to him, but by the time I take three steps he's already ten feet ahead of me, waiting for me at the door.

Maybe I should start working on my cardio.

What I really need to do is to figure out what we're going to do about our situation and how I'm going to bring it up. How does one politely say that they love having sex with you, but they don't want anything more than a physical relationship?

I feel like, if anything, Jake is the one person who would understand where I'm coming from. I highly doubt he'll be looking for a girlfriend anytime soon. Who would want to be tied down right before they start their career in the NHL?

He holds the door open for me and our footsteps become synced, as if he realized how fast his long legs take him, he slowed down just so I could keep up.

"I didn't know you had your own car," I say as he stops next to an old beige Jeep Wrangler. Every time I've seen Jake in a car it's either been Nate's or Kieran's.

He looks at me with that goofy grin still plastered on his face. "I got it when I was seventeen. Saved up for two years and had a little help from my dad. It's inspired by the Jeep from *Jurassic Park*."

My eyes roam over the vehicle, noting the red rims and trim lining the vehicle. Who knew Jake was such a movie geek?

Well, I guess I sort of did.

"Wow, *very* dorky of you." I muffle a laugh, and walk around to the passenger side, but before I can open my own door, Jake yells from behind me.

"Woah, hold up there." He reaches around me and opens the door, motioning for me to get in.

"Thanks." That stupid grin plasters across his face and it sends shivers down my body.

Okay, I need to get it together. I feel like it would be best to rip off the Band-Aid and talk about this *before* we're sitting in a restaurant full of people.

Jake climbs into the Jeep and tosses his bag into the backseat.

"Before we go anywhere, can we talk for a second?"

"What's on your mind, angel girl?" The nickname floats off his lips like it's his favorite word.

I secretly love the nickname he's become so fond of using, but it does make me a little nervous. Sure, friends have nicknames for each other, but angel girl sounds like something a guy would call his girlfriend. And I am definitely not Jake's girlfriend.

"I wanted to talk about our situation."

He leans back in his chair, his arm resting on the steering wheel. "Our situation?"

"I don't know where we stand after everything that's happened." I look at him, trying to gauge his emotion from his face—but all I can see is intrigue, so I continue. "I'm not looking to date. I just—I want you to know that I had a good time and I wouldn't mind doing it again."

"Are you insinuating what I think you are?" His tongue peeks out and licks the side of his mouth before giving me a cocky smirk.

I roll my eyes. "What I'm saying is that if you're open to it, I wouldn't be opposed to a friends-with-benefits situation. Sex is a good stress reliever, and you happen to be *very* good at it."

Jake's eyes are attached to my lips, watching every word come out of my mouth. Did he turn on the heat or did the car just naturally get hotter?

"Oh, I'm definitely open to it." He moves in, grabbing my neck and pulling me into him. Our lips crash against each other and I move myself from my seat so I'm now hovering over the center console.

His skin is soft against mine, he must've shaved this morning. His tongue sweeps into my mouth and the taste of mint overtakes my tastebuds. I didn't realize how hungry I was for his touch. *For his kiss.* Jake's hands move from the back of my neck to cup my face and I take this as an opportunity to climb into his lap. He grips my hips as I grind into him, not caring if anyone might see us as they walk by the car.

It isn't until he finally breaks the heated kiss to say, "Is it too forward of me to ask if you want to skip lunch and take this somewhere besides the student center parking lot?"

"I would love that, actually." I move back into my seat, buckling in. "We can go to my place. Maddie works after her classes and Sydney is on campus all night."

"Perfect." Jake moves the gearshift into Drive and has us pulling out of the parking lot and to my place in under ten minutes.

We barely make it through the front door before pieces of clothing are tossed haphazardly to the side. I think one of my shoes ended up in the middle of the living room and I have no idea where Jake's jacket ended up. All I care about is ripping off his jeans.

His lips are back on mine as he picks me up and holds me around my waist. *God*, I love being picked up and tossed around like I'm a rag doll.

Jake pushes me against the wall, his hands roaming across my waist and chest. We make our way to the kitchen and he sets me down on top of the countertop. *I've always wanted to get fucked on a kitchen counter.* It's a kinky dream of mine. I pull my shirt over my head as Jake pulls off his jeans.

"Condoms are in the top drawer next to the fridge," I tell him as I unclasp my bra.

Jake gives me a questionable look as I direct him to our designated clutter drawer. You can find everything in there from hair ties to pens to condoms. We probably should organize it better, but that's the last thing I want to think about right now.

Just as instructed, Jake pulls out a shiny square package and tosses it onto the cool marble next to me. He comes back to me, boxers still clinging to his *very* muscular thighs. The muscle is so defined I want to take a bite out of him.

This time I grab him and pull him into me. My fingers pull off his hat and thread their way through his thick curls. I think that one of Jake's most attractive features is his hair. Somehow he manages to have the curls perfectly tousled, even if they've been smothered by a hat all day.

Steamy breathes and moans fill the space around us, and I'm so glad we're home alone. Jake moves his hips in a circular motion, only the thin fabric of our underwear is keeping us apart.

A shriek that isn't mine carries across the kitchen and Jake stops all movement. I look over his shoulder and see Sydney standing in the doorway, mouth agape.

"Are you guys fucking kidding me!? I just cleaned!" Sydney slaps her hand over her eyes and turns out of the kitchen, dramatically stomping her feet on her way back to her bedroom, not before peeking through her fingers and giving me a thumbs-up.

She's something else.

I lean my forehead against Jake's chest, trying to stifle my laughter. This is mortifying but also hilarious at the same time.

"I thought you were on campus! I'm sorry!"

A shout comes from behind her bedroom door. "Just clean up when you're done!"

I've never been caught red-handed before. But looking at the expression on Jake's face, I can tell he must've experienced this a few times.

"Well, I hope she at least enjoyed the view." Jake wiggles his eyebrows at me and I playfully smack his chest.

"Should we take this into my room and save ourselves from getting caught by another roommate?"

Jake scoops me up and carries me down the hallway to my room as his response.

"Didn't you have classes to go to this afternoon?"

Jake shrugs. "One's about bees and the other is about environmental ethics. Both of which are entry-level courses that I could pass in my sleep." He plays with a strand of my hair before focusing his attention back on my eyes. "I would much rather spend the rest of my day in bed with you."

I clear my throat and sit up in bed, holding the covers over my chest. "Just in case I wasn't clear before—friends with benefits doesn't mean we're exclusive or anything. Anytime you want sex, just message or call me and I'll do the same. No jealousy, no romantic feelings—just friends who occasionally have sex. If you want to have sex with someone else, I won't hold it against you and vice versa. Deal?"

Jake leans back into the headboard. "Sounds like a dream to me, Ness."

Hearing him confirm he wants exactly what I do allows my body to relax into his and enjoy the tiny bit of happiness leaking into my life. I know most people wouldn't approve of our situation, specifically my friends, but I'm content with my decision.

Jake stretches and looks at the watch on his wrist that I didn't notice was there. "*Shit.* As much as I would love to stay in bed with you all day, Coach will kick my ass if I'm not in the weight room in fifteen minutes."

I groan as he leaves the bed, lifting the sheets and allowing cold air to swoop in. The bed is warm from our conjoined body heat and I quickly wrap myself back in the covers to keep the warmth in. I take a moment to appreciate Jake's physique as he grabs his clothes off the floor. As he pulls his shirt back over his head, his back muscles flex and I notice the small scratch marks I left behind. *Oops.*

Will the guys tease him for these marks in the locker room? Will he tell them who gave them to him? That's probably something we should discuss, but we can save that conversation for later. I don't mind if he tells his friends, but I think it'd be best if the whole team doesn't find out, especially Coach Wilson.

I find the strength to get out of bed and pull on a hoodie and sweats. I follow Jake to the front door as he grabs the rest of his belongings off the hallway floor. We stand there awkwardly at the front door, not knowing how to end this interaction.

Do I kiss him?

No, that's definitely not something friends would do. But I also feel like if I hug him, that's too personal. I settle for a handshake and he laughs, tucking one of his loose curls under his hat. "See you tomorrow, you goof."

The second he leaves, I can feel the heat rise to my cheeks.

A handshake? Who the hell says goodbye with a handshake?

"That man has the nicest ass I've ever seen."

"*Ohmygod!* Where the hell did you come from?"

Sydney stands behind me with her arms crossed and a mischievous grin plastered across her face.

"Some of us know how to be *discreet*." She walks by me into the kitchen, putting the kettle on the stove.

I follow her with an apologetic look. "I'm *so* sorry. I thought that you were on campus."

She moves to grab two mugs from the cabinet and plops an earl gray tea bag in each, "Technically I'm supposed to be on campus til nine, but I felt like skipping the rest of the day to finish an essay that's due at midnight."

Sydney grabs the boiling kettle from the stove and pours the water into both cups. "I guess in hindsight I should have messaged you to see if you were home. It definitely would've saved my poor innocent eyes."

My cheeks burn. "You are the farthest thing from innocent Sydney Archer."

Last semester she hooked up with a frat guy and forgot her blindfold and some other *interesting* items in the living room. Maddie and I teased her relentlessly for days after that.

"Well, it wasn't the *worst* view. His butt is perfectly round, like a peach I want to sink my teeth into." She smacks my butt as she walks by, before grabbing both of our teas. "C'mon, let's watch a raunchy rom-com and you can tell me all about Jake's magical dick and whatever the hell it is that you two are doing together."

I roll my eyes but reluctantly follow her to the couch. We settle on a random movie, knowing full well that we won't be paying attention to it. I blow on my tea before taking a small sip. Sydney situates herself so she's sitting cross-legged in the corner of the couch, her eyes locked onto me—patiently waiting for me to start talking.

"So, what's the deal? Are you guys fooling around? *Dating?"* Her eyes wiggle at the last word.

"We're friends." I push my glasses up the bridge of my nose, keeping them from sliding down as I readjust myself on the couch. "Friends who sometimes have sex. Y'know, no strings attached."

"Okay, who brainwashed you into thinking this was a good idea? Someone always catches feelings in these types of situations."

"Syd, you *know* how I feel about relationships. And we all know that Jake doesn't date either. It's just a healthy and convenient way for us to relieve stress. Nothing more." The last two words linger on my tongue like a bad taste in my mouth.

I don't want more. Just something fun. *Right?*

"All right fine, but when the two of you inevitably end up together," she leans in closer to me, "which we all know you *will,* I'm going to be standing there with a gigantic sign that says *Sydney was right.* And I will hold it over you for the rest of our lives."

She lounges back into the couch, grabbing her tea and focusing on the movie playing on the TV.

Maybe one day I'll be ready for a relationship—but today is not that day. For now, I'm content with the situation I'm in—and hopefully Jake is as well.

CHAPTER TWENTY-TWO

Big city anxiety

JAKE

Autumn is in full swing.

The lingering summer warmth has officially left Boston.

I'm a summer person. I miss the warm air and spending as much time soaking in the sun as possible. Growing up in a beach town will do that to you.

Vanessa, on the other hand, *loves* the fall. The other day she was complaining that the warm weather should be gone the second it hits mid-October. I think Vanessa likes the cold more because she can hide in thick sweaters whenever she gets the chance. She has this one pastel patterned fleece sweater that looks like something my grandma would wear, but according to her, it's *perfect* for cold mornings. I've caught her wearing it more than once to morning practices.

Since our recent agreement, we've been spending a lot more time together. Even outside of hockey and sex, I enjoy spending time with her. If we're not at the arena, we're on campus studying in the library or hanging out in the student center with our friends. We've decided to keep our arrangement a secret from the team. Vanessa is convinced it's for the best because she doesn't want the guys thinking of her in a certain way. I told her I'd smack them if they were to say anything, but I respect her choice.

We've been pretty sneaky these past couple weeks, but one morning Nate caught us sneaking out of the house. I used a classic excuse—we fell asleep while studying. It's not foolproof, but I think it worked.

I like hanging out with Vanessa. She doesn't bombard me with questions about hockey or stats. We talk about our interests like our favorite genre of music, even what podcasts we're into. I'm currently obsessed with this horror podcast but Vanessa refuses to listen to it after I played her a zombie episode. We also talk about our hobbies, our families, and childhood memories.

The other night we were hanging at the diner on campus, and I asked her what inspired her to go into photography. We've talked about the topic before, but never this much in depth. Vanessa went on about her grandpa who collected old photography magazines. After he died, she wanted to capture the beauty of the world and be featured in one of those magazines she was obsessed with. Her parents never understood her from what I've come to know.

I can only imagine the childhood Vanessa had growing up with parents who didn't support her dreams.

My parents have supported me ever since I could hold a stick in my hands. I was a kid with a silly dream, but with their unconditional love and support I've been able to live out that dream. They continue to support me in any way that they can. They attend home games whenever they get a chance, or if they're tied up at home, they'll stream it and call me afterward. And every now and again my family will come to support me at an away tournament. Which has me looking forward to this weekend.

We're heading out of town for a charity tournament in Nashville. Every year, a ton of teams from the eastern conference head down to Tennessee to play against each other in a charity tournament, not earning any points for the regular season. This allows us to bond and try to stifle any rivalries—but our competitive side is inevitable, even for charity events. We play on Friday and Saturday, leaving Sunday for us to relax before heading back home.

It'll be nice to see my parents and Autumn. I want to introduce Vanessa to my parents, but I don't know if that goes against our friends-with-benefits rules. All of my friends have met my family so I don't know why this should be any different.

"Jake, if you don't get your ass downstairs in five minutes, you can find your own way to Nashville." Kieran's voice echoes up the stairs.

I look around my room and finish packing the rest of my stuff into an overnight bag. I notice my BCU hoodie on my bed and make sure to grab it for Vanessa. Every time she's over she steals it, saying that I keep my room too cold. As much as she loves the fall, she does love to complain when she's cold.

I grab some last-minute items, phone charger, a pack of condoms, and extra socks—you never know when either of those might come in handy.

"Holy shit, Shep, let's get going. Stop looking at yourself in the mirror." Nate stands at the front door, waiting to lock up behind us.

"I was grabbing the rest of my stuff, asshole."

Kieran leans against the brown brick. "He was probably texting Vanessa a love letter or something."

"There's nothing going on with me and Vanessa," I lie through my teeth, hoping they'll drop the subject.

Nate locks up and we toss our bags into the back of Kieran's truck.

"Oh really? So, it wasn't Vanessa I heard screaming your name the other night. Good to know." Eli flashes me a wicked smile and I can almost hear his dirty thoughts forming. I guess we haven't been as discreet as I'd thought.

"Kieran, your room is right next to Jake's, didn't you hear it?" Nate accuses as he hops into the passenger side of the truck.

The guys have never complained to me before about hearing what goes on in my room. Up until now I'd always thought the walls were soundproof. Apparently, I was wrong. Vanessa is *not* going to be happy when I tell her this.

Eli and I settle into the backseat and I can visibly see his thoughts forming before he speaks.

"Well, if no one in this house is sleeping with Vanessa, I'll give her a ride."

I grumble, trying hard to keep my cool. *He's just joking, don't blow your cover.*

"When we go out Saturday night, I'll swing her around the dancefloor, show her my moves, and she'll be putty in my hands." Eli's pushing my buttons, and he knows it.

"I bet she'd make the softest sounds. I wonder if she keeps her glasses on during—"

"Don't finish that sentence." *Shit.*

"Y'know, I bet she takes them off. Wouldn't wanna break those while I'm tossing her tight little body around."

In a blink of an eye I'm grabbing Eli by his sweater, the cowboy hat on his head falls to the floor of the truck.

"Hey, idiots, it's too early and I'm too tired to deal with your shit today." Nate leans over his seat, pulling us apart. "You two are acting like five-year-olds fighting over a toy. Do I need to remind you that girls aren't toys?"

"Although I'm sure she's fun to play with." Kieran smirks at me from the front seat. I hit him upside the head, and he pretends to swerve on the road, acting as if I'd bludgeoned him.

"Will the two of you quit teasing him?"

"Thank you, Nate."

"Jake clearly gets upset when you talk about his girlfriend."

"She's not my girlfriend," I grumble as I cross my arms and sink back into my seat. Dammit, Vanessa's dramatics have started to rub off on me.

Eli picks his hat off the floor and places it back on his head. "Well, if Vanessa was so easy to give it up to Shep, maybe I should ask if she wants a turn in my bed. I can show her how a *real* cowboy fucks."

Before I realize what I'm doing, I reach across the truck, punching Eli. He puts up his arms, protecting his face as he laughs.

"For fuck's sake, quit it you two!" Nate almost falls over his seat trying to separate us. He grabs me first and tosses me back to the other side of the truck. It takes me a second to regain my composure, knowing full well I just outed myself to my friends. But what am I supposed to do, allow Eli to talk about Vanessa as if she's just another random hookup? *I don't fucking think so.*

"Can you two asshats stop bickering or else I'll drive us all into a pole and you two can explain to Coach why we're all dead."

"If we were all dead, how do you expect us to tell Coach it was our fault?" Eli fires back without letting a second go by.

I instinctively let out a chuckle. As much as Eli pushes my buttons, he knows how to quickly diffuse tension.

"Eli, apologize. *Now.*" Nate uses his stern dad voice, trying to calm the car down.

Eli puts his hands up in defeat. "All right, all right. I promise to stop making sexual jokes about Vanessa *if* you admit that the two of you are sleeping together."

I look to the front, where Nate is still turned around to face us and Kieran is now watching me through the rearview mirror.

Sometimes I hate my friends.

"Fuck, fine!" I scrub my hand down my face. "We've been sleeping together the past couple of weeks—but it's nothing. We're just having fun."

"Jake, don't tell me you guys are trying to do the whole friends with benefits shit?" Nate's eyebrow quirks up.

"Yeah."

The entire car is filled with groans.

"You're an idiot."

"I can't wait to see how this turns out."

"You have no idea what you're in for."

I shake my head at their comments. This is the main reason why I tried to keep it in the dark. I knew that they would all have their own opinions. But did they really expect me to say no when a beautiful girl asked me to casually hook up with her at both of our convenience? Especially when that girl is Vanessa. I would be an idiot to say no.

I ignore them for the remainder of the drive to campus, which lasts all of two minutes.

We park at the arena, grab our gear, and head onto the bus. It's almost a seventeen-hour drive so we're stopping halfway in Virginia to stay overnight. I was hoping to get some alone time with Vanessa before the weekend, but I have this lingering feeling that the boys won't let this be a peaceful road trip.

Almost half the team is already on the bus, knocked out cold. The nice thing about long trips is that we leave early in the morning that you're asleep for the majority of the ride. I head down the aisle and take a seat in my usual spot at the back. Kieran moves to sit in the window seat, but I block him with my knee. "I don't think so. Ness is sitting with me for the ride."

He shakes his head at me. "You are so in over your head, man." He turns around and sits down across the aisle next to Levi.

Kieran has no idea what he's talking about. Vanessa and I are just friends and I promised her we could sit together. It's the least I could do after the shitshow I caused on our last roady. This time I'm going to make sure we can make our time more enjoyable.

Even if we sleep the whole way, I hope her hair smells like that expensive shampoo she uses. It smells like coconut and vanilla. I used some when I was at her place and she almost killed me. She said something about only using a dime-sized amount of product, and I may have overindulged. And by that I mean I *really* lathered that shit on.

I feel her presence the moment she steps on the bus. My eyes follow my instinct and find her walking in between the rows of seats. I watch as she squints her eyes, the bus lights a little too bright for her this early. When her eyes land on me, she smiles and a weird feeling arises in my gut.

Oh shit.

Her mossy-green eyes have small bags under them. Her hair is pulled away from her face, resting in a bun on the base of her neck, those angel wings framing her face. I can't help but let a dirty thought sneak its way into my brain—her hair would look beautiful wrapped around my hand as I fuck her from behind.

I'm going to hell.

Her leggings make her ass look phenomenal as she squeezes past me to the window seat I reserved for her. The grey crewneck engulfs her small frame. It looks big enough for the both of us to fit into. She squishes her small pillow against her head and the window, immediately getting comfortable next to me. I have a feeling that she's going to pass out the second the bus starts moving.

"I made a playlist for the road. Some of your stuff mixed with mine." I pull my AirPods out of my pocket and pass her one of the earbuds.

She grabs it with a hesitant look. "There's no country on here, is there?"

"Nah, that's more of Eli's thing."

She takes my phone out of my hands and starts scrolling through the list of songs. Her fingers stop halfway through and she moves her attention back to me. "Jakey, have I ever told you how grateful I am that you have good music taste."

I cringe at the nickname she loves to call me. I think it's payback for all the times I called her "sunshine."

Eli eavesdrops from the seat in front of us and turns around. "There's nothing wrong with country, you two just won't expand your music taste to *real* music."

"Whatever keeps you sane, Eli," Vanessa whispers, settling back into her seat as she shuts her eyes and the rest of the world out. Unknowing to her, once you get Eli going, it's hard to get him to shut up.

"Once we get to Nashville, you'll realize what you're missing out on, darlin'." He inclines his hat toward her.

Vanessa quirks an eyebrow at him. "Are you telling me that when you're home and want to relax or study, you purposely pick a song that talks about late-night drives, drinking beer, and owning a plot of land with your small-town honey?"

I can't help the laugh that bursts out of me. That is *exactly* what Eli does. He was born and raised on his family's ranch in Tennessee, country is in the boys' bones.

"You bet your ass I do, Nichols. And you know what?" Eli leans over the armrest on his chair. "It gets me laid too. If you weren't so sassy, maybe I'd show you some of that Southern hospitality."

My mouth mimics Vanessa's, wide open and shocked as fuck. I can't believe he really had the balls to say that.

"Eli, it's too early to debate music with you. Keep your country music and your sweet talk to yourself. I'm sure you'll find some country puck bunny that'll worship the ground you walk on the second we arrive in Nashville."

"Oh, I'm counting on it. The second the girls see this smile along with my hat, they'll never want me to leave." Eli wiggles his eyebrows and Vanessa rolls her eyes at him.

Nate grabs Eli by his shoulder and pulls him back down to his seat. "Ignore him. It's too early for his brain to function properly."

"It's fine. If you forgot, I live with your sister. I can never truly escape country music. She blasts it through the place whenever she cleans. I was trying to edit a video the other day and I had some Zach Bryan song stuck in my head for the rest of the day."

"How's all that going by the way? Your term assignment and stuff."

Vanessa's eyes go big at Nate's question. "It's good. Well, as good as it can be, I guess. We have a big report due at the end of the month that's worth almost half our grade. Everyone has to compile all of their stats from each social media account and put all the information into a report with graphs and all that fun stuff. It's not hard, but it's tedious going through all the data, so I've been a little stressed."

She has seemed a bit stressed lately. Luckily, whenever it gets too much, she calls me for a little stress reliever. *A.k.a. my dick.*

A gift of Vanessa's is that she always loves to overexplain. If you ask her a question or if she's explaining a story, you better have five minutes set aside because she will go into every little detail and everything that connects to it. Some people might find it irritating when someone gets off track, but it's one of my favorite qualities she has.

"Nate and I were talking about how we've noticed you've been at the house a lot studying with Jake. Is he helping you with your project? Giving you some one-on-one exclusive content?"

At the sound of my name, she narrows her eyes on Eli. "Maybe you should focus on getting a goal rather than my whereabouts."

Her sassy comeback gets a reaction out of all of us. Eli settles back into his seat, crossing his arms over his chest. "Well, you don't need to be rude, *Vanessa.*" He snaps his head toward the window.

She laughs at his dramatics and settles back into her own seat.

"All right, quiet down back there." Coach stands up from the front and walks up and down the aisle. "We should reach Virginia in the early afternoon. We'll stay there overnight and then head to Nashville tomorrow."

Mumbles of agreement fill the bus and I focus my attention back on Vanessa as she gets more comfortable in her seat.

About an hour goes by and I'm about to fall asleep to the music when Vanessa shuffles next to me, still deep in her slumber. She moves her body, resting her head on my shoulder, her hand falling onto my lap. She starts mumbling in her sleep, but most of her words are incoherent.

"Mmm, warm." Her arm wraps around my torso, and her subconscious pulls herself closer into me.

That strange feeling in my gut returns and I'm starting to realize what it is.

I'm in deep shit.

VANESSA

I don't think I'll ever get used to long road trips.

Being stuck on a Greyhound for longer than eight hours should be illegal. Luckily Jake was prepared with a good playlist and snacks, or else I probably would've gone insane. He even convinced half of the bus to sing Taylor Swift karaoke with him.

Last night we stayed in Virginia to break up the seventeen-hour drive. A few of us hung out in Jake and Kieran's room playing cards. Jake taught me how to play euchre—a game that his family plays every holiday. It took him over an hour to explain it to me. Once I got the hang of it, Kieran, Levi, Nate, and Eli all played with us, staying up later than we should have. I think it's really wholesome that Jake and I can spend time together and not have it revolve around sex. We've become a lot closer since we've been spending so much time with one another. When we're not spending time in bed—or in the shower, or in my living room—we sit with each other and just *talk*. Our conversations have become one of my favorite pastimes. It feels so easy to talk to him.

It's funny how at the beginning of the semester I thought that being assigned as the social media coordinator for the hockey team would be insufferable. Looking at it now, I've gotten to experience so much and make new friends.

As I look out onto the ice and see my new friends warming up, my heartstrings tug. I'm so grateful for what this project has brought me. If I had been assigned to work for any other school club or sport, I never would've given Jake a second chance.

I grab my camera from my tote bag and start taking shots of the guys as they practice before their last game of the night. For special tournaments, they change the style to a round-robin tournament, something I'm actually familiar with. BCU has played two games so far today and won both. If we win this game then we make it to round two tomorrow morning. And if we win both games, we play another team for first place.

I pan my camera from the ice up to the stands, and I spot Jake's family right away. I haven't met them yet, but they're easy to pick out of the crowd.

Jake is the spitting image of his father. They are both tall, with broad shoulders—his coming from hockey while his dad's defined posture definitely comes from all his work in construction. His dad's hair is cut short, with streaks of gray peppering his light brown hair. The only difference between them is Jake's curls, which clearly come from his mother.

His mom is much shorter than his dad, but still looks taller than me, with peachy skin and gorgeous blonde curls. Her smile is so big as she watches Jake skate across the ice, waving at them. Standing in between his parents is his younger sister, Autumn. *Holy crap, they could be twins*. Everything from her blue eyes down to her wavy brown hair is identical to her brother. The only difference is the height. Autumn is about the same height as her mom. She has a smaller frame, but I remember Jake saying that she's been doing dance since she was four.

I could go over and introduce myself, but I don't know what I would say. *Oh, hi, I'm the girl your son is casually sleeping with.*

Yeah, I don't think that will go over well.

I think I'll just keep my distance and keep myself occupied with photographing the boys tonight.

We ended up winning the last game as well, putting us at the top of the tournament.

After the game, most people went out to dinner or explored the city with their friends. I decided to head back to the hotel to upload my photos and videos from tonight onto my laptop. I add them to my folder, organizing my posts for this upcoming week, and adding more information to my report.

The only stressful part about this class is our monthly reports. The actual work part is easy. Or at least for me it is. I thought that working with a ton of young athletes would be problematic, but they've been more than willing to help me with whatever I ask of them. I asked Jake if he would participate in a TikTok trend where the boys walk through the arena lip-syncing different parts to a song, and he had half the team volunteering to do it with him.

My stomach grumbles, distracting me from my work. I look at the time and realize it's late and most of the guys have probably already had dinner by now. I've never been to Nashville before, so I have no clue what time restaurants close or where the best places are, but there's one person who's been here multiple times who might want to tag along for a late-night snack.

I walk down the hall until I end up in front of Jake's door. On the other side I hear Kieran and Jake arguing with one another, but it's muffled, so I can't quite make out what they're talking about. I knock three times, loudly, and moments later Jake swings the door open. He looks down at me and his facial expression changes immediately from grumpy to happy.

"Hey, Ness, what's going on?" He leans against the door frame and crosses his arms over his chest, making his biceps bulge in his black BCU T-shirt. My legs quake as I study his tan, corded arms.

"I was feeling a little hungry and wanted to see if you'd grab food with me?"

He looks over his shoulder into his room and I follow his gaze. Kieran is sitting on his bed with his phone pressed to his ear.

"Just let me grab a jacket."

I start walking down the hallway to call the elevator for us, and Jake runs up at the same time the doors open.

"This is for you." He hands me a sweater, and as I unfold it, I realize it's his BCU hoodie that has his number on the sleeve. I always wear this when I'm at his place. "It's got a little chilly outside. Thought you might be cold in just your shirt."

I look down at my white long sleeve and realize I probably should've brought a coat.

"Thanks."

The material is soft as I pull it over my head. The hoodie is worn, but in the best way. You know it's been worn too many times when the former soft fabric pills inside from one too many washes. It's not technically soft anymore but now it's *cozy*.

My stomach growls, filling the small space with gurgling sounds.

Lovely.

"If you were that hungry, you should've grabbed me sooner." He laughs. "What are you in the mood for?"

The fresh air hits us as we leave the lobby and walk down the streets of downtown Nashville. The breeze is much cooler than it was during the day. I tuck my hands into the front pocket and walk alongside Jake on the sidewalk. The streets are packed with people—going out for dinner, heading out for a night of partying, or some simply enjoying the nightlife.

The air wafts around me, filling my senses with so many different options. I can smell smokey barbecue coming from the restaurant across the street. Coach Wilson took everyone out for lunch in between games today and I had the best crispy chicken sandwich. One thing Nashville knows how to do well is food, especially barbecue.

As I internally debate what I want, the most delicious smell goes up my nose.

Pizza.

Tucked in between a pharmacy and a smoke shop, there's a tiny pizza place with big glass windows and a giant neon sign at the front of the store. The New Yorker inside of me screams.

"I think pizza is the way to go. It calls to me." I place my hands over my heart, as if the food is my soul mate.

We enter the small shop and my mouth immediately starts watering. There are three large pizzas on the counter, one pepperoni, one cheese, and one pizza that has just about every topping imaginable. The tiles on the floor are checkered red and white and the walls are a basic yellow with multiple tacky signs. This place feels like it belongs in a movie from the eighties.

"Can I get two waters and two slices of pepperoni, please?" Jake pulls out his wallet before I can object.

"Thank you." I smile up at him as I grab my slice from the cashier.

My piece is bigger than the size of my head. The cheese is thoroughly melted and gooey, and the small circles of pepperoni have the perfect crisp to this. It reminds me of a place back home in New York that operates out of a small take-out window. It's one of those places where if you blink, you could miss it. The slices are the size of my head and they're only two bucks.

"What are you thinking about?"

"This place reminds me of a restaurant back home." I take a bite, a little drop of tomato sauce drips down my chin and Jake's there with a napkin, immediately cleaning it up for me.

"And how does it compare?"

With a mouth full, I cover my lips as I respond, "*Very* good."

He takes us to a park near the hotel so we can sit and enjoy our meal before we both finish devouring our food. Jake tells me about his normal pizza order—extra sauce, extra cheese, and a heaping amount of mushrooms and bacon. He tells me how his sister will only eat cheese pizza and nothing else, so pizza nights in their household were very entertaining.

"Each of us would order our own small pizza and sometimes if Autumn was feeling adventurous, she would try a piece of mine or my mom's." He laughs at the memory. "Almost every time she would end up pulling all the toppings off."

I love when Jake shares memories with me, especially ones with his family. He has no idea how lucky he is to have grown up in a loving home with a sibling. Being an only child seems like it's a dream—being the only one who gets all of your parents' attention, but it's lonely. I always hoped that one day I would have a sibling or that my parents would pay attention to me. But you can't always get what you want.

I finish my slice and toss out our paper plates.

As we get up to make our way back to the hotel, a shiver runs down my spine, causing goose bumps to settle over my arms.

"Are you still cold? Do you want my jacket?"

"No-no, I'm fine. It's chillier than I expected tonight."

Within seconds his denim jacket is placed on my shoulders, his warmth immediately engulfing me. The inside is lined with that sherpa material that keeps your body heat in. The goose bumps on my arms go away and the smell of him invades all of me. Sandalwood and something spicy.

"You didn't have to do that." Although I'm grateful he did. I really underestimated the weather here. I don't know why I thought Nashville would be warmer. I wrap the jacket around me, sealing in the warmth.

"You're always freezing. Especially at night when you put your cold toes on me."

"It's not my fault you're basically a furnace."

"I think if you started wearing socks around your house, your feet wouldn't be so damn cold all the time."

I stick my tongue out at him.

It's something I've done ever since I was little. I don't know what it is about me and socks, but as soon as I get home, they *have* to come off. Sometimes I'll get too warm or feel claustrophobic, and the second I take off my socks I feel better. Does that mean that my feet are normally freezing when I hop into bed? *Yes.* But that's something I choose to deal with.

We walk in a comfortable silence, allowing me to take in the scenery around us. I love exploring cities I've never been to, but I won't lie, sometimes I get big city anxiety. It's the fear of not knowing where anything is or the best way to get around. I'm pushed out of my comfort zone and have to figure out everything for myself.

"Can I say something vulnerable without being judged?" The words slip from my mouth.

Jake looks at me curiously. "You can tell me anything you want, angel girl."

The softness in his tone eases the anxiety building in my chest.

"When I visit a city for the first time, normally I get anxious. I know that sounds a bit bizarre since I come from one of the biggest cities in the country. Being surrounded by tons of strangers and not knowing where anything is unsettles me. But…" I trail off, thinking about how I'm going to say this without sounding like I'm in love with him or something—which I'm not. "Being here, in Nashville, with you—it's comforting. I don't find myself constantly looking over my shoulder or triple-checking the area we're walking in. I feel…safe."

Jake stops on the sidewalk and pulls me into him. "Anytime you need a comfort person, I'll always be here." His lips crash onto mine and the kiss makes me dizzy.

I don't know how long we stay outside, kissing on the sidewalk. But when he pulls away, my chest feels hollow.

We walk back to the hotel, which is only down the block. As we get to our floor, I turn around and take off Jake's jacket, passing it to him. "Thanks for hanging out with me tonight. Sorry if I interrupted something with Kieran earlier."

"Don't worry about him. Girl trouble, as always." He pulls me into a suffocating hug, "And don't thank me for hanging out with you, Ness. I love being around you."

My heart swells with his words. *Why does he have to say sweet things like that?* A girl could get the wrong idea very easily.

"I like being around you too." I press my card to my hotel room, unlocking it. "Good night, Jake."

"Night, Nichols." He gives me a quick peck that I wish was longer and then heads down the hall to his own room.

I close the door behind me, and all my suppressed feelings come to the surface. I can't shove them down any longer.

Could I be falling for him?

CHAPTER TWENTY-THREE

No feelings attached

JAKE

This morning we won two games, which advanced us to the final game against Boston College. *Our rivals.*

Of fucking course they would be the ones we have to face off with for the trophy. I mean, hell, the trophy is just a tiny piece of plastic that we'll probably toss away, but it's the principle of it. Boston College loves to mess with us during these nonseason tournaments—playing dirtier because it won't affect their regular season games. Jokes on them because we can give it right back to them.

There are only five minutes left in the third period, and we are absolutely demolishing the Eagles. I can already hear the sound of the buzzer and the boys cheering. The score is 4–2 and I had one of the most beautiful shots I've made all season. Nate scored our first goal with a slapshot in the first period, and then continued to make a hat trick, scoring two more goals in the second period.

Nate is always a high scorer. Every year he beats his previous record. He's going to make waves when he goes pro. I'll be shitting my pants if I have to play against him in the future. Having him on our team is an asset, but playing against him—all my bets are off.

At charity tournaments I try my hardest to not be a dick, but sometimes I can't help it. I especially can't help it when Andrew Meyers won't get his stupid body out of my way. Nate takes possession of the puck, but Levi is too heavily guarded for Nate to make a pass. I shoot Eli a knowing look, signaling to him that I'm going to try to create an opening for him.

I skate down the ice to try to help Levi out of a double-teamed situation. I shove one of Boston's defensemen into the boards as we fight for the puck. He shifts his body, forcing us to go behind the net.

This is his first mistake.

I'm good at making people feel claustrophobic, suffocating them with my presence. Call it a natural talent of mine.

The second mistake he made was not looking around, or else he would've noticed Levi swiping sideways and creating an opening. I flick my wrist and send the puck flying between Boston's defenseman, right into Levi's awaiting stick. By the time he realizes the mistake he's made, Levi shoots and scores another goal.

Take that, Meyers.

If only this were a regular season game, the points we would've accumulated during this weekend would easily toss us in first place—although I'm pretty sure that's where we're standing anyway.

The puck drops, sticks clash, and suddenly I'm thrown back into the game. My attention was misplaced for a second, but that single second allowed Meyers to fly past me down center ice with the puck. He slaps it over to his left wingman, but Eli is quickly on him, trying to steal possession.

Meyers moves to try to get past me and closer to the net, but I can skate faster than him. Within seconds I'm in front of him, bracing myself for his impending check. This guy has been all over me tonight and I just barely made my shot earlier before he slammed me into the boards.

Except this time, I'm one step ahead of him. I dodge to the side and he sends himself flying into the boards.

Fucking beauty.

"Hey, Meyers, you really should work on your footwork. If you were only a few seconds faster, you wouldn't be wiping ice off your jersey." I laugh as he uses the board to pull himself up.

I turn around in time to see that the Eagles lost possession and now Sebastian is skating toward their goalie, their defensemen distracted by someone in the stands. My eyes follow to where they're looking and find Vanessa bent over, picking up a different lens to use for her camera.

Fucking pigs.

I know, it's a bit hypocritical of me to call them pigs when I stare at her ass all the time, but the difference is she *knows* I look. She appreciates it when *I* look at her, not when random assholes look at her like she's a steak they want to devour.

The distraction works in our favor, Seb takes it as an opportunity to sneak by them. Sebastian is great at being invisible. He doesn't make too many goals, but when he does, the other team never sees it coming. Most players underestimate him because he's young, but they're all fools to believe the kid isn't wicked talented.

I linger back in our zone, keeping my eyes aware of my surroundings in case the puck comes back this way. As I skate by, I pass Vanessa in the stands. I give her a goofy smile and she winks in my direction, holding her camera up to take a photo of me.

God, she is so fucking hot. *And all mine.* I can't wait until this game is over and I can take her back to the hotel. I feel like I'm addicted to her. If we're not together I want to be. The second I get a whiff of her, I want to haul her into me and never let her leave. Even if that does sound caveman of me, I can't fucking help it.

"Shepherd, who's the little hottie with the camera?" Andrew's annoying voice comes up from behind me. He skates next to me, eyes falling on Vanessa, whose attention is now focused on the game at the other end of the rink.

Andrew is their center, so he *should* be with the rest of his team, defending their goalie, but he must realize that there's no way they'll be able to catch up. Instead, he's wasting time *and* getting on my nerves.

I keep my voice stern as I answer his question, "She's the team's social media coordinator."

"Oh really?"

"Don't even fucking think about it, Meyers."

"It's funny that you think I would listen to anything you say." He nudges my shoulder, which aggravates me more. "She's also a photographer, huh? Maybe I can get her to take some photos of me."

I let out a grunt, clearly showing my disinterest in this conversation. I skate away from him, moving closer to Kieran in case the puck comes back to our end. And just like the annoying little shit he is, Andrew follows me—still not paying attention to his team.

"Or even better, I'll bring her back to my hotel room and we can take some together. She's gonna love being on camera. I'm sure the guys would love to have a photo of her splayed naked to keep in the locker room."

"Fuck off, Andrew." I lightly shove my shoulder against his—making almost no contact because I don't feel like getting into a fight today.

"Oh, defensive." He skates around me, stopping close enough so what he's saying is almost a whisper. "You tapping that, Shep?"

I stay silent and try to focus on what's happening at the other end of the rink. Nate's circling the net, trying to get an open shot. I try to tune out the sound of Andrew's voice, but he's persistent.

"She probably lets the whole team pass her around. Sheesh, you guys have it made. A hot photographer and a puck bunny all wrapped into one. Mind sharing her for the night? I'd love to take her for a ride and see those big pouty lips wrapped around my di—"

I shove him back before he can finish his sentence. He laughs before shoving me back. *Oh let's fucking go.* I take my gloves off, punching Andrew in his nose. Blood gushes from his nostril.

Good.

I'll get an earful from Coach later, but this is worth it. Andrew whips his gloves off and his hand swipes at the blood running down his face. When he realizes he's bleeding, he looks at me and hooks his fist into my jaw, catching my lower lip on my bottom teeth. I feel my jaw rattle and I'm grateful that we wear mouth guards. I lick my bottom lip, feeling something there, and realize that the fucker cut my lip open.

"Don't worry, I'm sure she'll crawl into your bed as soon as I'm done with her."

His words send me over the edge and I tackle him onto the ice, both of us hitting the rink *hard*. My fist connects with his jaw this time, and I barely register the sound of the ref's whistle, and both of our teams skate over to see the commotion.

"Don't you ever fucking disrespect Vanessa like that again or I'll make sure the next time you don't get up off the ice."

"Fuck you, Shepherd." Andrew shifts and tosses me onto the ice under him.

In a second, Kieran and Eli are pulling us apart, and I hear Coach Wilson yelling my name, followed by some not-so-family-friendly profanities. Kieran extends a hand and pulls me to my feet. I run my hand along my jaw, it's tender but at least all my teeth are still in place.

"You good?" Kieran asks as he tears off his helmet.

I spit blood onto the ice as I take out my mouth guard. "The douchebag just doesn't know when to keep his mouth shut!" I say the last words louder, gaining Andrew's attention back on me.

"Do you wanna go again, Shepherd? I'll give you a black eye to match your fat lip." He tries to pull free, but Eli's grasp on his jersey keeps him in place.

The ref kicks us both off the ice for the remaining seconds of the game. I skate over to the bench, where Coach is waiting for me with a deep scowl on his face. I've seen this look before, the scrunched eyebrows, his crow's-feet in the corners of his eyes—he's definitely going to rip me a new asshole after this.

I park my ass on the bench and wait for the final buzzer to go off.

We win 5–2, but with the way Coach is looking at me, I shouldn't be celebrating with my team. The guys rush onto the ice, tackling each other. I move to follow the rest of the team, but Coach puts his arm on my shoulder, stopping me in my tracks. "I don't think so, Shepherd."

The tone of his voice is enough to scare the fuck out of me. It feels like déjà vu to a few weeks ago when Kieran and I were in shit. But now it's just me who's in trouble.

Fighting in a game never looks good, but fighting during a charity event definitely wasn't the right move. I feel my heart rate kick up as the team files into the locker room, leaving Coach and me alone in the hallway. *Oh, fuck me, this isn't going to be good.*

"Jacob, I don't know what's gotten into you lately, but whatever it is, you need to cut it out."

The use of my full name has the hairs on the back of my neck standing up. The only people who ever call me by my full name are my parents, and normally it's because I did something *really* stupid.

"Do you have any idea how fighting in a charity match looks? New Jersey is going to have a field day when they hear about this, and don't think that word won't get out, Jacob. You played like crap in a couple of games, you let yourself get distracted, and now fighting? Get your fucking head out of your ass."

I know I've messed up a couple of times this season, but everyone has a bad game. Just last week Sebastian got a penalty for tripping, but I don't see Coach beating down on him.

"Look, Coach, I'm sorry. This guy just got on my nerves and—" The look he's giving me tells me that he doesn't care for excuses. "I'm sorry, it won't happen again."

"You bet your ass it won't." He lets out a loud sigh. "You're a talented kid. You've got a bright future ahead of you—but petty fights like this could cost you your dream. You're so close to achieving it. I've seen you put your life into this sport, just remember to think about your future when you step onto that ice next time."

"I will. Sorry, Coach."

"Now go get changed and shower, you stink."

I feel like a dog walking away with his tail tucked between his legs. The worst kind of talk with Coach is when he tells you that he's disappointed rather than angry. I probably shouldn't have fought Meyers tonight, but I couldn't let him talk about Vanessa that way. It's not fair to her for people to assume she's some puck slut.

I head back into the locker room and grab my bag, making my way to the lobby to join the rest of my team and our families.

Dad is easy to spot since he towers over almost everyone. I'm surprised he never went into sports when he was my age. He could've easily been an amazing basketball player with his height, but instead he settled down with my mom and started his own business.

"That was a great game, honey." My mom's arms wrap around me first, and she tugs hard.

Boston Central University is only a two-hour drive away from home, but with hockey season and school assignments, it's hard for me to make it home as often as I would like.

"Yeah, so thrilling." Autumn's sarcasm never fails to make an appearance. "My favorite part was when you punched that guy and almost broke his nose."

I give her a warning glare and her smile immediately wipes off her face.

Dad lets out a sigh. "Can't say that was our proudest moment as parents. He better have deserved it."

"He did. He said some *choice* words about a friend of mine and I may have snapped. Sorry."

My dad's stern look fades as he watches the smile on my face, trying hard to move the conversation to something else.

"Do we know this friend?" My mom has always been nosey, that will never change.

"No, she's a newer friend."

"She?"

"Vanessa. She's our teams photographer and social media coordinator for the season."

Mom catches on to my mood, so she changes the subject and fills me in on what's been going on at home. Autumn's dance team made it to regionals, so they get to travel to Washington for her competition at the end of December. Unfortunately, it also takes place during our Winter Wonder tournament, but they've seen me play enough hockey. Autumn deserves a chance to shine in front of our parents.

Dad tells me how his construction business is going. It seems that everyone wants to either remodel or build, so he's been busy with different projects. It's nice to see that my family has other things going on to keep them preoccupied. Sometimes I feel like hockey keeps me away from them. That's why when I do get the chance to see them, or visit home, I cherish it a bit more.

Behind my dad, almost out of view, I see Vanessa talking with some douche wearing a backwards hat. I know I sometimes wear my baseball caps backwards, but I don't give off the douchey vibes that he is. I shift on my feet until I finally get a look at who she's twirling her hair for.

Andrew fucking Meyers.

"Hey—I'm gonna go meet up with some friends, but we're still on for breakfast before I leave tomorrow?"

"Yes, we'll meet you at the hotel in the morning." My mom hugs me again, but this time it's not crushing my ribs. My dad and sister both wave goodbye to me as they walk toward the exit. I go in the opposite direction, heading for Vanessa and that fucking idiot.

As I move through the crowd, I realize I've lost them. I swear to God, I will kill that asshole if he so much as touches a hair on her head.

"Jake!" Vanessa's voice calls from behind me. How the hell did she get over there without me seeing her? "I was looking for you. What the hell happened out there? One second you're all smiley and the next you're spitting blood onto the ice."

Her eyes land on the cut on my bottom lip and she moves to touch it, but I grab her hand, stopping her. "It's nothing."

Hell, a cut is better than a missing tooth.

"Who were you chatting with earlier?" I know it was Andrew, but I don't want her to think that I was spying on her.

Her cheeks immediately turn a pinkish shade. She's not seriously blushing over this guy?

"Oh, Andrew. Yeah, he came up to me after the game while I was waiting for you."

"You do know that he's the one I got in a fight with on the ice, could you not tell by his broken nose?"

"It didn't look broken to me."

"Did he say anything to you?"

"He asked for my name and number. Both of which I declined."

I let out a hearty laugh. Of course he did. He must think pretty highly of himself if he thinks that he could snag Vanessa. *Get in line, buddy.*

"Good."

"Good?"

"Yeah, that guy's a prick, Ness."

"Why are you laughing? You find it funny that some other guy asked me for my number as if it hasn't happened before?"

Happened before?

"Who else hit on you?"

She lets out an aggravated sigh. "It doesn't matter. Are you the only guy I'm allowed to talk to?"

And this is exactly what I didn't want her to think. I don't want her to think that I'm some alpha asshole type who only wants her to himself. I mean, I do want her to myself, but I'm also not a controlling manipulative piece of shit.

"Ness, that's not what I'm saying."

"Well, it sure as hell sounds like it. Did you forget the terms *we* made? No feelings attached, remember?"

The words hit me harder than Meyers's punch. I know the terms we agreed on, but fuck the terms. I don't care if she's friendly with other guys, but I don't want her flirting with them, especially if I'm in the same damn room. And maybe that does go against the terms of our situation, but I don't give a fuck anymore.

"Right." I give her a curt nod and turn around, ready to grab my shit and go back to the hotel.

She holds onto my arm, stopping me from walking out of the arena. "Jake, wait. Can we rewind? What's going on?"

What's going on?

256

What's going on is this stupid prick felt like he had the right to talk about Vanessa in a vulgar way and it aggravated me, so I hit him. I hit him because I have feelings for a girl who only wants to fuck me. I haven't admitted it to anyone, not even to myself until now, but fuck it, I *do* have feelings for her. I've never been in a situation before where *I* wanted more. I have no fucking clue what I'm doing.

"All you need to know is he said some shit about you and I didn't like it. So I hit him."

Her face changes into something like a scowl. Is she mad at me for defending her?

"So he said something about me, who cares? He's not the first and I'm sure he's not the last. I'm not your girlfriend, Jake, you don't have to get into fights over me because some random guy decided to be gross—especially when it can make you look bad." She says it so simply.

"You're right. You're *not* my girlfriend. I thought that friends should stick up for one another, but the next time a guy makes a derogatory comment toward you, I'll let it slide. Sorry, Ness, won't happen again." I pull away from her light grip and storm toward the doors.

I join the rest of the team outside.

"All right boys, last night means you get *some* freedom," Nate starts. "Back to the hotel to change, then we're going to party."

Nate sheds his responsible skin for one night on this trip, allowing himself and his teammates to overindulge. Which is great for me because I desperately need a distraction tonight. I'm going to drown out my thoughts with a bottle of booze and get so drunk I can't even think of Vanessa's name. Maybe I'll find someone else to occupy me tonight.

"Who's ready to get their country on?" Eli shouts.

"To the bars!" The boys shout with their fists raised over their heads like knights off to battle.

VANESSA

Nashville is nothing like I expected it to be.

Ever since our conversation at the arena, Jake's been actively avoiding me. Anytime I try to grab his attention he looks the other way or starts up a conversation with one of the guys. I don't know what his problem is. His emotions change more than Sydney's outfits when she's getting ready for a date. I've never been more confused by a guy in my entire life.

There's a small part of me that's been entertaining the idea of us being more than friends, but every time I allow myself to go there, my brain pulls me back to reality.

We could never work.

Jake loves to play the field and the word commitment sends fear running straight through my body. We agreed to be friends with benefits because we're always around each other, so it's convenient. That doesn't stop the jealous feeling that rises in my chest when I see Jake blatantly flirting with another girl right in front of me.

My head is spinning, and it's not from the whiskey. One second he's defending me and then a few hours later he's sitting in a bar entertaining some random girl.

How am I supposed to trust him if we get into one fight and he immediately ignores me for the rest of the day?

I distract myself from my ongoing thoughts and grab one of the shots from Levi's hand, turning my head slightly as I put the glass to my lips. Before I toss it back, my eyes land on Jake. He's standing at the other end of the bar with a blonde draped over him. I can tell from here that her platinum hair is completely fried and is probably going to fall out, but hey, if that's what Jake likes, then go right ahead.

Drink.

I slam the glass down onto the bar top, the cinnamon whiskey burns so badly that my eyes water trying to keep it down. I keep my gaze glued to Jake and the girl. I watch as his hands slide up and down her body, whispering something into her ear that causes her to laugh. Sebastian hands out shots to me and Levi, and I eagerly take it from his hands.

Another drink.

Okay, this is fine. *I'm fine.* Who cares who Jake's with? He can sleep with whomever he pleases.

Why was that again?

Oh right, because I said that we could be friends with benefits but still keep our options open.

I'm such an idiot, why did I say that?

Why can't I allow myself to have something more—something real? I feel like I've been protecting my heart for years, only letting people see what I want them to see. I wonder if I will ever fully allow someone into my life again. Loving someone is the best and worst feeling I've experienced.

Jake's the first person who's made me question all of my morals and rules. He makes me dream of what my life could be like with someone.

I shake my head of all thoughts of Jake and put my attention back to Levi. My friend who didn't ditch me for a blonde cowgirl.

"Want to do another shot?"

"Nichols, we might want to take it back a notch or else I'm scared you'll be throwing up the whole ride home tomorrow."

"I'll be fine." I lean against the bar, casually pushing my tits up a bit so they grab the attention of the bartender. The bar is packed, so if this is the only way I can get a drink then so be it. "Can I get another shot of cinnamon whiskey, please?" The taste isn't my favorite, but I've been knocking shots of it back all night, so I might as well stick with it.

My attention is once again drawn to Jake. Does he have some sort of magnet in his pocket? I watch as he moves closer to the girl, whispering in her ear. I'm not jealous. I'm *not* jealous. I'm...*okay I'm jealous.*

"Actually, make that *two* shots, please."

"You're gonna regret that in the morning."

I ignore Levi's warning and toss back both shots, letting the liquor warm me up and give me the courage to stay out with the team.

CHAPTER TWENTY-FOUR

Come dance with me

JAKE

I'm in a bad mood tonight.

And it's not because Eli convinced all of us to wear cowboy hats out tonight. They actually look quite good on us. Vanessa is the reason for my bad mood.

For the past ten minutes I've been watching her dance with some random guy, and I've never felt more jealous in my life. I want her to be looking at me, talking to me—not hanging out with some random fuckboy on the dancefloor.

I feel like a creep as I take a sip of my beer, eyes glued to her.

Sometimes I feel like there's more going on between us. We have this shared intimacy and yet she still keeps her walls up.

A random girl with big blue eyes and bleach-blonde hair clings around me, talking my ear off about the Music Hall of Fame, but I don't care about anything she's saying. She's nothing compared to Vanessa. No matter how hard I try to keep the conversation going and force myself to flirt with her, I realize how much I hate this.

I hate not celebrating with Vanessa. I hate how private we are. I hate not being able to touch her around my friends. All I want is to be able to dance with her and kiss her in public without her freaking out.

I always thought that I would just sleep my way through college until I got drafted and then try to settle down. I never would have expected that in my final years of college I would find a girl who makes me question everything.

"Y'know, if I were you, I would've asked her to be my girlfriend after the first hookup." Nate takes a swig of his beer as we watch Vanessa dance carelessly. "Shep, you gotta tell her how you feel before it's too late."

Sometimes Nate is *too* good at reading people. I feel like he knows what I'm thinking before I say it out loud.

"Who said I have feelings for her?"

Nate looks at me, giving an *are you kidding me* stare down.

"Okay, buddy. Keep lying to yourself. While you choose to ignore your feelings, someone else is feeling her up on the dance floor."

I watch as the guy she dances with runs his hands up her torso. I want to break each and every one of his fingers. Okay, maybe I do have feelings for her. But Vanessa and commitment don't go hand in hand. Why would I put myself in a vulnerable position only to be turned down again?

I arch a brow at Nate. "How come you always have great relationship advice and yet I never see you with a girlfriend?"

"We're not talking about *my* love life."

Eli clasps mine and Nate's shoulder, yelling over the music, "Yeah, 'cause Nate has horrible luck with women. Remember that girl you took out in the summer who thought a goal was a basket and brought you a baseball to sign so she could sell it when you go pro."

Eli breaks into a laughing fit and Nate shoves him off, shaking his head at his friend.

"Ignore him. You know I'm right—so when are you going to get your head out of your ass and do something about it?"

Nate is right. That's what aggravates me.

Vanessa is amazing. Once someone else realizes it, she'll be scooped up and I could miss my chance. I want to be the person she confides in and trusts. I want to be the person she turns to, the one to hold her when she's upset, the one she looks for in a crowd. I don't want to let her slip through my fingers. But I don't know how to talk to her about this because she's set her boundaries, and I need to respect them.

Maybe there's another way for us to take a step forward—starting with me interrupting her dance.

"All right, fuck it." I turn toward the bartender and order a shot of whiskey.

"Jake Shepherd needs liquid courage? Since when?"

"Shut up, Murphy. I can't wait for the day you fall for someone and decide to tell her about it. You'll be shitting your pants."

Eli puts his hands up in defense and backs away slowly. I knock the shot back and head toward the middle of the dance floor, where Vanessa is moving her gorgeous hips to the music.

She's in a world of her own, dancing with this stranger who I've become very envious of. The music changes from an upbeat twang to a slower song, and the guy spins her around, twirling her with one hand. Vanessa only notices my presence when she twirls around and I grab her by her belt loop. As I tug her into me, her belt loop breaks with the force of my pull, creating a decent sized hole.

"Hey!" Vanessa puts her hands against my chest, stopping us from colliding. *Fuck.* Her touch warms my entire body. As if she notices her hands are still on me, she smacks my hand away from her waist. "These were my *favorite* jeans."

A deep laugh escapes me as I look down at the hole along her hip bone. I slowly trail my eyes up her body, taking in all of her. When my gaze lands on her face, I notice she pulled her beautiful plump lips into a straight, taut line, her eyes narrowing on me, like a tiger ready to pounce on its prey. *She's so cute when she pretends to be mad at me.*

I lean low, down to her ear so I can talk to her over the music.

Her chest rises and falls quickly, and with all the confidence in the world, I whisper in her ear. "Don't worry, I'll buy you a new pair."

I grab her by her waist and pull her back into me. I can see the stranger from the dance floor still has his eyes on Vanessa. He looks at me briefly, giving me a look that says *what the fuck.*

I just stole his girl, and I don't give two fucks. Vanessa was mine first, and she always will be. Even if she hasn't realized it yet.

"Come dance with me, Ness." I nudge my nose against her cheek, begging.

Her eyes question me. "Why? Did the blonde ditch you, so now you've come for your second choice?"

Her question swallows me up. She was watching me tonight too? *Good.*

"You've never been a second choice to me, Ness." I grab her chin and bring her lips to mine. It's a risky move—one I don't know she would be comfortable with, especially since we're out with the whole team. But she doesn't pull away. She wraps her hands around me, her fingers immediately playing with my curls. *Fuck* I love when she does that. Her nails play with my hair and my scalp, sending an electric jolt down my neck. Vanessa could suck the life out of me with her kiss and I would thank her for it.

She tastes like cinnamon whiskey, which is unusual for her, but I like it. It reminds me of crisp leaves and late autumn nights spent by the fire.

Vanessa looks up at me, with a greedy smile. "I don't really care for the club, wanna go back to the hotel?"

Hell yes. I don't know if I can make it all the way back. I would take her here if there weren't a hundred watching eyes. I want to take her back and show her how badly I need her. I never want her to feel like she's a second choice when it comes to me.

in the elevator going up to her room. I want to take her in the shower, on the bed, on the desk—fucking everywhere.

I think I want it all with her.

But for now, I'll take her to her room and show her just how much I love being around her.

I pick her up by her waist, hauling her over my shoulder, and start walking toward the exit. On our way out I use my free hand to wave at Nate. He gives me a knowing nod, then focuses back on Eli and the rest of the team, who are taking shots at the bar with some players from the other teams. Normally I would be with them, celebrating and bonding, but I would rather spend my night buried in Vanessa.

We get outside the club and Vanessa pounds her fists on my back. "Let me down, Shepherd, before I hurt you!"

"You couldn't hurt me even if you tried, Ness."

I bend over and slowly put her down. As I do, she runs her hands down her outfit and I take a second to appreciate how fucking sexy she looks. She's wearing black jeans with holes across both knees—and a broken belt loop thanks to me.

Oops.

This girl has nothing else on but a little black tank top that I want to rip off her body the second we get back to the hotel.

"Are you okay to walk back or will your heels hurt your feet going that far?"

She rolls those gorgeous eyes at me. "I'll be fine. And if I'm not, I'm sure my amazing friend Jake will give me a piggyback ride." Her smile beams up at me.

"If your feet start hurting, just jump on." I pull her into me, hanging my arm over her shoulders, guiding us back to the hotel.

"Are you okay?" Her question throws me off. "Y'know, with the whole fight with Andrew. We didn't really talk before you stormed off."

I shake my head at her. "I'm fine. Meyers barely split my lip, it'll be healed in a day. Trust me, I've had *much* worse done to me."

Her eyes go wide when I say that. I can only imagine what she's picturing in that creative mind of hers.

"The worst hit I ever got was in my freshman year at BCU. It was one of our last games of the season and we were playing Northeastern. Their left winger came out of nowhere and checked me into the boards, knocking the wind out of me. " She winces and holds her side, as if she can feel a phantom pain. "I broke a rib and had a slight concussion."

"Yikes, talk about a rough sport." She blows out a whistle, in the cutest tune. "Should we talk about why you fought him?"

This girl never gives up.

"I feel like we should just forget about it. I didn't handle the situation properly and I've learned my lesson."

She nods at my response, allowing the topic to die, never to be brought up again. If I learned one thing, it's that Vanessa is very stubborn and independent. I know she appreciated me sticking up for her, but she didn't like the way that I handled it.

The hotel isn't far, but at the halfway point I lifted Vanessa into my arms. I knew those shoes wouldn't last long. Her lips are on me the second we hit the elevator. Traveling up her neck, I nip and suck at her gentle skin. The only thing stopping me from taking her right here is the ding of the bell indicating we've reached our floor.

Vanessa pries me off her and tugs me down the hall to her room. We're a heated mess of kisses and gentle touches as she gets the door open. She fiddles with the buttons on my jeans as I toss off my plaid jacket and white T-shirt. Vanessa pulls the jeans down my legs and palms me through my boxers. I'm already hard but her touch has me straining against the fabric.

"Is it rude of me to say that I've been waiting for this all weekend?"

The giggle that falls through her lips is soft. "No, you're just being honest. But doesn't waiting make the anticipation grow?"

I point down to my dick as I say, "If it grows any larger I might explode."

My statement causes her to laugh again, but this time it's a hearty laugh—that sound is going to be on repeat in my head all week.

Her pants and shirt find the floor and my eyes immediately fall onto her body, which is covered in the sexiest lingerie I've ever seen.

Holy fuck.

"Do you like it?" she asks so innocently, as if she's not the devil disguised as an angel.

The dainty black lace has red flowers embroidered over her nipples. The bra barely covers her, but I'm not complaining as the thin material holds up her beautiful tits. My eyes travel down her body. The black lace panties match the pattern of her bra. Her ass is so perfectly round, everything about her is fucking perfect.

As if she can hear the idea in my head she says, "You *cannot* rip these ones. This is my nice set." I hear the smirk in her voice as she says the last few words. *Her nice set.* I wonder how many other guys have seen it before. Actually, I don't give a shit if anyone else has seen her like this because right now *I* have her.

"What are you thinking about right now?"

I realize that I've been silently staring at her. "I'm torn whether I want you to keep this pretty little thing on while I bury my cock in you, or if I want to peel it off slowly, teasing you as I do it." My words come out thick with desire, and by the look on Vanessa's face, I know that she loves the husky tone.

"Did you bring your blue friend with you on the trip?"

My question causes her to immediately blush and tear her gaze away from mine.

"No…" *She lies so prettily.*

"Where is it?" I look around the room, finding her bag on the floor, tucked by the window. I walk over, shuffling her clothes around. I don't find her blue dildo, instead, tucked away in the front pocket, I find a tiny little purple vibrator.

Hmm, travel-sized. This will definitely come in handy.

"This little buddy and I are going to be great friends."

I toss the toy onto the bed and grab Vanessa. Her skin is cold from the night air, but it feels so good against my warmth. I mentally curse myself for not offering her my jacket on the walk over. I need to be a better gentleman.

I lay her down on the bed and my lips find their way back to her neck. I suck and nibble at her tender skin, trailing wet kisses down her body. The softest moans escape from Vanessa's mouth, encouraging me to go down farther—to the spot she really wants me to kiss.

I get to her lace panties but don't slip them aside. I would love to rip them off and offer to buy her a new pair, but I already promised to buy her new jeans because of my stunt earlier. Instead, I fan my hot breath over her, which makes her squirm under me. I place soft, featherlight kisses to her over her underwear. The intimate touch causes her to buck her hips, wanting more pressure.

I grab the small purple vibrator from the spot on the bed next to me. I turn it on, playing with the different settings. The toy has multiple vibrations, spanning from long and steady to short bursts, or a mix of the two.

"What do you prefer?" I ask. I always want to learn what gets her off.

Her cheeks are the prettiest shade of pink as she responds, "Long and steady."

"Of course you do."

I turn it on and place the purple toy directly on her clit. Vanessa immediately moans in pleasure, loving the way this feels against her swollen bud. I move the vibrator in small circles, making sure to keep just enough pressure without overwhelming her.

I use my other hand to slip under her panties and run my forefinger up and down her pussy. She coats my finger as it glides up and down, until I finally plunge into her. A gasp escapes her lips as I start to slowly thrust my finger in and out of her while simultaneously pleasing her with the vibrator.

Vanessa's fingers twine themselves in my hair, pulling gently on my curls. As I keep moving my finger in and out of her, I add a second finger.

"*Fuck,* please add another." Without any hesitation, I follow her command, and she moans in acceptance.

I accidentally move the vibrator a little lower and the sexiest rasp escapes her beautiful, parted lips. "Do you like that, baby?"

Her teeth bite down on her bottom lip as she nods.

I keep pumping my fingers and I can feel her pussy throbbing around them. "Jake, I'm gonna come."

"Good, come for me." I thrust my fingers deeper and rub the vibrator in a circular motion again, which sends her over the edge.

Her fingers move from my hair to my biceps, and she claws at me as she comes undone. Vanessa's body goes limp for a moment, and I allow her to enjoy the euphoria she's experiencing. I turn the vibrator off and toss it on the side table—I'm not done using that on her.

As I position myself next to her, she moves and peels my boxers from me. My dick practically springs free as the spandex material gets pulled off me.

I'll never get tired of the way Vanessa's eyes pop when she takes me in. I don't like to brag about how big my dick is because that's just an asshole move—but let's just say I'm packing enough that Vanessa's mouth waters as she debates how to proceed.

Her pretty white manicured fingers wrap around me, pumping me at an agonizing pace. Before another thought can make its way into my brain, she wraps those gorgeous plump lips around me.

Oh fuck, I could come just from her lips on me.

Vanessa's head bobs up and down as she takes me deep into her mouth. Most girls have issues fitting me all the way in, but Vanessa never backs down from a challenge. As her mouth works me, she has her hand still wrapped around my base, pumping as she moves up and down. The sensation sends a wave of pleasure through my own body and I can feel the familiar tingle in my lower back, telling me if she continues to do this even for another minute, I'm going to burst.

Slowly I lean up, cupping her face and bringing her to me.

"Please tell me you brought condoms." Her words are whispered against my lips.

My eyes scan the room until I find my jeans thrown haphazardly on the floor. "In my wallet, back pocket of my jeans.'

In an instant, Vanessa is upright scrambling through our discarded clothes until she finds the shiny wrapper.

She's back on the bed, ripping open the condom and sliding it down my dick. The feeling of her fingers on me again has me pushing back all the feral thoughts coursing through my head.

Vanessa adjusts her body, placing both legs on either side of mine. She holds my dick in place, slowly lowering herself onto me. The second the head of my dick enters her, I just about explode.

She wraps around me perfectly, as if she was molded just for me.

"Ness, *fuck,* that feels so good. Take all of me."

She follows my instructions and fully lowers herself onto me, taking me all the way in. Before I can even catch my breath, she's moving again. As she rides me, on the way down she grinds her pelvis into mine, which feels like fucking heaven.

Where has this girl been my entire life?

I put my hands on her hips, stopping her movements—because if I don't, I will bust right here. "Are you down to try something a little different, angel girl?"

She looks down at me with intrigue. "What do you have in mind?" Her voice is hoarse, filled with lust.

"Come to the edge of the bed and get on your hands and knees."

I move to stand at the end of the mattress, but make sure to grab the little purple toy on my way.

As I stand at the edge of the wooden bed frame, Vanessa positions herself so perfectly with her back arched. I trace small shapes on her ass, my thumbs gripping onto her soft skin by her hips.

I position myself at her entrance and enter her again. *Fuck*, it feels like coming home—as cliche as that sounds, I don't give a shit. I rock my hips, thrusting into her. Her hand immediately cups over her mouth, silencing her loud moans.

"Take your hand away right now. I wanna hear you moan my name so everyone on this floor knows who's making you come."

I grab the purple vibrator and turn it on—this time changing the setting to the small bursts of vibrations. My arm wraps around Vanessa's waist as I find her clit and hold the vibrator there.

"*Oh my god*, Jake." My name sounds smooth coming from her lips.

I thrust harder, burying my cock in her. I make sure to keep that vibrator pressed against her as I move my hips. That lower spot on my spine starts to tingle as I get closer to my own orgasm. My movements become quicker, building up to an intense release. As I am about to spill into the condom, Vanessa screams my name, clenching around me as she experiences her second orgasm of the night. My name coming from her lips will be my undoing.

Her pussy squeezes my dick and practically sucks the life out of me. As I come, my thrusts are hard and slow, wishing I was filling her and not the condom.

She exhausts herself, falling flat onto the bed. I fall right next to her, both of our breaths are shallow as our chests heave up and down from our workout.

"That…was amazing," she says in between breaths.

I peel the condom off, wrapping it in tissues and tossing it to the side for now.

"Yeah?" I lean on my side, resting my head on my closed fist.

"No one has ever used a toy on me while having sex. Most guys saw them as competition."

"Well, toys are my friends, not my enemy." Any guy who doesn't use them is scared that it'll outperform them. *Me?* I embrace them.

"Thank God for that." She smiles at me. Her big toothy grin sends a sharp tang in my chest.

We lie there for a moment, I stare at her as she looks up at the ceiling, mulling in the post-orgasm bliss. The only interruption is her phone lighting up on the nightstand. She leans over to look at the caller ID, immediately declining the call.

"Who's that?"

"My parents. They have been trying to get a hold of me to discuss our plans for Thanksgiving, but I don't want them to ruin my weekend." Vanessa peers up at me from her pillow. "I've had a lot of fun with you."

"I'm glad I was able to make your first visit to Nashville memorable."

She stares off into space, getting lost in the popcorn texture of the ceiling. I can tell that there's still something on her mind.

"What's on your mind, Nichols?"

It takes her a moment to come back to me.

She lets out a sigh. "I don't really want to go home for the holidays. I know exactly what it's going to be like. My mom is going to pretend that we live the perfect life in front of her family. My aunts will make comments on what I'm studying and my uncle will tell me that I'm wasting my life and my mom's money on a hobby. It's the same script every holiday."

I can't imagine how heavy this must weigh on her. Home is supposed to be comforting, filled with warmth. But Vanessa's family life sounds cold and harsh, filled with taunts and demeaning comments.

"I'm sorry that your parents are like that." There's not much else I can say to make her feel better. Some people have shitty situations and sometimes the best thing you can do is be an open ear for them. "Anything else you wanna get off your chest?" I try to change the subject, in hopes of making her forget about her family.

She quirks her mouth to the side, the way she does when she's stuck deep in thought. I've seen that look too many times during late-night study sessions.

"Well, there's been something on my mind, but I don't know."

"Ness, it's me, c'mon."

She bites her lower lip, taking her time. "Do you think maybe we could…never mind." She turns away from me for a moment, not wanting to make eye contact.

"What?" I press harder, wanting to know what she was about to say.

Vanessa turns back to me, her face has the familiar tinge of pink that she gets when she's flustered. "Feel free to say no, but I was thinking we could update the terms to our friends with benefits?"

I honestly have no idea what she's about to say, but whatever it is, I'm willing to do it for her.

"Like what?"

She fiddles with the blanket in her hands, twiddling her forefingers. "What if we were exclusively friends with benefits? So, I only sleep with you, and you only sleep with me. No jealousy or whatever that was tonight that caused you to rip my favorite pants."

272

When she offered the friends-with-benefits deal, it was like I had struck gold. But there's a selfish part of me that wants her all to myself.

I don't want to scare her by answering too fast, but I also don't want her to think that I want to see other people. Because I haven't been with a single person since we hooked up back in Vermont.

I rest my head on my fist. "You wanna make this a regular thing?"

She nods.

I steady my breath before answering. "I'd be cool with that."

Vanessa tries to hide her smile, but I get a glimpse of it before she directs her attention back to the ceiling. "Cool."

We lay together silently, and after a few minutes, I hear steady breathing indicating that she's asleep. I move slowly, trying to cause as little movement as possible, and grab my phone from my jeans.

Jake:

Is it cool if I bring a friend to breakfast?

Dad:

*Girlfriend? *peeking eye emoji**

Autumn:

Ooh is it the photographer?

Jake:

She's just a friend. Don't be weird about it. She was having a bad day and I thought you guys might cheer her up.

273

Mom:

Will the two of you stop teasing. Of course, she's
more than welcome to join us.

I tuck my phone back into my pocket and fall asleep with the small brunette in my arms.

CHAPTER TWENTY-FIVE

This is how it always goes

VANESSA

The light cascading through the open blinds wakes me before my alarm. Jake's arm is deadweight over my naked body, the thin white sheet draping low on his hips.

Last night was one of the best nights I've had in a while. Well, besides my parents constant interruptions.

My mom messaged me last night after I kept dodging her calls, asking for me to call her this morning. Normally I'd leave her on Read, but the *URGENT* and the *we pay your bills* is reason enough for me to reach out later. I've been avoiding them all weekend. I don't know how I'm going to get out of going home for the holiday weekend. Does it make me a bad daughter if I don't want to go?

I wonder what my relationship with my parents would be like if I became the girl they always wanted me to be. Someone who chooses her career based on money rather than something she enjoys doing. Maybe we would spend every holiday together, be able to laugh and joke with one another, we could have family dinners when they visit—maybe in another life they would've cared about my interests.

Seeing Jake with his parents this weekend, I got to witness what an actual loving and supportive family is like. I know that both of his parents are hard workers, but they still managed to come all the way to Nashville to watch their son play his favorite sport. Even his younger sister missed one of her recitals this weekend to be here.

Unconditional love and support from my family is something I've always yearned for, but I think it's time for me to come to terms that it will never happen. All I can do is fill my life with my chosen family, like Sydney and Maddie—even the boys at this point. I fill my life with people who actually care about me and my hobbies and don't put me down for wanting to break the norm of my family.

275

An alarm breaks my train of thought, some random chime of bells ringing loudly next to Jake.

Lazily, Jake turns over, lifting his arm off me to grab his phone and shut off the annoying sound. "Sorry," his deep voice mumbles, still half asleep.

"It's okay, I was already up," I say in a low tone, my voice still laced with sleep.

Jake moves to sit up in the bed, stretching his arms out wide and releases a sound that I can only describe as a groan mixed with a screech.

Slowly, he moves out of the bed and I get a peek at his very cute and very plump butt. They always say that boys who play baseball have the best butts, but I've seen enough athletes to know that hockey is definitely the supreme sport.

Every time I see him naked, I fight the urge to just take a little nibble of him.

"Do you wanna have breakfast with my family before we leave? They're just downstairs in the hotel restaurant." His voice is still groggy as he slips his jeans from last night back on.

His request takes me by surprise. I've heard countless stories about his family, so it feels like I already know them, but we haven't officially met yet. I watched them from afar this weekend, supporting Jake and his passion for hockey, but I never went up to them and introduced myself. Mainly because I have no idea if Jake has even mentioned me to them.

My stomach twists thinking of meeting them this morning, especially after sleeping with their son last night—it's a little unnerving.

"Uh, I—"

"It's okay if you don't want to meet them. I introduce all of my friends to my family 'cause they're a little intrusive with everything in my life." His confession lightens up the mood.

I wonder how they reacted to meeting Kieran. The dark and broody best friend. Or Nate, the stern but loving dad of the group. I'm sure meeting Eli and his bubbly himbo attitude made a good impression, and I can guarantee he hit on Mrs. Shepherd.

"No—I'd love to go for breakfast. I was just going to say that I need a minute to get dressed and pack my stuff."

I look around the room and realize that most of my belongings are already in my suitcase or are at least somewhat organized on the floor.

Jake chuckles at my awkwardness. "Take your time. I'm gonna run to my room to shower and change. Meet me in the lobby once you're ready." He pulls on his shirt and grabs his plaid jacket from the ground before heading out.

Okay, this is going to be fine. I'm sure his family is warm and welcoming, there's nothing to be afraid of. Well, except for them not liking me.

No, it'll be fine. It's just like when I had dinner with Maddie and her parents for the first time. We'll chat and laugh, and then it'll be over and I'll realize that I was stressing over nothing.

I find a pair of bootcut leggings and slip them on with a black sweater. We have a long bus ride home today, so as much as I want to look nice for Jake's parents, I also want to be comfortable for the ride back to campus. I brush my hair and my teeth and apply a tinted sunscreen to my face so I look a little more alive.

As I head out my door and down to the lobby, Jake is down the hallway with his bag in his hand, waiting for the elevator. He went for a similar outfit, gray sweatpants and his BCU hoodie. It's one of my favorites and I love wearing it every time I go to his place.

"My mom and sister both love to pry, so if they come across a little strong, that's just the way they are."

"Nosey, just like me." I do love to know what's going on in everyone's lives. I think I inherited that trait from Sydney.

We leave our bags outside next to our bus as everyone slowly wakes up and starts bringing their own luggage down.

As Coach Wilson walks out the front doors, we almost collide with him. He looks at Jake first, giving him a knowing nod, and then smiles at me. A sight not many people get to witness.

"Bus leaves at nine, so you make sure both of you are on it."

We head inside to the small restaurant that's attached to the hotel. Some of his teammates litter the tables, grabbing a quick bite before we all hit the road. I spot his family right away, sitting at the far booth next to a giant window, the morning sun peeking through the sheer curtains.

As we approach them, his parents both stand from their seats, immediately engulfing their son in a hug. It's bittersweet, standing behind them, watching parents hug one of their children that they love endlessly. I don't remember the last time I hugged either of my parents.

"Mom, Dad, this is Vanessa." Jake steps to the side, letting his parents see me.

I extend a hand out to his mom first, then his dad, whose grip is firm and fingers calloused just like Jake's.

"It's so nice to meet the two of you, Jake has told me so much about all of you."

The smiles on their faces are sweet and genuine as they motion for us to sit down, Jake taking the seat in between me and his sister. Jake and his dad immediately start talking hockey and my heart starts to beat at a more controlled pace as my anxiety starts to fade away.

"And I'm Autumn, but it seems my brother doesn't think I need an introduction." Her slender frame peeks out from behind Jake's chair, extending her well-manicured hand to mine.

"Ah, yes, the infamous Autumn. Jake's told me *a lot* about you." My mind flashes over all the information Jake has given me over the past month.

Autumn is a kind-hearted girl who has a passion for dance. She loves to tease Jake, but he has the biggest soft spot for her. I think she's one of the few people who Jake would do anything for. He told me that one year for Halloween he dressed up as a princess to go trick or treating with Autumn—like, c'mon, that's just *too* sweet.

"Hopefully he told you *good* things too."

"Maybe a little bit of both." I wink at her and she laughs. "It's really sweet of you to miss your dance recital to come out for Jake's tournament."

She flicks her hand, as if the gesture was nothing. "We already made it to regionals, this recital is just a chance for parents to see our routine before we perform in Philly. And my dance instructor loves me, so she didn't mind if I skipped this weekend."

She resembles Jake, but her attitude reminds me of Sydney. I wonder if Jake and Autumn bicker like Sydney and Nate do.

My phone buzzes on the table, rattling against the silverware. My mother's name flashes across the screen as I quickly silence the call, sending her to voice mail for the fifth time this week.

"Sorry," I mumble, but before anyone else can say anything, my phone immediately starts vibrating again.

Jake's mom stares at my phone with concern. "It's okay sweetie, you can answer it."

"I'm sorry, it'll only take a minute." I excuse myself from the table, silently cursing my parents for their impeccable timing.

I head to the hallway that leads to the bathroom so that Jake and his family can't overhear our conversation.

"Hello?" I answer quickly, annoyance clear in my tone.

"It's about time you answered." My dad's voice is curt on the other end. I hear the whisper of wind in the background and can immediately tell that they're both in the car, with me on speakerphone.

"Will you be joining us next weekend for Thanksgiving? Your Aunt Helen wants to host it at the Hamptons house. And since you missed the funeral, I'm sure everyone is expecting you to come." Her voice is stern, wanting to get an answer out of me quickly. Our conversations are never long.

I've already given thought to this upcoming holiday, and I've been dreading talking to my parents about it. We're getting to the end of the fall semester and I have a few big assignments coming up after the long weekend. I want to stay in the city and spend most of my time in my room. I'll order myself a pizza on Thanksgiving and watch the Macy's Parade by myself.

"Yeah, I don't know if I can make it, I have a huge project due for my social media class—"

"Social media? How does that even qualify as a course? You should rethink changing your major if you want to find a career when you graduate."

Her words are sharp, slicing small cuts into me. She does this every time we have a conversation. Mom always tries to make me feel like I'm doing the wrong thing and making horrible life choices. I thought that by now I'd be used to my parents' disapproval, but every now and again a pang of guilt swallows me whole, making me feel like I'm a failure.

"If it makes you feel better, I'm still taking a political science course every semester like you asked, but you *know* that I'm pursuing photography."

I hear a scoff on the other end of the phone, and then I hear my dad's calming voice in the background, trying to advocate for me. "At least she's taking some realistic classes. You never know, she could always change her mind."

This is how it always goes. My dad will pretend to support me, but once Mom hints at any sign of disapproval, he immediately shifts his opinion to agree with her. I'm always fighting the two of them alone. Some days I wish I had a sibling to share the burden of my family with. But then I feel selfish for wishing that upon someone else.

"No, Dad, I'm not going to change my mind. I've loved photography my entire life, why is this so hard for the two of you to accept?" I wish that they understood my passion, or at least pretended to care.

"I'll just tell the family she's busy with a case study and doesn't want to jeopardize her education." As if they ignored everything I just said.

"*Or* you could just tell them the truth." The words come out low, almost a whisper, as if I didn't really want them to hear me.

"And become the laughingstock of the family? I don't think so." Mom huffs out a breath before continuing, "Why can't you be more like your cousins? Mark is interning on Wall Street, Theo is finishing his last year of undergrad and starts his residency at Johns Hopkins next year, and even little Sarah got accepted into MIT for computer science. Do you know how embarrassing it is when they ask us what you're up to? While you're wasting away your education taking photos and partying, your cousins are getting their lives together. So, no, Vanessa, I will not be telling them the truth. If I did, I would never hear the end of it, especially from Aunt Helen."

Yeah well, Aunt Helen is a megabitch.

Sometimes I wonder if Mom ever gets exhausted trying to meet and uphold the standards of our family. She loves comparing me to my cousins because they're all following the life plan that their parents perfectly laid out for them while I've rejected mine since the day I learned the word *no*.

I'll never meet the standards of my family. Instead, I'll be the castaway. *The black sheep.* Eventually I'll stop being invited to events and I'll be the one who they whisper about during family gatherings. The saddest part of it all is that I'm used to it by now. I always get compared to my family. Someone is always outperforming me or doing something worthy of my family's attention. No one cares about me or what I've done. When I had my photographs displayed at a gallery back in high school, none of my family members showed up. They all claimed to have a valid excuse to not be present.

No matter what I do or how much I try to appease them, I know deep down that it'll never be enough. *I'll never be enough.*

I don't allow my parents to continue their teardown, so I end the conversation. "I'm sorry that you're so embarrassed by me that you feel the need to lie about my life. And I'm sorry I missed the funeral, but I won't be coming home for Thanksgiving, use whatever excuse you want."

My finger slams on the screen, ending the call. One single tear slips from my eye and I quickly bat it away not realizing how worked up I got during our conversation. One day I'm going to confront my family. I'll find the courage to tell them all off and make a life of my own without them.

I take a couple of deep breaths to soothe myself before I make my way back to the table. My face is smiling but everything else feels heavy. Sunken. *Empty.*

"Is everything alright with your parents?" Mrs. Shepherd asks innocently. Her gaze is tender, concerned—like a parent should be. She has no idea what my family is like, so I force a smile and shove down the dark feeling.

My relationship with my parents is rocky, but I never thought that they would blatantly lie to my family about my life.

It makes me feel like a disappointment.

Instead of spilling this to Jake's parents, I lock the feeling away so I can deal with it later. "Oh yes, my mom was checking in before the holidays."

"Are you spending Thanksgiving with your folks?" His dad's question tugs at my heartstrings.

I wish so badly that holidays with my family would be like everyone else's. Everyone would get together around a squished dinner table, trading stories about their lives and being grateful for everything that we have. Instead, my family gatherings consist of low whispers and judgmental looks.

"I'm actually staying in the city for Thanksgiving. My family travels a lot, so sometimes plans change unexpectedly."

It's not technically a lie—but I don't think breakfast is an appropriate time to air my family's dirty laundry.

Jake rests his hand on my knee under the table and gives it a small squeeze, silently letting me know that he's here for me. I'm sure he could tell by my expression when I got back to the table that it wasn't a good conversation.

"Well, you're more than welcome to come to our home for the holiday. It's not like we haven't hosted some of Jake's friends before, we have more than enough space."

His mom's offer warms my heart. It's not often you'll find someone willing to extend an invite to a girl they just met.

"No-no, I don't want to intrude."

Jake's dad interjects, "Nonsense. You and Jake can come out next Friday and spend the weekend. We love hosting. Hopefully the remaining leaves stay on the trees for another week. We've had such a lovely fall season so far."

I look at Jake and he smiles at me. His family is genuinely sweet and they're not offering for me to join them because I'm his girlfriend but because I'm simply his *friend*. It would be rude of me to decline.

"Okay, thank you for inviting me, Mr. and Mrs. Shepherd."

"Please, all of Jake's friends call us by our names—Amelia and Parker."

I give his mom a warm smile.

I spend the rest of breakfast listening to Jake tell his family about school and his other friends. They're attentive the whole time, listening to everything that he's saying. Autumn makes comments here and there, casually teasing Jake.

Maybe spending a holiday with an actual loving and supportive family will be exactly what I need.

I've never been more grateful to be back at school and not cramped on a Greyhound with tired, grumpy hockey players. I think my butt is permanently numb from those seats.

We got home early Monday morning and I ended up staying the night at Jake's house, not wanting to Uber from the campus back home or risk waking up Sydney or Maddie. Waking up for my class the next morning was brutal. I think the only reason I got out of bed was because of the aroma of the coffee beans wafting up the stairs from the kitchen. Jake brewed an extra-strong pot so we could all survive the day.

As I shove another salt and vinegar chip into my mouth, our front door whips open and Sydney walks in, her hands overflowing with textbooks, her laptop, notes, and other school supplies.

"Where the hell is your bag?"

She tumbles into the living room, dropping her belongings onto the couch next to me. "It broke! I was walking on campus and all of a sudden, *poof.*" Her hands flare like a firework. "All of my shit fell out and I had to carry it all back here." Sydney plops on the couch and dramatically flails her arms up, clearly agitated. "Ugh, anyway." She sits up and clears her throat before yelling, "Maddie! Get your ass out here."

It's silent for a moment, but then we hear the click of Maddie's door open and her footsteps rush to us on the couch.

"Oh good, we're all finally home." Maddie takes a seat, joining us. "All right, girl, fill us in on everything since you barely responded to our texts all weekend."

My cheeks blush thinking about the events of the weekend. I don't know where to start, so I spill everything to them in the span of thirty minutes, not sparing any details, even the nitty gritty stuff.

"Wait wait wait, so Jake punched him because he said he wanted to fuck you?"

"Yeah, something along those lines. He didn't want to go into *all* the details with me because he said it would make me vomit, so I let it go."

Sydney fans her face. "Wow, that's hot. If my friends-with-benefits companion punched a guy in his face for making a gross comment, I'd be naked in a heartbeat."

I roll my eyes at her. She believes that Jake and I are meant to be after I told them about our night spent walking around with each other.

Maddie sits quietly in the corner of the couch, picking at the skin of her nail beds. She only does this when she has something to say but is choosing to keep quiet.

"What's wrong?"

She looks up at me and then to Sydney, silently communicating before her eyes finally land back on me, giving me a stressed look. "That sounds very *boyfriend* to me. Same with meeting his parents *and* inviting you to Thanksgiving."

The honesty of Maddie's observation hits me. I've been trying to not think about it that way. Is going to Jake's home for Thanksgiving a step too far? A part of me is curious and wants to go. I'm almost excited to see his childhood home and the town where he grew up. I want to see old photo albums and the way he decorated his room.

Maddie's eyes go wide. "*Oh my god!* Are you guys dating?" Her face immediately turns to joy, Sydney's eyes popping at the accusation.

"No! No way." The excitement immediately fades from them as I continue, "We're just not sleeping with other people."

Sydney's brow raises. "So you're dating without labels?"

Maddie nods her head, agreeing with Sydney's question.

"Well...no. We're still friends with benefits, but now we're exclusively sleeping together."

"That's basically dating."

"Yeah, you guys hang out all the time, sleep together, study together. Didn't you say that he brought you a latte to practice? Sounds a lot like a relationship to me." Maddie agrees.

"Can we move on?"

It's not that I'm fully against relationships. But every time I feel like I'm ready to open myself up to someone, fear freezes me in place. Maybe one day I'll allow myself that kind of happiness.

"Okay, fine, we'll move on. You mentioned your parents called you at breakfast, what did Veronica and William have to say now?" Maddie spits their name out like acid.

She's never respected my parents because of the way they treat me. She and Sydney both have two parents who are very involved in their lives—sometimes I can see the pity in their eyes when I tell them childhood stories.

I take a deep breath before I open that wound. "Let's sum it up for you—I'm an embarrassment of a daughter, they told me that they constantly lie about my life to my family, and I'll never be enough for them." My voice hitches at the end of my statement, coming out more like a hiccup.

Sydney moves next to me and wraps me in a hug. "I'm sorry they're so shitty to you. Just know that *we* are both very proud of you and everything you've accomplished. Your family might not see how amazing and unique and gifted you are, but your friends see you."

I stifle a sob. I truly have the best friends on this planter. And Sydney's right, I don't need my parents approval. The only people whose opinions I care about are sitting in this room with me, showing me their unconditional love.

CHAPTER TWENTY-SIX

Even the dark bits

VANESSA

I've never been to Cape Cod before.

Growing up in New York, our summers were spent in the Hamptons—with extravagant parties, nights spent at the country club, and the occasional yacht hopping. That is, if my parents weren't on one of their excessive trips.

Cape Cod seems to be a popular summer home spot for residents of Massachusetts, but for Jake's family, it's their home all year round.

On our drive over, Jake told me more about his family and his childhood home. When his parents were young, before Jake was even a thought, they bought their small home in Falmouth—a small coastal town. The house only had two bedrooms, but as their family grew, so did the house.

Mr. Shepherd is a general contractor who owns his own construction business, Park and Renovations, so he's added multiple updates to their house over the years. Apparently he even renovated their old garage into a bar and converted the upstairs to a loft, where Jake permanently moved his room when he was a teenager.

My brain is trying to put the pieces together and imagine what the house looks like, but all I can conjure up is an all-white house with a picket fence and blue accents.

Lots of the homes we've driven by have alabaster siding and look like they were plucked out of an American colonial magazine. There are still some leaves on the trees, highlighting dull tones of yellows, oranges, and reds. All the flowers and gardens have become barren, awaiting the next spring to bloom again.

I can feel the heat of Jake's gaze on me as I look out the window, taking in the scenery. I know he's watching me, but I'm too busy being amazed by all the different shades of fall. No one appreciates fall because everyone views it as the *dying season*. All I can see is beauty.

The deep green blending into different hues of red, yellow, and brown. All the colors contrast each other giving a sense of warmth and comfort.

In New York, there's nothing but concrete—gray and cold. Skyscrapers, sidewalks, cars, and a small hint of greenery in Central Park. I'll always have a soft spot for New York, but Boston has my heart.

"I can't believe you got to grow up out here, in this *place*."

I imagine his parents teaching him how to ride a bike on a quiet street, no busy roads or honking taxis in the way. His dad probably set up a hockey net in their driveway for him to practice during the off season—something you could only do with a large yard at your disposal.

I turn to face Jake, whose face is frozen in a grin. I love his smile. The way the sides of his mouth tug upward, showing off one dimple.

He catches my staring and I feel the heat rise in my cheeks.

"I spent my teenage years at a prep school in Boston, where I stayed in a dorm, but nothing beats coming home. Except for the traffic, that's always the worst part."

"I come from New York, traffic is nothing new to me."

"It normally takes less than two hours to get to the Cape from Boston, but during the summer and holidays it's the *worst*. If you don't cross the bridge early enough, you'll be stuck in bumper-to-bumper traffic listening to the same radio commercials on repeat."

I imagine Jake making this drive alone, stuck in traffic, in a grumpy mood, listening to those endless infomercials they play about injury lawyers or loans.

"Well, hopefully I made this trip more bearable for you."

He takes one hand off the wheel and intertwines it with mine, rubbing gentle circles across my hand. "You *definitely* made it more enjoyable." There's a hint of teasing in his tone and I know it's from when I unzipped his pants and took him into my mouth when we were on one of the less crowded parts of the highway.

As we get off the main road, we follow the winding pavement, until finally Jake slows down in a neighborhood that's completely lined with trees. This place must be beautiful in the spring and summer with flowers sprouting and the green leaves canopying the streets, swaying in the wind. It looks like it was plucked out of a fairy tale.

"And this is home." He points to the house on the right, nestled between two other similar style houses. They all have that timeless Cape Cod architecture.

We pull into the long gravel driveway and suddenly my heart tightens.

Am I nervous?

I shouldn't be, especially since I've already met them, but I have no idea what to expect from this weekend. Spending a meal with his family is much different from spending a whole three days together.

The air is crisp with the late autumn weather, but there's still a hint of sea breeze wafting over that makes me wish it was still summer. I can imagine myself settling down in a place like this—propping my windows open so the smell of the Atlantic would fill my home.

I notice every detail of the house as we step out of the car. The main part of the house is all white siding and a grayish blue stone with a covered front porch that has one of those swinging benches. *I've always wanted one of those.* Imagine being able to curl up with a blanket and a coffee, and just swing while watching the neighborhood. I'm a sucker for people-watching, it's one of my favorite pastimes.

The bright white siding is accented by hints of dark navy trim on their doors and windows. The front yard is landscaped beautifully with colorful chrysanthemums in the garden and on the porch, and two big shrubs that are precisely trimmed.

My shoes crunch the gravel beneath my feet as I walk around Jake's Jeep to grab my bag from the trunk.

His neighborhood looks like it belongs in a Hallmark movie with giant trees in every yard, canopying the streets. All the houses have pumpkins, hay barrels, and other fall decor beautifully laid out.

This is what home *should* feel like, and I can't help but feel a little envious of Jake and the life that he has. The life that I've always wanted—a cozy home with a loving and supportive family.

Jake grabs both of our bags from the car, even after I protested that I could carry my own things, and leads us into the house. We walk up steps that lead us to a patio. There's a full living set with two couches, a couple chairs, a gas fire pit, and a flat-screen TV jacked to the wall. To the left of the patio, there are a few steps and a small porch that connects to what I'm assuming is Jake's loft above the garage.

We go past the furniture and dining set and head into the main house.

As we step inside, I get the full Cape Cod experience. The color scheme from outside floats directly in, with ivory walls, light gray couches, and navy blue touches everywhere. On one wall there's a massive stone fireplace with a sailboat sitting on the wooden mantle. The nautical theme is spread throughout the room in paintings and other decor to match.

"We're here!" Jake's voice echoes before we hear a response coming from further in the house.

"In the kitchen!"

Jake drops our bags by the door and motions his head to the right, silently telling me where to go.

We pass through an open entryway that leads into the open-concept kitchen and dining area that's renovated to the nines with state-of-the-art appliances and beautiful white marble countertops. This is a chef's wet dream.

In the middle of the room, partially covered in flour, is Mrs. Shepherd kneading bread.

"Hi, honey, how was the drive?" She has the cutest pink and white polka-dot apron fastened around her waist, and this is when all the aromas infiltrate my nose. There are hints of rosemary, thyme, and flavored oil.

"Hit a little traffic at the bridge, but smooth sailing after that." He walks around the island, giving his mom a hug.

More like suffocating his mom in a hug because Jake towers over her.

"Good, well, I hope the two of you are hungry. I'm just finishing the dough for tomorrow and then we can eat some dinner. Your dad made his famous chili for you."

"I *love* his chili." Jake's eyes are now filled with hunger as he eyes the pot on the stove. "Speaking of which, where is Dad?"

Both of us swivel our heads around, and I peek into the adjoining room, which seems to be another living room, but it's empty.

"Your dad had to quickly go into work to finish up some things, but he'll be home before dinner." Mrs. Shepherd wipes her hands on her apron and walks over to the door situated next to the dining area. She opens the door and yells down, "Autumn, come upstairs and say hello to your brother and Vanessa."

"I'm practicing my choreography! They won't miss my company."

Jake walks over to the open door, leaning his head down the staircase. "Autumn, we picked up some truffles and other desserts from Eataly on our way over, but I guess since you don't care we'll just enjoy them ourselves." He turns around and gives his mom a knowing look.

Within seconds I hear footsteps race up the stairs and Autumn runs into the kitchen, going right for the box of treats on the counter. She's wearing a matching turquoise workout set, her hair is tied up in a bun, with some shorter strands stuck to her neck with sweat.

"Did I ever tell you that you're my favorite brother?"

"I'm your only brother."

Autumn shrugs her shoulders as she shoves a tiramisu truffle in her mouth and mumbles out a thank-you before she runs back downstairs to finish practicing.

"Jake, why don't you give Vanessa a tour while I finish with dinner?"

His attention falls on me and he raises one of his thick eyebrows. "Do you wanna see the house?"

My head nods, maybe too eagerly. I want to see old photo albums, the place where he took his first steps, his first bedroom. I want to see it all and hear every story that comes with it.

Jake grabs my hand and leads us into the adjoining family room. Tucked into the corner by the sofa are boxes labeled DECORATIONS, patiently waiting to be opened and put up after the fall holidays are over.

"You should see this place at Christmas. Mom loves to decorate, so we have a tree in almost every room."

"Vanessa, don't listen to him! We only have *three* trees, and he always makes us wait to decorate them until he's home."

Blush creeps into Jake's cheeks as his mom yells from the kitchen.

I feel so happy being here. I wish it was Christmas and I could help set up the trees and decorate them with Jake. Maybe Sydney, Maddie, and I will get one this year and I can invite Jake and some of the guys over to decorate the place together. We could make a whole day of it with hot chocolate and Christmas music. I can already see Maddie's face turn with disgust when I put the music on. She royally hates Christmas and everything surrounding it.

We make our way through the entire house and I feel like we're on an episode of *House Hunters*. The bathrooms have all been updated, one with a beautiful clawfoot tub that I want to soak in. Each room is a different combination of white linens and blue walls. Normally blue is a more depressing color, but in their home, it brings the place to life.

Their basement seemed never ending, with a long hallway that leads into yet another living room. But this one is definitely more suited to his sister's taste—light pastels make the room feel bigger and not like you're underground. In the middle of the room, there's a white shag rug and an off-white couch strewn with pink pillows across it.

The living room leads to an attached bathroom and bedroom that Autumn currently occupies. Upstairs, they converted Jake's old room into a guest room—which is where I assumed I would stay. But apparently that's not the case.

Jake pulls me across the patio to his loft where the both of us will be staying for the weekend.

I wonder if his parents are okay with this.

He opens the door for me, but I had no idea what I was expecting on the other side.

The floors are gray carpet that's soft against bare feet. Next to the front door is a small bench and a walk-in closet, and directly across is a bathroom, decked out with a giant glass shower. The whole loft is open concept, with a mini fridge tucked in the corner next to a dark gray sectional. Along the wall across from the couch are two double-sized beds, fitted with fresh sheets that smell like lavender.

"This is like the ultimate bachelor pad." I collapse onto one of the beds, and my body sinks into the memory foam mattress.

Jake runs his fingers through his curls. "Yeah, it's a pretty sweet place. I used to have my friends over in the off season, it was easier if all of us could stay in one spot so we didn't disturb anyone in the house."

He sits down at the end of the bed, pulling me closer to him.

"Now as much as I would *love* to spend the rest of the day in bed with you, there's more to show you."

I groan as he heaves the two of us up from the bed, my body not wanting to leave.

Jake takes me downstairs to their old garage that their dad renovated. There's a huge bar made from white oak, with dark granite fitted on the top. The whole place is decorated in a rustic theme with dark wooden stools to compliment the lightness of the bar.

There's not one, not two, but *three* TVs pinned to the walls.

"Dad wanted us to be able to watch multiple games at once. He brought the sports bar home so we could all spend more time together."

I can't believe his dad converted their garage into a sports bar so he could spend more time with his son. He'd really do anything to get some quality time with his family.

Along the back wall there's an assortment of different arcade games, spanning from Pac-Man to pinball machines. I can only imagine how many wild nights and fun stories Jake and his family have in this garage.

"One time, my dad invited all of his workers over for a summer party and had me and two of my friends bartend." He saunters behind the bar with that goofy grin on his face, and starts pouring a bottle of rum from the shelf. "We made at least two hundred bucks each, and my dad got so hammered that he fell asleep in one of those stools." He points at the stool I decided to sit on and passes me a drink.

Rum and coke.

He knows me too well by now.

"My mom came down here in the morning and he was still passed out. I don't think he'll ever drink that much ever again."

"You bet your ass I won't." Mr. Shepherd's voice sounds from the door. *When the hell did he even get here?* "Vanessa, lovely to see you again."

I tilt my drink toward him. "It's nice to see you, too, Mr. Shepherd."

"Vanessa, you don't need to call me Mr. Shepherd. Parker is just fine." I feel the blush in my cheeks as he walks behind the bar, clapping Jake on the shoulders, giving him a hug. He grabs an empty pint glass and starts filling it with whatever beer they have on tap.

"Jake, how's the season going so far?" He grabs his glass and walks around the bar, taking the stool next to me.

"Fucking phenomenal. We've only lost two games this season, so not a bad start. Eli and I are *crushing* it this year. I have a feeling we're going to win the championship this year."

The smile that splays on Jake's face is full of hope and confidence. I can tell just by looking at Mr. Shepherd—*Parker*—that he's proud of his son.

Jake is doing something that most people are scared to do—following his heart and pursuing his dreams. He's lucky to have support along the way.

I sip on my drink quietly as I listen to Jake catch up with his dad.

"And how are you doing with school? Grades?"

"Same as every year, maintaining my three point eight GPA and all assignments submitted on time. How's the business? I'm shocked to see there's no renos going on at home right now."

His dad lets out a hearty laugh. "Oh, trust me, I'm sure there's something on your mother's to-do list for me."

They go back and forth for a while, discussing business plans, hockey statistics, and discussing *Star Wars* theories. I'm so wrapped up in their conversation that I barely notice Mrs. Shepherd and Autumn enter the room.

"Dinner's ready!" Mrs. Shepherd calls as she swings the door closed with her foot. She places a giant pot of chili down onto the bar top while Autumn is behind her with bowls and cutlery.

Jake leans over to me. "Dad's chili is the *best*. Just wait until you try it."

"I don't want Vanessa to get her hopes up."

"Don't worry, Mr. Shepherd—"

"Parker."

"Right, *Parker*, I can promise you it'll be better than anything my family has made."

I try to remember any time my parents made a home-cooked meal, but it was very few and far between.

My parents worked religiously, Dad always being on call and Mom always busy with a case. The only time we had family meals together was the holidays.

"Are your parents bad cooks or something?"

"Autumn!" Their parents are clearly taken aback by her bluntness. Her question makes me laugh, thinking of my parents attempting to use a pot or spatula.

"*What?*"

"It's fine," I reassure them. "My parents don't cook much. We had an in-house chef who prepared most of our meals, and on days he didn't, I would usually pick something up on my way home from school. My parents were always working, so dinners at home was few and far between."

"What do your parents do for work?" Parker asks.

"My mom's one of the lead lawyers at her firm and Dad's a doctor at Manhattan General."

Autumn's eyes go wide. "Yikes, and here I thought our parents' work lives were busy. Do you have any siblings?"

I shake my head. "Nope. It's just me."

I watch as the curious smile on Autumn's face fades as she imagines my life at home.

I don't like sharing too much, but being around Jake makes me feel comfortable and safe, and I get the same feeling from his family. Seeing their concerned faces and knowing how generous and sweet they were to me in Nashville, I feel like I owe them a part of me, even if it's small. That's something I can do.

"I'm not very close with my family. Things like *this*..." I use my spoon to motion to all of us sitting together at the bar. "We never did things like family dinners. We never sat with each other and talked about my hobbies, my friends, or really anything that was going on in my life. The most conversation my parents would get out of me is asking about my GPA and if I decided to pursue a real career. You guys are lucky to have such great parents."

I shove a spoonful of chili into my mouth to stop me from continuing. It's not overbearingly spicy, but there is definitely a kick. With a medley of steak and ground beef mixed with vegetables and beans, this is phenomenal.

"What would you like to pursue?" Mrs. Shepherd haphazardly asks.

The idea of being a freelance photographer brings an immediate smile to my face. Being able to share my photos with other people is my dream. To see my photos displayed in one of the magazines I idolized growing up, would be the ultimate goal.

"I enjoy photography. I've been applying to a few internships in hopes I can spend the summer building a better portfolio that's not just school assignments. My dream is to be a photographer for National Geographic or another nonprofit, environmental-based organization."

"That's why she's our social media coordinator. It's an assignment for one of her class projects. You should see the stuff she's been doing. The photos and videos she takes of us are so fucking cool. Maybe sports photography is your secret calling, Ness."

I stir the meat and vegetables around in my bowl. "I like trying different styles. Who knew sports photography could be so fun."

"My favorite photo she took is of the campus at the beginning of fall. The changing colors on the trees next to the student center and the ivy on the building…she definitely has a gift." He winks at me. How the hell did he find that photo?

Jake's words tug deep down into me. Hearing someone talk so positively about my work is something I'm not used to.

"You snooped through my things?"

He shrugs, acting as if it's not a big deal. Although a tiny part of me is annoyed he did, there's a part of me that's glad that he saw them.

Jake grabs his phone from his pocket and opens up his camera roll to show his parents all the photos he's saved.

He has a whole album titled *Vanessa's* and it's filled with photos from games and practices. The further he scrolls, the more photos I see that he must've sent himself from my phone. There are photos in the album that I took years ago. Some from my backpacking trip to Portugal, a couple from Central Park—but my favorite is the photo I took that night in Nashville. It's a photo of Jake and I hiding behind our slices of pizza. I can't believe he saved all of these.

"Vanessa, these are beautiful!"

"I should have you take photos of the houses we build and upload them to our website. These are really great."

I try hard not to blush, but I'm horrible at controlling my own emotions. "Thank you."

Hearing the compliments from his parents makes me feel validated in a way. I've never gotten my own parents' approval, so having someone else tell me that I'm doing a good job fills a parent-sized hole in my life.

The five of us fall into a comfortable conversation. Autumn tells me about the drama going on at her high school—looking for a prom dress, the ongoing friend and boy drama, and the never-ending cycle of popularity. Listening to her ramble on makes me realize that I don't miss those days at all.

Mrs. Shepherd tells us about her flower shop and how busy it gets around the holidays. She goes into detail about the special flowers she had to order because they're not in season anymore, and how her clientele has increased heavily since she made a website and social media accounts for her shop.

Mr. Shepherd spends a while talking about his business and how they just got a contract to build a few houses on Martha's Vineyard, and then the conversation switches to Jake and hockey.

I get a little lost in the technical terms but from what I've picked up, Jake's agent is talking with the New Jersey Demons about bringing him up potentially before the year is over.

When his dad mentions that last part, I can't help but feel a little upset. I've loved building my friendship with Jake and I'm scared that the second he gets his dream, he'll leave me behind—just like everyone else seems to do.

I have to keep reminding myself that Jake isn't like everyone else. He's not like my parents. He's proven that time and time again. I push that small feeling of dread far, *far* down, and enjoy the rest of my dinner with this family.

By the end of the night, I've come to one conclusion, I don't think I ever want to leave this place—this house, this family. *Jake.*

The weekend flew by quicker than I imagined.

After our laid-back Friday, we spent all of Saturday at Martha's Vineyard—a beautiful, and expensive, island off the coast of Cape Cod. I'm almost 100 percent positive that I saw Taylor Swift's mansion along the cliffside, but all of the multimillion-dollar mansions looked the same.

We ate at a delicious seafood restaurant along the water, shopped until my wallet hurt, and ended the day with saltwater taffy and a ferry ride at sunset. Jake bought us matching sweaters, which he insisted we take photos in. I may currently have it as his contact photo. It was previously a photo of him shoving a hotdog in his mouth after one of their home games, but I feel like this is more fitting.

This morning we were all a little tired after last night's festivities. When we got back from Martha's Vineyard, we settled into the dining room and played euchre until one in the morning. Normally I have no issue staying up late, but when you have to be up early the next day to start prepping a huge holiday dinner...yeah, it probably wasn't the wisest idea.

After delaying our wake-up by an hour, we found ourselves in the kitchen with Jake's parents. Mrs. Shepherd was up before us all, probably before the sun rose, working in the kitchen preparing for tonight's feast. They have a huge dinner planned for us, including homemade sourdough, a spiced turkey, stuffing, mashed potatoes, sweet potatoes, and parmesan-covered asparagus.

The one specialty I have is my brussels sprout salad, which I usually make during the holidays. I shred up brussels sprouts and bake them, then I toss them in a bowl with some toasted cashews and drizzle a homemade balsamic glaze over top. When I told Mrs. Shepherd about it, she was so excited to try it, she sent Autumn and Mr. Shepherd out this morning to get the ingredients for me to make it.

To be included in family activities is something I've longed for my whole life. When I would make this dish for my own family gatherings, it normally got picked over. Now that I'm thinking about it, I don't think anyone has ever complimented me on it. So hopefully it's not terrible.

Autumn lines the dining room table with fancy white and blue china, silver cutlery, and napkins that she folds into small swans.

The aroma of the food wafts over as we finish setting everything on the table. The rich spices coming off the turkey have my mouth watering like a dog looking at a steak. The garlic mashed potatoes look so light and fluffy, I know that those will be my demise tonight.

"Vanessa and I are gonna go wash up before we eat, we'll be right back." Jake grabs my hand and pulls us away from the room, leading us back to the loft.

"Are we actually washing up or were you just tired of listening to me and Autumn talk?"

I stand in the middle of the room, waiting to see if he's going to the washroom or if he has an ulterior motive for bringing us out here.

"Definitely the second one. But I also wanted to do this." He pulls me into him, tipping my chin up with his hand, and kisses me. Not just a regular kiss either. *No,* this is more intimate and softer. His kiss isn't hungry like last night when we were ripping each other's clothes off.

He pulls away and twists my arm so I twirl around him. "And did I tell you how fucking sexy you look in that outfit today?"

I look down at what I chose for today. I tried to look nice without overdoing it. I traded my regular jeans for dark green corduroy pants and paired them with a cream fisherman sweater. I added a simple golden necklace and a few rings to pull the look together. This isn't something *I* would consider sexy. I think Jake's hunger has gone to his brain and has taken over all rational thinking.

"You clean up nicely yourself."

He really does.

I'm used to seeing Jake in jeans and a sweater or a hockey jersey. Today he also decided to dress to impress. He's wearing black dress pants with a tight-fitting white tee and a sherpa lined denim jacket.

He doesn't just look hot, he looks so *handsome.*

Is it wrong of me to secretly hope that he dresses like this from now on?

"I just wanted to thank you for coming this weekend. You didn't have to accept my parents' invitation, but they're really happy that you did. *I'm* really happy that you did."

"I'm happy I came too. Your parents, they're so—"

"Weird? Nerdy? Obsessed with their kids?"

I laugh because even though his parents are all three of those things, especially his dad and his *Star Wars* collection, that's not what I was getting at. "No, that's not what I was gonna say."

"Sorry, continue." He sits down on the couch, playfully crossing one leg over the other and putting his hands in his lap, as if he's waiting for me to finish speaking before moving again.

"I was saying that they're so generous and kind hearted. I can see where you get your mushy side from." I see the red creep into Jake's cheeks before he puts on a neutral face, "They're really great people and I'm glad I've gotten to know them and your sister. Your family has made me feel more welcomed than mine ever has."

His face softens, the sharp features of his jaw and eyebrows eases, and he pulls me down to him on the couch.

"I hope you always feel like you're wanted when you're with me, Ness."

His words linger between us, and for a second I melt into them, kissing him again.

Jake kisses me tenderly, and this time I'm the one who's hungry. Hungry for him but also hungry for food, and my grumbling stomach interrupts us.

"I guess it's time for dinner." He smirks up at me.

We get off the couch and head back inside where the table is fully set and ready for us to devour.

The late November air decided to take a drastic turn by the time we arrived at the beach.

During the day, the sun kept the wind at bay, but now that only the moon and stars are out, the warm autumn air has turned brutal and cold.

I always thought that northeastern winters were brutal, but I never realized how cold towns along the coast can get. There are no big skyscrapers or busy streets to block out the harsh winds. Instead, the cold seeps into your bones and settles so deep that it feels like you'll get frostbite if you leave anything exposed for too long.

Luckily for me, Jake came prepared. Growing up out here, he knows exactly how to stay warm. He brought three blankets—one to sit on, and one for each of us to snuggle into, and made sure we bundled up in thick jackets and plopped a hat on both of our heads.

We brought a thermos that was filled with hot chocolate, and maybe a splash of Kahlua, that's now drunk dry, and our container of dessert sits next to us, empty. We devoured our pumpkin pie the moment we sat down. Who could blame us though? I think Amelia should change professions and become a baker rather than a florist.

I don't know how long we've been out here, but by the chill that's nipping at my fingertips, I can tell it's been well over an hour. I left my phone back at the house, but I don't feel like looking at the time anyway. I want to stay right here sitting in between Jake's legs.

"This is my favorite place to visit when I'm home." Jake breaks the silence. "When I was younger, my parents used to fight a lot, so I would sneak out at night to come here. I'd sit on the beach, listening to the crashing of the waves and studying the stars. It's where my interest in astronomy started. I'd come out here to look at the sky and suddenly nothing would feel heavy anymore. I would forget about everything and just breathe and find constellations."

His vulnerability hits home. Out of all of the conversations we've had, he's never talked about this before.

"If you look here"—he gently guides my chin upward and points with his index finger—"you can see the Big Dipper, and then if you lightly move your eyes down, you can see the little dipper. Those were the first two constellations I found—mainly because they're the easiest to locate."

I know how to find the Big Dipper, but I don't tell him that. I love all of Jake's little quirks. Everything from his morning peppiness to his love for stars and space.

"How often did you come out here?"

"One summer I came here almost every night. I borrowed a book from the library about constellations for beginners, and I bought an old telescope from a yard sale and just spent as much time out of the house as possible."

"Did your parents fight a lot?"

A subtle frown settles in his features. "When I was younger, yeah. That's one of the reasons why they put me and Autumn in so many extracurriculars. That way we'd be out of the house as much as possible." I remember one of our first conversations, he said that his dad put him into hockey to keep him busy. I never knew it was because of how hard things were at home. Looking at his parents now, I would've never guessed they had issues before.

It's crazy how much you can learn about someone in such a short period of time. A few months ago, I would have never expected Jake to be someone who loves to point out constellations. I expected him to be some glorified playboy who thought he was a gift to this earth.

Jake takes a deep breath, as if he's preparing to reveal a deep secret. "My mom cheated on my dad. It was when they were fighting. Dad was too preoccupied with work—early mornings and late nights. Mom was stressed because, not only did she have to deal with my ADHD ass and Autumn's stubbornness, but she *also* had a business to take care of. They never told me or Autumn, but when I was in the seventh grade, I overheard my mom having a conversation with her friend about it. I guess one day she had enough and went to a bar and kissed someone. She told Dad about it right after and that's when they decided to go to counseling. It saved their marriage."

The heaviness of what he said settles in me. I never would've expected this from his mom. Amelia seems like the sweetest woman, but I guess everyone has their breaking point.

It sends a shiver running down my spine.

"I've never talked to anyone about this before. Not even my parents. They have no idea that I know. All I ask is that you don't see my mom differently. She made a mistake, but they worked hard to get through it and be where they are today."

Infidelity is something I know too well, and I can understand why Jake was hesitant to talk to me about it until now. Even considering my own history, I don't think I could judge his parents or their situation. My situation isn't comparable to what happened with them—and frankly, I have no idea how they were able to work through it, but somehow they did.

I lean up and give Jake a kiss on the cheek. I can't relate to what Jake went through as a kid. As bad as my family is, the one thing I can say without a doubt is that my father loves my mom with every ounce of his body, and if they do fight, I've never been around to see it.

"Thank you for sharing that with me, Jake. Confession for a confession?"

He looks at me puzzled. "I wasn't telling you that so you would feel obligated to share more than you're willing, I just...I wanted to share that with you. I want you to know everything about me—even the dark bits."

I've never met a guy who was so willing to give up information on his life. Normally it's like pulling teeth with men, but it has only been easy with Jake. Well, *somewhat* easy.

"Okay, well I'm going to share something I've never really talked about before." I suck in a breath, pulling the blanket farther up my legs to feel warmer. "I'm afraid that the reason I'm so scared to commit to someone stems from my relationship with my parents. I use the excuse that I've been cheated on before and can't trust people, but the reality is, I don't know if I can trust *myself.* I don't know if I'll ever actually allow myself to be loved as much as I deserve because I've never had unconditional love before. It scares the hell out of me. So instead of being open to love, I make up excuses and stay closed off."

Jake looks down at me, his blue eyes full of pity. It makes me nauseous talking about my feelings so openly and being this vulnerable with him.

"Vanessa." My stomach fills with butterflies when he uses my full name rather than one of his many nicknames for me. "I want you to know that you *do* deserve to be loved unconditionally. And one day, you're going to let someone in, you're going to witness the good and the bad, and then you're going to allow yourself to fall. Somewhere down the road, someone is going to love you so much that you'll forget what it was like not to be loved unconditionally."

His honest words make me smile. Not a toothy grin, but just the tiniest smirk. I know that I deserve love, but I just can't seem to allow myself that.

I relax back into his body, lounging on the beach once again. I haven't felt this safe and at home in a long time. His warmth invades every inch of me.

My thoughts drift to the fantasy life I've been imagining recently. Jake and I together— he's a star NHL player while I do freelance photography. We own a beautiful home on the coast somewhere and raise two dogs and a cat, and *maybe* a kid in the far future. I've only allowed myself to think about this fantasy world a couple of times, because I know all too well how things can change in the blink of an eye.

"There's something else I want to talk to you about."

I feel like I already know the words that are going to come out of his mouth.

My heart stops as he speaks.

CHAPTER TWENTY-SEVEN

I almost dropped the turkey

JAKE

"There's something else that I want to talk to you about." The words leave my mouth on a shaky breath, not exactly how I wanted this to go. And by the look on Vanessa's face, I can't tell if she's curious or debating on fleeing the beach before I get the chance to say what's been on my mind for weeks.

"Are you going to say it or did your lips freeze together?" She raises an eyebrow at me in the quirky way that she does.

Fuck I want to kiss her so badly right now. *C'mon, Jake, focus.*

"I want you."

"Right now? It's kind of cold, and I don't really want sand in certain places."

Never in my life have I ever been so nervous. *Me of all people.* I mean, hell, I normally can get a girl without lifting a finger—but Vanessa is a whole different story.

"No, not like that. What I'm saying is—" I debate on continuing, unsure how she's going to react. "I-I want to date you."

I didn't think that her eyes could get any bigger with those damn glasses, but somehow they've opened wider in awe of my declaration. I had a feeling it would probably go this way.

Vanessa is like a jigsaw puzzle. There are so many pieces to her and they're almost impossible to find. Every time I think I have her figured out, she throws me another damn curveball.

"Now before you try to run into the ocean and drown yourself to avoid this conversation, because I know that you would—I need to get this off my chest." Her cheeks turn a darker shade of pink, this time from my words and not the chill that's settled around us. "I know you exposed yourself and your insecurities about dating, but I can't deny my feelings anymore. I want you, Vanessa. I want *all of you.*"

I grab her hand, gently squeezing it.

"I want to wake up to your grouchy attitude and fall asleep with you snuggled in my T-shirt. I want to hold your damn hand when we're in public, and *fuck,* I want to kiss you in front of the whole goddamn world. You pick and choose which parts of yourself you show me, but I want the unfiltered Vanessa. The Vanessa that you hide away from the world because you're too damn scared to let anyone love you. *But let me.*"

She's quiet. I pray she doesn't read too much into my words and realize I might've just let something slip. The only sound is the crashing of the waves behind us, and I'm debating whether *I* should jump into the water to escape this.

Her voice breaks between us. "Why?"

"What?"

"I don't understand why you would want me?" I don't understand why she thinks she's so undeserving. "I know that we hook up and we're friends, I just…I didn't think that you would ever *want* me. You have tons of gorgeous girls who practically worship you. I also just unloaded some crazy dark shit and did I mention that *I'm a complete mess*?"

It takes me by surprise that she hasn't figured me out yet. All I care about is her, no one else compares.

The wind sweeps her hair in front of her face and I move to tuck it behind her ear, keeping my hand resting on her jaw.

"Ness, I'm completely aware of you and your 'crazy dark shit.' That doesn't change my mind. I don't want anyone else, I want *you.* I want you and all of your little quirks."

She fiddles with her fingers again, then peers those gorgeous green eyes up at me. "Like what?"

There are so many goddamn reasons why I want this girl.

"Hmm, here's one. Every time we go out to a restaurant or for coffee, you always ask the server about their day. *Every. Time.* Another one is you poke your tongue out of the side of your mouth when you're really concentrating—mostly when you're editing. You immediately smile after the first sip of your latte, which is why I make sure to bring one to every practice." I pull her back to me, leaning her against my chest again. "I could go on all night about all the things I adore about you, but I'm afraid we might freeze to death out here."

She stays silent, and I can hear the rapid beating of my heart in my ears waiting for her to say something. *Anything.* I've wanted Vanessa since the moment I met her, but I was too dumb to do anything about it. I shoved the feelings out thinking they only existed because of our arrangement. But that couldn't be farther from the truth. I can't deny it anymore and I hope she can't either.

"I-I don't know what to say to that."

"The best answer would probably be 'I want you too,' but I can understand how intimidating my speech was."

She scoffs. Does she not feel the same way? Have I really misread all the signals?

"You're not scared that you're going to miss out on all the girls you could potentially hook up with? Or miss being one of the single guys on the team?"

"I can promise you, Ness, I'm not missing out on anything when I'm with you."

I hope my words are strong enough to break through those damn walls she has planted around her heart. I've had enough of this back and forth, trying to figure out what the hell we are. If she can't commit, then that's fine, I'm not going to hold it against her. But *fuck,* I can't continue to sleep with her if she doesn't feel the same.

"If it's too much, the whole commitment thing, we can stay friends. But we can't keep doing this anymore. *I* can't do this anymore, Vanessa. If we continued, it would just confuse the hell out of me."

She shifts next to me, pulling the blankets back so she can kneel in front of me.

Fuck, she's so beautiful.

Sitting here under the stars, even with the weather borderlining winter, she looks like a goddamn angel. Her hair is swept out of her face by the light sea breeze, and the moonlight highlights her features just enough for me to make out the expression on her face.

Is she smiling?

"I want you too."

I don't let a second pass before I grab her face and bring my lips to hers. This kiss feels different, like the weight of everything is lifted the moment her hands latch around my neck.

I hover over her, caressing the side of her cheek. My body doesn't register how cold it is because all I can feel is her warmth under me. If it wasn't practically winter, I would have her sprawled out on the blankets, legs wide and my face buried in her pussy.

"I think maybe we should head back to the house."

I love it when she reads my mind.

"Great idea." I lean down to kiss her once more then grab our belongings.

As we're folding the blankets, I notice something small and wet fall onto my face. Vanessa and I both look up at the moonlit sky, a few clouds hiding the stars now.

"Is that?"

"Snow? Yeah, I didn't realize it was *this* cold out. C'mon, let's get back." I tug at her wrist as we leave the snowy beach behind us.

By the time we get back to the house, our fingers are nearly frozen and I'm almost positive that my balls have shriveled into my body. I look over at Vanessa as she peels off her jacket and hangs it up in the closet. Even watching her do the most mundane things like putting her damn jacket away has me drooling.

As I remove my own layers, I watch her walk through my room, slowly taking in every photo on the wall and all the trinkets I've collected over the years—mainly hockey memorabilia. She pulls off her hat and flips her hair over her shoulder and walks over to the electric fireplace tucked into the corner of the room. I watch as she stands in front of it, putting her hands in front of the heater as it spews out warm air. The sweet smell of coconut wafts over to me and I can't stop myself from drooling. Her smell is intoxicating and it takes everything in me not to pick her up and toss her onto the bed.

Fuck it. I'm throwing all sense out the window.

She gasps as I lift her body into my arms, completely unaware I was that close behind her. Her hands clasp behind my neck and hold together in a death grip.

"What are you doing?" She laughs as I lay her down onto the bed.

I climb onto the bed and hover over her. "What does it look like I'm doing, angel girl?"

The use of her nickname has her shivering under me. I remember the first time I called her that—it was at her birthday party. And if my memory serves me right, she also shivered then.

She hasn't changed.

Vanessa pulls me down to her, crashing her full lips with mine. I don't know when she got the chance to put on ChapStick but her lips taste of cherry.

The things I would do to this girl.

The things I would do *for* this girl. I'll give her anything she wants without question. She could ask me to set the world on fire, and I would. She could start a cult and I'd be the first member, following her anywhere she goes.

I tug at her pants, the material is soft and buttery. I love these pants on her. The way they hug her curves and flow at the bottom. When she walked into the kitchen this morning I almost dropped the turkey as I was taking it out of the fridge. She stopped me dead in my tracks and it took everything in me not to let my mouth drop.

Vanessa always looks hot, but today was different. I don't know if it had to do with her being here in my childhood home, surrounded by my family—but fuck these pants might be the death of me.

As she slides out of her clothes, I waste no time in taking mine off. I make sure to lock the door and dim the lights so no one interrupts us. I highly doubt anyone is still awake right now, but I don't want to chance it. I've only gotten caught with a girl in my room *once*.

Let's just say it's something that Mom and I have *never* discussed since.

I walk back to my girl, who's now lying across my bed, with the cutest pair of pink lace panties on. She's lying there so prettily. And she's entirely *mine*.

"Are you just going to stare at me all night or are you going to fuck your girlfriend." She smiles at the last word and pulls her bottom lips under her teeth.

"Say that again?"

"Come fuck your *girlfriend*, Jake."

My response is my lips on hers, pushing her back onto the bed. I settle my hand along her jawline, gently squeezing every now and again. She goes crazy when I do that, rubbing herself against my thigh. I run my hand down her body, settling at the lines of her panties. Slowly, I pull them down, kissing her neck as I do it and a moan escapes her pretty little mouth.

"Condom?" Her question is breathless, rushed.

My lips detach from her neck as I lean over and open my bedside drawer. As I reach in to grab a condom, I find the box empty. *Fuck. My. Life.*

She notices my hesitation, "What's wrong?"

"We're all out," I say as I shake the empty box. "I can run inside and see if my parents have any."

The idea of rummaging through my house with a raging hard-on is at the bottom of the list of things I want to be doing right now.

"Well..." Vanessa fiddles with the rings on her fingers, then looks at me with those piercing green eyes. "I have an IUD and I'm clean."

Is she suggesting what I think she is?

"Unless you're not comfortable or—"

I cut her off before she can even finish that thought. "I haven't been with anyone since we started." I motion between the two of us. "There's *no one* else but you, Ness."

It's the truth. Ever since Vermont, it's only been Vanessa. I'd still flirt with other girls, but it didn't feel the same. It only feels right with her.

She looks between us, where our bodies are almost touching, and grabs my dick, stroking it slowly. *Agonizingly slow.* Fuck, her fingers are so soft I could come just from her touch. That's not what I want tonight. I want her tight pussy wrapped around me. No barrier between us.

I move and settle my face between her thighs. My favorite place in the world. I look down at her smooth and creamy skin, and the cutest pink pussy. If I had to choose a way to die, it would be with my face between her legs while she moans my name. She could steal my breath and I'd say thank you as I slip into unconsciousness.

311

My lips touch her and she bucks her hips, pushing her pelvis into me. I move my lips and tongue up and down her center, savoring her. She always tastes fucking heavenly. I slide a finger into her, ushering another moan out of her. She makes the sweetest sounds when I please her. My favorite song that I want to listen to on repeat. I thrust my finger in sync with my movement on her clit. Vanessa instinctively wraps her legs around me, squeezing me with her thighs.

My name escapes her lips as she comes on my tongue.

As her orgasm washes over her, I kiss my way back up to her mouth. She has this starry look in her eye as I break the kiss and position myself at her entrance.

"You sure?" I ask again, just to triple-check she's okay with this. I've never gone barebacked with someone before. It's been engraved into my brain from my dad to *always wrap it up*, so I've never had to think twice about it. Except now.

"Yes."

I don't hesitate as I enter her. Holy shit, this is definitely what heaven's like. Going in raw with nothing between us, I can feel her wetness and heat entrapping me. Her pussy squeezes me as I enter, and holy fuck I need to think about something else before I come in two seconds.

Dirty hockey bag. Locker room shower drain.

Okay, that does it.

I refocus my attention on the beautiful girl underneath me. As I move and thrust in and out, her eyes squeeze shut as she adjusts to me.

"Fuck, you take me so well, Ness."

I know she loves it when I praise her during sex. It's not only one of her kinks, but it's also one of mine. I love watching her come undone as I tell her what a good girl she is.

She clenches her inner walls around me again.

"I'm going to come if you keep doing that, angel girl."

Her devilish grin peers up at me. "Good."

She moans again as I drive into her a little deeper this time, pulling one of her legs up and resting it over my shoulder. From this angle, I know I've hit a *good* spot when her legs tremble and a cry tears from her.

I pause momentarily. "Are you okay—"

"Please, keep going!" she begs, her nails digging into my ass, making me move again.

Our eyes lock, and I lean in to kiss her as I continue grinding my hips into her.

This isn't like our regular hookups, it's more intimate. The eye contact, the slower kisses. Our breaths feel deeper, warmer. She pulls me in closer to her, one hand attached to the nape of my neck and the other digging into my ass. I'm sure she's breaking skin with those nails, but I couldn't care less right now; it's turning me the fuck on, and I'm ready to fucking burst.

"Ness, I'm gonna come soon."

"Good." She moans against me.

I grab her other leg and toss it over my shoulder. This angle moves her hips up, and as I barrel into her, I feel her walls clenching around me as I drive her into another orgasm.

"Yeah, baby, come all over my cock."

She cries out as she comes all over me. Her sounds alone are what send me over the edge. I feel the tingle in my lower back before I completely let go, filling her.

I swear I fucking see stars. I've had great sex before, *amazing* even. But nothing compares to Vanessa. Nothing compares to her or the way she makes me feel. I was never looking for a relationship, but I'm glad I found one because she is the best damn thing I've ever had.

I don't want to let her go.

CHAPTER TWENTY-EIGHT

Pineapple on pizza

VANESSA

"I have a boyfriend."

The words feel foreign on my tongue. I never believed I would utter these four simple words to my best friends, and yet here I am sitting in our living room, with the two of them staring at me as if I have three heads.

My life has done a complete one-eighty in the past week. It's weird to admit it to myself, but I think I'm finally allowing myself to explore the idea of love. Or what could become love. As scared as I am, I'm excited to explore this with Jake.

The chill of December has finally set in. I've kept the boyfriend secret to myself, but I caved the moment they cornered me into the living room with their detective hats on.

Sydney is the first to break the silence as Maddie sits on the sectional with her mouth agape. "You have a boyfriend? *You,* Vanessa Nichols, are in a committed relationship. Holy shit, if this is a joke, this is *not* funny!"

Maddie's voice finally comes back to her. "When? Where? How? Tell us everything!"

"Uh, Thanksgiving weekend. He asked me out on the beach."

"Thanksgiving? That was over two weeks ago!"

"You kept this information from us for *that* long." Sydney's eyes look like they're about to bulge out of her head. "Actually, that's quite impressive for you. Normally I give you one look and you cave."

Truer words have never been spoken.

It was and wasn't hard to keep this delicate information from my friends. When we got back from the holiday weekend, we were all wrapped up in our own lives, busy with classes, assignments, hockey practice, and games. Any downtime I had, I spent it with Jake.

"Our schedules have been all over the place, I didn't want to tell you over text."

Guilt rises in my chest. Sydney and Maddie are my two best friends, I should've told them the moment Jake and I became official.

The reason I didn't tell them was selfish. I wanted Jake and I to stay in our little bubble where no one's opinions or thoughts could penetrate. My heart was vulnerable enough that weekend, I didn't need another reason to overthink my decision. Which is something I'm prone to do.

As secure as I feel with Jake, there's still that underlying feeling of unease that's gnawing at my insides.

I don't think many people understand what it's like being raised in a household without love and support. I'm constantly worried that every decision I make is wrong—which makes it hard for me to be so trusting in relationships.

Especially after how my last one ended.

I still worry that Jake might find someone who better fits his life—someone with a loving family, a good head on their shoulders, a promised career, someone who could fulfill all his dreams and have significantly less family trauma.

Yup, and the overthinking has begun.

At least I'm trying.

"Well, I'm glad you told us. It's about damn time you two made it official."

Sydney flips her hair over her shoulder, "I'd like to point out that a few weeks ago I said you two would end up together. I'm such a matchmaker."

I roll my eyes at her. She *did* say that, but I won't be the first to tell Sydney she was right. "Anyway, I just wanted to fill you guys in before I leave."

"Leave?"

"I'm gonna head to Jake's for the night. There's practice tomorrow morning, so I was going to sleep there and catch a ride with him in the morning."

"You get a new boyfriend, neglect to tell us for weeks, and then drop this bomb on us only to leave to go to said boyfriend's house!" Sydney flails over the side of the couch, delving into her dramatics.

Sydney should consider changing her major to theater. She would *thrive*.

"I'm sure you two will be fine without me for the night."

"Yeah, but…I miss you. Can we *please* have a girls' night this weekend? I'll bake cupcakes and we can watch a Christmas movie and decorate. We'll be drowning in exams for the next couple of weeks and then it'll be time to go home for the holidays."

Maddie groans at the thought of Christmas. She's a grinch, and yet she still suffers through the baking, decorating, movies, and music—all because her two best friends are obsessed with the holiday.

Sydney's family usually goes away during Christmas break. Normally they choose somewhere warm with beautiful blue water. I think she said this year they were all going to Panama. I would love to go on a trip to a tropical island and walk around taking photos of the local flora and fauna.

Maddie has the same tradition every year. After her last exam, she hops on a flight and heads home until the new year.

Am I a bad friend for secretly hoping that their flights get canceled and we can stay in the city together?

I'm planning on staying in Boston. The last thing I need during my break is to visit my parents. It's their year to host Christmas with the family, and imagining all of us together at the condo in Manhattan sounds like a complete nightmare. Who knows, maybe they'll cancel Christmas and go on another vacation without me so I don't need to think of a lame excuse as to why I don't want to go home.

"Sounds like a date. After the game on Saturday we can watch *The Grinch* and eat so much junk food that we burst open."

"Perfect." Sydney purses her lips and sends a kiss my way. "Now go have amazing sex with your boyfriend. I can't wait to hear all the gorgeous details later."

"All I'm saying is that if you put pineapple on pizza, you're a psychopath." Eli grabs a slice from the box on the coffee table, complaining to Kieran for ordering a Hawaiian pizza.

When I walked into the brownstone twenty minutes ago, I had no idea I was walking into such a heated discussion.

"It's a *touch* of sweetness, it's not going to kill you to eat it," Kieran replies as Eli slowly picks off every piece of pineapple on his slice.

"You know how I feel about fruits."

Nate chimes into the conversation from the doorway that leads to the kitchen. "Your diet consists of chicken, pizza, pasta, and the occasional orange. I swear, you have the same palette as a damn child."

"Thanks, Dad, anything else you want to comment on?"

"Yeah actually, can you move your fucking socks and underwear from the dryer before I throw them outside?"

"Whatever, back to our original topic—fruit doesn't belong on pizza. End of discussion."

Jake nudges my arm and makes a face, letting me know he's about to stir the pot even more. "What about tomato sauce? Tomatoes are fruits, y'know."

Eli's eyes squint as he points to us with his pizza. "I hate *all* of you."

"Hey, what did I do?" I defend myself. I secretly agree that pineapple belongs on pizza, but there's no way in hell I'm going to confess that right now.

Eli fixes his attention on me. "*You* didn't tell me that you and Jake were dating. I had a feeling all along that this would happen, but you all kept denying it. I had to find out from Nate! *Nate,* of all people, he's always the last to know things."

"Actually, I knew they were sleeping together before any of you did."

Eli's mouth drops open dramatically. "Is that true?"

His eyes lock onto me and Jake again and my cheeks immediately turn red. Nate caught me leaving one morning. We told him we stayed up too late studying, but I had a feeling he didn't believe our lie.

"Hmm, yeah, I guess Nate was the first to know about us sleeping together."

"First, I'm forced to eat crappy pizza, and then I find out that I was the last to know about everything. And here I thought we were all best friends." He turns away from us and back to Nate. "Anything else you know? Am I getting kicked off the team for being too talented?"

"If you keep up the dramatics, maybe. You're starting to act just like my sister." Nate chuckles to himself as he takes another bite with a huge pineapple chunk on it, which almost causes Eli to vomit.

I would love to see Sydney and Eli in a room together. One overly dramatic person is enough, but those two? They might cause World War III.

"Screw this, I'm going to get wings with Levi and Sebastian." He tosses his half-eaten slice back down onto the table before grabbing his coat and heading toward the front door. "If there's any of *that* left when I return, I'm throwing it in the trash."

"When you get home can you remember to take your clothes out of the dryer or I will seriously throw them outside."

Eli flips Nate off before shutting the front door behind him.

"Well, that was...entertaining."

"Nichols, it's like this every day. You should hear Kieran and Eli go at it over soap."

"Soap?" I look toward Kieran and raise an eyebrow.

He sighs, as if explaining this story will drain him of all his energy. "I like a certain brand of soap."

"What, like *Old Spice*?"

"No, Vanessa, not *like Old Spice*." He does his best impersonation of me and all of us hold back our laughter. Kieran is normally all edgy and mysterious, it's fun to see his playful side come out.

"The brand I like is called Mister Suds. It's a natural brand that has a variety of scents, but personally I like the lavender and pine. Eli *also* likes the smell of it and thinks he can use it whenever he pleases."

"Why don't you hide it?"

Kieran lets out a frustrated sigh, indicating he's already thought about that. "I did! Fuckin' Eli went through my cabinet and *found it*. I went to shower and saw the sudsy bar on the damn floor with his hair stuck to it."

Nate starts chuckling to himself. "You should've seen the two of them. Kieran was running around chasing Eli, soaking wet with a towel wrapped around his waist. He slipped on the stairs and took both of them down."

A laugh escapes me and I slam my hand over my mouth when Kieran glares at me, laughing at probably one of his more embarrassing moments.

"I never would have pegged you for a lavender guy."

His dark green eyes settle on me, the playfulness slowly vanishing. "Is it a crime to like lavender, Vanessa?"

His voice is velvet smooth, sending shivers right down my spine, settling warm in my core. *Jesus, what is with these hot broody hockey men?* Kieran is a handsome man, and with his pensive stare, I can see why girls so easily fall into his bed.

I shake myself out of the spell he was putting on me. "Nope. Nothing wrong with it. Great scent, actually."

Jake chuckles, watching my cheeks turn pink as I fumble over my words.

"Well, on that note." Jake grabs our empty plates and walks over to the garbage. "Ness and I are gonna head out for a bit."

"Why? Is our company not entertaining enough for you?"

"I deal with you idiots twenty-four seven, I'm going to take my girlfriend out for ice cream. If you two are so lonely, why don't you go on a date."

Kieran flips him off in response.

Hearing the word *girlfriend* come from Jake's mouth has my palms sweating.

Jake grabs our heavy coats from the rack and holds it out for me. *Very gentlemanlike.* The weather has taken a drastic turn since we came back and I have a feeling snow will start falling *very* soon.

We leave as Nate and Kieran settle into the couch and boot up some random game where they are tasked to shoot aliens. I'm sure people are going to think we're crazy for wanting ice cream in the midst of December, but I can never say no to a sweet treat. A couple of blocks away, there's the Public Garden—the first botanical garden in America. During the winter months they decorate the entire park with Christmas lights. Trees are wrapped with string lights, some bigger bulbs filter through the branches, and the frozen ground is littered with multiple light displays ranging from candy cane sticks to reindeer pulling Santa's sled.

Last year, Sydney and I came here at the end of exams before she went away for the break. There were roughly two feet of snow on the ground at that point, and I'm a little thankful it's not that bad right now. We spent over two hours continuously walking through the park at night, sipping on hot chocolate while our toes froze. I want to go again so badly. Maybe Jake will want to go see the lights this year.

He leads us down a road that's lined with food trucks. There's a little bit of everything—tacos, burgers, grilled cheese, and desserts.

My all-time favorite food truck is Dairy Freeze. Although it's more of a glorified van than a truck. The owner is an older Italian gentleman who is one of the nicest people I've ever met. He named the truck after his granddaughter who would say she has a dairy freeze instead of a brain freeze. It's some of the best soft serve you'll ever have, and I believe it's because of the love he puts into his business. Their signature cone is a vanilla soft serve, dipped in chocolate and coated in peanuts. I've been telling Jake about this gem for weeks and he finally caved. He's more of a salty snack guy, whereas sweets are my kryptonite.

There's no one in line at the truck, which I kind of assumed. Most people would rather opt for a hot chocolate or some kind of warm beverage over an ice cream cone.

I swipe my tongue along the side of the cone, tasting the richness of the chocolate mixed with the creaminess of the vanilla. The crushed peanuts add the perfect amount of crunch and salt. I wish I could eat this every single day of my life.

I hear a moan come from Jake's throat.

"It's good, isn't it?"

He hums in agreeance. "Fuck, Ness. This might be my new favorite dessert. Well, besides you."

"Glad to know I'm in the top."

"You're always at the top of my list."

We stride back up the street, heading closer to the park. I wonder if Jake planned for us to tour the lights tonight without even telling me. The black iron fence lines the sidewalk next to us and we watch as families parade through the park, commenting on all of the light fixtures.

"I think Christmas might be my favorite holiday."

"Really? I didn't peg you as a Christmas girl."

"I love everything about Christmas, well except for family get togethers. I like gathering with my friends and exchanging gifts—side note, I am *very* good at picking gifts for people." I take the last bite of my waffle cone before continuing. "We always make a day of decorating and baking cookies, watching old-school Christmas movies like *Home Alone* and *National Lampoon's Christmas Vacation*. All that stuff. If I had to go home for the holiday break, I would probably stay in my room and not leave until the day I had to come back to campus."

Especially since my parents are hosting this year. I'm going to try my hardest to avoid going home. Not only do I have to deal with the hectic airport traffic, but I also have to spend a week wearing a mask and playing along with whatever story my mother spun.

"You could always come home with me."

My feet freeze in place. As sweet as it is for him to invite me to another holiday with his family—I feel like I would impose too much. I'm perfectly content spending the break in my condo, gorging myself on sugar cookies and online shopping.

"Well—" My words get cut off by Jake's phone ringing in his pocket.

"Oh shit, it's my agent. Give me a sec, I have to take this."

I nod, slightly grateful for the interruption. Jake puts the phone to his ear, and I'm not ashamed to admit that I eavesdrop.

"Hey, Charles, how's it going? Oh, that's great. Yeah. Yeah. *No fucking way, are you serious?* Yeah, yeah, send all of it to my email. Thank you, man, I appreciate it. Yeah, Merry Christmas to you too."

He drops the phone from his ear and jumps around like a little kid finding out they're going to Disney World.

"Yes, yes, *fuck yeah!*" The smile plastered on Jake's face is contagious, his gorgeous white teeth shining under the streetlight.

"What? What did he say?"

"Ness, you're never gonna believe this. My agent just got off the phone with Peter Savinsky, the GM for the Demons that I was telling you about." I nod as he continues, "Well, I guess he's been keeping up with me this season, and besides my little fight with Meyers, he's impressed by how I've been playing."

"That's awesome, Jake."

"There's more." His boyish demeanor doesn't falter. His dimples are peeking out with his wide grin, his eyes ecstatic. "The GM gave Charles their summer workout regime and the start date for training camp. Do you know what this means?"

He runs a hand down his face as if he's in shock. I'm sure my face is mirroring something similar. I'm so happy for him, so proud of him for fulfilling his dreams. Everything he's worked for is finally paying off...which means he'll be leaving soon after graduation.

"I was so worried about where I stood with the team, but hell, Ness—everything is working out. I know I have a spot secured on my dream team, I'm graduating this year, I'm playing amazing this season. I got you. I don't know what I did to deserve all this success."

Success.

The word triggers me, immediately thinking of my family and their obsession with outdoing one another. Everyone feels the need to compare their lives, as if someone's career status is more important than the rest of the family. I've spent the last six years of my life trying to get away from this ideology. Success isn't the only important thing in life—but to some people it's everything.

I shouldn't be thinking about this. Jake isn't like my family. He's getting everything he's ever wanted because he's worked his ass off his whole life to achieve it. I can be happy for him even though my insecurities are eating me alive. It's the least I can do.

"Jake, you deserve this. You've worked so hard to get to where you are today. You're allowed to freak out and be happy. Revel in it."

"Thank you." He pulls me in, kissing me deeply. The kind of kiss that makes you dizzy. "I think we deserve another ice cream cone to celebrate, what do you say?"

"Do you really think I would say no?"

We make our way back to the food truck and away from the Christmas lights and the cheerful sounds of families enjoying the park. I try not to think about what's going to happen next year when Jake's gone and I'm still here finishing my degree. I don't have a concrete plan of where I want to go, but at least I'll have my friends and Jake.

Hopefully.

It's pitch black outside as we all hustle out of the house to make it to morning practice.

As we make our way out of the house, I almost trip down the stairs on a pair of...*underwear?* My eyes adjust to the dimly lit street and realize that there is a hamper's worth of clothes strewn across their front porch.

"Are you shitting me right now?" Eli stands at the front door, rubbing the sleep out of his eyes.

Nate meticulously walks around the clothing, like a parent avoiding littered toys. "I told you."

"Yeah, yeah, fuck you. I'll meet you guys at the arena." Eli tosses his bag onto the ground and starts to round up his clothes, mumbling profanities to himself under his breath.

"Don't worry, if Coach asks why you're late, I'll tell him you were catching up on some laundry."

Eli flips us off as we head over to Kieran's truck parked down the street.

"I can't believe you actually did that."

"Oh trust me, Nichols. He deserves it. Eli is notorious for leaving his clothes in the laundry for *days*. Maybe this will finally teach him."

"Yeah, Ness, he's worse than you leaving your socks everywhere."

"Hey! Sorry that I enjoy letting my feet be free rather than constricted all the time."

I do have a horrible habit of leaving my socks everywhere. And when I say everywhere, I mean that I toss them wherever I feel like. I've found socks stuffed in couch cushions, in the hallway, hiding under the fridge—I don't even know how they get there.

I slide into the passenger seat and buckle up before Jake closes the door behind me and hops into the backseat. Nate tosses his hockey bag into the trunk with the others and settles in next to Jake.

"So Kieran, are you going to tell us where you ran off to last night?"

Kieran grumbles, clearly not enjoying my questioning this early in the morning.

Last night while the guys were midgame, he got a phone call and left abruptly. All he said was he had something important to do.

"A friend's house."

"Wow, always a man of many words."

"I like to keep my personal life to myself, Nichols. If you want to talk, should we chat about the noises I heard coming from Jake's room when I got home?"

My cheeks blush and that shuts me right up.

"Yeah, that's what I thought."

"Hey, asshole, cool it. No need to be a dick this early in the morning." Jake's tone is stern, coming from behind me. Kieran turns the music up to drown out any more questions. Jake reaches his hand around the back of my chair and settles it on my shoulder giving it a small squeeze.

The quick ride to the arena is silent besides the blaring music. Once we park, the boys are the first out of the truck, grabbing their gear from the back. Jake comes back around to open the door for me, and as I slide out of my seat to grab my tote, the worn handle finally tears. The burlap material rips straight to the bottom of the bag, dropping all of my contents onto the concrete.

Shit shit shit.

My gasp must've been loud because suddenly three tall hockey players are surrounding me as I grab my laptop, camera, and all the attachments.

Jake leans down, grabbing my extension lens and battery pack. He gazes over them, making sure nothing is broken or chipped. I take the lens cover off to make sure nothing cracked and I let out a breath as I realize nothing's broken. *Thank God.*

My torn bag looks scraggly, worn from too much use. I might be a little too attached to a piece of fabric, but I've had this bag with me for years. It's gone everywhere with me. I had it for most of high school, brought it with me to university, and have taken it on countless trips. There's stains and small tears throughout the bag, but it gives it character.

Well, it did.

That strap was the final straw. I guess it's time to be an adult and buy myself an actual camera bag for once. At least I'll look more professional.

"Thanks," I mutter as I grab my belongings from Jake's hands and shove them back into the torn bag. I'll have to stop at home and grab a backpack before my classes. I don't want to walk around campus looking like I'm carrying around a potato sack.

We make our way into the arena, and we part ways in the lobby—the boys heading to the locker room and I make my way to the stands.

Today I need to focus on updating the team's website with highlight reels from the past few games. Their Instagram and TikTok following has grown exponentially, and I have a feeling that my report will blow Professor Miles away.

I wonder how everyone else in my class is fairing out. I heard that the girl who got assigned to the chess team revamped their online presence and they've gained more members than any year prior.

I take my regular seat in the middle of the stands, sitting in front of center ice. Coach Wilson has his assistant setting up cones, getting ready for whatever drills he's going to put the boys through today. Every practice I'm more grateful I picked a hobby that doesn't require excessive sweating and sore muscles.

I plug my camera into my laptop and export all the photos and videos from the charity event and the games since then. Looking over everything I shot, maybe I should go into sports photography. The way I can focus on a single player or capture the perfect shot—I'm a damn good photographer, if I do say so myself. ESPN would be lucky to have me.

As I upload some videos to the website, the guys filter out onto the ice and begin their drills.

"Did practice interfere with your beauty sleep, Murphy?" Coach's voice carries through the empty arena.

Eli rushes onto the ice, "Sorry, Coach, there was a laundry incident I needed to take care of." Eli shoots his roommates a harsh glare as the three of them double over in hysterics. I think these boys thrive on pissing each other off.

Coach blows his whistle and the team starts moving. The harsh sound of skates on ice and pucks flying fades into the background as I bury myself in my photo gallery.

Before I realize it, the two-hour practice flies by, and Coach Wilson sounds his whistle for the last time, sending the boys off to the showers. I close my laptop and make my way to the lobby to wait for the boys.

Eli and Nate are the first to come out of the locker room—both bickering about this morning's practical joke. Kieran and Jake walk out shortly after, laughing at something one of them said. I fall into step with them as Jake slings his free arm around my shoulders as we walk to Kieran's truck.

"Shepherd, a word before you go." Coach Wilson calls from the front doors.

Jake drops his bag onto the ground, gives me a kiss on the cheek, and jogs over. Kieran picks up Jake's discarded bag and hauls it along with his over to his truck. They're too far away for me to eavesdrop so I follow Kieran, hopping in the backseat, leaving the passenger door open for Jake's return.

Nate left with Eli, feeling a little bad for making him late, he offered to take him out to breakfast. I could go for some greasy hash browns from the diner right about now.

"I'm sorry for being a dick this morning."

Kieran's words startle me. He's not giving me direct eye contact, but I watch his eyes occasionally glance at me through the rearview mirror.

"Oh…it's okay. I shouldn't put my nose in other people's business." Even though I'm dying to know.

His dark eyes soften, "Nah, I just…didn't have a good night and took it out on you this morning. I'm sorry, Vanessa."

I give him a forgiving smile. "Well, thank you. I appreciate it."

"Can I ask you something?"

The rawness in his voice has the hairs on my neck stand up. "Yeah, of course."

He turns around to face me this time, leaning his arm against the passenger seat's headrest. "This doesn't leave this vehicle." I nod, waiting for him to continue. "Let's say someone fucked up, and they wanted to make it up to someone, how should that person go about it?"

"Can I get any more details?"

"No."

Right, because asking Kieran to talk more than necessary is like pulling teeth.

"Okay, well how badly did this person fuck up?"

"I was an ass."

"*You* were being an ass? No way, that doesn't sound like you at all."

Kieran gives me a glare and I quit laughing. Guess he's not in the mood for jokes.

"Well, if I messed up with someone I cared about, I would apologize profusely. I would buy them their favorite snack, set aside some time for the two of us to talk and work out whatever issue caused the fight."

He nods, absorbing my advice. It's not the best advice, but it's all I can offer with limited information.

"Favorite snack, alone time, apology."

"Oh, and if it's a girl, grovel. *Grovel hard.* That'll get you bonus points."

"Thanks, Nichols."

"Anytime."

Jake climbs into the truck, giving us both a confused look as if he's trying to decipher what we just talked about. Kieran gives me a knowing look and I nod, the two of us silently communicating that our conversation doesn't leave the two of us.

"Anyone down to go to Tony's for a killer breakfast? I need it after that shitshow of a practice."

"Hell yes. Fucking Sebastian was hitting me with too many slap shots today. I need a breakfast burrito ASAP." Kieran puts the truck into gear and peels out of the lot.

We get to the restaurant and take our usual booth. Immediately my mouth is watering as the aroma of pancakes and coffee fills the air. I can't wait to scarf down a decent helping of hash browns and a pancake or two.

"What did Coach wanna talk to you about?"

Jake relaxes into the booth, slinging an arm on the cushion behind me.

"Peter Savinsky reached out to him over the holidays to talk about me. He said that once our season is done, he might pull me. So come April, I could be gone."

"Holy shit, congrats man."

I watch as the two of them clasp hands in what I refer to as a bro handshake.

"April?" I didn't intend for the word to slip from my mouth.

"Yeah. Once our NCAA season is over, the NHL can choose to pull someone from their roster if their college career is done. They did it last year, Travis Hayes was drafted to the Las Vegas Tigers, and after his school lost in the semifinals, Las Vegas pulled him and he got to play in the big leagues before they lost their spot for the Stanley Cup."

I try to absorb all the information he's throwing at me.

"What about graduation?"

"That's not 'til June. I'll be able to come back to walk the stage."

"So once you're done playing for BCU, New Jersey can pull you up whenever?"

Our waitress comes by with coffees and orange juice for Kieran. I take a sip before the coffee is cooled down, burning the tip of my tongue.

"Exactly." Jake shifts his attention back to Kieran. "Could you imagine if New Jersey makes it to the Stanley Cup and I get pulled just in time to play? Make my debut in a fucking championship game." Jake looks as if there are stars in his eyes, picturing his future. I'm so happy for him, but I'd be lying if I said a part of me isn't dreading the day that he leaves to pursue his dream.

Kieran takes a sip of his coffee before leaning back into the booth. "Just don't forget about us when you're all rich and famous."

"Never. I'll make sure you guys have seats whenever you want. I'll get a huge house you guys can stay at when you're visiting. It'll be like it is now, just in New Jersey."

The looming dread hangs heavy over me. Jake's going to leave, and sooner than I expected. I've always known he was going to leave for New Jersey, but I thought we would have a little more time. Our relationship is still new, are we going to be able to make this work when we both live in different states and have conflicting schedules?

I stay quiet as Jake goes on about his ideal life and his future with his friends. I don't bring up how he doesn't mention me in any of his plans, but then again why would he? *No one ever does.*

"I can picture it now. This time next year I'll be making so much money I'll have no idea what to do with it."

Our waitress comes back and sets our food in front of us. Kieran doesn't hesitate, immediately shoveling his breakfast burrito into his mouth.

"Man, it's crazy thinking about how much my life is going to change within the next year. I mean, who knows what's going to happen."

That was my exact thought too.

Where are *we* going to be this time next year? He's going to be busy training and playing in the damn NHL. I'll still be in college, studying a profession my family doesn't approve of, living my life as I always have—alone. Did we make the wrong decision?

Suddenly I feel like I'm twelve again, screaming for someone to pay attention to me, think of my feelings, acknowledge my existence in their life. Dad was always glued to his phone, talking to other doctors, being called in for an emergency surgery, or filling nurses in on his patients. Mom was usually in her office typing away on her laptop or organizing files for upcoming cases.

I was always shoved to the side so they could fulfill their own dreams, and it's starting to feel like that again, but this time with Jake.

I think I lost my appetite.

CHAPTER TWENTY-NINE

A few espresso martinis

VANESSA

"C'mon, Nate! You call that a slapshot? I could hit the puck harder in my sleep!"

Sydney yells from the stands as Nate's shot deflects off the goalpost. He looks over his shoulder and shakes his head at his sister, and Maddie pulls Sydney back down to her seat.

Personally, I love when the two of them come to games with me, but I can't say the same for Nate. I get to hang out with my friends while working, and I get to listen to Sydney talk smack to her brother all game. I don't understand how Nate can so easily tune her out. He always rolls his eyes and laughs when she says vulgar things or comments on how he's playing. It must be a sibling thing.

We're playing New Hampshire this weekend—a game today and then another tomorrow afternoon. These are also the last two games of the semester. After this weekend, exams start and the boys get a nice break until they come back for their winter tournament.

I'm secretly hoping Maddie and Sydney will be back by then so we can all celebrate together. Last year I spent New Year's Eve alone in New York—I opted to stay at the condo rather than going with my parents to my aunt Helen's party.

The Wolves have been playing phenomenally. Kieran has been on his A game, not letting a single shot get by him. Jake and Eli are also playing as if their lives depend on it. Eli has gotten two penalties so far for icing and elbowing, but Jake has picked up the slack when we're down a man.

I made sure to snap a few shots of Eli with a grumpy look on his face—these photos are pure gold. And I know the guys will love to see these. I made a small collection of photos I call *Pretty Penalties*. It's a curated album of each player who has spent time in the sin bin. Most of them are grumpy, some are yelling, and some—like Levi, look like they're staring into nothing.

But even with a power play, New Hampshire is nothing compared to BCU.

Ever since Jake found out that the GM of the Demons has been watching him this season, he's been playing like he deserves that spot on their team. Some would call him a show-off, but it's all pure, natural talent.

I've decided to shove all the thoughts about our future out of my head at least until exams are over. I need to focus on school rather than my relationship status. I want him to achieve everything he's ever wanted out of life, I don't want to be the one who ruins it for him.

The final buzzer goes off, and the score is 3–0. I wouldn't want to be on New Hampshire's team tonight.

I tuck my camera into my backpack. I *really* need to get a new camera bag, but my legs are tired and I don't feel like dealing with packed malls today. I swear, as soon as Thanksgiving passes, the mall becomes a frenzy of last-minute shoppers trying to get all of their Christmas gifts done.

Sydney, Maddie, and I make our way to the lobby of the arena to wait for the boys with the rest of the spectators. Littered in the main area are tons of students, parents, and faculty. Stationed right next to the doors that lead to the locker rooms is a group of five or six girls, patiently waiting. I notice one of the girls is Caroline, the rest I've seen at the games, but I've never introduced myself.

After twenty minutes I finally see Jake. I notice his wet hair first, followed by his wide-grinned smile. He hates to wait for his hair to dry after showering, even if it's below freezing outside, he'll still choose to leave it damp.

Before making his way over to the three of us, he gets sidetracked by the group of girls by the doors. He leans down to give Caroline a hug before getting caught in a conversation with her friends. As Levi and Kieran walk by, Kieran pulls Jake away from the group, leaving Levi in his place.

I can't even begin to imagine what it's going to be like when Jake joins the Demons. College hockey is one thing, but being in the NHL is a whole different league. He's going from small campus rinks to giant hockey arenas around the country. He'll have thousands of new fans throwing themselves at him. The days of sorority girls will be long behind him and he'll be thrown in with supermodels, singers, and other A-listers. He's going to be fresh meat and people are going to want to snatch up the NHL's newest treat.

Jake walks over and immediately engulfs me in a hug, his warm sandalwood scent filling me as he plops a kiss on the top of my head.

"Hey, you." He wraps his arms around me, resting his chin on my head. He feels so solid. *Ugh, I love his muscles.* "What are you girls getting up to tonight?"

"Girl's night. We're gonna do some Christmas baking and decorating. Maybe have an espresso martini…or five. Who knows what tonight will bring."

"Mm, that'll be fun. Maybe I'll sneak over later for dessert." He places a soft kiss to my temple.

Sydney shakes her head at the two of us. "You're disgusting."

Nate, Eli, and Kieran join us, listening to Sydney list all the different types of cookies she wants to bake tonight.

"Nichols, can you bring some to the house the next time you're over?"

Sydney whips her head toward her brother. "No. If you want cookies, you can make your own."

"*Please*, Syd. You know you're the best baker in the family."

"*Fine*. You're all annoying me. Girls, let's go." Sydney flips her honey curls over her shoulder and leads the way to the parking lot.

Instead of turning around to see just Maddie and I following, she finds the whole group trailing behind her. She huffs again.

"I will definitely be drinking multiple espresso martinis if I have to deal with you two and Christmas music all night." Maddie rubs her temples as if she already has a headache.

"Not a fan of Christmas?" Kieran's question sparks her attention, her eyes narrowing in on him as we walk out of the building.

"Used to love the holiday, now, not so much. I only put up with these two because I love them." She grabs Sydney and smacks her cheek with a kiss.

"Aw, here that, Ness—Maddie loves us."

Maddie sticks her tongue out. I love her and her grumpy attitude. Whoever falls in love with her, well—they better be able to handle her attitude.

Jake and I trail at the back of the group, peppering my head and cheeks with kisses.

"Did you see the goal I scored for you in the second period?"

"Yes, I did, it was *very* hot. I also saw you check that guy into the boards when he was going after Levi. You're such a big softy. Don't want anyone to hurt your friends, huh, Jakey." I poke his dimples as he smiles shyly.

He *hates* that nickname, but only tolerates me calling him that. Kieran once tried to call him Jakey and he tackled him to the ground faster than I could blink.

"I might have a soft spot for my friends, but trust me, baby, I'm hard in all the right places for you."

"Mm-hm, right." I wink at him as we stride to Sydney's car. "So…what did you and Caroline chat about?" I casually throw that into the conversation. I'm not necessarily jealous, but I know that he and Caroline have hooked up in the past.

"She was congratulating me on my contract."

How the hell does she know about that?

As if he can read my mind, he answers my question. "Her dad is a sports broadcaster, so he gets a lot of the inside scoop."

"Oh. Cool." I try to sound neutral, as if Caroline knowing more about hockey than me doesn't make me a little insecure.

We stop in front of Sydney's car and he spins me around so I face him. "So what are you girls actually doing tonight?"

It's funny that he thinks girls' night entails so much more than drinking and baking cookies—but that's exactly what we plan on doing. Although, it's always fun making Jake a little jealous.

"We'll bake some cookies, have a few drinks, and probably order a male stripper or two. You know, the usual."

"Hmm, well once the male strippers are gone, give me a call and I'll show you what a *really* good time is."

He winks at me, the simple look immediately taking effect on me. I want to say screw it to girls' night and go home with him—but I can't go back on my promise.

"What are you going to do without me for a whole night?"

Jake shrugs his shoulders, then runs a free hand through his mess of waves. "Eli wants to go out to a sports bar to catch the Boston game, so we'll probably get wings and beer. But the second you get too lonely, call me and I'll be right over."

Jake brings his lips down to mine, kissing me slowly and deeply.

"All right, go have fun with the girls. I'll see you tomorrow after the game?"

"Only if you win." I give him a wink before hopping in the back of the car, a grin sprawled across my face.

The second we pull out of the parking lot, Maddie turns around to face me as Sydney brings us back to the condo.

"Five dollars, he's over before midnight."

"Yeah right, it's girls' night." Sydney defends me.

"Exactly! We have too much baking and decorating to do."

I'm probably going to owe Maddie five bucks by the end of the night.

Midnight has come and gone and so far there's no sign of Jake.

Actually, I haven't heard a single peep from him since we left the arena.

I sent him a few texts keeping him updated on my night and sent over a photo of the cookies we decorated in case he wanted a specific one—personally I think my Christmas trees look better than Maddie's reindeer ones, but they all taste the same.

Even with pictures of the baked goods and a sneaky photo I took in the bathroom, there's still no response from him.

Sydney made her mother's sugar cookie recipe, and while the they were cooling, Christmas threw up in our place. We had originally planned on getting a real Christmas tree, but decided the trip out of the city would be too much. We ended up pulling out our old one from storage, the one we thrifted the first year we lived together. It's a basic green tree, about six feet tall with fake snow dusted on some of the branches.

For our decor, we like to stick with classic colors for Christmas, accenting the tree with deep red and gold tinsel, but we have all added our own ornaments to make a very odd collection. Sydney brought some older handmade ornaments from home, Maddie strictly likes gold and green, and I added a few special ornaments I've collected over the years from thrift stores and yard sales. If you look at our tree, it appears like it was decorated by children. To be fair, we were a few espresso martinis deep.

I lost count after the fourth.

"I vote we watch *The Grinch* and fall into a cookie coma, anyone else agree?"

"*Fine,*" Maddie mumbles from the couch, her face hidden in a pillow. She's had the most to drink out of us all and I'm willing to bet she's asleep before the opening monologue finishes.

"I'm gonna give Jake a quick call and let him know we're winding down for the night. You can start it."

Sydney makes a whip-slashing noise before grabbing one of many candy canes from our tree and settling onto the couch next to Maddie.

I head down the hallway that we've lined with garland and small fairy lights. It feels as if we were transported into a fantasy realm. I reach my bedroom, which doesn't have much Christmas cheer—just a themed throw blanket I put on my bed and a small Charlie Brown Christmas tree on my desk. My bed is soft and cozy as I plop down and pull my phone out from my sweatpants. I think Maddie made the martinis a little *too* strong because it takes me longer to find Jake in my phone and dial his number.

The phone rings for almost a full minute before he finally answers.

"Hello?" The noise in the background is overpowering his voice, making it sound like he's so far away.

"Jakey!" *Oh God, yup, I'm definitely more tipsy than I thought.* "Hi. I miss you."

"Someone is a little tipsy, isn't she?"

I accidentally hiccup right into the phone. *Yeah, not tipsy, definitely drunk.*

"A little. How's your night going?"

It's hard to hear his response over the talking and shouting in the background. It's past midnight, so the Boston game has to be over by now.

"It's good, just drinking and hanging out."

I think nothing of it, until I hear a group of high-pitched voices calling Jake's name. My stomach feels empty like when you're on a roller coaster. This feeling is all too familiar.

"What's going on?"

His answer is short and rushed, "Oh nothing, we're still at Wing Shack."

I'm surprised Nate didn't drag them out of the restaurant earlier. Especially since they have a game tomorrow.

"Oh, I thought you guys were only staying for food and beers?"

I can hear him having another conversation with someone else while I'm still on the phone, and it irritates me a little. I know that I called him while he's out with friends, but if he doesn't want to be on the phone then he could've just sent me to voice mail.

"Uh—yeah, that was the original plan. Then Car and some of her friends showed up. Are you girls done with Christmas decorating?"

"Yeah, we've been done for a while. I was going to see if you wanted to come by to watch a movie, but it seems like you're still busy."

This time I hear Levi's voice call out for Jake to join them for shots.

"I'll call you after we leave, okay, angel girl?"

Did he completely disregard what I said?

"Okay, good—" Before I can finish saying goodnight, I hear a dial tone.

He hung up on me.

He hung up.

On me.

I feel my cheeks heat and tears threaten to fall. I'm drunk and overstimulated, and I'm most likely making a bigger deal out of this than I should.

Actually, *no.* I'm not making this a bigger deal than it is. I think any girl whose boyfriend was out partying with girls and rushing them off the phone might put someone on edge.

Jake has been acting out of character all week and I'm trying hard to understand why. Deep down I know that it's because of hockey. More specifically, his contract with the New Jersey Demons. It's been looming over his head all semester, and once he finally got the confirmation he needed, he's acted completely out of character. I've tried putting it out of my head, but it's hard when the person I've come to know and adore is slowly slipping away. The other day I was running late to morning practice and Jake offered to get me my usual latte, but when I showed up, he completely forgot and barely spoke to me after getting changed, rushing off with the guys. I can't be mad that he's hanging out with his friends, but he's been pushing me to the side more and more every day.

It feels like he's purposefully putting distance between us. Maybe he wants to break things off. I wouldn't blame him. If I was going to the pros, I wouldn't want a girlfriend holding me back. I'd want to explore my options, and God knows how many options he's going to have.

All of it feels so heavy right now.

The fact that he's hanging out with a group of girls I don't fully feel comfortable with instead of coming here like he promised, upsets me even more. Especially since he used to hook up with one of those girls, and him actively avoiding me only fuels the anxiety building inside. This triggers me back to high school when my ex would ignore my calls and texts because he was busy sneaking around behind my back with my best friend.

Maybe my feelings *are* warranted.

What's stopping him from going back to the person he was before he met me?

Does he miss being single? Is that why he was so quick to rush me off the phone? Does he miss the attention he used to get? Who's to say that the attention ever stopped?

I see the comments girls leave on his posts. Anytime he's featured on the Wolves account, flocks of students comment. I can only imagine how insane his social media presence will be once he's gone pro, and how much attention he'll be getting.

My thoughts have taken control of my body, locking every bone and muscle. It feels like my life is crumbling beneath my feet. I thought that maybe for once I deserved to be loved. I allowed someone into my life, but I didn't think of the consequences. I didn't think about how I'd feel when Jake leaves for New Jersey. I didn't think about how we will always be in two different places. I didn't think about all these little things because I was so clouded by my feelings for Jake.

I'm such an idiot. How could I have ever believed this could work?

CHAPTER THIRTY

Oh dude, you're a fucking idiot

JAKE

Everything is not fine.

Why?

I'm nursing one hell of a hangover and feel like I could vomit all over the ice at any second. If Coach knew how much I drank last night and how shitty I'm feeling now, he never would've put me in the game.

After yesterday's win, the team decided to celebrate. It started off as wings and beer, but then we somehow ended up doing shots until two in the morning. We went harder than I expected, but hey, it's the end of the semester and we're about to go on winter break. Who really cares about the last game before the holiday. With exams starting this week, most of these guys have class on their mind, not how well we're going to play against a team that shouldn't even be in our division.

New Hampshire has lost almost every game of their season, including last night. But if I would've known that they were going to play like a fire was lit under their ass, then maybe I wouldn't have had those last few shots. I should've gone home at a reasonable hour like Nate.

Nate, being the responsible young adult that he is, tried getting us all to leave once the Boston game was over, but the team was pretty unanimous on our decision. Nate left us alone with our consequences, and fuck am I feeling regret today. Eli followed him shortly after, trying to make a good impression as the assistant captain.

I wasn't expecting to stay out as late as I did, but Caroline showed up with a few of her friends, and we lost track of time.

The buzzer sounds, ending the first period. We're up 1–0, most of us not playing as well as we should. Sure, we're up by one point, but a lot can change in the blink of an eye.

I'm sure Coach won't let us hear the end of this one.

I skate over to the bench, following the rest of my teammates into the locker room. If Wilson wasn't in the locker room with us, I'd be hacking into a garbage can by now. But I need to play it cool.

"What the hell is going on out there? Huh?" Coach's voice is too loud for my pounding head. "Last night we beat them three–nil. And today everyone is skating around as if your skates are filled with cement. Wake the hell up!"

The room fills with groans—no one is impressed by how we're playing, but none of us are going to tell Coach why we're doing so poorly.

"Captain? Do you have any inclination as to why we're playing like shit?"

Nate's eyes scan across the room, internally debating whether he should come clean and betray his teammates or shove it under the rug.

"No, Coach. But I'm sure everyone's going to *wake up* and get their shit together." The tone of Nate's voice is enough to get everyone to sit up straight. *Dad's mad.*

When Nate gives us orders, we listen.

"You're *damn* right! And if you don't, expect brutal practices when you all get back from winter break."

Coach takes a second to look at each of us. When his gaze lands on me, for a second I see disappointment in his face. At least I'm doing my part and keeping the puck away from the net, but that doesn't mean it hasn't come near our zone more than once in the first period.

"Have a drink of water, take a shit, I don't care what you do, but in ten minutes when you get back on that ice, you all better have your heads screwed on straight." Wilson smacks his clipboard onto the bench next to him and storms out, the rest of the coaching staff following close behind.

"What the hell? You guys promised if you stayed out late, it wouldn't affect your game."

"Sorry, Dad," Levi pipes up from the corner, deep bags under his eyes. He looks as pale as the ice.

Last night he left with Caroline, and I think the two of them might be seeing each other, but it's not my place to say anything 'cause it's not my business.

"How late did you guys stay out?"

"I came home around eleven. The rest of these idiots decided to go a little too hard last night. I think it was all the female attention they were getting."

"Coming from you, Murphy? You had Jasmine's tongue down your throat half the night."

"Yeah, but at least I left before you, Seb."

My head throbs again. Maybe if I rub my temples hard enough, the pounding will stop. I grab two small pills from my bag and toss back the ibuprofen with some Gatorade—blue because every other flavor sucks.

"Shep, I thought you were going over to my sister's place last night to see the girls?"

A loud gasp comes from our left—a freshman, Seth Donnelly, is sitting on the bench with his mouth wide open. "Jake's screwing around with your sister and you're letting him live?"

"Donny, how dumb are you?" Eli throws a towel at his head, which he dodges at the last second.

"Everyone knows Jake's seeing Nichols, you idiot. She's my sister's roommate."

"*Oh.*" Seth looks like a lightbulb just lit above his head. "Sorry, Captain."

I shake my head at him. The kid is speedy on the ice, but not as fast at keeping up with what's going on around him.

"It was too late by the time we were done, so I just came home and tried to get some sleep before the game."

"I thought she called you around midnight and asked you to go over?" Kieran pipes up from next to me. He gives me a conniving smirk, knowing the guys will *never* let me hear the end of this.

"*Woah woah woah.* You chose to stay out with us over going over to your girlfriend's?" Levi facepalms, dragging his hand down his face. "Oh, dude, you're a fucking idiot."

342

"No, she was having a girls' night. I didn't want to intrude." As soon as the words leave my mouth, I realize how stupid I sound.

I am an idiot.

I should've gone over last night. I should've left the damn bar and my friends.

One of the other seniors on our team, Trevor McAvoy, sighs loudly. "Oh, Sheppy. If my girl called me and asked me to come over—I'd be there no questions asked."

"Sheesh, okay, sorry. If you haven't noticed, I'm not used to being in a relationship."

McAvoy shakes his head. "Yeah, not gonna lie when I heard you and Vanessa hooked up, I was pretty shocked. I'm surprised you gave up the game."

I wasn't expecting to get a girlfriend in my last year of college. I always thought that I'd settle down after enjoying my time being single. Looking at my life now, I'm happy I changed my mind.

Nate starts hitting his stick on the ground, gaining everyone's attention.

"All right, enough about Jake's love life. We don't have time to discuss how hopeless he is, we need to get back on the ice. Move your asses."

We all hustle back out onto the ice, prepared for whatever happens next, a new fire lit under our asses.

The second period flies by. Wilson decides to do shift changes *constantly*, hoping that it'll give us a second wind and take a lead bigger than we had last night.

We make sure to time our switches perfectly, so we don't get a penalty for too many men on the ice. That shit is the fucking *worst, e*specially if you have some freshmen who don't clean their ears out and can't hear a damn play. Coach's strategy works, and Levi scores another goal for us before the buzzer goes off.

We spend our fifteen-minute break listening to Coach go over which plays we're going to make, and something about if we don't win by more than three, he's going to play Taylor Swift at every practice. Most of the guys groan about that, but Tay and I are good friends. Mainly because that's all Vanessa listens to in the car.

Damn, I can't wait to see Vanessa after this game. Hopefully she's not too mad that I didn't stop by last night.

As we walk back on the ice, I scan the crowd for her. Tucked to the side, near where the Zamboni comes out, she's holding onto her camera, and it looks as if she's scrolling through her photos.

I can't wait to give her the present I got her for Christmas. After her favorite tote bag broke, I've been on the hunt for something to replace it, and I finally found something. She's probably going to lose her mind when she opens it.

The third period starts off rough. And by rough, I mean I got tossed into the boards twice and the second time nearly knocked the wind out of me. Whatever distraction I was able to cause allowed us to regain control of the puck and Nate scored another goal.

After face-off, Nate passes the puck back to me. I take control, because *fuck it,* I deserve to have some fun after that hit.

The defensemen on New Hampshire seem to have smartened up overnight, because they're both prepared for me to barrel down center ice to them. Instead, I look over my shoulder and see Levi close behind—open. I whip the puck back to him, dodging one of New Hampshire's defensemen. I watch as he goes flying into the boards.

I hope Ness got that on camera.

Levi whistles, catching my attention. Nate and Sebastian have now joined us, and I fall back, idling the line at center ice. I see an opening, and luckily so does Levi. He skates around the player blocking him, tossing the puck to me, as I have a clear shot into the net.

Within seconds the puck is in my possession, and with a quick flick of my wrist, I send the puck flying past the goalie, right into the mesh of the net. Suddenly it's 3–0 and we only have a few short minutes left. This feels very déj*à* vu.

Now that most of us have hit our second, or third wind, we're ready to *really* push. With only a few minutes left, we completely take over. We act as if we're all starved wolves and the puck's a piece of meat. We do not let it out of our sight. And we *do no*t let the other team take what's ours.

I glance up at the clock as it ticks down, less than a minute remaining in the game.

Eli takes possession of a rejected goal, passing it back to Nate to take down the ice. Levi is right next to him, and McAvoy, who switched with Seb, glides past them, open for a pass. Nate shoots it over to McAvoy who passes it over to Levi. Levi swings around the net, passing back to McAvoy, who is now open and on the opposite side of the goalie—who's so lost that his attention is nowhere near Trevor.

He shoots and scores the final goal of the night, finishing 4–0.

The guys skate over to Trevor, tackling him as the rest of our team joins from the bench.

It must suck being on New Hampshire's team tonight. I definitely wouldn't want to be on *that* bus ride home. We've all been there before, tucking our tails between our legs and listening to our Coach bash on us and our performance for hours, but that's what made us a better team. Maybe it'll be a learning moment for them.

We head out to the locker rooms as the crowd starts filing out of the bleachers.

I change and shower faster than normal, washing only my body and letting the water run through my hair. I can wash my hair later, hopefully with Vanessa in the shower with me. *Maybe she'll even let me use some of her shampoo.*

As I make my way through the arena, trailing my hockey bag behind me, I scan the lobby for that familiar brunette. I pass by anxious family members and friends patiently waiting, until my eyes finally land on those gorgeous green eyes. The only reason I can see them from this far away is because of those damn glasses. I fucking love them though. They make her eyes seem two times bigger than they are, but I don't care because I get a closer look at those beautiful evergreen irises.

I swear her gaze pulls me to her because within seconds I'm halfway across the room.

"Hey, angel girl, enjoy the game?"

She drops her bag onto the ground as I pull her into me, inhaling that sweet coconut scent.

"You guys were great tonight. I mean, you always are, but two shutouts in a row? Kieran must be on cloud nine."

345

I look around the lobby to try to find him, he must've snuck out right after me.

"So, what's the plan for tonight? Wanna go back to your place? We could go to mine, but Eli invited some of the guys back to the house."

"I wanted to talk to you about something first—" A group of guys from the football team walk over to us, interrupting midconversation.

"Hey, man, *great* fucking game." Their captain, Jeremy Fields, tells me.

"That was a wicked goal."

"Great way to end before the break."

I smile and clap hands with a few of them. "Yeah, thanks guys, appreciate it. I'll check you guys at the New Year's party, yeah?"

"See ya later, Shep! Can't wait to see you on the big screen next season," Fields calls out before leaving the arena.

I fix my attention back on Vanessa. Her arms are crossed over her chest, giving me the vibe that she's not too happy.

"Sorry about that, what did you want to talk about, angel girl?"

She takes her bottom lip into her mouth before speaking. "Actually, I was going to ask if we could reschedule? I have a lot of studying I need to do. Maybe we can meet up this week in between exams?"

I can tell by her body language that something is up. At times like this, I wish I had mind-reading abilities.

"Is everything okay, Ness?"

Her eyes pan behind me then land back on me before she answers. "Yeah, everything's fine. I'll message you later, okay?" She stands on her tiptoes, placing a kiss on my cheek before slinging her backpack over her shoulder and leaving the arena.

Somehow I have a feeling that everything is far from fine. Most times I can read Vanessa's emotions without her even saying a word, but today I'm off my game. Maybe Levi knows what's bothering her. The two of them have gotten a lot closer over the semester.

"Brody!" I call out to him, jogging to catch up as he exits the front doors.

"Shep, what's up?" He fist-bumps me and motions for me to follow him to the parking lot. I pull my hockey bag behind me, falling in step with Levi.

"Have you talked with Vanessa lately?"

We reach Levi's SUV, and I toss his bag into the back as he opens the trunk door.

"Nichols? No, not really. I haven't spoken to her since last night."

"Last night?"

He slams the trunk closed, pulling his phone out of his pants pocket. "Yeah, she messaged me at, like, one in the morning. Just asking if I was still at the bar with you."

That's odd. Why didn't she just text me and ask if I was still there?

"That's it?"

"Yup. I told her that we were going to stick around for a little longer. I invited her out, but she didn't respond." Levi eyes me up and down, clearly noting my off-kilter expression.

When it comes to having a girlfriend, I feel like I know nothing at all.

"Why, what's up?"

I shake my head. "Nothing. I think I'm reading too much into something."

"Maybe Nichols is just stressed out. It's exam season, and our prints got messed up in the lab over the weekend, so she's been freaking out about getting her project finished on time. Either way, take the girl out for a night, get her mind off everything and I can guarantee she'll be putty in your hands, brother." He taps me on the shoulder as he moves to climb into his car.

"Okay, yeah. Thanks, Brody."

He puts his hand to his forehead as if he's saluting me. "Anytime."

CHAPTER THIRTY-ONE

Everything is fucked

JAKE

I fucking hate exam season.

I don't hate *my* exams per say, but I hate how busy and agitated people get.

For example, this morning Kieran lost his shit on me all because I didn't brew a new pot of coffee after taking the last cup. He complained about pulling an all-nighter for some economics class, but how the hell was I supposed to know that? I sleep like a damn bear. Once I'm out, I'm out. This semester, I've been lucky enough to be graced with easy classes, so I don't have to pull all-nighters to study or be hopped up on caffeine twenty-four seven.

My last exam is next Monday, and it's for my class on honeybees—a class I could pass in my sleep. Not all of my friends are as lucky as me when it comes to school. Kieran won't leave his bedroom except to grab food or to take a piss. Nate and Eli spend most of their time in the business center, since there are tons of conference rooms students can rent out to study in. So, I'm left here alone, twiddling my fucking thumbs waiting for someone to hang out with me.

Geez that makes me sound pathetic.

On top of my friends being slammed with school, Vanessa has been avoiding me all week and I haven't been able to figure out why.

Okay, maybe avoiding is the wrong word because she came over the other night to study together—although we didn't get a lot of actual studying done. But since then, I've only gotten one-word responses from her. I'd assume she's neck deep in textbooks, using all her free time to study, but something in my gut tells me that I'm wrong. I don't like feeling uneasy.

Tonight seemed to be the only night she wasn't held up in the library, so I'm taking advantage of that.

I took Levi's advice and found the perfect way to distract her. I'm taking her to see the Christmas lights at the Public Garden. She's been obsessed over it ever since we walked by, and nothing cures the exam blues better than a Saturday evening with her handsome boyfriend, a cup of hot chocolate, and Christmas lights to make her forget about her troubles around the holidays.

I pull my Jeep into one of the many visitor spots at her condo, they're lucky to have this much parking in the city.

"Hey, Greg, how's your night going?" I wave over at the front desk as I make my way through the lobby, heading for the elevators.

Their security guard knows me well by now. After Vanessa and I started sleeping together, she had me added to the list of approved visitors, which makes it much easier than waiting for her to come all the way down. The first time I came to visit, I had to wait for Sydney to buzz me up. While I waited the guard complimented me on the Jeep—another *Jurassic Park* fan.

"Mr. Shepherd, nice to see you again. How's that Jeep running?"

I put my index finger and thumb together, making an okay symbol. "Good as gold." The elevator dings as the doors open, and I wave again at Greg. "Have a good night."

The ride up to the fifteenth floor is quick. It feels like the elevator barely moves, then all of a sudden, the doors open to Vanessa's floor.

I've always liked the idea of living in a condo, especially now that I'll be moving to New Jersey this upcoming summer, I need to start looking into places. I'd like something similar to this—security guard at the front, back door access in case there's paparazzi out front, a gym and pool are a definite must, and a hot tub wouldn't be bad either.

I can picture myself winding down after a game and letting the bubbles soothe my aching muscles. Just like our trip to Vermont when Vanessa and I sat in the hot tub while she read that steamy book of hers. *I wonder if she ever ended up finishing it.*

I knock on the door, but don't have to wait because Maddie barrels out the second my fist connects with the door. She looks rushed, a little disheveled, and is wearing a black sweater that swallows her whole. *That sweater looks familiar.*

"Sheesh, Harper. Where are you off to in such a hurry?"

Her pale blue eyes look up at me as I take her in. Her long black hair is kept back in braids, an overnight bag hanging on her shoulder— *Oh Maddie's got a date.*

"Just a late-night study sesh." Her pale skin immediately blushes at her own lie, giving her away.

"Mm-hm, sure. Is Ness ready?"

"Yeah, she's just in her room. Head right in."

"Thanks, enjoy your date, Maddie."

"Thanks." Her eyes bulge when she realizes her mistake. "Don't tell them, *please.*"

I give her a silent nod. If she doesn't want her friends knowing where she's going, it's not my business to tell them.

And also, Maddie scares the absolute shit out of me. This girl *chose* to study dead bodies, and I know for certain she would know how to get rid of one.

I step in and I feel like I'm slapped in the face by Christmas. The place smells like fresh pine with a hint of a spice—cinnamon or nutmeg, maybe Sydney made gingerbread cookies. Their place is decorated to the nines with Christmas lights strung around the ceiling, garland lining the hallways, and a giant frosted tree sits in the corner of their living room next to the balcony doors. I guess they really did go crazy last weekend.

"Ness?" I call from the hallway.

"Coming! I'm coming!" She stumbles out of her room, hopping on one foot as she pulls her sock onto her foot. "Sorry, I'm a bit of a mess today."

I look her over and completely disagree with that statement. Her hair is tamed by a dark green toque that matches her eye color, and her curls fall loosely over her shoulders. If she thinks she looks like a mess, well she's at least a hot mess.

If I said that joke out loud, she would punch me.

350

"Ready?"

Sydney peeks her head out of her bedroom door, her hair tossed into a messy bun. "Where are you guys going?"

That girl does love to pry.

"It's a surprise."

Sydney's face lights up. I can only imagine the ideas roaming through that head of hers.

"Ness will fill you in later."

Her face falls at my statement, knowing I won't give any information up. "You suck. Have fun." She sticks her tongue out at us and retreats back into the comfort of her own room.

"Will you tell *me* where we're going?" Vanessa asks.

"Nope." I open the front door. "Just follow along."

She does as instructed and follows me out of the building into my Jeep.

The night is chilly, so I brought a thermos full of hot chocolate for us. I know that she would prefer a hazelnut latte, but if I have espresso this late I'll be up until three in the morning.

The drive from her place isn't far, but she stays quiet the whole way. I'm unsure if she was too involved with the music or the brightly lit city, but it makes me feel a little uneasy with how silent she's being.

I find a parking spot close to the entrance of the Public Garden, which is damn lucky considering how packed it looks tonight. Before heading in, I grab the thermos I had tucked away and pour the hot chocolate into two travel mugs I brought. This will keep them nice and warm while we walk around and take in the exhibits.

"Wait here." I climb out of the Jeep and jog around to the passenger door, opening it so Vanessa can get out.

"I thought Christmas lights and hot chocolate might be the perfect distraction."

The lights reflect off her glasses, and I watch as her eyes roam over the well-lit park. There are various light displays ranging from candy canes to Santa with his reindeer.

The trees are wrapped with multicolored lights that change with music that's playing through speakers throughout the park.

"I've been meaning to come to the lights, I just couldn't find the time."

"I know. You mentioned it a couple weeks ago."

She looks to the side, pretending to take in the display of stars, but I know it's a diversion.

"*Oh,* I didn't think you'd remember that." Her voice is soft, barely audible. That feeling in my gut returns.

Vanessa begins walking and I follow alongside her in silence. The bridge crossing the pond is strung with lights that reflect off the water, making it seem like the entire park is glowing. We walk through a small courtyard with evergreen shrubs that are lined with lights, creating different animals with the colors.

As we pause at one of the statues I look down at Vanessa. Her cheeks have turned a rosy shade from the cold. I study her as she looks at the display of lights. *Goddamn, she is the most magnificent thing I've ever seen.* The twinkling lights illuminate Vanessa. I could stare at her for hours.

The changing colors reflect off her glasses, and that's when I notice the look on her face.

Her mood has been off ever since I picked her up. *Hell,* it's been off all week, but I tossed it up to exam stress.

"All right, you've barely said a word to me all night. Are exams stressing you out?"

"No." She responds quickly, too quickly.

She stays silent for a minute. I watch as she rattles her brain, trying to decide whether she should tell me what's actually going on or keep it to herself. Knowing Vanessa, she's either going to ramble a bunch of nonsense, or she's going to shove it down and let it eat at her until it eventually boils over.

"C'mon, Ness. You can talk to me."

She lets out a deep breath before speaking. "These past few months have been amazing. I love the friendship that we have, but something feels wrong. I-I don't know if I can do this."

"Do what?"

What can't she do, our relationship? Everything has been going so well, I have no idea where she's coming from. Was it something I did? Did I say something wrong?

"I don't think I can be a part of your life anymore."

What the fuck?

"What? Why?"

I have no idea where my girl's head is at. I'm racking my brain trying to understand her, but every thought goes blank. I thought everything was going well. I'm not an expert on relationships, but I felt like things were going smoothly. We banter with one another, but we don't fight. Is that what's upsetting her?

"You are meant for so much more than me, Jake. You have this incredible life to live, but I was never meant to be a part of it."

"What the hell are you talking about, Ness?"

"Things change, and I don't think we ever fully thought our relationship through. There are so many moving parts, so many unknowns. I think we jumped into things too quickly."

Jumped too quickly? We spent months running around each other before I finally got her to settle down.

She starts fiddling with the gloves on her hands, not making eye contact with me. "After you got that call from your agent, things have been different. You've been different. It's had me thinking about our future and where we stand. I don't think I belong in your future. You've always known what you wanted out of life, knowing where your family and friends fit into place. But you never planned to have a girlfriend before going pro."

"Okay, *and?*" I must be an idiot because I'm not following.

"And you shouldn't have to change around your dreams to accommodate me."

"Ness, you're acting crazy. Plans change. Of course I'm going to accommodate my life to have you in it."

She finally looks up at me, those big green eyes have a shimmer to them, but I can't tell if it's from the lights around us or if she's about to cry.

"But you shouldn't have to."

"What the hell is that supposed to mean?"

"On the beach in Cape Cod, I told you about my insecurities. About never being enough for my parents, my family, or my ex. I was always an afterthought. My family's careers are more important than anything in their life, and that's how it's going to be with you, but it's not your fault. You've worked your entire life to get to where you are today, and who am I to stand in the way of your dreams?"

My dreams? Doesn't she understand that she's become a part of that dream? I never pictured molding my life to fit another person into it until I met Vanessa.

Before I can voice this to her, she continues, "This upcoming year will be so important for your future. You'll be gone for half the year, playing in different states, working harder than you ever had to make a name for yourself. I don't want to be a distraction. Our relationship is too new to go through something as big as this. Your career comes first, and you shouldn't feel guilty for that. I don't want to make you feel bad for choosing your dream. Your entire focus should be on hockey. Not us."

"Vanessa, baby." I reach for her, but she pulls away. *Ouch.* I stand up straight, acting as if her rejection didn't just kill me a little inside. "Listen, I know this next year is going to be tough, but we'll make it work. I know things between us are still new and we're still trying to figure it all out, but I'm not going anywhere."

"Jake, we have no idea what we're doing. We had our fun, but we never should've made this more than what it was."

Well, that fucking stung. Does she really think that little of me?

"Vanessa, c'mon. Where is all of this coming from? I thought we were good?"

"We're far from good. We're living in a damn fairy tale. Right now, it seems like our relationship is perfect, but it's not. We haven't had any conflict, anything to challenge us. We've been blind to what's right in front of us—*our future*. You're going to become preoccupied with your career and your social life, and I'll be put on the back burner like I have been my entire life."

Fuck. Vanessa is the farthest thing from an afterthought in my head. This girl is on repeat every damn day. Every morning when I wake up, I think about her. When she's asleep next to me, I can't help but stare in awe at the girl who aimlessly walked into my life and took my heart hostage. When we're not together, I'm constantly thinking about what she's doing and if she's thinking about me as much as I'm thinking about her. And when we are together, I can't stop fucking looking at her. She's done something to me, rewired my brain so its only thought is *her.* She's taken everything from me, I don't understand how she cannot see that. What do I need to do, scream out that I love her in front of all these people.

"Vanessa, you are more important to me than you realize. For fuck's sake, I think I'm falling—"

"I think we should break up." Her words come out faster than mine, cutting me off before I can finish my confession.

"What did you say?"

My shoulders fall, feeling like someone just put fifty-pound barbells on each side.

"I think we should end this." She motions her gloved hand between us. "Before either of us gets hurt. We took the whole friends-with-benefits situation too far. We were foolish for believing it could be something more when we knew you'd be leaving."

Her words barrel into me, I feel like I'm going to fucking puke. There are too many people around for a conversation like this. Parents and their children are laughing and having fun going through the light display while my girlfriend is trying to break up with me.

"You're talking nonsense, angel girl." I guide us down one of the less crowded paths. There are less lights this way, so it's not as busy as the rest of the park. "Can't we work this out? Isn't that what relationships are all about, talking things through, figuring out a way to make it all work.

"Jake."

She stops following me, stopping next to a park bench. She motions to it, taking a seat at one end. I reluctantly join her, keeping distance between us. A minute goes by before she speaks, "I've been wanting to talk to you all week about this, I-I just didn't know what I was going to say until now."

She's been thinking about this *all week?* How can she go from sleeping in bed with me one night to wanting to break up with me only a few days later? Even I'm not that fucking cold.

"So, you're breaking up with me because you're scared that my career will be too demanding and I won't have time for us? Even though I'm telling you otherwise."

"No."

"Okay, well then help me understand, Vanessa, because I'm really fucking lost right now."

She flinches at my swearing, and I internally curse at myself for making her feel uneasy.

"We want such different things out of life. Your career is going to take off and who knows where I'm going to end up. My photography could take me anywhere in the world. It's not fair for either of us to put our lives on hold and resent each other in the future for not taking certain opportunities that might come. You deserve to reap all the benefits, Jake. I won't be standing in your way anymore."

I can't believe any of the words coming out of her mouth. This whole conversation feels like it came out of left field. I've tried telling myself that nothing was wrong between us, but I guess I was an idiot for believing that. I should've listened to my gut after our last game. I should've pushed her for more information.

Well, I'm pushing now.

"Vanessa, you can't be serious."

Her relaxed brows furrow into a straight line. "*I am.*"

"This is ridiculous, I'm not buying it. Sorry to say this, but you're stuck with me, Ness." If she thinks that a little overthinking is enough to drive me away, she has another thing coming. "Baby, let's talk about this. This is our first fight, *if* you want to call it that. We can figure it out."

"Jake, I don't want to end up as some NHL player's trophy wife. I'm sure there are a million girls out there, like Caroline, who would love to be by your side. But I want to make a life for myself, be selfish for once. I've been fine on my own my entire life, I'll be fine on my own for a while longer."

She moves to stand up from the bench, but I'm frozen in place. It's not the cold that has me stuck in my seat, I've just lost all feeling in my body for a brief moment and my brain doesn't seem to be working. She's become my everything while I've become nothing to her. I have no fucking clue what I'm supposed to do right now.

"So this is it?" My voice breaks as I ask the question.

"I'm sorry." Her voice is soft, almost comforting.

I'm not a crier, but I feel that familiar sting spread across my eyes, threatening to spill if I let them. I let out a long breath instead. What the fuck just happened? *I need to get the hell out of here.*

I sit up. "Let's go, I'll take you home."

She takes a step away from me, and that's the second time she's recoiled away. I don't think my ego will ever recover from this.

"It's fine, Sydney's going to come get me."

My eyes dart down to hers. The warmth in her green eyes is gone. They've turned cold, like an evergreen in the midst of a winter storm. Threatening me as if I'm the wind that would sway her leaves in the dead of winter. Vanessa doesn't look sad. *No.* Her expression has gone completely neutral.

Over the past few months, I've been slowly falling in love with the girl in front of me. I'm such a fool for thinking she felt the same. I thought that we were on the same page, but apparently, we weren't even in the same damn book.

I nod at her. "Right, well, if this is what you want. Get home safe, Vanessa."

I don't look behind me as I make my way to the exit of the park, leaving behind what I thought was the best thing that came into my life. But now, everything is fucked. And there's only one way to forget about all of this.

I need a drink.

"Ness. Can we talk, *please*. Call me when you get this."

I'm pathetic and drunk. That's the fourth voice mail I've left her tonight. If Kieran was here, he'd tell me that drunk calls lead to no good, but I don't give a shit. The whiskey I've been drinking has helped ease the pain at least.

I've tried texting her but that also hasn't worked. I don't understand how we went from zero to a hundred in the span of one night. I think she's overthinking our situation. She let her fear of commitment completely take over her rational thinking, and that's what caused her to break things off. *Right?* I wish she would pick up the goddamn phone so we can sort this out.

I found myself at Shaker's. Ironically, it's the bar where I first met Vanessa. Maybe I ended up here on purpose. I've been here sulking for the past two hours, and the bartender and I have become great friends. We made an unspoken rule, anytime he sees my drink empty, he needs to replace it.

Speaking of which, I lift my hand, signaling to the bartender for another. He nods and pours me another double shot of whiskey on the rocks. I decided to torture myself tonight, and nothing does that better than straight alcohol.

"Jake?"

My head turns at the familiar voice. *Caroline.*

I raise my newly filled glass and grumble, "Car! Hey, what're you doing here?"

"Geez, you look like ass. What the hell happened to you?"

I laugh as I take a sip of my drink.

What *is* wrong with me? Well, besides the fact that my girlfriend just broke up with me. If only Vanessa knew how I really felt. If she picked up the damn phone, maybe then she would know just how much I care for her.

"Woman troubles," I mumble.

"*You're* having women troubles? Well shit, I need to hear about this." Caroline takes a seat next to me at the bar. My eyes roam down her body, she's wearing a black lace top that ties at her chest and is open around her abdomen. I don't think Vanessa would ever wear an outfit like that. *Although I'd fucking love to see her in a lace top again.*

Why won't she answer? Did she really mean what she said? Was our relationship really a mistake? *Fuck no.*

I type out another message, but as I try to read what I just sent, I realize that my vision is a little blurry. Calling would be better. I should call her. As my finger hovers over her contact info, it's pulled out of my grasp.

"Hey!" I whine as Caroline tucks it into her bag.

"No drunk dialing. Nothing good comes from a drunk phone call, *trust me.*" I guess she does have a point. "Instead, we drink until we forget who we wanted to call…which I'm assuming is Vanessa?"

I nod at her. "She broke up with me tonight."

Caroline's eyes go wide and she immediately calls over the bartender, ordering two shots. She grabs both glasses and hands one to me. "To shitty relationships. We deserve much better than the hand we were dealt."

I don't know if I agree, but I clink my glass to hers. For the next hour we sit there, drinking and talking. And soon, I start to forget those deep green eyes, the big round glasses, and her pouty lips. My words start to fumble as I reach drink number who knows.

Caroline leans to whisper in my ear, the music getting too loud to hear each other without being this close. "I'm going to get us a ride home."

She ruffles through her bag, grabbing her cell phone. I hear her make a call to someone for a ride. The conversation is short, but I hear her mention my name to whoever is on the other line.

I should have another drink while I wait. One drink while waiting for our ride won't hurt.

Right?

I wave at the bartender again, this time giving him my credit card to pay my tab. I'll look at the damage in the morning. Nothing matters to me anymore.

Well, someone still matters. But I'm too drunk to even think about that right now.

My vision is starting to fail me and I think I'm starting to have hallucinations because I swear the last thing I see before I keel over to vomit is Kieran and Maddie rushing over to me, attempting to help me out of the bar.

CHAPTER THIRTY-TWO

I don't believe in love

VANESSA

There's no sun today, which is quite fitting for my mood.

I've been staring out my window since early this morning, watching the gray clouds take over the sun, snow threatening to fall. If only the ground would open up and swallow me whole.

I should probably be studying for my final tomorrow, but I can't focus on anything. All I can think about is the look on Jake's face when I broke things off last night. It was about four in the morning when I finally cried enough to the point of exhaustion.

I'm the first to admit that I have my faults. The biggest being I let my insecurities run my life. Or should I say *ruin* my life. I started to question whether our relationship was one that would last or if it would easily fall apart the second things got tense. I felt insecure and let my thoughts run wild. I allowed myself to imagine the worst, which led me to sabotaging everything, just like I always do. I didn't care what I said. I didn't think. I acted on my own stupidity. My words shaped themselves into a knife, slicing Jake with every vowel that came out of my mouth.

I was the one scared of Jake breaking things off, and yet it was me in the end who put us to rest. I let my intrusive thoughts burrow in my brain like an invasive species. I planted the seed, thinking that Jake would act just like my parents and our relationship would be doomed before it started. I watered that seed and let it grow until it blossomed into a full-blown mental breakdown.

This pattern has been present my whole life. When I start to feel too comfortable in a position, the overthinking begins and it takes over my rational thoughts.

Why can't I allow myself to fall in love? I mean, that's what was happening. I was falling in love with Jake fucking Shepherd and that scared the shit out of me. It scared me so much that instead of embracing it and telling Jake how I feel, I decided I wasn't worthy of that kind of love.

I pushed Jake away, and now I'm left here, broken in pieces all from my own doing.

His friendship mended something in me. At first, it was small gestures like bringing a latte to early morning practices or carrying my bag for me on campus. The gestures turned into us staying up late and him listening to me babble on the phone about nothing for hours, playing my favorite video games, watching each other's favorite shows, and even listening to Taylor Swift. There were so many small things he did to show how much he cared for me.

And I threw it all away.

My reasons might have felt like they were out of the blue—but these insecurities have been here the whole time, bubbling under the surface until they finally boiled over. And when they did, I allowed myself to think that Jake would treat me the same way my parents do. I tricked myself into believing that once Jake's life starts to take off, he'll toss me aside like I've meant nothing to him.

I'm too big of a coward to swallow my pride and admit to him that I'm scared. It's a fatal flaw of mine—pushing people away when things get too heavy.

"Ness," Sydney knocks at my bedroom door, "are you okay? Can I come in?"

I shuffle off my bed, wrapping myself in my blanket and unlocking my door for her. As soon as she sees me, she engulfs me in a hug and my tears begin to fall again.

"Syd...I-I'm so stupid."

"Are you going to tell me what happened? You've kept yourself locked in here since last night. I had my ear pressed to your door to make sure you were still alive."

I sniffle and take a deep breath. *Stop crying.*

"I broke up with Jake."

Sydney pulls away from me, her eyes almost bulging out of her head. "What? What do you mean you broke up with him? I thought you guys got into an argument."

"I was going to talk to him about all the stuff I told you and Maddie, but it didn't turn out as I had planned."

"Okay, sit down. I need to know everything from the start to finish." She grabs my hand and leads me back to my bed, where the sheets are ruffled from a restless night.

"I've been feeling anxious thinking about our future. I've never cared for someone this much and it fucking terrifies me, Syd. I'm scared that I'm going to fall so deeply in love with him and he's going to leave. And instead of waiting for him to break my heart...I broke his."

"Oh, Vanessa." She pulls me back for a hug, "That boy is so head over heels for you, Vanessa. If you asked him to jump off a bridge, he would. If you asked him to wear a pink tutu to practice, you bet your ass he would strut on the ice in it and not give a single fuck what any of the guys say."

"What are you talking about?"

"I know you need glasses to see, but are you *that* blind? That boy has been in love with you since the second he laid eyes on you. It's just taking him a long time to admit it to you."

Does he actually love me?

Sydney sees me questioning her and continues, "I know your parents' relationship sucks, but you need to realize that not everyone is like your family. There are good people out here, *people like Jake*, who love you. He wants to be with you, Vanessa. If he didn't, he wouldn't have asked you to be his girlfriend."

Maybe she's right. If I was feeling this way, maybe Jake is too.

I put my head in my hands. "What should I do?"

Sydney rubs her palm over my back in the soothing way she always does to comfort me. "What do you want to do, Ness?"

I want to take back what I said last night. I want to run over to Jake and tell him that I'm falling in love with him. Hell, I want to tell him that I'm *in* love with him. I think I have been for a while, and I've been too stupid to acknowledge it. I want to apologize for all the things I said and tell him I didn't mean it.

"I want to fix this. I want Jake."

"Okay, so how about you call him and see if he's willing to talk?"

I rustle around my bed until I find my phone buried under my pillow, dead. *Great.* As I plug it into the charger, it turns on and a ton of notifications pop up on my screen.

Nine missed calls from Jake. Fifteen unread texts.

"Shit."

"What?"

"He called me last night." We both look at my phone as if it's a foreign object. I press Play on the first voice mail.

"Ness"—the crack in Jake's voice pulls at my heart—"I'm sorry. I shouldn't have left you at the park, I should've stayed and fought for our relationship. I'm…I'm an idiot, okay? I don't know how to fix this, but please, please call me back."

I hit Play on the next voice mail.

"Hey, I know I just called and this probably sounds pathetic, but I need to talk to you. I need you in my life. I *want* you in my life. Just tell me what to do to fix this, and I'll do it. Vanessa, please pick up."

As each voice mail goes on, my heart breaks even more at every apology. Eventually his words start to slur and there's loud music behind his voice. I decide to delete the rest, I don't need to listen to any more to realize how wrong I was last night. I need to make this right.

As I rummage through my drawers, I look back at Sydney, who is studying the texts on my phone.

"Do you think he's going to forgive me?"

"Well, based on these"—she shakes my phone in her hand— "I'm sure he's willing to give you another shot. This boy is so in love with you."

My heart warms at the thought. It's time to end the self-sabotaging cycle.

"I think I'm in love with him too."

Her eyes go wide at that four-letter word. "Did you—did you just admit to loving Jake?"

I look at her and nod my head.

"*Oh my god.* I need to document this. What day is it?" She gets up from her spot on my bed, now standing on my mattress. "Ladies and gentlemen, Vanessa Nichols is FINALLY in love!" She acts as if she's shouting this from a rooftop and not from my bedroom.

I let out a breath and quickly look over myself. I have on Jake's BCU Wolves hoodie that I stole weeks ago and a pair of leggings—not the sexiest thing in the world, but I don't care.

"Is my face still puffy?"

"You look fine, now get your ass moving and go get your man back!"

I head to the hallway closet to grab a pair of Converse. As I slip them on, we hear sleet hitting our windows, quite hard.

"Here." Sydney grabs her car keys off the table in the hallway and tosses them to me. "Take it as long as you need. Knowing Jake, I'm sure you're about to have some crazy makeup sex."

"Thank you." I smack a kiss on her head. "And thank you for being such an amazing friend and dealing with my crap."

"No need to thank me, I love you like a sister. Just make sure to give me *all* the dirty details when you get home!" she calls out as I race out the door.

I sped out of our parking lot, not wanting to waste any more time. I've already let more than twelve hours pass, and I don't want to wait any longer. I don't expect Jake to forgive me right away, but I'll do everything in my power to make this right.

The rain lightens up and the big raindrops turn into giant snowflakes as I park in front of Jake's brownstone.

I lock the door behind me as I make my way to the stairs of Jake's place. As I'm about to turn the handle, Maddie comes barreling out.

What the hell?

I stumble back onto the porch, allowing Maddie to stand outside with me. I take note of what she's wearing, or what little she's wearing. She's in a black T-shirt that goes past her hips and a pair of plaid boxers peek out from underneath, exposing her pale legs.

"Maddie, what are you doing here?"

"It's a long story but…" She looks over her shoulder, looking into the open entryway behind her. "Ness, let's go home, okay?"

Kieran appears behind her, his tattooed arms crossed around his bare chest and his sweats hanging low.

Oh. I think I get it now. All those secret glances and late nights—all the puzzle pieces are finally fitting together. I want to ask Maddie a million questions, but I can do that later.

Priorities.

"Can this wait till later? I need to talk to Jake. I made a mistake and I need to apologize. I'll fill you in later, I promise. But this is *really* important."

"Vanessa, it might be better if you come back tomorrow. He's not…in a good mindset right now." Kieran moves next to Maddie, his body blocking my path.

Hearing that makes my heart ache more. *I did this.* I'm the one who broke his heart and left him shattered in pieces for his friends to pick up. I can only imagine what the boys must think of me.

"I said some things that I didn't mean and he…he needs to know how I really feel." I look up at him, but his features are stone cold. He's like a damn robot. "Kieran, *please?*"

He sighs and uncrosses his arms, giving Maddie a sorrowful look. They're silently communicating, and I hate that I can't read their minds. Reluctantly, Kieran moves aside, allowing me access into the house. I make my way through the living room, ready to spill my feelings to Jake. I'm ready to tell him that I was stupid and wrong, and that I love him. I just really hope he forgives me.

My feet pause when I hear a familiar female voice coming from the kitchen.

I know this voice.

My stomach immediately sinks. I retreat my steps back and that's when I see Caroline sitting on the counter wearing one of Jake's faded T-shirts. My eyes scan back and forth between her and the shirtless man standing in front of her. *Jake.*

No. *No, no, no, no. Please, tell me I'm hallucinating.*

The floor creaks beneath my feet, gaining Caroline's attention. She looks at me over Jake's shoulder as I stand in the archway, frozen in place.

Move. Run. Do something besides standing here like a complete idiot.

Caroline's face immediately changes from a lighthearted expression to horror. My stomach feels like there's acid shooting up my esophagus.

Jake takes notice of her shift and turns around, eyes going wide when they land on me. He wasn't expecting me to come here. For a second, I can read him like a book—*he realized he just got caught.* His face immediately hardens, turning into something more stoic, cold, unloving.

I desperately try to hold back the tears that are stinging my eyes. Here I was, coming over to apologize and tell him that I made a mistake and I'm sorry for hurting him. I was ready to tell him that I love him, and he's shirtless in his kitchen with another girl, only hours after we've broken up. I didn't think he was capable of doing something so malicious.

Caroline hops off the counter, making her way to the door. "I'm gonna go." She slips by me, not making eye contact on the way out.

My body finally defrosts and I'm able to feel my legs once again. In a second, I'm across the kitchen, standing in front of Jake who refuses to make eye contact with me. My neck cranes up to take him in. Normally I would be fawning over his messy curls and stubble, but right now I'm feeling too many emotions. *Anger. Betrayal. Disgust. Hurt.*

I know I was in the wrong last night, but how the hell did we get here? How could his feelings change in the blink of an eye? Last night he was calling, *begging* for me to see him— to work things out. And somehow, in the span of a few hours, he was able to move on. If his feelings could change this quickly, were they ever real?

My stomach feels like it's being repeatedly kicked in.

"Did you hook up with Caroline last night? Be honest." I blink back the tears that won't stop forming.

Jake keeps his gaze fixed on the cabinets on the wall behind me, refusing to meet my eyes.

"We broke up yesterday, Jake. *Yesterday.*" I move to stand directly in front of him, but he still refuses to look me in my eyes. "You have nothing to say all of a sudden?" I ask him, hoping to get something out of him. *Anything.* It's like he doesn't care that he's shattering my heart into a million pieces.

"I listened to your voice mails. I-I came here to tell you that I'm sorry. That I was wrong for pushing you away and that I…" I swallow the words he doesn't deserve to hear. "I was going to beg you to forgive me and give me another chance but…" The words feel like fire on my tongue.

I can't believe I came over here ready to ask for his forgiveness. What would've happened if I didn't show up this morning and decided to talk to him later? Would he have told me he slept with someone else, or would he keep it as his own dirty little secret?

"Never mind."

I turn to leave, and I only take a couple of steps before his voice finally breaks.

"*You* broke up with *me,* remember? What the hell did you expect me to do?"

I turn on my heel, hot tears streaking my cheeks. "I didn't expect you to fuck someone the same night!"

He stands before me, face stern and unmoving. "You're the one who broke things off, Vanessa. You said our relationship wasn't working and you wished we never got together. You were worried that I'd revert back to old ways, and I guess you were right."

Those stupid words I said to Jake last night get thrown in my face like an insult.

I wipe the tears away from my eyes and try to stand tall, although I'm nothing compared to Jake's tall stature. "You're right, it is my fault. I shouldn't have come here. I should've just left everything as it was."

This time when I turn to leave, Jake stays silent. And somehow, his silence slices into me deeper than his words. My biggest fear came to fruition. He doesn't care about me. I don't know if he ever did. I never should've opened my heart up to him. I should've kept him at arm's length and I never should've agreed to be anything with Jake Shepherd. Because here I am, once again, caring about someone who doesn't give a fuck about me.

This is why I don't believe in love.

JAKE

I lean back against the counter as I hear the front door slam.

Fuck. Fuck. Fuck me.

What the hell was Vanessa doing here? Last night she made it very clear that she wanted nothing to do with our relationship, and then she shows up unannounced, wanting to get back together. I've never been more confused in my entire life.

It takes only a matter of seconds for Maddie to steamroll through the room, smacking me upside the head as she yells, "What the fuck is wrong with you?"

Yeah, I should've seen that one coming.

She didn't smack me hard, but hard enough to rattle my already throbbing head. I think I might be done with whiskey for a while.

"Well? Are you going to say anything or are you just going to stand there with your dick in your hands?" Why does Maddie always say the most out of pocket shit? "Why did Vanessa run out of here bawling her eyes out? What the hell did you do?"

I did what was best for both of us. I bet she only came here to apologize and ask to be friends for the sake of the team. I didn't need to listen to her pity apology. She probably wanted to cover her tracks and make sure things could remain professional between us. I guess I kind of fucked that up, but whatever, it's for the best.

"I'm sure you're smart enough to put two and two together, Maddie."

"Hey, watch it." Kieran walks into the room, standing firm behind Maddie.

Memories from last night come flooding back. I remember being absolutely plastered to the point where Caroline had to get us a ride home. I didn't know she called Kieran until he and Maddie showed up. They were both dressed in Kieran's sweats, and I connected the dots from there.

"I told Vanessa I fucked Caroline." I walk over to the fridge, grabbing the cream so I can make myself a coffee and hopefully get the fuck out of this conversation. But by the sound of her gasp, I don't think I'll be so lucky.

As I turn around to turn on the coffee maker, I notice the daggers that Maddie is throwing at me. For a split second I think she's about to smack me again, but instead she rolls her eyes at me.

"Guys are such idiots. What the hell is wrong with you, Shepherd?"

I groan, running my right hand through my hair. Hangovers and arguments don't go well together. "What do you want from me, Maddie?"

"I want you to tell the truth because I know for a fact that you didn't sleep with Caroline. At least not last night. The two of you were in no shape to walk to the car let alone sleep with each other. So, you better tell me why the fuck you just lied and broke my best friend's heart, or else I'll kick you so hard in the balls that you'll feel them in your throat."

I look down at her, the small pale body that's barely covered by Kieran's T-shirt. This five-foot-five girl could kill me in a second, I don't doubt it. Maddie may be a little unhinged, but it's fueled by her love for her friends. Kieran picked a good one.

"Vanessa broke up with me last night."

Her harsh exterior changes immediately. *She had no idea.*

"Wha—"

I decide to answer her question before she finishes her sentence. "Vanessa decided that she no longer wanted to be a part of my life and our relationship was a mistake." I pour the cream into my mug and stir, "She said that we never thought about our future and we were living in a fairy tale, whatever the fuck that means."

The coffee pot starts brewing and the kitchen starts to fill with a robust aroma. I really fucking need this.

"Oh shit." Maddie puts her head in her hands, shaking it in disapproval.

"What, Vanessa didn't run this by the groupchat first?"

"When we had our girls' night, she told me and Syd that she's scared things aren't serious enough between the two of you. She has it in her head that when you move away you'll regret being with her. She's scared that since you two will constantly be in different places, you'll be around all your hockey buddies and temptation isn't easy to turn down."

Fuck. Why didn't she tell me this last night instead of breaking things off? If I had known she was scared, I would've done everything I could to make her feel safe.

"She told us that she was going out to talk to you last night, but I didn't think she was going to break things off. It doesn't make any sense, that girl loves yo—" Maddie stops herself.

The word is ringing in my ears, so I push, "She what?"

Maddie sighs, realizing her mistake. "Vanessa loves you, Jake. I could tell the moment she came back from Cape Cod that she was in love, even if she wouldn't admit it."

"Did she say something to you?"

"Well…no. But you know Vanessa. I'd be surprised if she ever said the word out loud. She has a whole mess of trauma and yet…" She pauses for a second, carefully choosing her next words. "And yet she still chose you. In the three years I've known her, I've never seen her this head over heels for a guy. She messed up because she was scared."

And I fucked it all up. How didn't I notice this? This entire time, she's felt the exact same way as me, and I was too damn blind to see it. I need to fix this.

"Shit, *shit, shit, shit.*" I start pacing around the kitchen, trying to figure out how the hell I'm going to fix this. I turn back to face Maddie. "I didn't sleep with Caroline. I-I just said that to make her feel how I felt last night. I'm such a fucking idiot."

"We already knew that, buddy," Kieran chimes in again, now more relaxed than he was earlier.

"Maddie, what the hell do I do? I really fucked up."

She bites her bottom lip. "I think you'll need to give her some space. If she thinks that you hooked up with Caroline, there's no way in hell she'll want to see you *or* talk to you. Let me go home and I'll see if she'll talk to me." She pats my arm before heading out of the kitchen, stopping in the archway. "Jake, I'm not saying this to make you feel worse than you already do, but you might have to come to terms with the fact she might never forgive you."

The truth hurts, but if she chooses to never forgive me, I deserve it. The coffee pot beeps, but I don't think I need coffee anymore. I take a seat at the kitchen table, a million and one thoughts racing through my head.

"I've royally fucked this one, didn't I?"

Kieran pulls out the chair next to me, sitting down. "I mean, I personally wouldn't tell someone that I fucked someone else the same night we broke up, but I guess we all do things differently."

Fuck, I can't lose her.

Kieran clasps his hand on my shoulder, "Don't worry about it. Maddie's gonna talk to her and I'm sure everything will be fine."

Something deep inside has me feeling otherwise.

CHAPTER THIRTY-THREE

A complete dumpster fire

VANESSA

It's been three days.

Three days since I've left my room.

Three days since I've talked to anyone.

Three days since my heart was set afire and turned into ash.

I've only left the comfort of my bed to get food from the kitchen or to write an exam. Maddie and Sydney have both tried talking to me, but my mouth comes up empty every time I try to open it. There's nothing to say anyway. My brain is exhausted from studying and overthinking. I think I've given myself a permanent migraine.

There's been an internal battle going on in my head, debating whether I should be mad or upset, or let the numbness take over.

I'm sure most people would say that Jake didn't cheat on me because we were broken up that night. Those same people would agree that Ross and Rachel were on a break.

To me, it's all the same. I've been wracking my brain trying to understand how Jake could sleep with someone else only hours after breaking up. I know I broke his heart, I'm not innocent here, but how does that give him the excuse to go sleep with someone right off the bat?

I was sulking in my bed that night while he was in someone else's.

I can't get the image out of my head. I didn't need to see it firsthand to let my mind play it out for me. Imagining all the things he used to do to me, the things he probably did to her. Did he caress her face? Did he kiss her entire body and tell her how beautiful she is? I'm sure he did much more than that.

This is the spiral I keep going down.

I never should've let my guard down. You never know when the rug is going to be pulled out from under your feet.

I've kept my phone on Do Not Disturb since that night, not wanting anyone to bother me. I should block his number. I know I should, but every time I try, my finger hovers over the button, too scared to move.

Geez, I'm so pathetic.

"Vanessa?" Maddie's voice carries through my closed door as she knocks. "Are you okay?"

No, I am far from being okay.

"I'm studying. Can we talk later?"

It's a lie, but she doesn't have to know that. I'm not the best company to have around right now. I'm sure she wants to talk about what's going on and make me feel better, but I'm not in the headspace for conversations right now.

A few seconds pass before I hear an "Okay" whisper through the door and her retreating footsteps.

My friends have tried to comfort me—be a safe place, but I'm in no mood for comfort. When I came back from Jake's the other night, Sydney was waiting for me in the living room with a soft blanket and a cup of tea. I have a feeling Maddie warned her before I got home. But instead of sitting on the couch with Sydney, I kindly took the tea from her and barricaded myself in my room instead. I built up a wall of silence, wanting to sit and wallow in my room until I turn into a crazy cat lady.

My alarm starts blaring next to me, shaking me out of my head fog.

Shit. If I don't get out of bed right now I'm going to be late for my last exam if I don't get out of bed. My feather duvet is heavy and cozy, I don't know if I *want* to leave.

At least I'm lucky enough that my last final is for my film class. The study material consisted of me sitting in front of my laptop streaming all the films we watched this semester and going over class notes.

The first movie I watched for this class was *The Godfather*.

With Jake.

That usual butterfly feeling I'd get when thinking of him has been replaced with an empty, sinking feeling.

I change out of my day-old clothes, swapping my dirty sweatpants for a pair of clean jeans. I have zero motivation to do much else than toss on a baggy sweater and pull a toque over my head. Somehow, I find the energy to brush my teeth and put moisturizer on so at least I don't feel like a complete mess.

The condo is quiet. It's still early in the morning, so I tiptoe across the hardwood, trying to avoid my friends on my way out. Sydney and Maddie have both finished all of their exams, and I can't wait to get this over with so I can officially be on winter break.

And, girl, do I need a break.

Campus isn't a far walk from our building. I'd rather face the cold and freshly fallen snow than have to wait for a crowded city bus. And it gives me time to listen to music and clear my head. Music seems to be one of the only things that keeps me busy.

By the time I make it to campus, I can feel my cheeks burning from the icy wind. I'm sure they're the same shade as a rose. The quad looks bare in the winter—snow covering the picnic tables that normally are crowded with people in the warmer months, trees stripped of all their leaves, nothing left besides footprints in the freshly fallen snow.

"Vanessa!"

My heart drops into my stomach at the sound of his voice.

Jake.

This is not what I needed this morning. Was it really too much to ask for an easy, uninterrupted morning? All I wanted was to finish my last exam then go home and curl into the fetal position in my bed.

I turn around to see him jogging over, his backpack hanging over his shoulders, bobbing as he makes his way toward me. It takes only seconds for his long legs to cover half of the quad and stand near me. He's smart enough to keep some distance between us.

"What do you want?" I keep my tone cold and my words short. He is the last person I wanted to run into today.

"I-I wanted to know if we could talk?"

"I have an exam in ten minutes." My words come out stronger than intended. I thought from days of crying that my throat would be hoarse by now.

"Okay, how about after? I can wait for you and we can get coffee."

I want to feel angry toward him—*but I can't.* The old me would've told Jake to get lost and to go kick stones. But the Vanessa he's looking at now is broken.

I mask my emotions so he can't tell how destroyed I am seeing him face to face. "I can't. I'm leaving for New York tonight."

It's not a full lie. I'm not leaving tonight but I am going home for a week to spend the holidays with my family. I wouldn't normally accept their invitation, but I'd rather be anywhere but here.

He huffs out a laugh. *"Really?* You'd rather lie about visiting your family than give me ten minutes of your time?*"*

"Not that it's any of your business, but I *am* going home. And you don't deserve *any* of my time. Not anymore."

His cold blue eyes narrow on me, trying to read if I'm lying. *The fucking audacity.*

"Why would you choose to spend a week with them knowing they're just going to tear you apart?"

I spent a lot of time thinking about that. I made the adult decision to put everything behind me for now so at least I won't be alone during the holidays.

"Y'know what, Jake, what I choose to do with my life is none of your *damn* business anymore. You lost that privilege when you were balls deep in Caroline." I turn away, about to make my way toward the student center, but the little green monster inside of me wants to hurt Jake. "I'd like to say it was great seeing you, but it wasn't. And the next time you see me, pretend you don't."

I don't wait for his response. I pump my legs faster until I reach the inside of the student center. My cheeks finally start thawing as soon as the heat hits my face, but the warmth also seems to unfreeze my tear ducts. I bat away a couple loose tears, I don't want to be that girl crying on campus before an exam.

Before heading to the auditorium, I run to the washroom to do a once-over. My eyes are puffy from nights of crying and my cheeks are still a little red from the cold. At least my fogged-up glasses have cleared up.

I just have to get through this exam and then I'm free. Free to go home for the holidays and probably hate my life the entire time I'm there. Maybe by the time I'm back on campus for the Winter Wonder tournament, I'll be ready to face Jake without wanting to curl up into a ball and cry.

By the time I left campus the sun had been captured by gray clouds and the tolerable midday chill turned agonizingly cold.

The second I got home I shed all of my winter gear and huddled myself in a thick pair of sweats.

While I was trying to find a hoodie to put on, I found myself finding things of Jake's—his Wolves hoodie, many of his T-shirts, and his favorite pair of black sweatpants he left here back in November. I remember the night he gave them to me. He came over after a home game, promising me great sex and a cozy night. We stayed in my room, ordered dinner, and spent hours watching *The Office*, gorging ourselves on snacks. He even tried a salt and vinegar chip that night—he gagged after taking a bite.

Goddammit. My stupid emotions.

Every thought, every memory of him swallows me whole, drowning me in a sea of sadness. I'm stuck between wanting to eat a pint of ice cream while crying in my bed or burning everything in sight that reminds me of him.

Okay, that might be a little too dramatic.

Instead of doing either, I find myself collecting the things that remind me of him and packing them into an empty box. Everything—his clothes, the custom camera strap he got for my birthday, the postcards I collected from each city we had an out-of-town game, and other memorabilia from the time we spent together. All of it fits perfectly in the box, as if it was made to tuck away all of my memories, never to be opened again.

As I tape the box shut, I feel a sense of relief wash over me. I don't feel completely better, but closing the box made me feel lighter.

I hear the front door swing open and close and a wave of guilt rushes over me. Maybe it is time for me to talk to my friends. I shouldn't leave for winter break without speaking to them.

My door squeaks as I open it, finding Maddie in the hall undoing her boots.

"Hey."

Her head whips in my direction. "Hi. How are you feeling?"

I shrug. "Is now a good time to talk?"

"Yeah, yes, definitely, my ears are wide open." She grabs her boot and flings it off her foot.

I motion my thumb to the living room. "Couch?"

We settle onto the sectional as Sydney walks through the door.

"Oooh, just in time for girl talk! Wow, I have great timing." She squeals, running into the room, not caring that her snow-soaked boots are getting all over the hardwood floors.

Sydney slides off her black platform boots, chucks them toward the hallway, and shimmies out of her coat as she settles comfortably on the couch with us.

"What'd I miss?"

"Nothing, we literally just sat down."

The two of them look at me, patiently waiting for me to talk first. Sydney sits with her legs crossed and her freshly manicured hands folded in her lap. This is might be the longest we've gone without speaking—all by my doing. For the past few days I've been lost. I didn't want to say anything to them because I don't want to come off pathetic, because I *do* still care about Jake. As much as it pains me to admit.

"So…how were exams?"

They both look at me with dead eyes. *Yeah, that's definitely not what they wanted to hear.*

"Nope. You're not weaseling you're way out of this conversation. We want all the details, Vanessa. We've given you your space, allowing you to sulk and mope around for days, but it's time to share what happened with Jake. We hate seeing you like this." Sydney leans over toward me, putting her hand on my knee.

"What do you want to know exactly?"

"*Everything.* One moment you were ready to win Jake back, and then literally forty minutes later you come home in tears."

I let out a long sigh before starting, "I went over to Jake's to apologize. And when I got there…" I close my eyes, picturing Jake's shirtless body standing in front of Caroline. He looked so relaxed, his broad arms encasing her on the counter. Before I can stop myself, my brain imagines what they did together and I swallow back the sob that wants to break free. "He slept with Caroline."

Sydney's mouth drops open in an *O* shape.

"You're kidding me?" She rolls her sleeves up to her elbows. "Oh, I'm going to fucking *kill* him. I'll call Nate right now. Maddie, you study dead bodies, surely you know how to get rid of one."

"I mean, you're not wrong."

"Guys, it's fine." It's not, but isn't that what people normally say in this type of situation? "I ran into him today."

Maddie squints her eyes, focusing on me. "What did he say?"

"He asked if I'd go for coffee with him to talk."

"And?"

"And I basically told him to forget that I exist."

Sydney nods her head at my response, understanding where I'm coming from. She's had her fair share of bad breakups, so if anyone knows my situation best, it would be her.

"Do you really think he slept with her? Maybe you should hear him out."

Maddie's suggestion has both me and Sydney whipping our heads in her direction.

"Why the hell should I do that?"

"I don't know, but if he's trying to reach out to you, there has to be a reason why. Maybe he lied about Caroline just to hurt your feelings. I mean, you broke up with him, maybe he wanted to even the score and hurt your feelings?"

Even the score?

I can't imagine Jake lying to me about sleeping with someone only to hurt me. Why would he do that? Why would anyone do that?

The anger I so badly want to feel toward Jake now comes to the surface, but instead of it being directed at him, it's narrowed in on Maddie.

"So what, you're defending him now?"

She holds her hands out in defense. "No, I just thought you two could come to an understanding, since you guys are going to be around each other until the season is over."

Sydney's eyes bounce back and forth between us as if she's watching a tennis match.

If Maddie wants us to talk so badly, who's to say she didn't tell Jake I was on campus today. It would make sense, because how else would he have known I'd be there today at that specific time?

"Did you tell Jake that I was going to campus today?"

The look on her face answers my question.

"What the hell? Maddie, why would you do that?"

"I think the two of you need to talk, that's all. I was there that night. If he and Caroline did hook up, Kieran and I would've heard it."

"Wait, hold up. You were with *Kieran*? You were there when all this went down and you didn't tell me? I hate being left out of things." Sydney tries to lighten the mood but it fails.

As practical and honest as Maddie sounds, my brain doesn't want to hear it. There's no excuse for Jake's behavior. Even if they didn't sleep together at the house, who knows what they did *before* they got home.

"I'm done with this conversation. I have to pack."

I storm off to my room, not wanting to listen to Maddie take Jake's side in all of this. Maybe a trip home will do me some good.

Or it could be a complete dumpster fire.

I grab my suitcase from my closet and start packing. I'm only staying for the week since I need to be back by Boxing Day. The Wolves have their annual winter tournament the following weekend, and I need to prepare a crap ton of social media posts for them.

My body mindlessly moves around my room, grabbing enough sweaters, shirts, and jeans to last me my entire trip. I'm not paying much attention to where I'm going, until my foot catches on something that makes me fall flat on the floor.

The box of Jake's things.

Fuck this box and fuck Jake Shepherd.

I lift the box into my arms, glad that it's not overbearingly heavy, and walk back out into the living room, finding only Maddie occupying the space.

"Here." I drop the box in front of her feet. "Can you give this to Jake the next time you're visiting Kieran?"

She pauses the show she was watching and looks up at me with those pouty blue eyes.

"Sure." I'm about to turn back to my room when Maddie grabs my hand. "I'm sorry for telling Jake where you were today. He's been asking about you every day and I thought if the two of you could just talk, then maybe he'd leave you alone." She sighs. "I'm sorry, I shouldn't have meddled."

Suddenly my anger melts away. It's so damn hard to stay mad at my friends because they genuinely want what's best for me. Even if sometimes we don't agree on everything.

"You're lucky it's hard to stay mad at you." I join her again on the couch, tucking away all thoughts of Jake. "So, what's this thing going on between you and Kieran? Anything serious?"

"It's…complicated. I'll fill you in when we figure it out."

It seems like everyone's life has been complicated lately.

CHAPTER THIRTY-FOUR

Am I that pathetic?

JAKE

The drive home for the holidays is lonely. I've taken this route home a million times, but today it feels wrong. Vanessa should be here with me, but I'm the only one to blame for why she's not.

A month ago we were on the same highway, flipping through radio stations until we landed on a song we could both belt out. I'd give anything to listen to her sing classic rock songs with me in the car again.

I don't think she'll ever forgive me.

I thought that surprising her on campus might've given me an advantage, maybe taking her by surprise would be beneficial.

It wasn't.

I wanted to tell her I made a mistake and that I lied, which, in hindsight, was a big fucking mistake. I only hurt her because her breaking up with me was the worst pain I have ever felt. I gave Vanessa my heart on a silver platter, and she grabbed a steak knife and sliced it to pieces. I was ready to go to the next step and she wasn't. For all I knew, she couldn't care less about me. I wanted her to feel like her heart was ripped out of her chest, just like me. It was wrong of me to do that. I know that makes me an asshole, and I have to live with the consequences.

I don't want the consequences to be having Vanessa completely out of my life.

Although that's how it feels. The other night, Maddie dropped off a box of my things at the house. The gift I got Vanessa for her birthday, photos, and trinkets from our time together—our entire relationship was shoved in that box.

I pull my Jeep into the gravel driveway, just like I've done a thousand times before. The snow crunches under my tires, it seems like the Cape got hit with a storm last night. I'm sure Autumn will want to build forts and have a snowball fight the second I walk in the door.

I grab my duffel bag from the back seat, leaving the presents for later. I'll sneak out tomorrow night to get them and stuff them under the tree so they're there when everyone wakes up on Christmas morning.

"I'm home!" I call out into the empty living room, my words echoing off the walls.

I drop my bag onto the heated hardwood floors, another upgrade Dad added to the house a few years back. The door to the basement is left slightly ajar, and I can hear voices wafting up the stairs.

As I get to the bottom, I find my family gathering all the Christmas decor from under the stairs.

"Ah, perfect timing." Dad notices me first, tossing me a box full of decorative pillows.

"You're not seriously decorating on Christmas Eve's Eve?"

Mom peeks her head out from under the stairs, a cobweb stuck to her hair. "We wanted to wait for you!" We decorate the house together every year. Normally I try to come home in between exams to help set everything up, but there's been so much going on lately that I didn't get a chance to come home sooner. I also may have been putting off coming home because I have no idea what to tell my parents about my relationship.

"I was grateful at first, not having to lug all this stuff upstairs without you, but Mom has had us working *all morning.* I wanted to go outside and start working on my snow fort for our snowball fight later, but she used her secret Mom powers and convinced me to organize her collection of Santas." Autumn huffs a stray hair out of her face, her arms full of mini-Santa Claus statues. Mom loves them and every year she seems to add more to her collection.

"Don't worry, even if you worked on your fort all morning, there's no way in hell you'd win in our fight."

She maneuvers the statues in her hand and flips me off. *She definitely missed me.*

"Well, now that I'm here, put me to work. You guys head upstairs and I'll grab a few more things and follow you up." I place the box of pillows onto the ground and sift through the rest of the decorations.

Ten minutes later and the dining room is filled with a ridiculous collection of tinsel, reindeer, and knickknacks. Dad and I bring up the Christmas tree from the basement, setting it up in our main living room. Mom goes through each room, placing a smaller evergreen in each, decorating them with different colored bulbs and ornaments.

Each room is color-coded. The living room has soft whites and gold, the kitchen has red tinsel and bows hanging from the cabinetry, and the nautical-themed family room is decked out in deep blues and light grays.

I wasn't joking when I said Mom goes all out on Christmas. I wish Vanessa was here to see it. At Thanksgiving, I thought she would be here with me.

"Hey, can you help me bring in some firewood from out back?" Dad clasps his hand on my shoulder, breaking my thoughts.

"Sure. Let me toss my stuff into the loft first. I'll meet you outside."

I grab my discarded bag off the floor and run across the deck, tossing it inside my room before making my way behind the house to the shed. Dad is already there, making a small stack of firewood for each of us to bring in.

"How was the drive?"

"It was fine."

I lean down, scooping a handful of logs into my hands, not caring if I get a splinter.

"And how are you?" Dad's tone changes, and I know what he's secretly asking. He wants to know why I'm home for the holidays *alone*.

I swallow the lump that settled in my throat. "I'm good, same as always."

I give him a curt nod before heading back inside. I don't feel like hashing out my feelings with my dad before Christmas. I can deal with all this shit after the holidays. I can pretend to be happy for the next few days, I just can't think about Vanessa.

If I don't think about her then the next few days will go by in a breeze.

"I think my head is going to explode." I poke my head into Autumn's room. She's sprawled on her bed, a book resting in front of her.

"Are mom's candles giving you a headache too?"

I enter her room and plop down next to her, grabbing a fuzzy black pillow and tucking it under my head.

"No. Well, okay yeah, the cinnamon maple one is burning my eyes, but that's not it. I can't seem to get Vanessa out of my head."

"Aw, you're so in love with your girlfriend you can't stop thinking about her. How sweet."

"Ex-girlfriend."

She stops flipping the page of her book, and turns to me, shock written across her features. "You finally get into a real relationship, and it only lasted a week? What the hell happened?"

Her insult doesn't affect me. Growing up with Autumn, I'm used to her constant teasing and brutal honesty. I also think she's going through a bit of a rebellious phase because the last time I was in her room it was bright pink with fluffy pillows and now it's dark gray walls filled with posters and vinyl records.

I shrug. "She broke up with me."

"What did you do?"

I sit up, leaning on my arms. "Commitment issues mixed with me being an idiot."

"Okay, elaborate please."

"Vanessa broke up with me because she thinks we want different things out of life, and she doesn't want either of us to resent one another." I save her from the rest of the messy details.

"And you didn't fight for her? Tell her that she's crazy and you wanna marry her."

"Autumn."

"What? I'm just saying what we all know." She gets up, putting her book on top of her dresser. "When you came home for Thanksgiving, you were so *goo goo ga ga* over her. Mom didn't shut up for *weeks* after. She and Dad kept saying, 'Jake found the one.'"

They never said anything to me after we left. They told me they were excited for her to come back for Christmas, but other than that, our conversations mainly consisted of hockey, school, and what was going on at home.

"Yeah, well, I kind of fucked up too."

She crosses her arms over her chest. "I knew it. What did you do, asshat?"

"You've gotten meaner since I've left."

"I've always been mean, stop dodging the question."

She's good. She knows all my diversion tactics.

"Vanessa thinks I slept with someone the night we broke up."

Autumn's face turns cold. This is the first time I've ever felt a little scared by my younger sister.

"She came by my place and a friend stayed over. Nothing happened, but I was hungover and still pissed from the night prior, so when she showed up unannounced and assumed I did something, I let her believe it."

Autumn smacks her forehead. "Jesus, Jake, you are such a big, stupid idiot. I can't believe New Jersey wants such an airhead on their team."

"I wasn't thinking."

"Obviously! What possessed you to be such an asshole all of a sudden? I knew you weren't into relationships, but I thought maybe once you got into one you would change."

All right, that one hurt a bit.

I know I don't have the greatest track record, but I would *never* cheat on Vanessa. I'm a fucking fool for letting her believe I screwed Caroline. I made a stupid decision in the heat of the moment, and I don't know what I'll do if I can't tell Vanessa how sorry I am.

"I tried fixing it, but she won't even speak to me."

"Can you blame her? If I was Vanessa, I would've slashed your tires and egged your house."

I lie back down, letting out a long breath. I should've kept this to myself. Sometimes it's nice talking to your sibling about life, getting a different perspective on things, but Autumn's definitely laying it on thick. I deserve it.

"Maybe you should talk to Mom and Dad. They'll probably give you better advice than me."

"I'd rather cut off my balls than talk to Mom and Dad about this. So don't bring it up."

"*Whatever.* You're just cranky because you screwed up with Vanessa *and* I beat you at Catan the other night."

"I would've won if you didn't take away my longest road card."

"It's called strategy, Jake. Wanna play *Mario Kart* till dinner's ready?"

Memories from Vanessa's birthday graze my mind. Her eyes lit up walking through the house, seeing all the decorations and everything we put together. I just want things to go back to the way things were.

We play for a while, Autumn kicking my butt more times than Vanessa has. She's about to win the final race when Dad calls down the stairs for us to come up for dinner.

It smells fucking heavenly as we enter the dining room. On the table there is a spread of turkey, mac and cheese, mashed potatoes, asparagus smothered in parmesan, fresh buns, and gravy. My mouth waters on instinct. We each load up our plates. Me and Dad both add heaping scoops of mashed potatoes and gravy onto ours. It's winter break, so my diet is on pause for the remainder of the week.

For a few minutes the only sound in the room is forks scraping against plates. I think we starved ourselves all day for this meal.

"So, did I miss anything important these past few weeks?" I ask no one in particular.

Autumn nods as she shoves a spoonful of mac and cheese into her mouth. "I got into Florida State."

"Autumn, it's not polite to talk with your mouth full." Dad's voice is stern.

That's not something I'm used to. He only uses that voice when he disapproves of our choices. Like when I was twelve and broke my elbow rollerblading with my friends. In his defense, we thought it would be fun to race down a hill and try to jump off a ramp. His tone was valid.

"Dad isn't thrilled I applied there."

I raise my eyebrow, looking at Dad. "Why?"

"It's a party school. It's out of state. I don't know why you don't want to go to Boston Central like your brother."

"They have a great dance program in Florida, Dad. I can't live in Massachusetts forever!"

Mom smiles at the two of them as they bicker. It's always been like this. Autumn is Dad's favorite, but it doesn't hurt my feelings, she is the one who lives with them all the time. I've always had a close relationship with my parents, but it's different with Autumn. She's the baby of the family, so he's more protective of her.

"Well, either way, it's not decided yet. I applied to other schools, too, including USC and Tisch."

"Once you hear back, then we'll sit down and discuss it." Mom's voice is soft. She'll cave and let Autumn go anywhere she wants, and then she'll be the one to convince Dad that he's overreacting.

Mom takes a sip of her wine, then sighs. "I wish Vanessa could've come for Christmas. Can we give you the gift we got her? I'm sure you will see her before we get the chance to."

Shit. We've gotten through most of the day without bringing her up. I really thought I'd be in the clear.

"Yeah, sure."

"If she lets you within five feet of her." Autumn fires under her breath and I elbow her side, giving her a look without my parents noticing. Christmas dinner is not the time to bring up my failure of a relationship. If my parents found out how poorly I acted, they would disown me.

But I know Autumn. In order to get the heat off of her, she'll change the subject to me. "Hey, Jake. Where did Vanessa go for the holidays? It's so weird you haven't heard anything from her."

I keep my face neutral, not trying to give my parents any more information. They don't need to know about this. As far as they know, she went home for the holidays to spend quality time with her family.

"She's, uh—in New York, with her parents. She's probably just busy, I'll give her a call later."

Mom grabs my hand and gives it a squeeze, her face full of joy. "Aw, I'm glad she got a chance to be with her family during the holidays. I know Thanksgiving was hard for her. Maybe we can call her later and wish her and her family Merry Christmas."

"Yeah, if she picks up." Autumn takes a sip of her drink.

That little shit disturber.

"She might be busy, Amelia. We don't want to intrude on the girl's holiday."

Mom shrugs, ready to let the topic die, and I couldn't be more grateful.

"Maybe next year we'll invite her and her family for Christmas," Dad says before shoving a heaping spoonful of mashed potatoes in his mouth. "We have more than enough space for her and her parents."

Autumn huffs a breath, and I know she wants to spill my secret. She only wants to tell our parents so it forces me to deal with it, and that's the last thing I want right now. I give her a warning glare that screams *Don't you fucking dare.*

Her smirk grows and I know I'm screwed.

"*Maybe.* If Jake can win her back by then." Autumn conveniently takes another sip of her drink while our parents' attention is now locked on me.

I'm going to kill her.

Dad clears his throat. "What do you mean, win her back?"

"We broke up." I try to keep it simple, hoping that they'll drop the subject if I seem uncomfortable.

390

"What?"

"Oh no, sweetie, what happened?"

I open my mouth to answer, but Autumn steals my words. "Vanessa broke up with him and then Jake told her he slept with someone else instead of fixing things."

"For fucksake Autumn."

Mom gasps and Dad gives me a very discerning look. Dad's long sigh is what tells me that I'm fucked, and they're disappointed.

"*Jacob Anthony Shepherd*, why would you do that?"

I'm shooting daggers at Autumn. She's lucky it's Christmas or we'd be throwing hands like we used to when we were little. I would like to clarify that I've never brutally harmed my sister, but we've definitely thrown punches a few times—her more than me, but her tiny hands can pack a punch.

"It's nothing, can we just drop it?"

I need this conversation to be over. I don't want to hash out my feelings or my relationship at fucking Christmas dinner.

"Jake's upset because he made a mistake and now things aren't going his way." Autumn smiles wickedly at me, she knows now I can't escape talking with our parents. She meddles more than fucking Mystery Inc.

I drop my fork onto the table, and the clanking against my plate causes my mom to flinch. "Is this really a discussion to have at the dinner table?"

"Actually, I think everyone's finished. I'll excuse myself and get us all dessert while you three talk." Autumn collects our empty plates, bringing them into the kitchen, her ears still perked waiting to eavesdrop on our conversation.

"Jacob, what happened?"

This subject is a touchy one. It's been a long time since he and Mom had problems, but I know my situation is only bringing up old emotions for them.

Fucking Autumn. I hate that she brought them into this.

I avoid all eye contact. "I don't know."

Out of my peripherals I see Dad giving me a stare down that has me realizing I won't be leaving this table until I come clean.

"I went to the bar and my friend Caroline showed up. We got wasted and she stayed at the house. She puked on her clothes, so I gave her something to wear. The next morning Vanessa came over and, well…I'm sure you can imagine what she thought." I look away, not wanting to make eye contact with either of them, so instead I look at the wreath hanging on the wall. "I was upset. Pissed off. *Hurt*. I didn't know she was coming by to get back together. I wanted her to feel as shitty as I did. I-I was stupid and I made a mistake. One I'm paying for."

"Stupid isn't the word I would've chosen to describe your actions." Dad sits with his back straight, the look of disappointment still transparent on his face.

"Jacob." Mom reaches for my hand again, but I pull away. Hurt flashes across Mom's face for a second before going neutral again. *She understands.*

"I know I screwed up, okay? As soon as I realized the mistake, I tried to fix it. I tried calling, texting, showing up in person—but she doesn't want anything to do with me. So what the hell am I supposed to do now?" Saying it out loud brings out emotions I tried shoving down.

I'm not some hard-ass who won't admit to having feelings, because I do, and I'm fucking upset. I'm already disappointed in myself, but seeing my parents look at me like this, it fucking *kills* me. I know they're my parents, and they're going to try to understand, but I can tell just by the look in my dad's eyes that he's not impressed with me or my actions.

We sit in silence, the only sound is Autumn in the kitchen cutting into dessert. I watch as my mom places her hand on my dad's, his harsh exterior softens, the hurt and disappointment melting off at Mom's touch.

"Parker." They silently communicate, my dad's nod is his only response to her before he gets up.

His eyes fall back on me, and with a tick of his head, he motions to the door leading to the patio. "Let's go."

Is he kicking me out?

I don't hesitate to follow him. My dad is a big guy, and if he tells me to do something, you bet your ass I'm doing it. I grab my jacket off the hook by the door, slipping it on quickly. We head down the patio steps to the garage bar.

"You're not a kid anymore, but this is still going to be hard to hear." His breath collides with the cool air around us.

The door opens with a slight creak. We flick the lights on, the heat immediately relieving the brief cold. Dad walks behind the bar and motions for me to sit down on one of the stools. He grabs a bottle of bourbon off the shelf behind him and pours us each a shot over ice. I grab the glass from him, taking a sip. It's smooth with a butterscotch aftertaste.

"When you kids were younger, your mom and I were going through a rough patch." His voice is low, sounding *embarrassed*. "We didn't want to tell you—"

"I know."

He looks up from his glass. "*You do?* How? Did your mother—"

"Dad, I was a kid, but I wasn't stupid. It wasn't a coincidence that you conveniently put me into hockey the same time you two were constantly fighting."

His shoulders sag with the weight he feels. *Fuck,* I didn't want to make him feel like shit.

Back then, I pretended like I knew nothing. But parents are sometimes a little careless. Mom would put their counseling sessions on the family calendar and label it as *Doctor's appt.* At first, I thought nothing of it, but when the appointments became a monthly thing, I knew one of my parents was either sick or they were covering up something. And as any sleuthing kid would do, I snooped through their things until I found out their doctor was a marriage counselor. It wasn't until months later, when I overheard Mom's confession to her friend, that I learned why they went to counseling. I decided to keep my mouth shut and pretend I was oblivious to it all.

"It was hard. Your mother and I went to counseling, but it took years for me to trust her again." He tips the glass back, the amber liquid disappearing as he tosses it back. "Why'd you do it?"

His question hits harder than a full-body check.

I've been asking myself this question a lot lately. I was so quick to be guarded, maybe it's the defenseman in me. That night all I wanted to do was drown out the thought of Vanessa. The next morning, when I saw her standing in my kitchen, my brain stopped working. Instead of running to her and telling her how sorry I was, all I felt was embarrassment. I was embarrassed that the girl in front of me, the girl I love, didn't want to be in my life anymore.

I've never felt small or insignificant, but I did then. I should've heard her out before shoving my own foot in my mouth. Not a day goes by that I don't regret my decision.

"I guess I'm just an idiot."

Dad laughs at my statement. *All right, he didn't have to agree so quickly.*

I swallow the remainder of bourbon, letting the smoky and sweet flavors rest on my tongue. "It's the first time I've ever felt useless. I think I'm in love with her, Dad. And for her to break up with me out of the blue, I guess you could say I had some resentment. There was a little piece of me that was happy to make her regret her decision. Until I realized how in the wrong *I* was."

Dad grabs the empty glasses off the bar top, placing them in the sink to wash later.

"I think if I was able to forgive your mother for a kiss, Vanessa will forgive you for lying. But if she doesn't, then you'll have to live with the consequences of your actions. And if she does forgive you, there's no guarantee she'll fall back into your arms. You broke her trust, and that is not an easy thing to get back."

"Yeah, I understand."

"Try talking to her again. She might not want to hear it, I know I was reluctant to give your mother another chance, but I'm glad I did. Look at the life we have now." He places a hand on my shoulder. "You're a good kid, Jacob. We're human, and we all make mistakes. Be honest with her, open that big heart of yours and I'm sure everything will work out."

My dad and I don't always have heart-to-heart conversations, but I am grateful for the few that we do.

"C'mon, let's head back inside. Your mother made her signature German chocolate cake, and if we don't go in soon, Autumn will hoard the entire thing to herself."

My sister does have an intense sweet tooth.

We head back inside to eat dessert and open presents. I sit on the couch across from the fireplace with Autumn while Dad starts separating the gifts. My parents got me a new shaker bottle for my protein shakes and a new hockey bag that has multiple compartments. Mom said it's to help me stay organized, but we all know that within a few weeks, the bag will be far from organized. Autumn got me more hockey tape and a Blu-ray copy of *Dazed and Confused*, our favorite comedy to watch together.

Finally, it's my turn to hand out gifts. I grab my presents from under the tree and pass them out accordingly. I got Mom a new pair of shears, her last ones bit the dust this past summer. For Dad, an aged bottle of his favorite whiskey to add to the bar. Autumn was probably the easiest to shop for, and that's because she told me exactly what she wanted. A pair of these fluffy brown slippers that I guess every teen *needs* to have.

After presents, the Shepherd family traditions continue as we watch a Christmas movie together before heading to our separate rooms for the night.

I hope Vanessa is having a good Christmas. I don't know if her family has any traditions that they upkeep every year. From what she's told me about her family, I highly doubt they do.

The gift I got for Vanessa stays hidden in a box under my bed back in Boston. I wish she was here with me and I could watch her open her present. I wanted to get her something sentimental for Christmas. I tried for weeks to find a replica of the tote bag she loved so much, but I guess it was one of a kind and even eBay couldn't help me. Instead, I found a girl on social media who makes custom tote bags out of California. I sent her a photo of Vanessa's old one and had her create something similar but with some modifications. This tote is a sandy burlap material, and she embroidered a circle of flowers and vines on the front, with a beach in the center to remind her of our trip to Cape Cod. I had the girl add extra pockets and interior compartments so Vanessa's camera accessories have their own spot rather than being thrown together in the bag.

Worst case scenario, I'll give the gift to Maddie and she can say that she bought it for her. Even if she never forgives me, I still want her to have it.

I just hope that her Christmas is going better than mine.

CHAPTER THIRTY-FIVE

Men, most of us are assholes

VANESSA

The holidays suck.

I never should've agreed to come home.

The first couple of days were easy. My parents were both busy with work, so we barely said more than a few words to one another.

I was able to explore the city like I used to, walking around with my camera, taking photos of anything that piqued my interest. Boston is a big city, but it doesn't have the same hustle and bustle of New York. Who knew I'd miss the crowded sidewalks and rude motorists shouting at people on the street. Although I think I missed the single-slice pizza from Pinoppio's the most. Nothing beats a fresh slice of pepperoni on a cold day to warm you up.

My parents decided to host Christmas at our condo in Manhattan this year rather than the house in the Hamptons, although it's not much of a difference besides not being right on the beach. My parents' condo is something you'd see in a movie. It has two floors, six bedrooms, six bathrooms, and a massive balcony that wraps around the entire place. The building also comes with its own amenities like a private elevator, a pool, a private gym and sauna, and a relaxation room—which is basically just a glorified office space with small water fountains and a juice bar.

Everything is the same as when I moved out three years ago. Bright marble flooring, and white cabinets and walls—no warmth to be found besides a small vase of flowers sitting in the middle of the island. The furniture is all modern with glass coffee tables, sleek black leather couches, and a beige area rug to *add color* as my mom once said.

That's why my place in Boston is full of color. I don't want people to feel as if they walked into a hospital rather than my childhood home.

The only spot in this entire place that feels like home is my room.

I packed up most of my belongings and took them to Boston, but I still have a few of my things left here. My old bed, with a custom-made quilt I purchased from a flea market, sits in the middle of my room, I covered the hardwood floors in the bedroom with multiple area rugs, all ranging from earthy greens to dusty blues. The walls are still full of my photos— some I took when we went on vacations, and a few that won me prizes in school.

It's as if my parents hadn't opened my door since I left.

I tried to stay in my room as long as possible today, but once the family started arriving, Mom forced me to be social—which is why I'm currently sitting in the living room with a glass of wine, far away from everyone who's chatting about the upcoming election and what everyone's been up to, a.k.a comparing lives to see who's outshining who.

My parents look like they've been plucked out of a *GQ* magazine. Dad's hair and beard are trimmed perfectly, the gray of his hair almost matches the color of his sleek suit. Although he looks a little unkempt with his dress shirt unbuttoned at the collar. I'm sure Mom will give him a backhanded compliment later.

Mom went for her signature look—dark gray slacks with a white cashmere sweater. The chestnut curls that I've inherited from her are pulled back tightly into a ponytail, not one hair out of place. I decided to stick with my regular wardrobe, light-washed blue jeans and a tight black turtleneck. It's basic, but still somewhat dressed up. You'd think for the holidays my family might want to relax, wear more comfortable clothes, but my family is the opposite. Holidays are for fine dining, classy outfits, and catty conversations.

"Vanessa?" A deep voice comes from behind me, taking my focus off our family that's congregating near the dining room.

I turn around to find my cousin Theo and his boyfriend, Curtis. They both look so put together—Theo's in dark brown plaid dress pants and a black turtleneck, the fit is similar to mine, tight fitting and showing off his muscles. His dark hair kept short, and his beard is well-groomed and maintained, looking as if he just got a fresh trim. Curtis is the opposite of Theo. Curtis is the opposite of Theo, with curly blond hair and a tall slim build. His dress shirt is also unbuttoned, but open enough to see his chest and the pendant necklace he's wearing.

"Theo, hey." I get up to hug my cousin. "It's good to see you. How are you guys?"

They walk around the couch, sitting down across from me.

"Good." He looks over at our family that's huddled with their red wine and scotches. "Glad to find someone sane in this house." He motions his glass to me, and I toast him.

I guess I'm not the only one who feels out of place here.

Theo has his life together for the most part, and everyone in the family adores him. I need to remind myself to not spill *too* much. You never know who you can trust in our family.

"How's school going?"

"Oh, uh…" I think back to the conversation I had with my parents a month ago, Mom insisting that she tell the family I'm undeclared and still haven't made my mind up.

Well fuck that. I'm tired of lying to my family. If they're disappointed in me, then so be it, but I'm done hiding who I am.

"It's going great. I'm working with BCU's hockey team, managing their social media accounts."

"That's pretty cool." Theo leans back into the couch, extending his arm behind Curtis. "Are you still into photography? I remember you used to always have a camera in your hand growing up."

Memories of running around with a disposable camera, taking photos of myself, my cousins, and our whole family come rushing back to me. Memories that I kept locked away. I used to take pictures everywhere. Whether we were at someone's house or on vacation. I've always felt the need to capture everything.

"Yeah, I'm majoring in journalism with a minor in film and photography. It's been really great so far."

"Good, I'm glad to hear that at least one of us has pursued our interests."

His answer comes as a surprise. "Are you not excited about your residency at Johns Hopkins?"

Curtis moves his hand to Theo's knee, giving it a slight squeeze. The gesture doesn't go unnoticed. Jake used to shake his knee when he was anxious, and I'd always put my hand on it to calm him down.

Theo takes a sip of his scotch before leaning in closer to me, his eyes panning back and forth from us to the rest of our family, making sure they can't hear. "I'm not going to Johns Hopkins."

I nearly spit out my wine. "What?"

"Curtis and I are moving to Seattle, and I'm going to do my residency there. We haven't told the family yet."

My mouth hangs open, still shocked. The last I heard, all my cousins were doing so well, becoming so successful and making the family proud. I don't want to say it's nice to hear that one of my cousins is like me, but it's nice not feeling as alone.

"Curtis's job is transferring him to their office in Seattle, and we thought that it's the perfect opportunity to get away from, well, all of this. I don't know if you've noticed, but our family can be quite exhausting." He motions around us. I know the stresses of our family all too well, he's preaching to the choir.

"I'm so happy for you two. I hope it goes well. I've always wanted to see Seattle."

"You're more than welcome to come visit us once we're settled. I'm sure your camera would love to see some of those beautiful sights in Washington." Curtis smiles at me, and all I feel is warmth. For once, I'm okay with a family gathering.

"So, give us the gossip, what's going on in your life? Friends? Boyfriend? Girlfriend? It's been ages. I wanted to catch up at the funeral, but your parents said you came down with a cold and couldn't make it." *Hmm, good lie.*

"Oh…yeah, I had the flu." I know I shouldn't cover for my parents, and I could easily out them for lying, but I decide to let it go. "My life isn't too exciting. Same friends—Sydney and Maddie, my roommates."

"No love life?" Curtis asks.

I take another sip of wine, not wanting to answer *that* question.

"Oh, I can tell by that look in your eyes that you have something juicy."

I shake my head. "No. There was this guy but…things didn't work out."

"*Men.*" Theo sighs. "Most of us are assholes."

"I wish I could say I don't agree, but I do."

"What'd he do?"

I'm about to open my mouth and answer when we all get called over for dinner. We walk over to the open-concept dining room. The long quartz table is filled with an assortment of meats, cheeses, and side dishes. Everything from a roasted turkey down to mashed potatoes and brussels sprouts. The table is decorated with tall candles, scattered pinecones, poinsettias, and greenery.

I take the seat next to Theo and my dad, my mom sitting next to him at the head of the table. *Very fitting for their relationship.*

The sound of forks hitting plates and scooping food immediately fills the silence. Everyone's passing around plates and bowls, grabbing a little bit of everything. Soon, the conversation starts. Uncle Richard goes on about how his friend is running for governor, and Aunt Helen boasts about helping with the campaign. For a while, the adults chat about their lives, comparing everything from vacations to what events they were invited to.

I don't know why I agreed to come here.

That's a lie.

I was lonely and vulnerable and thought that getting out of Boston would help clear my head. Nothing is working. I can't stop thinking about Jake and our situation. There are moments when I think I should reach out and make things civil between us. Like Maddie said, we'll have to be around each other for the remainder of the season. I don't know if I can forgive him for what he did, but I can try to pretend to be okay until this is over.

We make it through dinner and dessert, and I barely say a word the entire time except for my small conversation with Theo and Curtis. My other cousins, Mark and Sarah, decided to spend their Christmas with their grandparents. I wish my dad's parents were still around so I had an out too.

"Vanessa, why don't you grab that silly little camera from your room so we can take a family photo." Mom waves her hand at me, her insult hit its mark.

Theo sees me tense, and I'm ready to let my entire family have it, all this pent-up aggression I have toward them. I'm tired of feeling like I need to tone myself down to fit into the family standard they've created.

"It's not a '*silly little camera*,' it's what I'm going to school for. I've pursued photography since I was a kid, and you still refuse to recognize how important it is to me."

She looks taken aback by my comment. *Good.*

Her smile doesn't falter, instead she keeps her teeth clenched as she addresses me for talking back to her in front of our family. "Vanessa."

"*No.* I've been here almost a week, and you've barely said more than five words to me. You don't care about me. You don't care about my hobbies or my passion. I don't even know why I agreed to come home."

"You shouldn't speak to your mother that way, she's the one who pays for all your expensive hobbies, your schooling, and your accommodations," Aunt Helen mutters from across the table.

My eyes land on my aunt, the cold-hearted bitch that she is. "Maybe *you* should take a hard look at yourself and figure out why your kids don't want to spend the holidays with you. *News flash*, it's because you're selfish and you also don't care about your kids besides how successful they are."

The room fills with gasps. *Screw it, I've already gone this far, might as well give them all hell.*

"You should all take a hard look at yourselves. Look at this family—all of you competing with one another, trying to be the best. The only thing that you're all successful at doing is ruining this family." I make sure to eye each and every one of the adults present.

The room is full of hard stares and silence, until a muffled laugh comes from Theo and Curtis. They love that I'm finally unleashing my feelings onto the family. My dad, on the other hand, isn't as impressed.

"Vanessa, how about we excuse ourselves for a moment?"

I throw my napkin onto my plate and get up without waiting for him to follow me. I head to my room, my pace faster than it should be, but I need to get out of here. This was a mistake.

My bag is still on the floor by my closet, I grab it, tossing it on the bed to start packing. I'm rummaging through my bathroom grabbing my toiletries when my dad finally walks in.

"What the hell was that?"

I roll my eyes at him. A gesture he's more than used to by now.

"This family is ridiculous. I don't know how you put up with them, especially after all these years, but I'm *not*. I'm going back to Boston."

"Vanessa, it's Christmas."

I turn around swiftly, meeting my father's eyes, which are identical to my own. "*Exactly,* Dad. It's Christmas. A time when families gather to spend time with one another. They talk and laugh and have fun. Our family sucks the life out of every holiday and I'm over it. I'd rather be home alone eating takeout than spend another day here."

I exit the bathroom, walking back into my room, placing my products into my bag.

"I know your mother's comment upset you."

"*Upset me*? Dad, she's never supported me or my love of photography. *Neither* of you have. All you two care about is making me look good in front of this family."

"That's not true."

"*It's not*? Please, enlighten me then."

"Vanessa, of course we care about you. We want to make sure that you're set up in life and that you can provide for yourself. With or without a family. We don't want you to have to depend on anyone but yourself."

I have to stop myself from laughing in his face. They wanted me to be independent and yet disproved of all my life decisions. Isn't that a little contradictory?

"Well, in doing that you two really fucked up the relationship you have with your only child."

"Let's stop it with the temper tantrum. You have a beautiful life. We've provided everything for you—all the tools you need for success. Most people would kill to be as privileged as you."

I never once forgot how privileged I am in this life. But I do not need to sit at a family dinner and get degraded.

I shove the remaining clothes in my bag before zipping it up. Dad's standing next to the door with his arms crossed over his chest, not happy that his daughter is finally standing up for herself.

"You wanted an independent daughter, well congrats, you got one."

I walk out of my room, my carry-on in tow behind me. My flight doesn't leave until tomorrow morning, but I'd rather spend my Christmas night sitting in an uncomfortable chair at the airport listening to a baby cry than deal with my family for another minute.

CHAPTER THIRTY-SIX

Hide behind the mask

VANESSA

It's been four days since I got home from New York, and I've spent those four days alone with my thoughts.

My parents tried calling me once my plane landed but I declined. I sent them a text telling them I made it back to Boston and left it at that. They want me to call them on New Year's and pretend like nothing happened during this trip, but I think I'm finally done trying with my family. There really is no hope for them.

I don't care if they decide to cut me off and kick me out of the condo. At this point, I have enough in my savings that I can live off. I might have to scrounge a bit and only eat ramen, but I'd rather not have an extra penny to my name if it meant I'd be done with my family.

Sydney and Maddie are both still with their families. They're supposed to come back tomorrow for New Year's Eve, but I'm scared that the post-holiday traffic and packed airports will delay them. I might end up celebrating alone.

I spent the last few days working on the Wolves' website and their social media platforms. I updated the photo and video gallery, and rearranged their highlights on Instagram. Now they look more aesthetically pleasing than they did before I got my hands on them. Their accounts have all gained more followers since I've taken over, so I think I'll pass this class with flying colors.

Not to toot my own horn, but maybe I should get into media and communications. It's not as mundane and aggravating as I had originally thought it was.

The boys have their Winter Wonder tournament this weekend, and we're broadcasting it live for those families who can't make it to Boston. I bet the Archers are going to have it screening in their home theater with the whole family around to watch.

Coach Wilson asked if I could do some pregame interviews with the team beforehand. Ask about their holidays, talk about their hopes for the season—all that kind of crap. It's easy stuff. What's not easy is knowing that I have to interview Jake. I knew I'd eventually have to face him. I just wish I had more time to prepare myself.

My hands are clammy, so I run them over my jeans to try to absorb the moisture.

The lobby of the arena is warm, almost *too* warm. Maybe that's why my hands are sweaty and not because of my anxiety that feels like an elephant is sitting on my chest.

At least I was smart enough to swap my regular latte for a chamomile tea—Maddie would be very proud of me. She's the tea drinker in our group, and normally I wouldn't touch the stuff, but today I needed something to relax me.

"Miss Nichols, you're here quite early." Coach Wilson's voice startles me as he walks out of the doors that lead to his impromptu office in the locker room.

"You know what they say, the early bird gets the worm." I wink at him. *Okay, reminder to self—never do that again.*

"The boys should be showing up soon. You can use the office for interviews if you'd like." A smile stretches across his face, and I notice that he's groomed his mustache differently today. Normally it's thick and bushy, but it looks like he got a clean trim, and the edges are upturned in a handlebar fashion.

"That would be great, thank you." I lug my heavy backpack over my shoulder, desperately wishing I bought myself that camera bag I saw back in Manhattan. "I like the new look. The mustache seems more sophisticated."

I swear I see a hint of blush creep into his cheeks. He nods at me then disappears behind the doors to the arena.

I don't care what anyone else thinks, that man is so adorable.

I walk through the swinging doors and down the hallway to the office adjacent to the locker rooms. This office is much different from the one in the athletic building. For one thing, it's a lot mustier—clearly from years of moisture exposure. There's an old oak desk positioned in the middle of the office, one that you would find in a '90s catalog. There's a filing cabinet and a small bookshelf positioned on the back wall behind the desk, but other than that and an empty whiteboard, the office has minimal decor. His trophies and accolades are on display in the athletic building.

I set up my tripod and position it in front of the desk, planning to have each player sit while I conduct the interviews. To keep it quick, I'm only going to ask a few questions. Ask the boys about their holidays, see how they're feeling about today's tournament—little things like that. By the time I end up interviewing the entire team, I'll have over an hour or so of footage that I'll have to go through. The less content, the easier it'll be for me to edit so I can have it out by New Year's Day.

As I finish setting up the office, a knock comes from behind me. I whip my head around to find Levi leaning against the doorway with one arm grasping the top frame.

"Hey, Nichols, Merry Christmas." He strides in, engulfing me in a hug.

"Merry Christmas Brody. How was your break?"

"Meh, the usual. Dad ordered takeout, his new girlfriend got me a new pair of Chuck Taylors I've been wanting. Yours?"

I shrug my shoulders at the thought. "The usual."

"We live such exhilarating lives." He plops down into the desk chair. "Let's get this show started."

He shimmies out of his black peacoat, revealing a beautiful dark gray suit with a black dress shirt and tie. I can't deny that Levi is handsome, but I don't think I could ever see us being anything more than friends. He's like the sibling I've always wanted. We get to share our music tastes, help each other with our photography, discuss new crime documentaries, and compare our similar home lives. It's nice to have someone else to talk to about these things.

"Since when do you like doing interviews?"

"You gotta have the best go first. I'm a tough act to follow." He motions up and down his body, putting himself on display. He gets a laugh out of me. It feels foreign, like I haven't laughed in weeks.

Maybe I haven't. When was the last time I genuinely laughed?

"Fire away, Nichols."

I go through my list of questions, asking Levi about his holidays, his New Year's resolution, and how he feels going into the first game since their break. He smiles as he answers each of my questions, his resolution being my favorite response—he wants to try every combination of pizza at a local dive bar in Boston. They have too many different combinations that equal to about a hundred different pizzas.

I told him I wouldn't mind helping out with that one.

Levi gets up and gives me another hug before heading into the locker rooms to get changed before warm-ups.

The rest of the team starts to filter in behind him. A few of the freshmen seemed nervous talking to me, barely making eye contact. As one of them leaves, a senior on the team, Trevor McAvoy, walks into the office.

"Are you too scared to talk to me too?"

He laughs and sits down, interlocking his hands behind his head, leaning back in the chair. "Those guys are scared of Jake. I, however, don't give a fuck."

"What do you mean scared of Jake?"

Trevor raises his eyebrow at me as if I asked a redundant question.

"Because the two of you...y'know. You're together. They don't wanna step on his toes."

"We're not together." My answer comes out fast.

Trevor studies me for a moment but decides to drop it. "Ask your questions, Nichols."

By the time we finish, Nate and Eli show up, insisting on taking their pregame interviews together, thinking their captain and assistant captain dynamic will bring in more views to our page. I didn't fight with them on that one.

After filming we chat for a bit before Nate hears commotion coming from the locker room. I wave them both off, deciding I don't want to know what's going on behind those doors.

My list of players dwindles down to two. I know Kieran will probably opt out of the pre-game interview, so that only leaves one.

Jake.

Maybe he'll skip it. That would be a blessing.

"You still doing interviews?". *I spoke too soon.* Jake's voice is hoarse, his hands are tucked into his pant pockets

He's wearing a navy-blue suit, white shirt, and a dark blue plaid tie. I'm upset at how my body responds to him. My heart slams in my chest and my fingers itch, wanting to run themselves through the mess of curls on Jake's head. *What the hell is wrong with me?* It feels like my body betraying me.

Get it together, Vanessa. He broke your heart, this is pathetic. You shouldn't be feeling anything for him right now.

I pretend that his presence doesn't faze me and I try my hardest to put on a neutral, or possibly annoyed look. Maybe if he thinks his presence irritates me, he'll go to the locker room with the rest of his teammates and leave me the hell alone.

"Yeah, you're the last one besides Kieran, but I know interviews aren't really his thing, so I'm not gonna hold my breath."

We stare at each other for a minute. The only sound is our breathing. He keeps his face plain, but I can see in his eyes that something is wrong. As if he's internally battling with himself. I don't know if I can handle any more uncomfortable silence and prolonged eye contact. I stand up from the chair and point to it as I walk over to stand behind the tripod. Time to be professional. *Hide behind the mask, Vanessa.*

"Sit."

Without hesitating he moves across the room in two strides. I momentarily forgot how fast he could go with those long legs. He used to always slow his pace knowing my short legs couldn't keep up.

"Okay, like it stated in the team email, I'm going to ask you a couple of basic questions." He nods and I continue, "How was your break? Did you celebrate a holiday with your family—if yes, do you have any traditions that your family follows?"

I wonder what Amelia and Parker do every year. I bet they have a few family traditions, they seem like the type. Something cute, like binging Christmas movies or having an annual gingerbread house competition.

Jake watches me as I ask the questions. He sticks his tongue out of the corner of his mouth to wet his dry lips. "My family celebrates Christmas, and our family tradition is decorating the house together and having a family game night. And, um overall my break was okay."

I didn't know what to expect of this, but I at least expected more words out of him. I realize now that he's not looking at me but toward me, like he's focusing on something right behind or beside me, avoiding my stare.

It's weird seeing Jake so quiet.

"Okay, uh, next question. What is your New Year's resolution?"

He takes a moment to think it over. "Mend broken promises and put my friendships first."

His answer feels like a bullet to the heart, but I pretend like it doesn't affect me. *Keep this professional, you don't want to seem like a crazy ex.*

"Great." I force the fakest smile. He definitely knows it too.

"Last question, how do you feel about the Winter Wonder tournament? Do you expect to win every game like the past two years, or do you think the other teams have a fighting chance?"

This question causes a small, micro smirk to appear on Jake's face. "I think we're going to take the trophy for the third year in a row. The other teams, especially Boston College, are tough competitors, but this tournament doesn't count toward the NCAA points. We're all just here to have some friendly competition and fun."

He's going to do so well in the NHL. Jake's personality is so bubbly and energetic, I'd be surprised if people didn't fall in love with him solely from his press conferences.

I realize that I've been staring at him for too long, long enough for him to notice and for him to become curious. He opens his mouth to talk but I snap out of it and cut him off before he can mutter a syllable.

"That's all I need, thanks." I turn away to start dissembling my camera and tripod. I hear the chair squeak as his weight is lifted off it.

"This is for you. From my parents." I watch as he sets a small, wrapped box onto the desk, then walks out of the office without saying another word.

I'm frozen. My tripod is half disassembled in my hands and yet I can't move. I stare at the small, green, wrapped gift on the desk. Is this really from his parents or was that a ploy?

I shouldn't open it. We're not dating; I should give it back. It would be rude of me to accept a gift from Jake's parents.

Did he tell them that we broke up? Maybe not, and that's why they still gave Jake the gift to give to me. If that's the case, then it would be rude *not* to open it.

I grab the box and carefully peel off the solid green wrapping, exposing a beautiful gold box. I take the lid off and my heart stops. Inside is a small gold bracelet that I was admiring on our trip to Martha's Vineyard. Autumn and I were fawning over everything in the small jewelry shop, but this bracelet stood out the most to me. It's nothing fancy, just a simple solid gold chain with a singular pearl in the middle. So delicate and beautiful.

I take it out of the box and notice a note tucked underneath the Bubble Wrap. It's a handwritten note from Amelia.

Vanessa,

You are such a beautiful and smart individual, and we are so glad that Jake has found someone who makes him smile. Autumn picked out this gift for you, but I added a little something extra. Wishing you and your family a Merry Christmas and Happy Holidays. There will always be a spot at our table for you.

With love, Amelia (and Parker... and Autumn too).

I look back in the box to see what else could be hiding. Tucked underneath everything is a polaroid. I flip it over to see a photo of Jake feeding me a French fry at the seafood restaurant we went to during Thanksgiving weekend. Autumn was playing around with an old camera we found in the house and she must've snapped this photo when we weren't paying attention. Jake's face is broken out in a full smile as he watches me bite into the crinkle-cut potato.

The photo nearly breaks me. We were so happy, so full of hope. My heart breaks all over again, imagining the life Jake and I could've had together. So much has happened to lead us to where we are now, I don't know where to go from here.

I tuck the photo, the note, and the bracelet back into the box and put it in my bag. I'll cry about this later when I'm in the comfort of my own bedroom.

I finish tearing down the rest of my gear, only to lug it all to the arena to set it up all over again. I position the tripod in the upper corner of the stands so I can capture the entire rink and use my second camera, my Canon EOS R10, to take up-close action shots during the game. Coach Wilson likes to have a lot of footage, especially for when he reviews plays with the team, something I've learned over the course of the semester.

I try to focus on the game, but my eyes keep going to that little box in my bag and the boy who gave it to me.

I wish things were different.

CHAPTER THIRTY-SEVEN

It's because I'm an angel

JAKE

We won the Winter Wonder tournament for the third year in a row, just like I predicted.

It's not a shock though. Our team is the most organized and well developed in our division. Boston College gave us a run for our money, but in the end, Andrew Meyers got one too many penalties, which lost them the game due to a power play on our end. After that, we played Northeastern in the finals and won with a close game, 4–3.

I didn't play my best during this tournament but thank fuck it didn't count for regular season points.

Seeing Vanessa and being in the same vicinity as her for a few minutes is what did it for me. I haven't been able to talk to her for more than two minutes these past weeks and seeing her yesterday wearing those mom jeans that drive me crazy…it was a lot.

I felt like I was suffocating in that room and Vanessa was solely responsible for the air in my lungs.

I know she doesn't feel the same way about seeing me. She couldn't get out of that room fast enough. The second I was done answering her questions, she already had her camera disassembled.

I think I took her by surprise with my parents' gift. Her eyes practically jumped out of her head when she saw it. I told my parents that she probably wouldn't want it, but my mom insisted on giving it to her. Originally, I planned to give it to Maddie or Sydney and have one of them give it to her. But I seized the opportunity when it arose. If that was the only chance I had to speak with her, I'm glad I took it.

I wish she was here tonight. The guys decided to host a New Year's Eve party, so I can only imagine how crazy it's going to get tonight. I'm not in the partying mood. I want to be with Vanessa, sitting on the couch watching dumb movies. I want to drown myself in her laughter and get high off her coconut shampoo.

I tried to catch up with her after the tourney yesterday. She was still in the lobby when I got out. I called out her name, but the second she saw me, she ran off with Levi. *That lucky bastard.* I watched them at first. The way she smiled up at him, laughed at something he said. The way she pushed her glasses up higher on her nose as she focused on whatever he was saying. I'd do anything to have it all back.

I'm just a fucking idiot who messed it all up.

"Can you stop moping around and grab the keg tap from the basement." Nate chucks a pillow at me from the opposite end of the couch.

Since we got back, everyone's been in high gear, getting the house ready, or *idiotproof* as Nate likes to say. If it wasn't for Nate, we'd have two cases of beer and a bag of chips for the whole night.

"Sure."

It's probably time I move my lazy ass. If I'm going to be in a funk all night, the boys aren't going to want me around. And I think there's a box of chocolate chip cookies hidden somewhere in my room. I can preoccupy myself with those and a movie tonight.

Who says you need to party on New Year's Eve?

The basement is dingey and not as nicely renovated as the rest of the house. The floors are still concrete, and the walls are only half-drywalled. Dad always jokes about buying the place and fixing it up, but I don't think he'd ever pull the trigger on that.

I grab the tap and head back upstairs. The same time I walk into the living room, the front door bursts open, Sydney and Maddie almost toppling over each other, slamming the door and the cold behind them.

"What the hell are you guys doing here?"

"Wow, nice to see you, too, Shepherd. How about instead of being an ass, you help us with all of this shit for *your* party." Sydney motions to their hands full of bags with everything from groceries to party supplies.

Nate immediately comes rushing in from the kitchen, muttering thank-yous as he and Eli grab the rest of the things from the girls.

Maddie walks over to me, placing a medium-sized brown paper bag in my hand. "Here. This is for you."

"*What is it?*" I bring the bag to my nose, silently praying this isn't a bag of dog shit. I inhale deeply and spices immediately drift to my nose. Thai food? *Fuck, this smells so good.*

"Kieran said you've been moping around since you guys got home. Coincidentally, Vanessa has *also* been at home moping around. She might get mad at us, but we think it's for the best. This is your in, Shep. You better take it."

Her cool eyes settle on mine. Maddie may seem to have a dark exterior—and interior, to be honest—but somewhere deep inside, she's a softie.

Sydney walks over, leaning her elbow on Maddie's shoulder. "I personally thought this idea was insane, but Maddie convinced me. You're a slut Jake, but I know you have morals and wouldn't cheat on my best friend. So, you better fucking make it up to her. Or else you'll have to deal with *me*."

I shake my head at them. They're delusional if they think that Vanessa is even going to give me the time of day. "There's no way she's going to talk to me."

"You at least have to try, Jake. Is she not worth it?" Sydney crosses her arms over her chest, the look in her eye is more deadly than I've ever seen before, even from Maddie.

"You know that's a ridiculous question, Syd."

"Is it?"

"Yes. She's fucking *everything* to me. She's brightens my day. She makes me smile all the damn time. She deserves the world, and I will spend every damn day of my life giving it to her. I want to make her feel like she's the best goddamn thing on this earth."

Sydney smiles, as if she's been waiting to hear that. "Well, you better hurry up and get there before the food gets cold. She won't be as willing to hear you out if she has to reheat the noodles."

I smile at the two girls in front of me. They didn't need to help me. They could've easily written me off the second Vanessa asked. Maybe the only reason they're helping is because Maddie knows the truth. At this point, all I want is for Vanessa to hear me out. She deserves to get an apology from me. *A sincere one.* Even if she wants nothing to do with me after this, I need her to know how sorry I am, how much regret I live with. I don't know if I'll ever be able to make it up to her, for causing her so much grief. I can't have her believing that our relationship meant nothing to me. Because it meant *everything*.

I hug Maddie and give Sydney a kiss on the top of her head, then haul my ass out of there. Screw the party, I have a girl I need to see.

My girl.

I don't care to grab a jacket before I run across the street to my Jeep, but I remembered to grab Vanessa's gift from my room. It's cold as balls outside, but I only need to deal with the cold for a few minutes. *Hopefully.*

The roads are jam packed, bumper to bumper—everyone's en route to their parties and plans for the evening. It takes longer than it should to reach Vanessa's condo. My Jeep is warm by the time I pull into the parking lot. I turn off the engine and sit in the warmth, giving myself a second to figure out what the hell I'm going to do.

What am I going to do? What the hell do I say?

I gotta be my own hype man right now.

If Kieran were here, he'd tell me I'm an idiot and to try not to say anything dumb. He'd also tell me to get the fuck out of the car and untuck my balls, but I think my ass is glued to the seat. I don't know if it's from the guilt or the stress of the situation.

Get out of the car, Jake.

This food is going to get cold, and if I don't come bearing some sort of peace offering, I think she'll slam the door in my face faster than I can say *hello*.

Without wasting another second, I step out of my car. The outside of the building is still lit up with Christmas lights. All the trees in the courtyard flash in sync with the music playing over the speakers. Vanessa probably loves this. I bet it's one of the reasons why she loves this place.

"Greg. Hey, Happy New Year, man. How were your holidays?"

"Mr. Shepherd, it's been a while." He walks over and shakes my hand. This guy is one of the most pleasant security guards I've ever met. "The holidays were great. Kids were spoiled as always. Yours?"

"Good, good." My knuckles clench the paper bag in my hands. I hope the sweat on my hands doesn't ruin the bag.

"Tell Miss Nichols Happy New Year. I haven't seen her all day."

"I'll tell her. Have a good night." I nod at him, making my way to the row of elevators. The door chimes as I step in and suddenly my heart sinks.

What the hell am I doing?

I'm not going to lie, I'm scared shitless that she's going to take one look at me and slam the door in my face. Or worse, she might not even open the damn door.

I stare at myself in the mirror wall of the elevator, mentally judging myself. Fuck, I should've at least tried to dress up for her. I didn't think to change out of my sweats before I left. I just wanted to haul my ass over here as quickly as possible. I thought I'd be spending New Year's Eve sulking in my room, not in Vanessa's building, arguing with myself in the elevator.

Jake, don't be a pussy.

The worst thing that can happen is she rejects me.

The best outcome would be her agreeing to listen to me.

If I can get her to talk to me for five minutes, I think I can straighten everything out. I will beg on my goddamn knees for this woman because I know it. I know it deep down in my gut, in my bones, in my whole goddamn being that she is *it* for me.

The elevator shifts as it comes to a stop on her floor.

This is it.

Within the next few minutes, I'll have my answer.

VANESSA

Sydney and Maddie are taking way too long to come home.

They messaged me only an hour ago, saying they were back in the city and grabbing food on their way home, but since then it's been complete radio silence. Their last updated location was Nate's house. I know they were dropping something off there, but I have a feeling they got distracted. Nate said they're having a party tonight and invited the three of us over. I turned down the idea right away, I wouldn't be any fun tonight anyway. Sometimes I get into these moods and it's easier for me to deal with it on my own than surrounded by my friends.

My stomach growls and I send another message to the group chat requesting an update. The only reply I get is from Maddie.

Maddie:

Food is on the way!

Within two seconds of her text message, there's a knock at the door that makes me jump off the couch. They must have their hands full.

I walk over to the door and unlock it, pulling it open without checking to see who it was. I should've checked the peephole.

No fucking way. Standing in front of me, with a brown take-out bag in tow, is Jake. I watch him for a moment. He keeps looking up and down, shifting on his feet.

Yesterday, I tried so hard to avoid him. Every time he tried to get my attention, I'd book it the other way. At one point, I grabbed Levi and dragged him out of the arena just so I could avoid him and now he's here. He's here at my door with food and a puppy-dog look on his face that is making my knees weak.

Stay strong, Vanessa.

Every other time I've opened this door for him I've wanted to jump his bones. But right now, I feel sick to my stomach. Those pesky butterflies and emotions try to break free of the restraints I put on them. They succeed in their prison break and spread through my body, making me feel all tingly inside. Every thought of him, every feeling that I've pushed away for these past few weeks comes barreling out.

Shove them down.

"What are you doing here?"

"Sydney and Maddie sent me. I brought you dinner." Jake motions to the paper bag. *Of course they did.* I love my best friends, but the two of them need to stop meddling in my life.

"Great. Thanks for delivering, but I'm not giving you a tip."

A small laugh escapes his lips. *Of course he finds that funny.*

He notices my glare and clears his throat, pretending he wasn't thinking of a crude joke.

"Good one." He passes me the bag and I debate whether I should slam the door in his face. "Can we talk?"

The way he so casually asked that has me on edge. Did he think that he could bring me food and I'd forgive him? Does he think that little of me?

As if he can hear my thoughts, he continues. "Five minutes. You can set a timer and once it's up, I'll leave. You'll never have to speak to me ever again. *I promise.* I know you probably hate me, and I know I fucked up. Just let me talk, and after if you still want me gone, I will disappear from your life. *Please*, only five minutes."

I shouldn't be feeling pride right now, but him practically begging for me to listen to him does something to me. It makes me feel powerful. As if I'm in total control of this situation.

Good.

"Five minutes. Don't make me regret it."

I swing the door open, a silent gesture for him to come in. I make my way to the couch, not waiting for him to follow. I drop the food on the coffee table, not caring about the contents inside. My appetite flew out the window the second I saw him.

I take a seat in the corner, wrapping a blanket over my legs. The cold from outside feels like it's seeping in through the glass doors, and even though I have a thick crewneck on, I still feel the chill hitting my bones. I don't know how Jake is surviving in only a hoodie and sweatpants.

I shouldn't care if he's cold or not. *But I do.*

Jake walks around to sit on the other end of the couch. Smart choice. He leans his elbows on his knees, holding his face in his hands. He drags his fingers through his hair, letting out a breath before sitting up straight, those deep blue eyes immediately finding mine.

I can't look at him. Every time I do, I'm reminded of what he did. I picture Caroline kissing him, sucking his neck, and God knows—

No, I don't need to picture that.

I remind myself of how much he hurt me so I won't cry in front of him again. That's one thing I've promised myself.

"I'm sorry." His voice cracks. "Vanessa, I need you to know, I swear on my whole fucking life that nothing happened between me and Caroline."

Those words feel like a slap to my face. Seeing her in his kitchen wearing his shirt with no pants on, how could I believe otherwise?

"If you're going to sit here and lie to me, then we're done."

I move to get up, but Jake grabs my wrist, his eyes pleading for me to stay.

"I'm not an idiot, Jake. And I'm not one of your puck bunnies that will fall at your feet and forgive you."

"Vanessa, I promise you that I'm telling the truth. I fucked up, but not in the way I led you to believe. Let me explain."

I pull my wrist out of his grip and look down at my watch. "You have *four* minutes."

420

He watches me as if I'm glass that could shatter at any moment. He doesn't realize that he already shattered my heart to pieces.

"I lied to you. When you showed up that morning and Caroline was over, I knew you'd assume I fucked her." I flinch at the word. "*Sorry.* At the time I was hurt and angry with you. I wanted to hurt you back so I let you believe it."

What the hell?

"I wanted you to feel the same way I did. The night before, I felt like our relationship meant nothing to you. You were so quick to break things off and to leave me, I barely had a second to fight for you. To tell you how much you fucking mean to me, angel girl."

My body aches at the sound of the nickname he gave me. It feels like a lifetime ago.

"Vanessa, I'm sorry for not making you feel wanted or important in my life. That's one of the biggest mistakes I've ever made. But I'm here now. I'm here and I'm fighting for you. Even if you don't want me back, I need to try because you're fucking everything to me."

We sit there for a moment before I can gather words. The alarm on my watch starts going off, indicating his five minutes are up.

He looks at me, waiting to tell him to go, but I don't. I deserve closure.

"Why would you do something like that? You can't say I'm your everything but then do something so cruel. Let's say you are telling the truth, why wouldn't you tell me right away? You let me believe for *weeks* that you did the worst possible thing to me. What did I do to deserve that, Jake?"

He runs his hands through his curls again. "I tried to talk to you, but…" But I turned him down that day on campus, rightfully so.

"So, what? You've come here to apologize for lying? You want to clear your conscience so you can feel better?"

"No, I don't want to clear my conscience. You deserve to hear the truth. You didn't deserve what I did to you. I want to own up to my mistake and tell you that this is the worst thing I have ever done. Hurting you—lying to you—was the biggest mistake of my life. I know that there's no possible way for me to make it up to you, but I'm trying, Vanessa. For the past few weeks, I've only been thinking about you and how shit I've made you feel. You didn't deserve any of it. I'm so sorry."

I look up at him, tears brimming his own eyes. Fuck, maybe he *is* telling the truth.

"I was an idiot who decided to fight fire with fire. I know that was stupid. Trust me, *I know*. I thought we were in love, but then you broke my heart so easily. I know that's not an excuse for my actions, nothing about what I did was okay. But you need to know that I would never cheat on you. I'm ashamed of what I did, and I just needed you to know that. You don't need to forgive me, but you deserved to know the truth. You deserve so much better than the way I treated you."

Wait, what did he just say?

"You thought we were in love?"

His eyes dart to mine, not realizing that's the statement I was referring to. "That night at the lights, I was going to tell you that I was in love with you. This isn't exactly how I wanted to tell you, but I guess I have nothing to lose now."

Was. He *was* in love with me. Is he only saying this to coax me back to him?

"I was in love with you and I'm still in love with you. I know I've done some stupid shit, but before all of this blew up, are you telling me you never realized how I felt about you?"

It's impossible for words to form, so I shake my head.

"I've been in love with you since that night in Nashville, but there was no way in hell I was going to tell you then. I know commitment scares the absolute hell out of you, and that's why I didn't say it. I thought that if I told you too soon, it would be the final nail in the coffin. I was selfish and terrified. I didn't want to push you away, but I guess I ended up doing that anyways."

He moves closer to me, resting his hand on my knee. I could easily pick it up and toss it aside, but the gesture feels comforting. My body doesn't shudder at his touch, it craves it. It wants his hand to trail up my leg and keep exploring.

C'mon, Vanessa, get it together.

"I have been obsessed with you since the first night we met. That night at the bar, you were the only one in the room who I cared about. You're the only one who matters to me. I can't breathe without thinking about you. When I'm not with you, I crave you. I miss your laugh and your sporadic texting. I miss your gross movie snacks and the way you fall asleep wearing your glasses. I miss finding your socks in random places and the way you would always ask, 'How did those get there,' when we both knew you were the one who took them off in the first place."

"I'm not here convince you to forgive me. All I want is for you to know that you're worth everything to me, Vanessa. I understand if you don't feel the same way. And if you don't want to forgive me, I understand that too. You deserve to feel loved every day of your life. If you're willing to give me another chance, I'll spend the rest of my life proving to you how much you mean to me. I believe you're it for me, Ness. But I understand how my actions contradict everything I've said."

A tear escapes, running down my cheek. How the hell do I respond to that?

I spent the last couple of weeks heartbroken because of the man in front of me, but I'd be lying if I said I didn't love him too. As messed up as our situation is, I can't help but feel for him. We all make mistakes. I made the mistake of breaking things off prematurely and Jake lied. A horrible, gut-wrenching lie.

Can I even forgive him for this—for betraying me and losing my trust? If he's telling the truth and didn't actually sleep with Caroline, how can I guarantee he won't ever lie to me again?

"After everything you've put me through, do you really expect me to forgive you?"

"I don't expect you to do anything, Vanessa. If you tell me right now that you don't want to see me again, done. I'll leave and you can pretend I never existed. I'm not expecting to win your trust back with one conversation, just like I'm not expecting you to forgive me in the blink of an eye. I want you to know that I truly am sorry. I fucked up. I made a horrible, fucking immensely stupid mistake. You deserve more than me, but I needed you to know that you were the best thing to ever happen to me."

As much as my head is screaming at me, telling me that this could all burn and turn to ashes, my heart is willing to burn with him. I won't pretend like these past few weeks didn't happen. And there's still a whole lot of insecurities we must deal with, but I want to do it. I want to do it all with Jake.

"You're such a fucking idiot."

He looks up at me, his blue eyes bloodshot from his tears. "I know."

"You made a stupid mistake. One that cost you my trust."

"I know."

"And yet…" I look away from him, it's the first time I really broke eye contact with him during this entire conversation.

"And yet?" His eyes watch me carefully, holding on to that last bit of hope he has.

I take a deep breath before I let the words escape, ready for him to hear them. "And yet I can understand why you did what you did. I don't condone your behavior, but I'm telling you that I understand you were hurt. This doesn't mean I've forgiven you, but…I'm willing to work on things."

His eyes waver back and forth across my features, as if he's confirming what he just heard.

"W-wait, are you saying…"

"What you did hurt me so bad, Jake. I know I hurt you, too. After I broke things off, I knew I made a mistake. I pushed you away because I couldn't come to terms with the fact that I was falling in love. Instead of voicing my concerns to you, I did what I do best and ran. I don't want to run anymore."

"You…you were in love with me too?"

"Were. *Am.* If you promise to be a man of your word, I will promise to stop pushing good things away."

"I promise. I will do anything for you, Vanessa. If you want a star, I'll buy you one. If that's not good enough, I'll get in a fucking rocket and won't return without the cosmos. I fucking love you so much."

"I love you too."

Those four words float off my tongue. I never thought I would have the courage to say them aloud. My gaze flickers from his eyes down to his mouth, hoping he takes the hint.

Within seconds his hand is on my jaw, pulling me close, kissing the absolute hell out of me.

I melt into him, losing all self-control. His mouth is warm and soft, welcoming me back. Goose bumps rise on my skin as his hand moves from my jaw, settling on the side of my neck. My fingers immediately find Jake's curls, gripping them, bringing him closer to me.

We haven't been this close in weeks. I don't even remember the last time we kissed. All I know is that right now, I want to be suffocated by him. By his love for me. Something I never thought I would have.

He breaks the kiss first, breathing heavy, but still holding my face in his hands. "I love you, Vanessa Nichols. And I will love you for as long as you allow me to."

Jake brings his lips back to mine. This time the kiss is soft, less demanding and yet I can still feel the hunger he's holding back. *Hell, I'm holding back.* He breaks the kiss again and I savor the look on his face. It's like he can't believe that I'm real and in front of him, forgiving him, telling him that I love him. But I am. It won't be easy for Jake to gain my trust back, but I'm willing to give him time to prove to me that he's remorseful for his actions.

For now, I'll let him show me how much he loves me.

Jake leans back into the couch, pulling me with him so I'm lying on his chest. He brushes my hair with his hand, tucking a loose strand behind my ear.

"Ness, I need you to know that I will do whatever it takes to gain your trust back. I know it's going to take you a while to fully trust me again. Just know that I promise I will do my best every single day. You ask it of me, and I'll do it. Whatever you want, name it."

I don't even have to think before I answer, "You."

"Done."

CHAPTER THIRTY-EIGHT

Happy New Year

VANESSA

Jake whisks me into his arms and I let out a squeal. I've missed his toned arms wrapped around me, making me feel weightless. I always feel so small and protected by him.

It's only been a few weeks, but oh my god, I've missed him. I missed the feeling of his calloused hands roaming my skin, teasing my clit, his lips nipping at my breasts and sucking on the tender skin behind my ear. I missed the way he would whisper sweet nothings into my ear, knowing how hot and bothered it got me.

Jake carries me from the couch all the way to my bed in what feels like seconds. He places me down gently, then climbs on top of me, keeping me imprisoned between his muscular thighs. *God*, I love his thick thighs. Thank the world for hockey men.

"I've missed you so much, angel girl." The nickname sends a wave of heat straight down to my pussy. I'm probably going to come the second he thrusts into me—which I hope is any minute.

Slowly he peels off my clothes, as if he's savoring every second he has with me. I don't want him to go slow. I want him now, hard and fast. We have all night to take things slow, but I need him now. I feel like a starved animal and he's the first piece of meat I found.

Am I salivating?

I lift my hips up to help him pull my pants down my legs more seamlessly, but he pushes my hips down in an almost primal way. That has me throbbing with anticipation.

As he pulls down his sweats, I see the outline of his dick straining against the spandex fabric of his boxers. The fact that he's hard enough to stretch an already stretchy material to its limits should scare me, but my heart only beats faster in excitement.

Jake tosses my pants onto the floor and starts kissing his way back up to me. Starting at my ankle, leaving a trail of warm and wet kisses up my leg, onto my bare stomach, my breasts, my neck, and finally his lips find mine again.

"Tonight is all about you, baby. We can go as long as you want, but I want you to be coming as the clock strikes midnight so you start the year off right."

Well, shit.

I look over at my clock, it's only a little after nine. Does he plan on having sex for three hours? I mean, I won't complain.

He brings his mouth back to my right nipple, sucking and grazing with his teeth. Every time he does that, my back arches, wanting more. He slips his fingers past the thin material of my underwear, lightly dusting over me, torturously. His calloused hands roam over me, barely touching me. I start to grind my hips to try to gain some sort of friction. If he thinks he's going to tease me, he has another thing coming.

"I thought you said you would do whatever I asked."

Jake looks up at me through his thick eyelashes, ones I would *kill* to have. "Tell me what you want, Vanessa."

Normally I'd be a little shy asking him for something, but all my anxiety has gone out the window.

"Make me scream."

"Anything for you, princess."

Princess?

I don't have time to react to the new term of endearment because his lips are on me faster than I can finish my thought. He immediately finds my clit as if he knows my body better than the back of his hand. I'd like to say that I'm surprised he's so good at this, but I'm not. I know what he's capable of, which is absolutely life-shattering, leg-shaking orgasms.

Jake runs his tongue down my center, before thrusting his tongue in me while using his thumb to rub circles over my clit. My fingers grip my duvet as I push my hips up, giving Jake easier access. He swaps positions with his tongue and finger, now back to sucking the bud of

427

nerves while plunging two fingers into me. I grind my hips into his hand as he thrusts in and out of me while his tongue continues to drive me crazy.

His teeth graze my clit the same way they did to my nipple a few minutes ago. My core tightens and I can feel the orgasm coming. A moan escapes my lips, and Jake can tell I'm close. *He can always fucking tell.* He adds a third finger, still sucking and grazing my clit at the same time, and suddenly I come undone, his name slipping from my mouth. My vision goes a little hazy in the corners and my head feels light. *Jesus, did that orgasm give me vertigo or something?*

"Hmm, the moaning was nice. But I think you asked me to make you scream, didn't you, angel girl?"

I look down at him and his eyes are wild, like he's gone completely feral.

His lips are swollen and pink. I wanna kiss the hell out of him.

"You're right," I say between breaths, still trying to get air back in my lungs. I grab him by his hoodie, tugging him back up to me. I want to feel his chest and muscles against my bare body.

I tug at the hem of his sweater and he pulls the heavy material over his head. I take the time to do the same, but as I get the sweater over my shoulders, Jake grabs it, pulling it the rest of the way off.

"You're so fucking perfect."

I can be fully nude in front of this man and be comfortable, but the second he compliments me, my cheeks turn redder than a rose.

"Your perfect lips." He kisses me again. "Your perfect neck." He continues down until my breasts are in his hands. "Your perfect tits."

"The only perfect thing is my body?"

"Fuck no." He makes direct eye contact with me, as if I'd just asked the most idiotic question. "I'd say your eyes are perfect, but you're half-blind. The shade of green has become my favorite color, though. Everything about you is perfect, Ness. I'm just letting you know about all the *other* parts I love. All the parts I want to give *special* attention to."

That shuts me up.

He kisses me again and this time I open my mouth, letting him invade me, dominate me with his tongue. I glide my hand down his body, feeling every hard, toned muscle on my way down. I reach between us and grab his dick in my hands.

Holy shit, has it always been this big?

I swear the last time we had sex it wasn't this...wide? Girthy? I don't even know the proper term, all I know is that my neighbors are probably going to hate me after tonight. Maybe the New Year's Eve parties will drown out my screaming.

I run a delicate finger over his head, using his precum as a makeshift lube, I start pumping my hand up and down, making him moan into my mouth.

"W-wait, I have an idea."

He jumps off the bed, fully naked, and starts rummaging through my drawers.

I lean up on my elbows. "Something I can help you find?"

Jake pulls open the bottom drawer of my nightstand and pulls out my small purple vibrator.

"What are we gonna do with that?"

"I think you know exactly what we're gonna do with it, yeah?" He raises an eyebrow at me in such a cocky way.

"Put your legs up here for me, baby." He pats his shoulders, telling me where to position myself. The use of pet names would normally annoy me, but right now, it's so hot. So, I oblige. He places a pillow underneath me to give himself better access.

I think I'm about to get pounded into a different dimension.

"You're so fucking wet for me, baby."

Jake runs the tip of his dick up and down my clit and pussy. He holds his dick in his hand and positions it at my opening. He slowly puts the tip in, making only shallow thrusts. It feels too good. *I need more.* I let out a soft whine—one that's begging for him to fill me.

"What was that, angel girl? Use your words." He stops thrusting altogether and I'm about ready to lose my mind.

"Fuck me, *please*."

"Anything for you."

He grabs my ankles and moves them both more inward so they're still sitting on his shoulders, but closer to his neck. The pillow under me helps with our height difference; without it, my ass would be floating in the air.

I slap a hand over my mouth the second he starts sliding into me. Jake does it slowly, *agonizingly slow*, but it allows me time to get adjusted to his size.

Yeah, he definitely feels bigger.

"Nuh-uh. You said you wanted me to make you scream. How are your neighbors supposed to learn my name if you're not screaming it all night?" Jake grabs my wrist softly, pinning it next to my head. I feel myself clench around him, squeezing him as he enters me fully. *Oh my god.* He's so big, if he moves, I might die.

Okay, I'm definitely being overdramatic, but I once thought that his dick could split me in half; tonight it might finish the job.

He takes his hand off mine and grabs the vibrator. Jake starts moving his hips, thrusting at a steady pace. Then I hear the buzz come from the small purple toy. As he continues to thrust in a good rhythm, he positions the vibrator on my clit, making small circular motions as he does it.

The vibration working with his dick is about to send me over the edge. Jake takes his other free hand and slides it up my leg.

"*Fuck,* Ness, you feel so good, baby. I've missed you so much."

Jake trails his hand back down my leg and leans more into me. The angle change has him hitting me deeper than before, which I didn't think was possible. He keeps pressure on the vibrator and pinches my nipple.

My head starts to feel light and my legs start to shake. I'm going to come at any second.

"I love you, Vanessa." He leans down to kiss me, putting my legs almost behind my head. For a second, I think about how I probably look like a pretzel, but his soft words and kiss melt the thoughts away.

His thrusts get harder, deeper, and my orgasm builds and builds. With the click of a button, he changes the speed on the vibrator and I'm screaming his name as I come completely undone, my body feeling like liquid.

Jake turns off the toy and lowers my legs. Both of our breaths are ragged as we lie next to each other.

"You think your neighbors heard that?"

"*Shut up.*" I bat at his chest, but he catches my hand—his reflexes much faster than mine.

He looks at me in the way that would make me soak my underwear, except I'm not wearing any.

"Make me."

His demand sends a chill up my spine and suddenly all of the energy that was sucked out of me has returned. I feel like I could run a marathon right now. But instead, I'm going to ride my boyfriend.

Boyfriend.

I straddle his waist, hovering over his body. "Do we...are we..." The confusion is evident on his face, so I point back and forth between us. "Are we back together?"

Jake palms his face. "*Jesus,* Ness. You're about to hop on my cock and you're asking me if we're back together?"

I remain frozen in place but nod my head. "Well, we never clarified."

Jake's shoulders sag and he shakes his head. "You are the most amazing thing on this goddamn planet. Would you do the honor of being my girlfriend, *again?*"

I pretend to think for a moment, hoping to make him sweat, but he sees right through my act.

"Hmm, I guess so."

"You're such a brat."

"Mm-hm, I know. Now lean back."

"I like it when you're bossy."

I lean on my knees to position myself above him. I use one of my hands to guide him in, and I watch him as I do it. His eyes are locked, watching me put his dick inside me. He fills me again, but this time I'm in control. I get to set the pace and the rhythm.

I start moving my hips, grinding my pelvis against his. I go up slowly, then grind on my way down his shaft. He takes my jaw in his hand and brings my lips to his again.

We're a mess of wet kisses and clashing teeth.

"*Fuck, Ness.* Keep doing that, baby." He shudders when I grind in a circular motion at the base of his dick. I move faster, making sure to do the same thing every time I go down.

Jake's thumb finds its place on my clit, rubbing circles over the tender bud. The kissing and touches are enough to set me off. That plus the friction from his pelvis and his dick hitting a damn button inside of me, I'm ready to detonate.

I cry out, "I love you."

My words seem to be the tipping point, sending Jake over the edge. I slow my movements as he crushes his lips to mine.

I lie down next to him, taking a second to catch my breath before I have to get up and clean myself off.

"Holy fuck, I think I'm seeing stars."

"It's because I'm an angel," I say smugly.

He bellows out a deep laugh, and I realize how much I've missed that sound. His *true* laugh is much deeper than his regular one. A laugh that only a really good joke or tickling his pelvis could get out of him.

We move to the bathroom so I can clean myself up, but instead we end up in the shower, touching each other's bodies all over again.

After we're both squeaky clean, I climb back into bed while Jake rummages to find his discarded clothing.

"Where are you going?" I ask as he reaches for my bedroom door.

"I forgot something in the Jeep. I'll be back in five minutes."

"You better be! It's getting close to midnight."

"I'll be right back." He plops a kiss on my forehead before heading out. I wonder what he could've forgotten.

I don't have to wonder for long, because just as he said, he's back in my room within a few minutes, but this time with a gift box in his arms.

"What's this?"

"Your Christmas present. I've been waiting for the right moment to give it to you."

Present? I completely forgot about his gift I stashed at the back of my closet until now. I scramble out of bed, tripping over our mess of blankets to retrieve it. I grab the rectangular frame from behind a stack of old CDs, and keep it hidden behind my body as I walk back to the bed, where Jake has now taken his previous spot.

"Who should go first?" I ask.

"You first. I've been wanting to give this to you for weeks and I'm so fucking happy I get to give this to you in person."

He passes me a medium-sized box wrapped in red and white paper. I hold the box in my hand, feeling the light weight of it, trying to guess what it is before opening it.

"Well, are you gonna open it or keep staring at it and hope it unboxes itself?"

"All right, stop being so pushy."

I tear at the wrapping paper, not caring about the mess I'm making on the bed. I open the box and find a burlap tote.

There's no way.

I pull the bag out of the box and unfold it in front of me. On the front, there's a circle of vines and flowers, including some of my favorite varieties, like lilies and snapdragons. In the center of the circle is a landscape of a beach, reminding me of the night we spent in Cape Cod together, watching the snow fall onto the sand.

"Jake, this is…so beautiful."

"I saw how upset you were when your favorite bag broke and you couldn't sew it back together, so I went on the hunt for a replica. Come to find out, that bag you had was one of a kind. I found a girl who makes custom tote bags and had her add some pockets and compartments inside for your camera and all of your gear, so this way it won't break as easily."

I think I might cry right now. This is one of the sweetest things someone has ever done for me. The fact that he remembered and knew how much I loved that bag…I can't believe he put that much thought into this gift.

"Do you like it?"

I put the bag down and practically jump into his arms. "Jake, this is the best gift I've ever received. Thank you so much."

"I'm glad you like it."

"I don't just like it, I *love* it!" I hold the bag up one more time, admiring the intricate stitching and embroidery, before placing it back in the box and grabbing Jake's gift from behind me. "Your turn."

He takes the wrapped frame from my hands and wastes no time tearing the paper off. I watch as his eyes land on the photo in front of him, his eyes looking a bit glossy.

"Vanessa. This picture is amazing. You took this?"

My cheeks blush as I nod. In the gold frame is a photo I took of the guys the night they won their tournament in Nashville. It was the night Eli convinced them to wear cowboy hats out to the bar. Nate and Eli are grinning like they heard the funniest joke. Kieran and Levi look like they want to gouge Eli's eyes out for the outrageous idea. Jake is in the center of their group, smirking at his friends, showing off that signature dimple.

"What made you choose this photo?"

"It was the moment I knew I was falling in love with you, Jake."

"Ness." He puts the frame down and grabs my chin, pulling my lips to his as his way of saying thank you. "This is such a precious gift, I love it. And I love you even more."

We move our gifts off the bed and get comfortable under the covers once again.

I lie on his chest, drawing small circles over the freckle above his left pec.

"Oh shit, we forgot about the pad thai…it's probably cold by now, huh?"

Of course Jake's thinking about food right now.

434

"We can always reheat it, or we can order something else."

"Mm-hm." He nestles his nose on the top of my head before kissing it. "If you think I'm going to leave this bed anytime soon, you're terribly mistaken. I don't think I'm going to let you out of my sight for the next twenty-four hours."

I look over at the clock on my bedside table, it reads midnight.

"Oh no, we missed the ball drop!"

Jake leans over, checking the clock, and curses. "Shit. I'm sorry, baby."

I shrug. It's only the ball drop. "We can always watch it next year."

"Happy New Year, Vanessa."

"Happy New Year, Jake."

His hands are soft as he takes my face in his palms, kissing me like I'm his source of oxygen.

This year has thrown my life in a million different directions, but I wouldn't change any of it. The good, the bad, and the ugly, I'll happily take it all, as long as I have my friends and Jake by my side.

CHAPTER THIRTY-NINE

This is a good life

VANESSA

FOUR MONTHS LATER

Jake pops a bottle of champagne, putting his finger over the open bottle as he shakes it and sprays his fellow teammates with the sparkling liquid.

The team and coaching staff flew back to Boston this morning after winning the Frozen Four against the University of Minnesota. They held the play-offs, and previously, every year that they hosted, they've won.

Until this year.

Boston Central dominated them, winning 5–3.

The game was super close, both teams showcasing their amazing offensive and defensive skills. What won us the game was a hat trick by Jake. He made three goals in the final period, which for a defenseman is surprising.

I don't know if he wanted to show off during his last NCAA game, but he definitely proved to everyone why New Jersey picked him.

Eli passes out plastic champagne flutes, which are filled to the brim with the bubbly drink. I guess we *are* celebrating after all.

"Ladies." He flashes his white, dreamy smile at Maddie, Sydney, and I.

Sydney and Maddie both flew out to Minnesota for the game to support the boys and keep me company. We all shared a hotel room, so it felt more like a girl's trip with a hockey game right in the middle. After the game, we spent the night in the hotel bar with the team, drinking, laughing, and at some point, someone brought out a karaoke machine.

Now that we're back in Boston and finals are just around the corner, it's time for a *proper* party. Or at least that's what Eli said—which is why we're all crowded in their brownstone.

Working with the team all year has changed my life. It sounds corny as hell, but it did.

Coach Wilson even thanked me after the game for everything I've done to help the team. With my behind-the-scenes videos, photos, and interviews, the Wolves had the highest in-house attendance ever recorded. I'm so glad that my work was able to connect the players and their fans. I think my working with the team even made some people more personable— and I'm talking about Kieran on that one.

I've gotten to know so many of the boys in this room—I've learned things about them that I never could've imagined. If I hadn't been assigned to be their social media coordinator, I wouldn't have known that Eli's family owns a ranch in Tennessee, or that Levi loves anime and photography, or that Nate collects magnets from every place he visits.

"I'd like to make a toast," Nate calls out from the middle of the kitchen, raising his glass in his hand. "This year has been absolutely *fucking* amazing. You all worked your asses off for us to get here. Even though some of us won't be coming back next year, moving on to greater things, the foundation we built is going to carry this team to the championship next year. Especially with Eli leading you all." He tilts his cup toward his friend, his assistant captain who had recently been promoted. "Here's to all of us. *Cheers* to friendships, hockey, and a hell of a good time."

Normally Nate's speeches would be more direct and well, *parent-ish*. But tonight, he's acting fun and goofy like the rest of his teammates. I don't know if the reality hit him yet or not that this was also his last college game. But come the fall, he and Jake will both be playing professionally. I can't wait to watch the two of them play against each other for once.

We all clink our glasses against each other's, I take a long sip of my champagne. I don't know who decided to spend so much on these bottles, but it's so smooth, the bubbles feel like they float on my tongue.

Jake comes up behind me, resting his body against the wall, he loops his arms over my shoulders, giving my head a kiss before taking a sip of his drink.

"I can't believe you guys aren't going to be here next year. How the hell am I going to wrangle all these idiots on my own?" Eli motions to the group of athletes scattered in the living room. "At least this year there were *two* of us. Next year I'm gonna have to be Daddy Nate."

The group of us break into laughter at the thought. Nate was always the responsible, sensible one, hence the nickname. Eli on the other hand, he's the farthest thing from responsible. He's like the cool uncle who sneaks us beer and lets us stay out past curfew.

Nate clasps his hand on Eli's shoulder. "Don't worry, buddy. It's not as much responsibility as you think. Just make sure everyone is keeping up with their training, academics, show up to practice on time, don't miss any games, monitor their partying…" Nate continues on his tangent, Eli's eyes growing bigger as he continues down the list.

"I think I'm gonna need another drink." Eli saunters over to the fridge, cracking open a can of beer.

"You're so dramatic, Eli. I could easily get these boys to do anything I ask," Sydney says.

"There's no fucking way any of those idiots would listen to you."

"Oh yeah." Sydney motions her head. "Watch."

Sydney saunters over to the doorway leading to the living room. "*Sebastiannn*, we ran out of ice. Could you run to the store and get some more."

Sebastian's head immediately pops up at Sydney's request. "No, yeah, for sure I can." His Canadian accent leaks out a little.

He grabs his keys from his pocket and is out the door in less than a minute. I look over my shoulder to see the cooler still full of ice.

"See? It's that easy." Sydney flips her hair over her shoulder as she passes by Eli, before jumping up to sit on the counter.

"That's only because you're Nate's little sister."

"Their respect for me doesn't come from my brother. It's because I'm a badass and they'll do anything I ask. Isn't that right boys?" There's a murmur of *yeahs, mm-hms,* and *yeses* that come from the teammates in the living room.

Sydney smirks at Eli as if saying, *I told you so*. "I'm sure that by the end of summer, they'll fall in line. Use your training classes as an opportunity for everyone on the team to see you as a leader."

Coach Wilson announced that Eli will be running their annual summer training camp. Jake told me that every year Coach picks a player to help him over the course of the summer to work one on one with each player, working to improve any weaknesses.

Coach also asked me to return as their social media coordinator and photographer next year, to which I obviously said yes. I couldn't imagine being here next year and not being a part of the Wolves.

"So is *anyone* going to be home with me this summer besides Levi?" Eli raises an eyebrow at the group.

Jake straightens up behind me, his arms stretching over his head. "Nate and I will both be at our own training camps this summer."

"I'm taking a few courses in Scotland this summer, so I'll be gone for two months," Maddie answers. She's always wanted to travel to the UK. I don't know what her fascination is with the place other than Harry Styles and Highland cows, but her program offers an exchange for the summer term and she got accepted last month.

"I'm going on a backpacking trip through Europe with Ethan for a couple of weeks," Sydney says.

"You're taking Ethan with you? Did Mom and Dad make you?"

"No. Ethan actually *enjoys* hanging out with me, unlike my other brother." She darts her eyes at Nate, but he rolls his eyes, shoving off her comment. I will say, he has been better at including her in plans—that might be because of me, though.

She hops off the counter and engulfs Maddie in a hug. "And I'm obviously stopping in Scotland on my way home to say hi to my bestie."

"What about you, Nichols? Any plans for the summer?" Levi directs the question at me.

"Well." I look up at Jake and his gargantuan smile.

He nods his head, excited for me and my summer plans. "Tell them."

"I applied to be a photography assistant for a retreat in Costa Rica. I'll be there for a few months assisting the director and main photographer, capturing photos and videos for a documentary they're going to air on the nature channel."

I've kept this a secret from everyone—well, everyone except for Jake. He was actually the one who saw the posting and sent it to me. I never in a million years would've thought that I'd be chosen. There were three spots, and from what I heard there were over two hundred applicants.

"Holy shit, Ness! I can't believe you didn't tell us." Sydney and Maddie run to me, both of them wrapping their arms around me.

"I can't wait to see all of the amazing photos you take. You have to promise to send me every single one. Even the dirty ones." Jake gives me a devilish smirk.

"Oh, trust me, I'll send you one naughty photo for every day that we're apart."

"Damn, baby, you keep getting sexier and sexier." Jake leans down, crashing his lips on mine. He tastes of mint and champagne, the spearmint from his gum lingers on my taste buds and I want more of him.

I give him one look and he knows exactly what I'm thinking.

"And on that note, we're going to bed." Jake grabs my hand and pulls me toward the patio doors, our friends making kissing noises behind us.

The morning sun is desperately trying to shine through Jake's dark curtains. After months of protest, he finally bought new shades after realizing how much light his old ones let in. Anytime we would sleep here, we'd always get woken up by the sun. And trust me, in the summertime that's such a great feeling. But when you've been partying all night and want to sleep in, it's not as much fun.

I reach out to the nightstand to grab my phone. I'm too lazy to grab my glasses, I can see well enough to make out what's on my screen.

I check my socials and the first post I see is the one I made on the BCU Wolves account. It's a photo of the team holding up the trophy from the Frozen Four. Each of the boys has a gigantic smile plastered on their face. Jake and Eli are both yelling in the photo, I want to say they both were shouting *hell yeah!* Or something along those lines.

I lock my phone and turn it over to inspect the Polaroid I have tucked into my case. The photo was taken in Minnesota. Jake and I stand in the middle, microphones in our hands, belting out a Taylor Swift song on karaoke, Maddie and Sydney sitting to our left with their drinks raised, and the boys—Kieran, Eli, and Nate—on our right, arms around each other's shoulders. We all have these goofy ear-to-ear grins—probably from drinking a little too much, but it was one of the best nights I've had in a while.

Jake curls his arm around me, pulling me against his body, letting me know that he's awake. "Good morning, angel girl." He kisses the top of my head, then leans his own on mine.

I curl more into him, wrapping my arm around his torso, snuggling in. "Good morning."

His body is still warm from sleep, the blankets keeping his heat in. He still smells of his cologne from last night, like deep woods and the smell of rain melded perfectly together.

"Should we get up and get some coffee?" The deepness of his voice never fails to amuse me. The amount of times he's gotten laid because of it would be too many to count.

"No, I wanna lie here a little while longer with you."

He chuckles, moving his fingers to grab my chin. "Whatever you want." He slowly tilts my head back, kissing me deeply.

His eyes are still heavy with sleep, but the blue of them is so vibrant. Like the ocean on a warm summer day, glistening in the sun.

"I love you."

"I love you too, Ness."

This has been the best year of my life. Even though I have gone through many ups and downs, the people I've met this year and the friendships I've created—I wouldn't change any of it.

Yeah, this is a good life.

THE END

EPILOGUE

I think your sister is hitting on me

JAKE

THREE YEARS LATER

I don't think I've been more nervous in my entire life.

I wasn't even as nervous during my first professional game. I was more excited than anything.

But today—today is an *important* day.

I've flown our closest friends into town, and all of them are currently setting up the best engagement party ever planned.

Well, that is if she says yes.

I've been planning this engagement for months, everything from the location down to the flowers. Sydney and Maddie have both been very helpful in the ring-buying process and thank fuck for them because this isn't something I'd be able to do on my own. Who knew there were so many different cuts and styles of rings? And apparently diamonds are on their way out, according to Sydney.

My mom and Autumn have also been an amazing help to me. Planning something on this scale is hard when you're on the road for half the year. Autumn made sure the caterer had everything correct and checked the menu over multiple times. Mom donated all the flowers for the party including the custom flower arch in the backyard and the various bouquets positioned around the house. Even after I insisted on paying her, she refused my money.

I check my phone for the third time tonight, but still no word from the group chat.

The movie is almost over, so I'm really counting on everyone to pull their weight right now. I'm also praying that Vanessa hasn't noticed how many times I've taken my phone out.

I glance over at her, but her focus is solely on the Disney movie we're currently watching. Some princess is singing about how she's sad or something, I'm not really sure what's going on because my brain has been a little too preoccupied.

I send another message to the group, hoping to finally get a response.

Jake:

Is everything set up?

Nate:

Ice rink ready to go *thumbs up emoji*

Eli:

Food is piping hot and so am I *checkmark emoji*

Kieran:

Your mom finished setting up the rose petal trail.
Did you really need this many flowers?

Levi:

Jake, your sister is hitting on me. Please hurry

The last text makes me laugh. I shove the phone back in my jacket pocket as Vanessa gives me a weird look. I guess now *isn't* the time to laugh during the movie.

For the rest of the film, I sit and fidget with the box that's hidden in my pocket.

This is my first day back after a long eight-day roady. I told Vanessa we could do all of her favorite things this weekend, but she has no idea what the grand finale is.

We started the morning with breakfast at her favorite cafe, La Rochelle, and I ordered her favorite, a hazelnut latte and a cheese-stuffed croissant.

We spent the rest of the morning browsing multiple bookstores. I think we left with two bags full of novels she wants to read—all recommendations from Maddie. I'll have to thank Maddie for fueling Vanessa's newfound hobby. *A very costly one.* But as long as it makes Vanessa happy, I'd buy her a whole damn library.

Maybe I'll ask Dad to build some more bookshelves. At this rate, Vanessa will have her own library by the end of the year.

I continue to watch Vanessa rather than the movie, because hell, she's much more entertaining. There hasn't been a dull moment in our life since we met, and I wouldn't have it any other way. Every day I'm grateful that she decided to give me another chance, because if she didn't, who knows where I would be right now. *Probably sitting at home, alone, and watching reruns of The Office.*

The credits roll and I wipe my sweaty hands on my pants.

"I can't believe that movie made me cry."

I laugh as she tries to wipe away her dried tears. "I can, you cry at almost *every* Disney movie."

"It's not my fault. I swear they purposefully make them sad."

Yeah, they definitely make them more sad than they need to be. This is the same company that made you love a dog and a fox and then cry at the end of the film.

"So where to next? We still have a few hours before the sun goes down." I open my Jeep door for her, letting her climb into the seat. Most guys buy a new car within their first year of playing, but I will never get rid of my Jeep. I'll run this thing into the ground before I get something new. And even then, I'd rather put thousands of dollars into fixing it than buy a newer model.

"I'm thinking maybe ice cream?" She furrows her brows. "Or I guess we should get dinner first."

The one thing I've learned over the years about Vanessa is that making decisions is *not* her strong suit. Especially when it comes to food. But luckily, we're not doing either. I'm only giving her the illusion that she has a choice.

"Let's stop at home first. If we're going out, I wanna shower quickly." It's a lie, but I need to make up some excuse to get us back to the house.

Her eyes sparkle at that. "Maybe we can just stay in and order takeout from that new sushi place? Snuggle on the couch. Maybe do some other things." Her fingers trail up my arm as I start the car.

The whole way home she's peppering my neck with light kisses, whispering sweet nothings into my ear.

Fuck. I hate being on the road. When I'm gone, we find time to call or text, but nothing beats being home with Vanessa. She's made our house into a home, one that I never want to leave. Maybe I should call Autumn and tell everyone to go home so I can fuck my girlfriend properly.

Okay, no. I shouldn't do that. We all put a lot of work into getting this night right.

As we pull into the driveway, I notice the lights are out and everyone was smart enough to park their cars on different streets. Vanessa has no clue what's coming her way.

Our house isn't a mansion, but it's one Vanessa and I spent months finding. When I started playing for New Jersey, I purchased a two-bedroom condo in downtown Newark. We stayed there for about two years until we found this place. It's in a small suburban area on the outskirts of Newark, close enough where my commute isn't long, but far enough that we don't need to hear sirens going off at two in the morning. Living in our condo downtown was enough city living for the both of us.

We settled on a two-story, colonial-style home with white siding and dark green shutters and trim. The wraparound porch is what sold Vanessa on this place. It took me a little more convincing, but once we saw the big backyard with a patio, gazebo, and beautiful willow trees and greenery that lined the back fence—yeah, that's what got me. We put an offer in the second we got home.

We've been in this house only for a couple of months, but this will be the first holiday we've celebrated here. Thanksgiving is just around the corner, and I thought, what better time to ask Vanessa to marry me then the anniversary of when we became official for the first time.

I know she loves sentimental gestures. Her romance novels are riddled with that kind of stuff.

I put the car in Park and kill the engine. Swiftly, I grab my eager girlfriend and kiss the hell out of her. If we didn't have our family and friends waiting inside for us, we probably wouldn't leave these seats. It wouldn't be the first time we got it on in the car.

"C'mon, I have something to show you." I break the kiss and slide out of the car.

I walk around to open the door for Vanessa, her face pure lust and shock. I know she's probably racking her brain trying to figure out what I'm up to. The one good thing about being with her for so long is I learned how to master my poker face. She never knows what I'm going to pull out of my sleeve.

I grab her hand and have her follow behind me. We walk up the driveway to where our fence meets the garage. The second I open this gate there is no going back. It feels like my heart might physically jump out of my chest.

I push open the gate, and immediately hear Vanessa gasp.

Well shit, our friends really outdid themselves.

Warm-colored string lights hang from the willow tree branches and are draped throughout the backyard, connecting from the gazebo to the patio. Floral arrangements line the poles of the gazebo, rose petals of all shades of red and pink litter the walkway that leads to the homemade ice rink. I can't believe the guys were able to pull that off.

"W-what is all of this?" I watch as Vanessa takes it all in, her eyes shimmering from shock but also what I can only assume to be more tears.

I keep a hold on her hand and walk her over to the gazebo. The rose petals lead up the stairs to a giant heart in the middle of the floor. Candles are lit along the rails of the gazebo, lighting up the entire space along with more string lights that intertwine with the flowers and greenery.

Okay. This is it. It's now or never.

"Ness." We stop in the center of the heart. Her eyes are practically bulging out of her head, her glasses magnifying them even more. Fuck, I'm so in love with this woman. She watches me closely, her eyes never leaving mine as I lower myself onto one knee, pulling the small velvet box out of my pocket.

"*Oh my god.*"

"Vanessa." Her eyes pop at her full name; it's very rare I call her anything but Ness or angel girl.

I take both of her hands in mine. Looking at her, I see my future—my wife, the mother of our future children, my soul mate.

"I love you so *fucking* much. There is not a single person on this earth I want to spend the rest of my life with besides you. Who knew that a little over three years ago, I would meet this stunning, amazing girl at a damn bar. A girl who turned my life upside down. For the better of course."

She rolls those gorgeous green eyes thinking back to the night we met. I still remember that black dress she wore, *fuck I love that silky dress*. I should pull it out of her closet and have her wear it again for me.

"I wasn't lying when I said that you're it for me. I wouldn't change a single thing about our love story, Vanessa. I would do it all over again to get you. You are everything to me. You give me the energy to wake up every day. You make me strive to be a better person. I want you by my side for the rest of our lives. I want to wake up next to you each morning. I want to go through life with you, experiencing everything the world has to offer for us. I want to live the rest of my life with you by my side, rolling those beautiful green eyes at me."

I look up at the most amazing person who's graced my life and I can't fathom how I was so lucky to get her. I don't know what I did to deserve her love, but I'm going to hold onto her forever.

"I fell in love with your kind heart, your generosity, and your sassy attitude. But mostly, I fell in love with you because of who you are to me. You're my best friend. The one thing I couldn't and wouldn't want to live without."

I swear she makes a sound so high pitched, dogs could hear it.

"So, angel girl, I have a question." Her eyes well with tears as she starts furiously nodding her head, already knowing the question I'm about to ask.

"Vanessa Lilian Nichols, will you marry me?"

"Y-yes, of course I will."

I grab the dark emerald ring out of the box and slide it onto her shaking finger.

She holds her hand out, admiring the deep-green stone I picked out specifically for her. Maddie and Sydney have been secretly sending inspiration photos from her Pinterest so I would at least get this one thing right.

I rise, grabbing her face softly with my hands. As soon as my lips are on hers, the backyard fills with cheers. Our friends and family pour out of the house, clapping, cheering, and wooing at our engagement. I barely get a second to kiss my fiancée before she's pulled away.

"Lemme see, lemme see!" Sydney grabs Vanessa's hand, admiring the ring. "Holy shit, Shepherd, you did a *fabulous* job."

"Well, I did have some help." I motion my head to her and Maddie.

"What are you guys doing here?" Vanessa looks around the backyard, finding all of our friends and family emerging from their hiding spots.

Sydney puts her hands on her hips. "Do you really think we would miss a moment as big as this?"

"You both knew and kept it from me? You guys are horrible friends." Ness crosses her arms in the sassiest way possible.

"Girl, shut up, do you know how hard it was to keep this from you? I pretended to be working on a grad school paper just so I didn't have to talk to you this past week. 'Cause I know if I did, I would've spilled the secret."

I leave the girls to scream and obsess with each other so I can join my family.

"You guys are fucking incredible. I can't thank you enough for all your help." I grab Autumn and pull her into one of those sibling-crushing hugs.

"Well, as a thank-you, I'd kindly ask for you to *let me breathe, Jacob!*" Autumn squirms in my arms before I let her go.

Immediately she runs over to Vanessa, fawning over the ring with the rest of the girls. The two of them have become so close over the years, sometimes I feel like the third wheel when we're all together.

Mom comes over next, engulfing me in a hug. "I'm so happy for you. You two are the epitome of love. Looking at you together, it's like I'm watching one of my Hallmark movies."

She wipes a tear that falls down her cheek. Leave it to my mom to start the waterworks. If Vanessa sees this, she'll be blubbering all over again. You should see the two of them watching a romance movie together, not a dry eye in the house.

A hand clasps my shoulder, and I turn around to find Kieran with a smile spread across his face—a sight that used to be rare to see.

"Fuck man, congrats. How are you feeling?"

I run a hand through my hair, *how am I feeling?*

"Honestly, I feel like I'm on cloud fucking nine. I knew she was going to say yes, but my hands were sweating more than they do in my gloves."

Kieran shakes his head at me, not liking the comparison I used. But hey, my hands *do* get pretty fucking sweaty in my hockey gloves.

We both move our attention to the girls still freaking out in the gazebo.

"She's perfect for you, man. You really hit the jackpot."

"Thanks, buddy."

The sound of a utensil clinking glass grabs everyone's attention, and we all look over to my dad, who's holding a glass of champagne. Levi, Nate, and Eli start passing out flutes filled with the bubbly liquid.

"I'd like to make a toast."

Vanessa rejoins me at my side, and I sling my arm around her waist, pulling her into me, placing a kiss on the top of her head. The rest of our family and friends gather around us, champagne in hand waiting for Dad to continue.

"A few years ago, Jake asked if he could bring a friend to breakfast. Normally we'd think nothing of it, until he told us it was a *girl.* And not just any girl, but Vanessa."

Kieran and the boys make *oohing* noises and I shake my head at them. Everyone here knows our story.

"He didn't notice, but I was watching them the entire meal. The way his eyes were stuck to her, watching her every emotion. He'd be telling a story, but his attention was always on Vanessa. I've never seen him so distracted, and that boy has ADHD.

"When they came home for Thanksgiving, that's when I knew this was it for him. Jake, you remind me so much of myself when I was your age—courageous, selfless, and you put your family above all else. I am so proud of the man you've become and the family you've created for yourself. Vanessa, you've been a part of this family for years now, but we couldn't be happier to have you as our daughter. Cheers to the future Mr. and Mrs. Shepherd!"

I take my glass and clink it against Vanessa's. The second she pulls the flute away from her lips, I take her chin and tip it up to kiss me. Her lips are wet from the champagne, but fuck she tastes as heavenly as ever.

"I love you, soon-to-be Mrs. Shepherd. I can't wait to spend the rest of my life loving you."

"Mrs. Shepherd? Hmm, I think I could get used to that."

She kisses me deeply this time, pouring all her love into it.

Yeah, I think I could get used to this too.

ACKNOWLEDGEMENTS

Thank you to my husband, Dylan, for always believing in me and being my biggest supporter throughout this whole process. I don't know how many husbands would be willing to travel to another province to see a hockey game for inspiration for their wife's book, but you take the cake. I wouldn't have been able to do this without you constantly telling me how proud you are of me. I could cry at the amount of support (emotional and physical) you continue to give me. Our love story is worth its own book, but I hope you see pieces of us in Vanessa and Jake.

Maddie, where the hell do I begin? Thanks for being my go-to gal for this book (and the entire series). You were with me when I wrote the first words and you've been by my side with everything since. I cannot thank you enough for dealing with my sporadic texts, chaotic voice memos, and listening to me go on and on about scenes and characters. The only fitting way of repaying you is by making a character inspired by you. I hope Maddie Harper lives up to her inspiration. I wouldn't have been able to start this series without your help. You are an amazing friend, and I will cherish you until the end of time. Thank you for continuing to put up with my nonsense as I continue to write the rest of this series (you're the best!). Also…sorry for killing Jax (IYKYK)

To my family and friends, thank you for being so patient with me. This book has been a long time coming, and it feels so freeing to finally share it with you. Also, never look me in the eyes ever again. It feels like a fever dream to finally have something published, and your support helped make my dreams come true. I wouldn't have been able to get this out to the world without your constant love and support. Special thanks to Gabby for listening to me drone on and on at work and being a helpful ear.

Beth and Lucija, I cannot express enough my gratitude for our friendship. Your kindness and encouragement kept me motivated when self-doubt crept in. I hope you'll figure out which characters I based off you and which personality traits of yours I applied to many characters. This book wouldn't be the same without our friendship as the basis. I love you sisters.

Paisley, my amazing editor, you took my baby and made it into the best possible version of itself. A Regular Thing would be nothing without you, and I cannot thank you enough for everything you've done for me. (Sorry for the millions of emails, hehe). It's amazing to find an editor who takes such good care of your book but it's even better when you find a friend through the process. I hope you're ready for book two...three...and four.

Thank you to Acacia, for designing such a fabulous cover. You took the images out of my head and made them into something real. I've envisioned a million different covers, but you somehow found the perfect combination of them all. I cannot thank you and the team at Ever After Design enough.

And finally, thank you to my readers. Without you, this book would be nothing. I hope you loved reading Vanessa and Jake's love story, and I hope you're excited to explore the other characters in the books I have planned. Next up is Maddie and Kieran...hold on to your hats because this will be a tough one.

About the Author

ALEXANDRA SERRE IS A SMALL-TOWN CANADIAN author that lives with her husband and four cats, writing everything from contemporary romance to fantasy.

When she's not writing down a million book ideas, you can find her snuggled under blankets watching trashy reality TV or curled up on her porch with a good book.

www.ingramcontent.com/pod-product-compliance
Lightning Source LLC
Chambersburg PA
CBHW021840010726
47493CB00005B/1479